William Knox Wigram

Five Hundred Pounds Reward

A novel

William Knox Wigram

Five Hundred Pounds Reward
A novel

ISBN/EAN: 9783337028534

Printed in Europe, USA, Canada, Australia, Japan

Cover: Foto ©Andreas Hilbeck / pixelio.de

More available books at **www.hansebooks.com**

HUNDRED POUNDS REWARD.

A Novel.

By A BARRISTER.

NEW YORK:

HARPER & BROTHERS, PUBLISHERS,

FRANKLIN SQUARE.

1868.

FIVE HUNDRED POUNDS REWARD.

CHAPTER I.

ONE day, during Easter Term, not a great many years ago, two barristers sat down to breakfast in chambers, at No. 8 Stone Buildings, Lincoln's Inn.

John Worsley was the name of one: Paul Petersfeld the name of the other.

Worsley, of whom I shall hereafter speak in the first person, being no other than myself, was the actual proprietor of the rooms in question. There I lived and worked and slept; making the most of them, both in their professional and domestic capacity.

Paul, an old college friend, and some three years my junior, owned fashionable quarters in the Albany; and beyond placing his name upon my door, and dropping in pretty regularly once a day, to ascertain that he wasn't in the least wanted, took his brieflessness as a matter of course, as if it had been one of those unimportant ailments which naturally cure themselves as people grow older.

"Energy, Worsley!" he exclaimed suddenly, in answer to some observation of mine, the tone of which seemed to strike him as objectionably paternal, "I like that! To charge me, of all men in the world, with want of energy, is too good. What on earth do you suppose I am in Lincoln's Inn for at half-past nine this blessed May morning? Is there any thing so astonishing about your chops and coffee—both capital by the bye—as to induce a fellow who wasn't a perfect miracle of energy to pound all this way from Piccadilly before most people are quite awake? Wrong for once in your life, old fellow. Think again!"

"Not I. You are here simply because, as I truly told you, dawdling down some time between eleven and twelve in a hansom, with a cigar in your mouth, looked preciously unlike work in a three-months' barrister, and would infallibly damage your professional prospects, whatever these may be. I quite admit that you have put on a famous spurt this morning, and I advise you to stick to the plan."

"All right," returned Petersfeld, proceeding leisurely with his breakfast. "But, do you know, Worsley, I begin to suspect that what you are pleased to call professional energy, is a confounded delusion in my case, and nothing else. What's the good of energy to a man who never has any thing to do? Where's its use to a man bound hand and foot to a profession where he can't get a chance to show it? Isn't it like a good appetite to a man who hasn't got a chop like this before him—like Robinson Crusoe's tarnishing doubloons in a land with no tailors and nobody to take a bet? But, to say that I haven't got energy! Give me the chance to show it—that's all! Give me what Archimedes wanted when he offered to shunt the world! Give me—"

"Give me the coffee. What's the good of blowing off steam at this rate? Who said you were not energetic? Of course you are, in your own way—in any ready-made pursuit which happens to take your fancy. I have no doubt, for instance, but that you are, at this moment, about the most energetic volunteer in the 'Devil's Own.' Only there are two sorts of energy, Petersfeld—male and female—as an old writer rather happily distinguishes them."

"Interesting couple, I should say. Which is the lady?"

"Female energy," I replied, "is the energy which waits for its work. It works well enough with what actually comes to it; but its work must come, do you understand? Female energy waits for its work."

"Like the spider. Were you aware that spiders are all females? They are, though. What's the other?"

"Male energy doesn't wait for its work—it finds it—makes it—does it."

"Like the policeman. By the bye, policemen are supposed to be all males. Curious coincidence. What next?"

"I simply advise you not to wait for your work. You look too far ahead. You always, in chambers at least, talk and dream of what you will do some time or another—not of what you are going to do to-day."

"To-day, my dear fellow," replied Paul, with a slight yawn, "my numerous engagements may be summed up approximately as follows:—I shall devote the next hour or so to the consumption of a pipe of cavendish and the perusal of the *Times*. From eleven till one, I shall hold quiet communion with some standard author upon the principles of equity. At one, or thereabouts, I shall take my seat in the luncheon-room of Lincoln's Inn. Immediately afterward, I shall array myself in complete c nonicals, and proceed to inhale 'the atmosphere' of the Courts,' until four o'clock. I shall endeavor to look, as much as possible, as if I had been called six years, instead of half as many months, and as if I were 'waiting for the next cause,' instead of a cause in which the plaintiff is probably at this moment employed with his coral. At four precisely my presence, as the most valuable sergeant in No. 9 company, is imperatively required in the Temple - Gardens. That's about what I'm going to do to-day. After five, a lawyer's time, you know, is entirely his own. What do you say to that, for a day's work?"

It so happened that I was at the moment adjusting my wig and bands before the glass over the chimney-piece, with my chin rather in the air, preparatory to going into court for the day. Otherwise my reply—" Do you call *that* work?" would hardly have been resented as implying, what it certainly was never intended to imply, a disagreeable comparison.

"Call it work, indeed! It's about all the work ·I'm likely to get if I stick to this confounded profession till I'm as old as Adam. It's all very well for you, my boy, who've got solicitors for friends, and go into court every day of your life, with three briefs in your bag, like a little Daniel, to ask me if I call that work. If you'd got a plate of chops and I'd got a plate of sawdust, you'd ask me, I suppose, why I didn't peg away like you, and whether I called *that* eating. What next?"

"Male energy," replied I, arranging my papers. "Don't wait for the chops. Peg away at the sawdust now. That's your work, if you only choose to make it so. But by your own admission you don't. You are not half in earnest about it. Give it up, if it doesn't suit you; but don't dawdle away the best years of your life under false pretenses. There's a bit of my mind for you."

"A nice large piece too. However, there's sense in what you say, old fellow. If I don't see the result pretty near, I never do work with more than half a will. That's about it, I expect."

"Exactly. You wait for work which is to show a result at once, and in the mean time do nothing worth doing at all. You don't find your work—your real work—either in the profession or any thing else."

"Which is a state of things to be immediately rectified," observed Paul. "Just so. Now let's see what I'll do—I'll—what! going already? Why, it's hardly half-past nine."

"I've a consultation with Buttermere at the quarter to. We're in the first cause in to-day's paper."

"*Au revoir*, then. I perfectly agree in all you've said. I can take advice like a child, provided I get the article genuine. Hand me the *Times*, will you? I must have a smoke over all this. And, when I once do make up my mind, why then Foig-a-ballagh! as the Irish say at Donnybrook."

CHAPTER II.

"BY the way, Worsley," inquired Mr. Buttermere, as, consultation over, we walked from his chambers toward the court, "you've a man of the name of Petersfeld with you in Stone Buildings, have you not?"

"Yes; we have shared chambers since his call last January."

"Nice, amusing, gentlemanly fellow," pursued Buttermere, in his peculiar soft, soup-eating tone. "Met him at dinner the other night. One of the Westmoreland Petersfelds, I believe. Isn't he an eldest son, and on his way to some sort of property there? I fancy I have heard something about his family."

"Some day or other he comes, I believe, into a very considerable estate, with a baronetcy into the bargain. The present baronet is an unmarried uncle. In the mean time his father gives him no option but to follow the law."

"Ha! well, he couldn't do better. Does he seem to take to it, Worsley?"

"Oh yes; fairly enough. He is a man who may do a great deal if he chooses; and I have a strong idea that he will come out in due time. Petersfeld is one of those dashing, reckless fellows to whom our work is rather a grind at starting."

"Ha! yes. My son, who was with him at Trinity, tells me that he was first-rate on the river—a sort of recognized leader in every thing in the way of a lark. That I take to be about the best sign after all in a young man. I want to ask him to dine with us some day. Will you come and meet him?"

"I shall be delighted, I am sure."

"That's well. You shall hear from Mrs. Buttermere in the course of a week. But here we are—and just in time."

I could not help secretly smiling as I followed my leader into court. Report said that three blooming olive-branches in muslin sat around the prosperous table of Mr. Buttermere.. Moreover, that that learned gentleman was bound, under high connubial pains and penalties, to 'bring home' every eligible or promising young man whom he could pick up in court or elsewhere, to be looked at by Mrs. Buttermere and, if found eligible, appropriated, if possible, for the benefit of one or other of the three sedate vestals aforesaid. It was a beautiful instance of male and female energy, combining toward a virtuous end.

My own position, I may at once say, was scarcely such as to warrant Buttermere in bringing me home. I was getting on well enough for a comparative beginner, and that was all. But Paul was handsome, dashing and attractive; and moreover blessed with ultimate prospects which were of infinitely greater merit and importance in the eyes of all sensible people. So I felt that I was only to be asked for the sake of making the thing rather less palpable; and, giving Paul credit for being very well able to take care of himself, gave myself no farther concern about the matter.

Our case came to an end rather sooner than we expected, and, having no other court business on hand, I leisurely returned to chambers. Ours were on the top story of Stone Buildings, a fearful and wonderful height for human habitation. You ascend by exactly one hundred steps from the pavement outside to a suite of rooms nice enough with one rather serious exception. A long, narrow aperture, some seven feet from the ground, extending across the room just below the ceiling, is the sole substitute for a window. Through this slice of glazing, when you can reach it, you may look between the interstices of a massive stone balustrade upon the fair breadth of Lincoln's Inn Fields. To a couple of acrobats such a window would probably be the source of unmixed enjoyment, as they might regale each other with alternate peeps the whole day long. But, practically, the necessity of arranging and climbing upon furniture every time you wish to look abroad, becomes irksome and irritating sooner than one would easily believe.

I found Petersfield striding backward and forward under this exasperating casement—his fine bronzed face on fire with excitement. His arm-chair had been sent sprawling upon its back—his pipe lay extinct upon the table—while he crumpled and flourished a sheet of the *Times* as he walked, like a sort of preposterous pocket-handkerchief.

"Found it, Jack! Found it! Told you I should! Never knew such luck in my life!"

"What's up now?"

"Up? Why look here! Not in a hurry, are you? Sit down and read THAT!", continued he, thrusting into my hands the page containing that mysterious "second column," at which most of us glance every morning.

"There, Jack—that's the place:—'Five hundred pounds reward,' it begins. Read it out, will you, old fellow? I want to hear how the thing runs. Come, fire away!"

So with Petersfield stalking backward and forward before me, looking so defiantly resolute, that it was all I could do to avoid laughing outright, I took my seat upon the edge of the table, and read as follows:

"FIVE HUNDRED POUNDS REWARD!—Disappeared lately, a YOUNG LADY, aged eighteen, of very distinguished appearance. She is slender and of middle height—dark hair and eyes—pale clear complexion, and is in manner peculiarly graceful and self-possessed. She had with her a very considerable sum of money; but, it is believed, no personal luggage whatever. She was dressed, on leaving home, in a brown silk dress, purple cloth jacket, white straw hat, trimmed with black velvet, and grebe feather. Wore a curious oriental gold bracelet, plain gold guard-chain, and watch by Rosenthal, Paris. Whoever will bring her to Mr. Bloss, solicitor, No. 14, New Square, Lincoln's Inn, or give information leading to her recovery, shall receive the above reward. Thursday, May 1."

"Now then, Worsley, what do you think of that?" exclaimed Petersfield, as I threw down the paper. "Did you ever hear of such a chance? Give you my honor, I never did!"

"What on earth do you mean? Are you going to find her?"

"Find her! Certainly I am. My good fellow, don't laugh. This is exactly what I wanted! Now you shall see something like energy! I take my oath I'll find her, that's to say, if—"

"If you can," suggested I, quietly.

"If she's above ground, Worsley! Of course, if I can't, I can't; but I tell you I will. I'll make it my business to find her. I give you my honor I never felt as I do at this moment. *Now*, I've a direct object in life. Just you watch me while I pursue it; and then tell me I've no energy, if you dare," concluded Paul, picking up his arm-chair, and arranging his necktie furiously at the glass.

"You don't mean to say that you are going to begin this moment?"

"Don't I. Why should I lose one hour's start? I'm going at once to Bloss. I shall pump him; get all the information I can, and probably leave London in one direction or another, by an afternoon train."

"Petersfeld! unless you have really gone barking mad, stand still for one minute. Will you listen to reason, or will you not? If not, say so, and I have done."

"Reason!" retorted Paul, looking slightly piqued; "are you going to advise me not to try? You needn't do that."

"Nothing of the kind."

"Then can't you see that there is no time to be lost. In a case of this sort every minute may tell. What's the good of conversation?"

"I really gave you credit for more sense, Petersfeld! You are just now in a mood to make a mess of the whole thing. You'll ruin your chance at first starting."

"Talk away, then," returned Paul. "Perhaps I was a little too hot, after all, but then I had considered more than you think, before you came in. Really, I ought to be very much obliged to you for taking so much trouble. So I am: that's the fact."

I am ashamed to acknowledge that the extravagant absurdity, the utter wantonness of the whole proceeding, did not strike me as distinctly as it ought to have done at the first blush. I so thoroughly entered into Petersfield's overwhelming desire to engage in an adventurous, exciting chase, in which every energy of mind and body might be strained to the uttermost, and in which success would afford such a glorious omen of future victories, that I simply wished to prevent his rushing into immediate and vexatious failure through sheer impetuosity in the first instance. But, in fact, any attempt at dissuasion would have been perfectly idle.

The hot spirit of pursuit was upon him—that strange indelible brand of the forest imprinted upon every human heart. Jaques was quite wrong when he piped over the stag, whose

"Big round tears
Coursed one another down his innocent nose."

Who that ever hunted, considered the stag's dislikings? Who has pitied the wise and wonderful fox, or the hare so docile and original, so glad to be an affectionate diverting fireside companion, instead of that changed and ghastly fugitive which nobody who has ever seen flying, can ever forget? Whoever suggested that a woodcock minded being winged? What sailor ever gave a thought to the feelings of his chase, while overhauling her hand over hand to the glorious banging of his big bow-gun? And if a young lady of eighteen objected to being dogged about the country by an exuberant young barrister of three-and-twenty, for no earthly reason except that he wanted occupation, and had made up his mind to catch her, had she any special ground of complaint, after having advisedly placed herself in the catalogue of *feræ naturæ ?*

"All this will cost money, Paul," I observed. "No use going into an affair of this kind unless you mean to spend. Hast thou ' put money in thy purse ?' "

"Good Iago, be easy upon that score. I had an odd twenty guineas or so, which I was keeping for Switzerland in the Long. They will shortly be in my cigar-case for this especial purpose."

"It will also cost time," pursued I. "Our courts won't be up this week."

"All the worse for them. What can a few days, more or less, matter to me? Our Easter vacation begins almost directly, and I shall have the whole of that quite free. Anyhow, I go to-night; that is, if I see reason."

"One more question : do you know Bloss ?"

"Not I. I shall call upon him in consequence of his advertisement. Isn't that regular enough ?"

"Suppose you take my card. Bloss and I come from the same part of the world, and we always nod when we meet. Scratch out my name, in pencil, and write your own. It may serve as a sort of introduction ; at least, I think he'll consider it as such."

"Thank you very much. What sort of a fellow is he? By the way, how had I better begin? That's the point I hadn't quite considered."

"Bloss is a great, fat, good-natured fellow, who will talk and laugh with you for half an hour together, without letting you be one bit wiser than he chooses. I should say that the more frankly you go to work the better. Don't let him, at any rate, fancy that you are laying traps for him. If you do, he'll shut up in an once. Go in and win. Shall we meet in Hall ?"

"Haven't an idea. All I know is, that I'm down upon Bloss within the next two minutes."

CHAPTER III.

At five o'clock on every evening during Term time, we Chancery lawyers hold pleasant festival in the great dining-hall of Lincoln's Inn.

At the tables, running lengthways, toward the lower end of the hall, sit the students, divided into messes of four. Above, at the cross-tables, distributed in the same manner, dine the barristers; while higher still, entrenched behind a sort of oaken rampart, and raised upon a dais, the benchers of the Inn regale themselves—it is believed—upon the fare of the rich man's table.

That the assisting at a certain number of these dinners should be an indispensable preliminary to a call to the bar has always been a fruitful subject of pleasantry among people of the "funny" class, who are perhaps unnecessarily numerous. Of course I am not going to explain, in these casual pages, any of our esoteric doctrines—our calm, professional mysteries, which *propter simplicitatem laicorum,* we habitually keep to ourselves. That would never do. But I can safely declare that I have enjoyed few dinners more than those at which I "ate my terms," while for plain fare and good company, I ask nothing better than the bar-table at Lincoln's Inn.

Petersfeld and I entered the hall almost at the same moment.

"Just seen old Bloss," he whispered. "Got a mess? Tell you all about it afterward."

And so the dinner began.

Our two comrades at the board were Brocklebank and Millworth : one a large, red, lusty, noisy man ; the other singularly composed and quiet, with an olive complexion and a soft voice. So remarkable an advertisement as that which had just roused the curiosity of half London in the morning papers, was not likely to pass without comment at the bar-table.

"I say," exclaimed Brocklebank, who was lecturer in some branch of jurisprudence at Lincoln's Inn, "seen that queer advertisement to-day, Worsley, about the beauty in brown silk? Richest thing I've known this long time ! By George, I expect to find my class empty to-morrow. All our students will be after her."

"You must have a very mild opinion of all our students," observed Millworth.

"Lord bless you, why ?" retorted Brocklebank, with his strong, loud laugh. "You'll be after her yourself, Millworth, I shouldn't wonder. I can fancy the sly, innocent way you'll go purring and peeping about, and how you'll come back with your eyes half shut and a perpetual smile, asking us all, confidentially, if we know of a nice snug investment for £500 or so !"

"I assure you," said the other, with unchangeable suavity, "you do me far too much credit. Besides, if I were really such an egregious rascal as to undertake the experiment, I ought to have made my fortune long ago."

"Well done, Millworth!" said I, while Petersfeld flushed perplexedly, embarrassed with the weight of his own secret. "How do you know that I'm not on the track myself?"

"If you are, I wish you joy of it," returned my neighbor with his easy smile.

"You have had the benefit of a candid opinion, at all events. But, seriously, Worsley, what a hideous state of mind must that man be in who could undertake such an adventure for the sake of the paltry reward."

"Not so paltry, after all. Besides, one offers —the other earns. Is there any harm in that?"

"Worsley, you are a gentleman. If you wish to test the utter baseness of such a pursuit, just consider what the young lady herself would think of the man who could be vile enough to follow and molest her without any conceivable inducement or excuse, beyond the miserable hope of pocketing some few hundred pounds. Of course we are all now speaking in joke, but I should really like to tell that man my opinion of him. I should indeed."

"Isn't that Millworth all over?" shouted Brocklebank. "What a virtuous man he is! Now, I've no doubt whatever but that this young woman is as thorough-going *franche aventurière* as ever met Monsieur Gil Blas. Where did she get the 'very considerable sum of money' she seems to have sidled away with in her dainty pocket? She's a naughty little fashionable thief in my opinion. She has robbed somebody who was fool enough to tru█ her; and, I'll bet you what you like, ought not only to be caught, but whipped into the bargain, for all her distinguished appearance."

"To my mind, noo," came a deliberate northern voice from the adjoining mess, "I've listened to two vara indifferent opinions, where I would have thought to have heard two wise ones."

"What's the matter now, Kinghorn?" cried Brocklebank. "Don't you believe she's a thief?"

"Do you want any more of my mind about hunting her?" inquired Millworth.

"I think ye may be both strangely in the wrong. I think ye have both taken extreme views; neither of which was there any need to take."

"*In medio tutius ito,*" suggested Millworth.

"As to this young lassie," continued Kinghorn, placing his elbows square upon the table, and helping himself to a stupendous pinch from the snuff-box which forms part of the regulation-furniture of every bar-mess, "I can detect no reason whatever for concluding her to be a thief. Far more likely to my mind she is █te innocent and virtuous, and has rin awa' from home through some love trouble, which was na kindly taken by those about her. Many girls do flit away for the like reason. As to the lots of siller spoken of in the advertisement, what would be quantities to Mr. Brocklebank or myself, mightn't be so much out of the ordinary to a well-to-do lassie. Anyhow, she has fled away from the bosom of her family, or those who have the caring for her, which is indubitably the right place for her at eighteen. And it seems to me that he who can recover and win her back before she falls into some terrible pit of misery, and may be of sin, which may happen to any girl of that simple age wandering alone, would well deserve five hundred pounds and more for the good office."

"Well, we must let her alone for the present. They're going to say grace."

"Petersfeld," said I, as we rose from the table, "are you off for the evening, or will you smoke your pipe in chambers first?"

"Certainly. I want to tell you what happened this afternoon. Are you going there now?"

"Yes, and I'll bring Kinghorn. He has a first-rate head for a matter of this kind. If you have any thing to discuss, you couldn't have a better adviser."

"Is he safe, do you think? You know what I mean. I mustn't have this talked about."

"To be sure he is. Besides, he has committed himself, you see, to the doctrine of intervention, and Kinghorn never changed his mind in his life. Go on, and I'll bring him."

And so, within ten minutes' time, we were all three seated in that legal eyrie, of which I have already made mention, with pipes alight, coffee brewing upon the hob, and ready to dispose of any conceivable question which could be submitted to a council of counselors.

"I am well satisfied to be here," began Kinghorn, quietly adopting to himself the arm-chair and footstool of our chamber establishment; "because I'll advise with you, Worsley, upon a point of copy-hold which was much pressed upon me this morning. Hereditaments parcel of the Manor of A., and held—"

"Pardon me one moment, Kinghorn. We want to ask your advice upon a point which concerns our friend here, personally. Would you mind clearing his mind upon a private matter, in the first instance, before we go to the Manor of A.? Afterward, my time for the rest of the evening is quite at your disposal."

"By all means, my dear Worsley—by all means! It is I who should ask pardon. Of what would you speak?"

"Of the young lady whose case we just now discussed in Hall. Petersfeld is going to find her."

"That's news, indeed!" exclaimed Kinghorn, with a look of unqualified interest. "I am glad, on my soul, that such a pursuit should be undertaken by a gentleman so likely to bring it to a creditable issue. May be you are acquainted with the lassie's whereabouts, or have some other information to guide you? Is it so, sir?"

"Wish I had," returned Petersfeld. "I got some information this morning—rather less than I should have liked—from Mr. Bloss, whose name you may remember in the advertisement. If you could help me to make head or tail of it, I should really be obliged. Every man's opinion is worth taking at the outset in a case like this; and yours, of course, Mr. Kinghorn, would be a great favor."

This was said rather in the sort of blunt shy way in which, of olden time, we who were not then very old, were wont to avail ourselves, as a disagreeable convenience, of the opinion of our elders.

"You have only to ask my mind to know it,"

replied Kinghorn. "Well enough do I remember Bloss. If I had a hind leg to be talked off I'd take it to Bloss. But, in the mean time, let us hear what he said; and give me, if you have it, a copy of this advertisement, which is the chief matter after all. Thank you. Proceed now, Mr. Petersfeld, if you please."

And Paul, seating himself astride of a chair with its back toward us, as if delivering his experience from the top of a small and unusually stiff-necked pony, detailed for our benefit the result of the first step instigated by those euphonious syllables—"Five hundred pounds reward!"

CHAPTER IV.

It may seem scarcely fair upon Petersfeld to intercept him from giving, in the first person, his own account of the interview between himself and Mr. Bloss. But an historian is bound to consult the convenience of his readers, even at the expense of strict justice to his *dramatis personæ*. And, in the present instance, it demanded so much conversational cross-questioning to extract the story entire, that I intend to undertake it myself, as the shorter and more intelligible course.

Lincoln's Inn clock had just struck two, as Paul arrived at the great yellow door, No. 14 New Square, which bore the inscription in large black letters, "Mr. Bloss."

As the postern of the forty thieves unlocked itself spontaneously upon the very shallow suggestion "open sesame!" so did Mr. Bloss's outer oak spring backward, as of its own accord, at Petersfeld's decided rap.

Within was the indistinct vista of a passage, terminating in a green-baize door; with certain pens or pews on the right, in which the work which we barristers conventionally depreciate as "clerical," was apparently in course of performance.

"Yes—?" inquired the voice of the invisible gentleman, who had pulled the string, which raised the latch, which opened the door. "Yes—?"

"Yes," replied Petersfeld, with composure. He was now fairly embarked on his enterprise, and it would never do to be trifled with at starting.

A round sleek face appeared over the nearest pew door; and the owner having satisfied himself that Paul was what he inwardly designated as a "swell," at once let himself out, and appeared in the passage.

"Wish to see Mr. Bloss, sir? What name shall I say?"

"Be good enough to say that Mr. Petersfeld, of Stone Buildings, would be glad of five minutes' conversation. Have the kindness, also, to hand him my card."

"Certainly, sir," replied the clerk. "Mr. Bloss is just at this moment engaged with a gentleman from Oxfordshire; but if you'll sit down for one minute or so, he'll be happy to see you. There, that's his bell! Go in, Tommy."

Tommy, whose clerical duties were apparently exercised in an adjoining pew, at once obeyed orders, and presently returned with a considerable tin tray which filled the whole outer office with a savor of beefsteak and onions, and upon which an empty pewter tankard suggested that those delicacies had been pleasantly washed down.

"Now, sir, I'll take your card in," said the first clerk; and whether the gentleman from Oxfordshire had been smuggled off under the tin tray, or how otherwise his exit had been effected, as it most certainly had, must be left to the conjectures of the inquisitive. At all events Petersfeld was at once ushered through the green-baize door, and found Mr. Bloss alone.

"Happy to see you, Mr. Petersfeld — very happy indeed," exclaimed the solicitor. "I find your name upon Mr. Worsley's card. Always glad to meet any friend of Mr. Worsley. Know his family well."

Here Mr. Bloss pushed back his arm-chair from the table, and courteously motioning Paul to an opposite seat, inspected him with a jolly, benevolent air, as if the departed gentleman from Oxfordshire had left him in a most even and enviable frame of mind.

It would be a rare world, indeed, and not without its recommendations, which should be peopled exclusively with gentlemen cut out after the exact pattern of Mr. Bloss. Fancy our streets crowded with nothing but enormously protuberant, white-waistcoated, elderly men, with immense flaxen faces, no hair to speak of, pitcher lips, three chins apiece, and unsteady blue eyes which float ever so long right and left before they seem to lay hold of any thing in particular. Fancy them all lolling and bobbing about, perpetually saying, "ha, ha!" and what a fine day it was, to each other, never grumbling, never discontented, never in any thing but the best of spirits, and think how charmingly we should all get on.

"Happy to meet you," repeated Bloss, rolling his plump white hands together, and kicking his immense legs into a listening attitude. "What can I have the pleasure of doing for Mr. Petersfeld?"

"I have troubled you, Mr. Bloss, in consequence of an advertisement, mentioning your name, which appeared in the *Times* this morning. I have a strong idea that I can find the young lady."

"Ho, ho, ho!" chuckled Bloss. "Delighted to hear that. Heartily hope you can. You haven't got her outside, have you? Not left her to play with those good little boys in the office, I hope,—hey?"

"Certainly not. I shall take better care of her than that. I ought however, to explain that my object in troubling you, at present, is simply to ask whether you can give me any information beyond that contained in the advertisement — the young lady's name, residence, and so forth, for instance."

"I can give you one very material piece of information," replied Bloss, settling himself cosily in his chair, and tapping a paper-knife upon his desk—"and that is, that the £500 will be paid across this very table, upon production of the young lady. That's a point, sir, which, perhaps, you took for granted; but it ought to be gratifying to a practical man like yourself, considering how these sort of things are sometimes managed—in fact, how they are managed every day. The check is, in this drawer, sir. And this is the key."

"I never doubted it for one moment, Mr. Bloss; the advertisement being in your name."

"My name! ho, ho, ho! That's true enough; but I'm not the advertiser," interrupted Bloss, with his comfortable laugh. "The advertisement is not mine, my dear sir, one bit more than yours. I'm to pay—that's all. I hold the money, and wait for the lady. I'm a cat's-paw in the affair—nothing else. I can't give you any farther help, not I. I'm not instructed to do it. I'm told not to do it. Bring the lady—take the check. That's all."

"In that case," returned Petersfeld, not a little disconcerted, "I'm sorry I troubled you. Worsley told me that I might expect from you the ordinary information, whatever that may mean. However, if I am simply wasting your time and my own, I had better wish you good-day at once, and beg pardon for intruding."

"No, no, no!" replied Mr. Bloss. "Sit down again, my dear sir, do. Don't run away as if I wouldn't give you every sort of information in my power, because I will. Only, unluckily, the best piece of advice I can give you—always supposing that you don't know more than I do about this business—is to let it alone."

"If that's the case," retorted Paul, "what's the meaning of this confounded advertisement?"

"Ha, ha, ha! What, of course? Well, the fact is," continued Bloss, struggling between the keen enjoyment of an interesting mystery, amusement at Petersfeld's absurd crotchet, and the obligations of professional reticence—"the fact is, speaking to you, Mr. Petersfeld, as a barrister, and wishing, of course, to afford you every assistance in my power—the fact is, that this young lady escaped, eloped—levanted is, I believe, the correct word—upward of a fortnight ago."

"The deuce she did?"

"Ha, ha! it's a fact though. Her—father," continued Bloss, cautiously balking himself before every word which might betray more than he intended—"knowing old customer as ever lived, naturally thinks to himself, 'least said, soonest mended'—keeps all quiet in the first instance, and simply sets two Scotland Yard detectives upon her track before she had been twelve hours out of his gates. Don't you see, it was every thing that the scandal of this sort of escapade shouldn't get wind in the county?"

"To be sure! and so the detectives failed?"

"Failed! I believe you. As I said just now, they were hot-foot after her before she was well over the lawn. They knew all that you know from the advertisement—and more too. Much more, of course. Yet not one trace of the girl did they ever manage to discover. Not a bit of it. From that day to this she has just as much disappeared as if she had been sunk in the sea. By the way, that reminds me: every likely port in the kingdom has been watched day and night; so I'm told. It's the most extraordinary thing I ever knew, Mr. Petersfeld; and that's the fact. Ha, ha, ha!"

"And the present advertisement?"

"Why, don't you see? She must be somewhere. The detectives have done their outside. They've come home and said 'no go.' Therefore, the only chance is to appeal to those who've got her. £500 is a good lot of money, Mr. Petersfeld, as we both know; and if that doesn't tempt them to hand her over, or lead to some account of her, why," continued Mr. Bloss, rolling himself up more cosily than ever, and stabbing himself playfully with his paper-knife, "why, that's about the end of the story, I take it."—

"You said something about being a mere cat's-paw in the business. You'll excuse my curiosity, I am sure. I shall not trouble you again."

"Oh law! don't mention it. Ask what you like, Mr. Petersfeld. Cat's-paw, indeed, ha, ha! that's just what I am. Don't you see, this clever old gentleman who would manage it all himself, advertisements and every thing, didn't want his own solicitors' names to appear in the matter. There was a reason for that. If they had, all their clerks would have guessed directly who the young lady was. Their house had acted for her father in a chancery suit, to which she was a party. However, never mind about that. He didn't want those clerks to get wind of the thing, and go talking right and left—as of course they would. Law, you've no idea how clerks do talk. So he just told his people to put it into my hands, so far as the reward was concerned; that's all. My chaps here know no more of the family than the man in the moon, so they can't tell tales. The other chaps, there, not having the thing popped under their noses, as it were, don't think about her more than any body else. In fact, my name appearing, you see, they're cock-sure the matter doesn't concern any of their clients. It was a neat dodge, that, indeed—ha, ha!"

"I will trouble you with only one question more," said Petersfeld. "The advertisement mentions a considerable sum of money."

"So it does. Large sum, indeed. Very large. Quite a little fortune. Just about the funniest part of the whole affair, that is. But really, Mr. Petersfeld, I shall be telling more than I ought if I don't shut up soon, and upon my honor, I've told you a great deal. Hope you don't think I should have done as much for every body, ha?"

"Certainly not," replied Petersfeld rising.

"You have told me every thing which as it seems I could, under the circumstances, fairly ask, and I am exceedingly obliged. Good-day, Mr. Bloss. I am afraid you must wait until next week for the young lady!"

"Good-day—good-day!" laughed the jolly old gentleman, ringing his bell. "Law bless me, what a funny start it is, to be sure," repeated he to himself, long after Petersfeld had disappeared in the passage "Only to think of the advertisement of a runaway girl in a newspaper, setting a young chap wild like that! What upon earth does he want with her? Is he going to take his reward out in love or money, I wonder? Ha, ha, ha!"

"And yet," continued Mr. Bloss, musing to himself, "what a strange round things do run, to be sure! That I should have drawn that will more than forty years ago! That I should have had charge of that child when she first landed in England! And now, that this boy should come to me for information about her—knowing just as much of Miss Helen, as I do of next month's baby! Almost wish I had told him more. Give a good deal to think she was in safe hands again. But it would have been no use—no use at all! Very strange the whole thing is, but as for Petersfeld—ha, ha, ha!"

And so diverting did Mr. Bloss consider his recent conversation, that he merrily recounted it that self-same evening to his son and heir, Mr. Eldon Bloss, barrister-at-law, over a chosen bottle of port, with strict injunctions not to let the cat out of the bag upon any account whatever. Unluckily Mr. Eldon's bag was about as unsafe an enclosure as his papa's. But whether or not this piece of paternal and after-dinner confidence was justified by the result, must be discovered in a future chapter.

CHAPTER V.

"Well," exclaimed I, as Petersfeld concluded his narrative, "Bloss has been a great deal more communicative than I should have expected. I suppose he felt himself a cat's-paw, as you say, and behaved accordingly. But, after all, are we much wiser than before? If we are, I don't seem to see it."

"How does it strike you, Mr. Kinghorn?" inquired Paul, quietly disparaging my remark. "Worsley, there, never does see things. He'd be chancellor one of these days, if he could."

"It strikes me," replied Kinghorn gravely, "that this visit of yours, Mr. Petersfeld, has been by no means unproductive. I am inclined to opine that it throws a new light altogether, upon this advertisement."

"You think so!" cried Paul, immensely pleased. "Well, now, if you wouldn't mind telling us what you think about the whole matter, I should be really obliged. Of course I gathered something from Bloss, but I have hardly had time to think it into shape, yet."

"Very strange," observed Kinghorn thoughtfully, "was the foolish failure of those detectives, placed upon the track as it were, just the minute the lassie escaped from bounds, and yet dumbfounded from the outset. A private man may indeed be a great fule, which need never be wondered at, seeing he may have been taught no better. But these men, one would suppose, were trained to their trade, and that a young girl should all at once outwit them, and flee away from under their noses, without leaving trace or track behind, passes my comprehension altogether. The present reward would make me think they were not ill-fee'd, and yet they must have been strangely remiss."

"We shall come to about the same conclusion, Kinghorn, after all," observed I.

"By no means. For mark you this: when I cast my eye over the advertisement this morning, it never occurred to me that the 'considerable sum of money' mentioned therein, need be more than a weel-filled purse of gold, such as any young lady of rank and position as the present undoubtedly is—might be supposed to have at her command. You may recollect that I stated as much just now in Hall. And indeed, £500 would be no more than friends might well offer for the recovery of such a girl, without any respect to her belongings. But now Bloss has told us that this sum of money is another thing altogether! Quite a little fortune, you say, were his own words. This alters the case most strangely. Heaven help her, she must have purloined it!"

"Purloined it!" exclaimed Petersfeld with an indignant start. "Impossible! You are joking, Mr. Kinghorn."

It was useless to struggle against the explosion provoked by this fiery and unlooked-for bit of championship. Luckily Petersfeld saw the matter in our light, and laughed as loud as we.

"Still, Mr. Kinghorn," he persisted, "I don't see why you should come to any such conclusion without even the shadow of evidence to support it. There is nothing that I know of, either in the terms of the advertisement, or in what Bloss has told us, inconsistent with the money having been her own."

"How do you suppose she may have earned it, sir?" inquired Kinghorn dryly.

"Earned it! I am not going to suppose any thing of the kind. But why may it not have been left to her—been her own fortune, in fact? Nothing more likely."

"Left to her? her own fortune?" repeated Kinghorn, looking at Paul, with a half curious, half compassionate expression. "Why now, a parson's daughter might have propounded to me that query well enough, but surely not Mr. Petersfeld of Stone Buildings. Will you tell me this, sir—Who would have taken her receipt?"

"True enough," rejoined Paul, after a moment's reflection. "Of course at eighteen she could not give a discharge for money."

"I doubt if there be a young lady—heiress

or no heiress—aged eighteen, within the united Kingdom," pursued Kinghorn, abstractedly, with the tone of one who has been in contact with ignorance, "who at this moment could lawfully put, say a couple of thousand, into her pocket, and proceed to expend it after her own sweet will—let alone in gallanting about the country on her own hook. It could not be, sir."

"What are we to conclude then ?" demanded Petersfeld, with a gasp of despair.

"Let us conclude nothing against the young lady's probity without farther testimony. Many a suspicious matter admits of being explained easily, which is incomprehensible for want of knowing one simple fact. When I employed the word 'purloined,' I made use perhaps of a term for which there was no need. But now, observe. From whomsoever's custody or keeping that money was removed, as it undoubtedly was, it must have been carried away in notes, or paper of some sort. And, knowing thus much, it scarcely can be difficult to discover that person's name and abode. And thereupon, you have made a grand step at once."

"He would advertise, you mean ?"

"Surely. What man do you suppose would sit down and blink, with his hands before him, in such a state of affairs. He would stop the notes—if notes they were—at the bank, and advertise in all the papers. You may depend upon that. And he would do so, mind you, the first moment he discovered his ill-fortune, which, according to your information, may well be some weeks ago. This is but a suggestion, you'll observe, Mr. Petersfeld, which you must work out for yourself. I only affirm that if this 'very considerable sum of money' has not been already advertised, it is more than strange : and that, if you are only canny enough to pick out the right advertisement, you will have made a strong beginning."

"It's a good idea, anyhow," exclaimed Petersfeld. "But suppose after all she happened to carry it away in cash ?"

"Whoo, now ! that's a bright notion, truly ! Why, man, a couple of thousands, even, in sovereigns, is more than any lassie living would travel under far, were it all she had to keep her forever. Besides, though I've seen the value of such a sum in a house, or a steamer, or may be a drove of black beasts, I never yet saw it together in stamped gold, except at the mint indeed, neither I'll wager did you."

"Well, I've no doubt but you're right. Can you suggest any farther clue ?"

"I can. Have you not just heard that the lassie disappeared some three weeks back ?"

"All the worse for me, I should say."

"Not quite. It is indubitably discouraging to find that she has been pursued by detectives so long in vain. Nevertheless, to my mind it opens just this chance. The advertisement I hold in my hand is not addressed, you see, to herself."

"No. To use Bloss's words, it is addressed to those who've got her."

"It is. And you recollect he added that the scandal of this escapade, as he named it, was to be avoided by all means. That's just why the present step, careful as it is, has been so long delayed. That's why they don't give you an address, or an initial even, don't you see. But I would engage that some notice intended for the young lady's eye alone has already appeared ; and knowing what you now know, or may adroitly discover, there's no saying but that it might supply a link at least. In short, you must just lay side by side every thing that you can find out any way which seems likely to bear upon the present matter, and I doubt not' but that, with perseverance and good luck, Mr. Petersfeld, you may at last lay hold of the clew-hope ; and then, with a long pull and a strong pull, who knows but you may even end by hauling in the young leddie herself. Never was neater description laid on paper than that with which her friends have provided you in this present advertisement. And so I wish you the needful luck very honestly."

"I'm immensely obliged indeed," returned Paul. "You'll excuse me, I'm sure, if I leave you at once. I shall just drop down to my club, and look through last month's file of the Times. Good-night, Worsley. I shall send you a line some day to let you know my whereabouts. And, if I shouldn't turn up in a hurry, don't put me in the paper, that's all."

"Strange, vary," muttered Kinghorn, as Paul disappeared. "Is he gone off, think you, without bag or baggage, to seek after this anonymous hussy ? According to the advertisement, she's just as ill provided. So they'll make but an untidy couple."

"Oh, dear no. We share chambers here during the day ; but Petersfeld has his own, or rather his father's, rooms in the Albany. He comes down here pretty regularly—as early as breakfast now and then—just to show that he is really one of us."

"I see. One hundred fi' pound notes is a handful indeed. He would like it ?"

"Like it ? Probably he would. However, I'm quite certain that's not his object in this present instance. I believe that, so far as Petersfeld knows his own mind, he is entirely actuated by a restless adventurous spirit, which must cut out immediate work for itself, the more ardous the better. Besides, in this instance, there is a tinge of romance—curiosity to gratify, with perhaps a bit of gallantry into the bargain. Surely this is enough to account for the whim of an unemployed and impetuous young man."

"Undoubtedly. And I wish him winning luck with all my heart, for he's a nice gentlemanly lad indeed. But faith, Worsley, to run your nose into places where you're neither asked for nor expected, is just the Deil and St. Dunstan over again. And we all know what happened of that. The present is not a common case, I am certain ; and I'd have your friend look out for something besides purring.

and velvet paws. Not that I would dissuade him from the adventure altogether, since he has set his heart upon it. But he may cry 'would it were bed-time and all well!' like old John Falstaff at Shrewsbury, before he finds himself fairly through the business, and safe out on the other side. And now may be you'd not mind turning over with me the copy-hold query, of which we began to speak awhile ago?"

"With the greatest pleasure," returned. I. And we were soon deep in the discussion of an entertaining controversy, touching the exact position of the representatives of a defunct copy-holder, late tenant of the Manor of A.

And the same hour beheld Petersfeld seated in the most sequestered corner of his club library, diligently conning over the last month's file of the *Times*, between a towering pair of silver candlesticks, which he had ordered the waiter to place beside him, upon either hand; so that no possible mistake in his investigations should occur through want of sufficient light.

And here it becomes necessary to divert the course of our narrative, in order to make room for other people whose turn has come to appear upon the stage.

CHAPTER VI.

FOUR or five days, if I remember rightly, had elapsed since the occurrences of my last chapter, during which I had heard nothing whatever of Petersfeld. I knew his independent, unbusiness-like habits better than to expect him to write, without any particular necessity. In fact, to take any sort of trouble "for fun," as he called it, was altogether out of his line. And, being at the time unusually pressed with work, I took very little heed of his absence, satisfied that he would turn up, some fine morning, just as easily as he had disappeared.

The first news I heard of him was in a letter, bearing the Paris postmark, which I found with two or three others, upon my breakfast-table. It was short:

"Grand Hotel, Boulevard des Capucins, Tuesday.

"DEAR WORSLEY:—In Paris, as you see. Full on the scent, thanks to Kingborn; but just now at a confounded check. Expect me at Stone Buildings some time to-morrow. Yours, ever, PAUL G. PETERSFELD."

Another note, written in a clear, feminine hand, said:

"Mr. and Mrs. Buttermere request the honor of Mr. John Worsley's company at dinner in Harley Street on Friday next, the 9th instant, at seven o'clock."

There was a corresponding envelope addressed to Petersfeld; evidently a counterpart of mine, and which I accordingly took the liberty of opening and answering in his name. I had no objection myself to the capital dinner which Buttermere always hung out; and I knew that Petersfeld liked to extend the circle of his visiting acquaintance in all respectable directions.

Moreover, nothing vexes a man of the world more than to have left an invitation of any sort unanswered, even for a single post. It is one of those cases in which excuses count for little; being a simple crime in itself, like sending letters without stamps, or calling people by wrong names.

Perhaps the reader may like to accompany these twin notes of acceptance to their destination, and make acquaintance at once with the three young ladies of whose existence he has already become aware.

"There, girls!" exclaimed Mrs. Buttermere, tossing the notes upon the table, at which her daughters sat engaged in various feminine occupations around the evening lamp. "That's fortunate. We shall just make up fourteen at dinner on Friday. Mr. Worsley and Mr. Petersfeld are both coming. Here's our list; so you may set to work and arrange it among yourselves. I'll just look in and tell your papa that it's all settled. He'll like to know."

Whether that eminent Queen's counsel liked to know any thing unconnected with the contents of the great white briefs, which he systematically devoured after dinner, and digested until bed-time, is not so certain. But, at all events, their mamma's absence gave the young ladies the opportunity of discussing that fashionable domestic puzzle—how shall they sit—entirely at their leisure.

Charlotte, Louisa, and Belinda were the names of these damsels. Collectively, however, they were better known as "Lotty, Loo, and Linda" among those of the junior members of our fraternity who had the luck to enjoy an *entrée* to the house in Harley Street. And, to tell the truth, there were a good many stories current touching transactions between various young gentlemen whose first wig was still crisp and curly, and the several partners in that elegant firm. This, however, is no business of mine.

Now, whensoever there chance to be three maiden daughters of one house, it invariably happens, if the experience of centuries is to count for any thing, that the youngest is all that is nice and lovely; the elders jealous and unkindly disposed.

From the age of Khosrou Schah, whose unparalleled matrimonial disasters are recorded in the Arabian Nights—from the birthday of Cinderella, or that of the unlucky Beauty of Beastly memory—from the time of Regan and Goneril—the rule has constantly held good. Nobody, therefore, need be surprised to find that Linda enjoyed the proper advantages, and paid the peculiar penalties of her birthright. But more of her in her turn.

Lotty, the senior partner, was of the venerable age of twenty-one. She was blonde, moderately handsome, and the victim of a dissatisfied spirit. The world, according to her thinking, was not altogether as happy a place as it might have been. Its grapes hung high, and were probably sour and dusty. Whether she had been disappointed in her own private gleaning, is more than I can tell. But it was early days to disbelieve in that ladder of Gold—so long delayed, so often raised when least expected.

One remembers a cynical French saying—that in thinking over the misfortune of our best friend, there is always the germ of a pleasant sensation. In the present instance, the theory received an illustration. Whatever may have been Lotty's particular crosses, they attracted a very mild amount of sympathy from her junior partners, who, on the contrary, were in the habit of posting up in the private ledgers of memory all her peevish sayings and doings, for reproduction at inconvenient opportunities.

In every contest for a favorite cavalier—seat in a carriage, or place at a picnic, it was so atrociously delightful to be able to say—"Oh, Lotty doesn't care for this sort of thing. She's so good she won't mind;" a quiet process of annihilation which would probably have disconcerted a saint, had Lotty been such in good earnest.

Loo, the second partner, was some two years younger than her sister—handsomer, cleverer, and any thing but used up. Her first object in life was to cut out Lotty by some splendid coup in the matrimonial bazar. Her second, to escape being cut out by Linda, who was bent upon winning, and in fact coming up at a dangerous pace. The very idea, good gracious, of the celebrated firm coming to grief that way, and suddenly collapsing into "Lotty and Loo—spinsters," was a great deal too dismal for sober realization. Unluckily, it appeared any thing but an improbable wind-up of the existing business.

Fair, like her sisters, Linda's figure was *petite* and faultless, while her delicately-modeled features had that peculiar and indescribable charm which so rarely survives the school-room. Very few faces retain that bewitching air of *naïveté* and innocence up to the time when its value would be beyond all price. And hers, to use an expression which is at least intelligible, was a regular little kitten-face; now so deliciously demure, now, in an instant lighting up, as if fun or mischief were the only things in the world worth living for.

Her complexion was the most perfect thing you ever saw, and her hands—oh those wonderful little white hands! ought to have had a chapter all to themselves in Dr. Bell's Bridgewater treatise. To call those twinkling fairy fingers "organs," was plain profanation. Any one could see that they were not constructed for mere every-day useful purposes. They had, indeed, much more destructive work before them, and had already endangered many a young gentleman's peace of mind. And they would probably continue to do so again and again, until at last one of them should be imprisoned in a tiny gold circlet, by way of pledge that they, one and all, should thereafter keep the peace, and do mischief no more forever.

Besides these advantages, Linda dressed better than her sisters, partly, perhaps, from better taste—partly, certainly, from more extensive opportunities. For Buttermere, who was quite foolish over his youngest pet, had a way of every now and then giving her his gloves to mend; when, owing doubtless to the prodigious amount of fees which diurnally traveled through the hands of that learned gentleman, a stray sovereign or so was frequently found lodged in the thumb.

And it was quite a treat to see the paternal visage expand, as Linda jumped upon his knee with the resuscitated gloves, exclaiming, "There papa! Aren't they nicely sewn? Do you know, I don't wonder you found them uncomfortable! If you only knew the no end of work I've had clearing all sorts of rubbish out of the fingers!"

Now it is no part of my business to tell tales of my characters, or even allude to their failings unnecessarily. Therefore, lest any thing which it may fall within my province hereafter to relate should happen to convey a disadvantageous impression of little Linda, I wish every body. distinctly to recollect that her chances and education had been sadly against her, and to lay the saddle upon the right horse.

Her mother, a mere worldly woman of little sense, would have spoiled most girls in her unblushing attempts to pitchfork them into matrimony. "Train up a child in the way she shouldn't go, and when she grows up will be time to depart from it" is a maxim neither safe nor sound, albeit acted upon by wiser people than Mrs. Buttermere. Her father's petting was scarcely less injudicious, and placed her in a false position with regard to her sisters; who, in their turn, were perhaps in some small degree less inexcusable for uncharity toward a sisterly rival.

Such, however, was the firm; in which, if the partners didn't see their way toward pulling all together, there was quite as much cordiality, and probably less discord, than I have known in certain grand commercial houses doing real business in this city of London.

But it is time to return to the drawing-room table.

"Read out the card, Linda!" exclaimed Loo. "Don't keep it all to yourself. We want to know who's coming."

"All right, Loo, my dear. First of all Mr. Justice Brindlebun and Lady Brindlebun."

"Well, that settles itself. Papa takes my lady. Mr. Justice waits on mamma. Who next?"

"Mr. and Mrs. Springletop—Mr. and Mrs. Poppit. Hands across, don't you see?—that's all. Married people ought to dine with married people and entertain one another about their families."

"Much you know about the matter! However, you're right for once," remarked Loo. "The fact is, Mr. Springletop and Mrs. Poppit do flirt so desperately whenever they get a chance that they not only entertain each other, but, every body else. Poor little Mr. Poppit! He does get so aggravated, and then drinks like a fish and shouts out questions across the table to Mr. Springletop, which he knows he can't answer, on purpose to make him shut up and look foolish."

"How many more?" demanded Lotty.

"Only three—all bachelors—Mr. Goldwin, Mr. Worsley, and Mr. Petersfeld."

"Well?"

"Just what we want," rejoined Linda. "You shall have Mr. Goldwin, Lotty, my dear, because he's a beautiful dark dandy with diamond studs and an eye-glass, and all that sort of thing: much too good for small people like me; and Loo shall have Mr. Worsley, because, though he's rather a muff, he's going to be Vice-Chancellor or something, some day, papa says. And I'll dine with Mr. Petersfeld, because there's nobody else left. Nothing could be more capital."

Naturally enough this cool appropriation of the new guest, about whom a great deal of curiosity, to say the least of it, existed, was not received with acclamation by the elder sisters.

"You are quite welcome to Mr. Petersfeld, Linda," observed Lotty in a freezing voice.

"Quite," added Loo, with a slight toss of her head. "We wouldn't stand in your way upon any account."

"Why, what nonsense! You know perfectly well that there's no choosing in the matter. He's the youngest of the three and can't well be sent down before them; and I'm the youngest of you, so we must go together—hey?"

To this unsatisfactory truth the sisters could only reply by a mitigated, young-lady-like snort.

"I can't conceive what you mean, either of you," resumed Linda, almost out of patience. "You seem to want a quarrel, and to expect me to begin."

"I wish you were back in the school-room!" broke out Loo, impetuously. "It's too bad that such a chit as you should always interfere with arrangements. Mamma should get a great big school-boy with short trousers and a silver watch for *your* partner. Then you wouldn't make a fool of yourself, and of us into the bargain."

"I'm afraid what Charley Lavender said of you at his club—yes, up in the smoking-room, before goodness knows how many men—is only too true," murmured Lotty. "I wish you were aware, Linda, of what men *do* say of girls who come down stairs before they know the way of the world, or what's what in society."

"Perhaps Mr. Petersfeld likes that sort of thing," continued Loo. "I hear he is eccentric. Isn't he to have ever so many thousand a year, and to be a baronet some day, when somebody dies?"

"Don't ask me," growled Lotty. "I know nothing whatever about Mr. Petersfeld. Linda has it all pat, I'll be bound."

To this petulant explosion of ultra-sisterly jealousy Linda disdained a corresponding reply. To place an angry person plainly in the wrong is to pull the bone from a snarling dog. He

must have something to worry, and ten to one if you interfere with his occupation as it stands, you will divert it with very little advantage to yourself. I don't mean to say that she was not considerably annoyed at the moment; but, however that may have been, she came down upon her sisters with a brilliant flank movement, which disconcerted them both.

"Come!" said she, her sunny little face lighting up, as if with some delightful idea. "I couldn't be as old as Lotty, of course, if I tried; and as to being as wise as you, Loo, my dear, that's still more out of the question. However, I beg to decline the school-boy, and to offer you both a bet if you only dare to take it."

"A bet!" exclaimed Lotty contemptuously.

"Certainly. Mr. Petersfeld, you'll observe, is none of my choice. Moreover, I have never set eyes upon him in my life. Now, we are engaged to go to the Zoological Gardens on Saturday with those dreadful country cousins, the whole clan of the Bunnytails—are we not?"

"Dear me, I had forgotten it, I declare," replied Loo. "Why on earth we need be so frightfully civil to them every time they think proper to come to town, passes my comprehension altogether!"

"My gracious, Loo, don't you know better than that? Members of Parliament, like papa, must take notice of their constituents, even when they aren't their own brothers-in-law, as Mr. Bunnytail is. Why, papa would have been turned out last election, if it hadn't been for Mr. Bunnytail and his friends, the farmers. If he and aunt were ten times as dreadful, they'd have to be rubbed the right way. But no matter for that. We are going to the Zoological Gardens, are we not?"

"I suppose we are. Worse luck to us. I do hate dromedaries and all that sort of thing like poison."

"Never mind the dromedaries. Listen to me. I bet you each a pair of new gloves that Mr. Petersfeld shall not only talk to me all the evening after dinner, but that he shall appear at the Zoological Gardens next day, and talk to me, and me alone, and follow me about all the afternoon like a regular showman. There, now! Say 'done,' if you dare!"

"Well, you are too dreadful, Linda!" gasped Lotty. "Do you mean to say that you'll actually ask him to come sweet-hearting, like a housemaid? I do hope to goodness gracious he's a modest man, or got some rag of decency left him, that's all!"

"Fiddlestick, Charlotte! I give you my honor I will never even allude to the Gardens, if either of you will simply let him know we are going. Now, there's a fair wager. You have called me all sorts of contemptuous names. Now, I defy you both! Why don't you say 'done?'"

"Who's to be umpire?" demanded Lotty, with a supercilious air. "Are we to believe our own eyes, or only what you may please to tell us?"

"Judge for yourselves, of course!" replied Linda. "What do you suppose I should care for victory, if I didn't make you acknowledge your defeat?"

"Done with you," said Loo, desperately. "A pair of new gloves at three-and-six."

"Done!" echoed Lotty, who 'didn't see exactly what else to say, though she had uncomfortable misgivings as to the result. "I'm utterly ashamed of the whole thing, Linda; but if willful will, why willful must. I only hope you'll get a right-down, good lesson, without disgracing any body besides yourself. Of course Mr. Petersfeld may be fool enough for any thing, for all we know."

"Part of my chance!" retorted Linda laughing. "Recollect, my number is six and a quarter, and my favorite color bright chocolate. Recollect, also, that I leave it to your honor to tell fairly about the Zoo. I promise not to say a word myself."

CHAPTER VII.

It was not until four o'clock of the very day of the Buttermere dinner, that Petersfeld made his appearance at chambers, on his way from the terminus at London Bridge. I had naturally begun to feel not a little uneasy at his absence, for it is no joke to have forged a man's acceptance to a note of invitation, and to be obliged to confess the fact with shame, at the last moment, to a justly irritated and disappointed hostess.

His arrival, therefore, was a welcome relief, although I was too much engaged at the moment to listen to the story of his adventures. Accordingly, he soon took his departure, promising to appear in Harley Street at seven punctually, and engaging me on the other hand to accompany him, after dinner, to the Albany, and hear all he had to tell, even if we gave the whole night to it.

Three facts, indeed, were all that I had time to gather during our short interview. First: that he had actually ascertained the name and late abode of the missing young lady, beyond all possibility of mistake. Secondly: that—like the detectives themselves—he had signally failed in discovering any clue whatever to her actual whereabouts. Lastly: that he had arrived at the irrepressible and uncomfortable misgiving, that all was not as it should be upon the part of her friends—to use his own words, that there was foul play somewhere.

This belief, indeed, had worked itself so deeply into his mind, that the idea of a mere exciting chase, brilliant with adventure, and perhaps closing in romance, was no longer—as I could easily perceive—the principal motive for continued exertion.

Lightly as the pursuit had been taken up, it might as lightly have been abandoned, but for a grave change in the aspect under which he had begun to view it. Wondering even to himself at the blind and headlong manner in which he had rushed recklessly into what was—in the outset, certainly—no business of his, a gradual conviction had possessed his mind, that by a sort of providential chance, he had blundered into an affair in which he was, as it were, a predestined actor, with a duty and a responsibility deservedly cast upon his hands.

Is there any thing in this to smile at? Did you yourself, reader of these pages, never encounter some sudden, some unexpected occasion, upon which you might have made yourself the instrument of untold good, had you only chosen to interfere? I use the word "interfere" advisedly, for in its base and secondary sense, it has probably furnished as much excuse for plain neglect of duty, as any in the English language. Was it not, if you recollect, one day when you passed on, happy to be able to assure yourself that the matter was no business of yours? No? Then you are fortunate, indeed. I have: and the recollection has embittered many a moment since. It was an opportunity offered me, a chance of service, the reward of which was, assuredly, not in this world. But I passed on, with the dreadful, the irrevocable truth upon my lips, that the affair was no business of mine.

However, since nothing can be more foreign to my purpose than to regale my reader with melodramatic extravagance, I may at once say that Petersfeld was altogether wrong in his suspicion that any thing like foul play had occurred in the present instance. That, in his hot inexperience, he may have had strong apparent reason for coming to the conclusion which he did, is quite possible, but another thing altogether, as in due time will appear. Meanwhile, it may be as well not to be late for dinner.

As I happened to be the first arrival in Harley Street that evening, I had not only the pleasure of being very kindly welcomed by the family present, but of entertaining myself with watching other people as they entered the room.

Those who study character, should always avail themselves of such an opportunity, where a great deal that is suggestive may often be picked up in a few moments.

The fact is, that although the entering a drawing-room before dinner is a feat which many people perform several times in the course of each week of their lives, yet such are the conditions of complete civilization, that between the clatter and clang at the hall door, announcing the first arrival, and the welcome apparition at the drawing-room door of an obsequious personage in black, shortly after the arrival of the last, there is generally an embarrassing interval, which a recent Chinese embassador used to rejoice in, as the only portion of the day during which he found himself reminded of the ineffable proprieties of his own Flowery Land.

It is a *mauvais quart d'heure*, during which nobody appears to be naturally alive—when wits are shy and beauties dull, and when middle-aged gentlemen, who in ten minutes' time are going to be jolly for the rest of the evening,

B

talk grievous platitudes with a miserable show of being quite serious, and positively amused in good earnest.

And, as each successive visitor alights within the spell-bound circle, it is with such reckless resignation to the exigency of the moment, that to guess from first appearances what he or she may be like in more lucid intervals, or may probably turn out after a short course of soup and sherry, presents a problem well worthy the attention of any unoccupied philosopher.

Thus Mr. and Mrs. Poppit sidled in first, with a conscious simper, as if they had just been privately married in the cloak-room.

Mr. and Mrs. Springletop came next, with radiant air and ambling steps, looking as people are bound to look upon such occasions, in tip-top spirits, and full of the pleasantest anticipations imaginable.

Then arrived Mr. Justice Brindlebun and his lady, smiling like a well-to-do couple in the farming line; the former with just a touch of the hippopotamus in plain clothes, but as jovial and easy an old gentleman as one would wish to meet.

Immediately afterward, Mr. Goldwin sparkled in, all wristband, studs, and eye-glass, with his flat hat under his arm, and pulling off his white gloves, to all appearance just landed from some magnificent planet, and bewildered in plain wax-candle-light.

Last of all came Petersfeld, elaborately got up certainly, but as easy and unembarrassed as if strolling into our own chambers before breakfast. He was happily unaware of the intense interest which his appearance created in the minds of the three partners respectively; and, after gracefully making his salutations to host and hostess, allowed himself as easily to be introduced to Linda, as the young lady whom he was to take down to dinner.

Preoccupied as he was with other thoughts, it was not in his nature that he should be indifferent to her pretty face and figure, lustrous with youth and health. Whether the knowledge that those snowy muslin flounces had been arranged for his especial benefit—that those glossy sheaves of auburn hair had been parted and smoothed with such elaborate attention for the same purpose, and that even the tiny locket which danced like a star upon her dainty bosom, had been carefully selected to flash fascination upon him alone, would have made any difference, is perhaps an awkward question. And what might have been the result of a suspicion that his own performance that evening had been betted upon as freely by the young lady herself as that of a colt at Newmarket, is a speculation better left alone.

Buttermere himself moved about the room a perfect picture of happiness and hospitality. The old boy enjoyed nothing in the world, out of court, so much as these snug little dinners. Fourteen was his regular number, partly because it just suited the dimensions of his modest dining-room, partly because it was one of the numbers which admit of such an arrangement as seats a lady on each side of her host, a gentleman on either side of his hostess, with alternate lady and gentleman down both sides of the table. And upon this latter point Mr. Buttermere was minutely particular—a place for every body, and every body in his or her place—being in his opinion one of the many secrets of success in one of the most arduous responsibilities which can be undertaken by a citizen of the world.

Another secret—the happy selection and combination of one's guests—he flattered himself he had not overlooked upon the present occasion. In short, it was with feelings of more than every-day complacency that, having carefully counted his visitors backward and forward, he turned to Mrs. Buttermere with the stereotyped smile and expression customary in such cases, and meekly said:—"I think I may ring for dinner, may I not? We seem to be all here."

Oh no, Mr. Buttermere, oh no. Not by any manner of means. You may count your company and ring your bell; but we are not all here. Not all!

For there arose a sound of conversation upon the staircase, at first simply mysterious and irregular; then louder and more energetic, as if somebody was being punished. And then the drawing-room door was suddenly flung open, and a vague voice announced—"Mr. and Mrs. Bunnytail!" and was gone.

It was the transaction of a moment. So are many of the casualties of life.

An enormous woman, followed by a short sunburnt, stubble-headed man, sailed steadily across the room, like a frigate with prize in tow. And such a cruiser! She really might have been shown for money at the town-fair, and described to the sound of the drum. You never saw such a fat, florid face, cascaded on either side with floods of golden ringlets, shiny sleek. You never saw such magnificent fat arms, such a breadth of bosom, such girth of waist, and exuberant, well-developed weight. If the tough little gentleman astern had any thing to do with it—I mean in the professional administration of oat-cake, swedes and mangold-wurzel, or any better adapted esculent, I should like to walk with him through his home farm, and pat and pinch the remainder of his stock. He ought to have won the medal of every known society whose aim it is to encourage unwary beasts in overeating themselves, and disfigure our shops at Christmastide with bloated and unwieldly carcasses, only fit to be devoured in darkness, amid the bellowing of all the giants.

But, if Mrs. Bunnytail's appearance was commanding, her attire, when you had leisure to consider it, was quite as worthy of wonder.

I suppose it was, in point of fact, the dream of some Arcadian modiste, inspired by one of the plates in a French Fashion-book. Of course, as a bachelor, my connoisseurship in such matters will be taken for what it is worth. I only recollect that she seemed to set us all in a blaze with a crimson satin gown glittering with bugle lace, while her neck and arms, which rivaled the dress in point of complexion, were festooned with outrageous jewelry, producing a result which I think she would like me to describe as "gorgeous."

Moreover, notwithstanding her ample circumference, she positively rolled top-heavy under the frightful weight of flowers, lace and feather stacked upon her head. It looked, I declare, as if some insane tropical bird had built its nest upon that stupendous summit—indeed it may have been hatching there at the moment, for aught I know to the contrary.

"Well, Sister Carlo!" she exclaimed, steering straight for Mrs. Buttermere, "you know you said you hoped we'd dine with you often, as long as we could stay in London; and so here we are, you see, though goodness knows if I'd only known who you'd got here, I wouldn't have come;—anyhow I wouldn't have brought Bunnytail. And now I do hope and trust we bring no inconvenience with us; though that's like talking about spilt milk, isn't it, because really, what between the cat and the parlor-maid, as to keeping any thing at our lodgings, the thing's impossible, and to go straight back again, would be just going to bed at once; and as you recommended the apartments, it makes finding fault more unpleasant than ever, doesn't it?"

Mrs. Buttermere had been in the act of rising from her chair at the moment of this unparalleled intrusion. Her first impulse was to sink back again and faint away dead. Her second, an injudicious one, to exclaim, with a dreadful face, "Who are you?" and command that the Bunnytails should be forthwith hustled into the street as a couple of sturdy impostors. But, alas, the indignant volubility with which Mrs. Bunnytail would only too clearly proclaim her identity, was matter of very plain prophecy; and terror held her dumb.

Could a word have consigned Mrs. Bunnytail and her consort to the uttermost part of the Red Sea, or landed them both within the crater of Cotopaxi, I suspect the worthy couple would have vanished upon their travels in less time than it takes me to write this line. What would the Brindlebuns think?—what would the Poppits say?—how should she ever look the Springletops in the face again? And as to Petersfeld, why had he ever been "brought home" on that horrible night?

"I thought you were going to the theatre this evening!" she gasped at last. "Oh, why didn't you go!"

"Why that's true enough," retorted the great sister, nothing abashed. "We were going, sure alive, and meant to go, only Bunnytail, don't you see, has a wonderful knack of asking questions; so he asks and asks, and at last he makes out that these performers, or whatever you call them, don't finish up till some outlandish time to-morrow, anyhow long after twelve o'clock to-night; and if Bunnytail ain't in bed before the clock strikes ten, why he goes to roost wherever he is, and snorts like his own bull. So, don't you see, the theatre was no place for us; and we had, as it were, to cast about how to spend a companionable evening; and, as luck would have it, I says to him, says I, Law, Bunnytail, good man, why not spend it with Sister Carlo? Let's dress up at once—."

"Oh, my goodness!" shuddered poor Mrs. Buttermere, on the verge of hysterics, "Charlotte's my name, if you'd only leave it alone! Couldn't you go down stairs—or up stairs—or do any thing but stand there?"

Lucky it was that Mr. Buttermere had exactly the tact and aplomb necessary for encountering the most desperate emergency. Had he been in court, before the chancellor himself, he could not have shown more conspicuous generalship and self-possession.

"My dear Mrs. Bunnytail, say no more. We are delighted to see you. How are you, Bunnytail! Just the man we wanted to fill our only spare place." And in the twinkling of an eye the unlucky couple were introduced all round. Petersfeld and Linda, as the junior couple, were begged in a whisper, the one to escort Mrs. Bunnytail, the other to pass to dinner under Mr. Bunnytail's wing—then to assume their proper places, side by side, as if nothing had happened, leaving their morganatic partners to edge in where they could.

And so, in five minutes' time we found ourselves upon the staircase, rather the better, if any thing, for recent troubles, during which Lotty had looked on like a vestal insulted at the altar, Loo with the more intolerant feelings of a maiden of this world, while Linda laughed outright.

CHAPTER VIII.

"Well," exclaimed Mrs. Bunnytail, cramming herself into a chair next to Petersfeld, who had Linda on his left, "this is comfortable indeed, and as smart as you please! You live in London, sir, I dare say, and living and lodging comes all natural. But just you come up from the country as we do. You'd wish yourself back again often enough. But law!" continued the lady, glancing round at the épergnes, cut glass, spun-sugar and hot-house flowers, "what's the meaning of all this? It looks more like a dessert than a dinner, to my mind. We're never going to dine backward, are we? Not that I mind, only Bunnytail's got a short temper, and if he doesn't soon get his tooth into something wholesome, he won't like it, I know. Lucky for him he would step in for a snack this afternoon at the 'Six Bells.' I dare say you know it well, sir. A public-house with a blue door and plate-glass window, just off Charing Cross. It reminded him, don't you see, of the old sign where he takes his dinner market days. La! I do declare here's a dish of hot broth, and I never saw it come; and yes, my man, I'll take a glass of wine, and it's just what I was wanting, thank you."

But it is high time to put a padlock at once upon Mrs. Bunnytail's tongue. In spite of her voluble conversation, to which Petersfeld listened apparently with the most winning interest and attention, Linda was not neglected; neither did she forget to improve the shining hour to the very best of her ability, which was indeed far above the average.

I need hardly say that the only too palpable manner in which she was rapidly coming over Petersfeld was watched by her sisters with unmitigated displeasure. Lotty pretended to herself that she was scandalized, when in fact only jealous; while Loo's exasperation proceeded to the extent of seriously interfering with her dinner. They were only too delighted at the incessant interruptions of Mrs. Bunnytail, whose running commentary upon the whole entertainment, intermixed with her experience of life in London, as contrasted with housekeeping in the country, were loudly audible across the table.

It would be a great mistake, however, to suppose that Linda was trusting to her own personal attractions, or pretty flow of small-talk, alone, to win the chocolate gloves, and drive her sisters in confusion from their own ground. Quite the contrary. She had a famous piece of artillery in reserve, which she hesitated to let off *à propos* to nothing, but which nevertheless lay primed and loaded, and which, come what might, must be discharged, at all hazards, before the ladies left the table. Luckily, almost at the last moment, she was spared the trouble of finding an excuse for the shot.

"By the way, Buttermere," suddenly exclaimed Mr. Justice Brindlebun in his sonorous voice, "have you ever, among your many clients, chanced to learn the meaning of that strange advertisement in the *Times*, the other day? Five hundred pounds reward, if you recollect, offered for the recovery of a lovely and mysterious damsel, who seems to have walked off with her pockets full of gold and silver."

"No, indeed I have not, Sir John," replied Buttermere, from the lower end of the table. "There's a romance of real life, depend upon it, at the bottom of that story. It was talked about a good deal when the notice first appeared, and the singular thing is, that nobody I ever met, even pretended to know any thing about it. Never yet heard a bit of scandal discussed at the club, when somebody or other didn't say he only wished he was at liberty to tell all he knew."

"She ought to be caught, I should say," observed Mr. Goldwin, in the tone of one accustomed to deliver weighty remarks *ex cathedrâ*:—"caught of course, if only to satisfy the public, whose curiosity she has so unfeelingly tantalized. Wonder if they'll tell us, if they do catch her. Very likely not, I should say. Wonder where she is now?"

"Last seen near the London Tavern, hailing a hansom," said Mr. Springletop. "Poppit jumped in after her."

"What, my husband!" exclaimed Mrs. Poppit, with a little affected scream.

"It's a dreadful business, in my opinion," remarked Mrs. Springletop. "Only to think of having one's face and dress paraded in all the newspapers, with a reward for one's conviction, as if one was going to be removed in the van."

Mrs. Springletop's experience in criminal law having been chiefly derived from a perusal of the daily police report, suggested this as the final doom of the wicked; in England, at all events.

"I'm not so sure that a month in the House of Correction would be at all a bad lesson for her," observed Mrs. Buttermere, by way of promptly discountenancing any such escapade as matter for imitation in her own family.

"What's all this? For goodness' sake somebody tell me what we're all talking about!" exclaimed Mrs. Bunnytail.

"Isn't it odd, Mr. Petersfeld," remarked Linda, in a low tone, and with the most captivating air of innocent confidence—"isn't it odd that I should know more of this mysterious affair than all these good people put together?"

"You!" exclaimed Petersfeld, with a start of astonishment. "Is it possible?"

"Pray—pray, Mr. Petersfeld, don't jump again like that, or we shall have every one looking at us. Yes. It is not only possible, but perfectly true."

"I beg your pardon, I'm sure," said Paul, "but really if you had told me that the young lady was under the table at this moment, I should scarcely have been more surprised. Will you tell me her name?"

"Not for five hundred pounds!" replied Linda, with a playful shake of her head. "I assure you, Mr. Petersfeld, I can keep a secret. How can her name have any possible interest for you, unless as a mere point of curiosity?"

"It happens, however, that I am very much interested in the case," returned Petersfeld, gravely. "As to her name, I assure you I know that as well as you."

"Oh no—no! Else why did you ask me? You are not serious, I am quite sure. Tell me the name, and I shall begin to believe you."

For an instant, the ungracious suspicion flashed across Petersfeld's mind that his pretty companion was making fun of him. She might possibly have heard of his late proceedings, and thought it fair sport enough to get a "rise" out of him after dinner. So he replied to the challenge by a shake of his own head, implying that the conversation had come to an end so far as he was concerned.

"You doubt my word: I see that," persisted Linda, pretending to look vexed. "I am not suspicious myself, and I do not choose to be suspected by others. I will be the first to tell. Only there's my sister looking as hard at us as if we were talking high treason. You can speak on your fingers? Well, watch mine—

quite promiscuous, you know—while I speak to Mr. Worsley across the table."

Of course, in her simple artlessness, Linda knew of no better way than this to convey an important piece of information. Of course she hadn't the slightest idea that those little nimble fingers could be doing any other business than passing it silently and secretly to her attentive neighbor. Of course, if the pretty twinkling telegraph, working with such bewitching neatness, should make him long to snatch and work it himself, and keep it for his own private use all the rest of his life, it would be an exceedingly odd result; but no affair of hers. It was obviously a quiet careful way of imparting a secret, and adopted accordingly.

Quick as thought, then a surname, were spelled out. Then the name of a country house. Then the little fairy hands clapped thrice, as if in the glee of childish triumph—folded themselves pleasantly together, and were still.

Nobody was a bit the wiser; except, indeed, Mrs. Bunnytail, who, conceiving at once the sensible idea that this might be the way in which town-bred young ladies explained the state of their feelings to favored young gentlemen, was much edified by the performance. Not being an adept at the manual alphabet, the various symbols, as she considered them, were naturally perplexing; although, as to the meaning of one or two of them, she felt there could be no possible mistake.

Paul sat thunderstruck. It was evident that Linda knew all. "May I ask you one more question," he began, breathless and confused at this astounding revelation.

"Not now. Look! Mamma's signaling to Lady Brindlebun, and can't catch her eye. We shall be going up stairs in one minute. Another time."

"I am not asking out of mere curiosity."

"No, no, I dare say not. But you should have asked sooner. See, we are going; I can tell you no more now."

And in that rustling sweep of silk and muslin with which ladies disappear from a dining-room, was Linda borne away.

I have not thought it worth while to say much of Mr. Bunnytail's behavior during dinner, because, in point of fact, beyond being very quiet and clumsy, I can scarcely say that he behaved at all. Fishes, I believe, are proverbially supposed to drink very often and speak very seldom, which was precisely the case with my neighbor. However, just after the departure of the ladies, and almost before Buttermere had assumed his position at the head of the table, he suddenly exclaimed, after a thump of his fist, which set every wine-glass jingling:

"She should ha' come to Bunnytail Bottom!"

"Hey—who should have come?" exclaimed the judge, looking down the table, his rosy face on the *qui vive* for a joke. "Are you speaking of the young lady, Mr. Bunnytail?"

"Aye, my lord," returned the farmer slowly. "She should have come to Bunnytail Bottom. She would have been safe there. Safe enough. My house is my castle."

"To be sure! She wouldn't get away again in a hurry—eh? Well, now, if she came to me, I should take much the same view. I should think twice before I parted with her for five hundred pounds. I think I'd keep her—economically, of course—and stand out for the thousand."

"Saving your presence, my lord," replied Bunnytail, upon whose elocution a liberal bottle of port had bestowed an almost judicial solemnity, "if I could harbor such a thought—in the way, mind you, of putting it in act—I should deserve nothing better than to be tossed by my own bull. Nothing I should hate more, you understand; but I'd take it, if I so deserved it, like a cheerful man."

"Just so," rejoined Brindlebun, mischievously, "I see exactly what you mean. If you had the young lady, and I came to molest her, you'd run your bull, and let him carry the answer. That's it, I think."

"Ho, ho, ho!" chuckled Bunnytail. "I'd give a pound, any time, to see Solomon do it! There'd be no mistaking what he'd got to say, would there? So that's law, my lord?"

"Come, come, Mr. Bunnytail! I'm not going to be let in for a legal opinion after dinner; especially where I'm a party concerned. It would be quite enough for me, I take it, if it turned out to be a fact."

"Fact!" retorted the farmer, over whose faculties the predestined hour of roost was rapidly stealing. "Aye, fact. I'm a juryman of twenty years' standing and more—I am. Many's the judge I've seen sitting penned up like a pig with a medal, and not a word to say for himself, till we gentlemen made it convenient to step back into court and tell him what o'clock it was by the fact. Facts are facts, sir. And if ever there was a fact with a tail and a pair of horns to it, that fact is my bull, Solomon."

"What a pity it is, Mr. Bunnytail," suggested Petersfeld, whose excitement during this desultory conversation had become unendurable, and who felt that he must explode in unexpected confession, if he kept silence a moment longer. "What a pity it is that this forlorn young woman can't be made aware of your kind intentions. If we could only contrive to let her know that there was one spot, at least, in England where peace and protection awaited her, and that that one spot was Bunnytail Bottom—what glorious news to carry!"

"Carry it yourself, young gentleman," replied Bunnytail, whose conversational faculties were in process of rapid eclipse. "Carry it yourself, if it's no trouble, and say I sent it. Just you bring her there, any time between milking in the morning and half-past nine at night, and see whether Laban Bunnytail isn't as good as his word! Let the Beadles come. Let any body come. The more the better, I say. To be sure. The more the better. While she wants to stay she stays. When she wants to go she goes. And if any man would lay his finger upon her, within my gates, except in the way of kindness, Laban Bunnytail will know the reason why. That's all I shall say."

Nothing could have been truer than the last remark ; for Mr. Bunnytail thereupon fell immediately into a snoring sleep from which nothing short of violence could have aroused him. And a few slight attempts in that direction, made as we quitted the dining-room, having been received with unmeasured obloquy, there was nothing for it but to leave him in his chair, with orders to the servants upon no account whatever to disturb him.

So the latter, in clearing the table, laughed as gently as possible, and not liking to leave their master's guest entirely in the dark, compromised matters by lighting a flat-candlestick and placing it reverently before him.

And there Mr. Bunnytail was found, an hour later, by his buxom partner ; his chin buried in his waistcoat, and his hands folded complacently across his stomach—looking like a weather-beaten Chinese Joss, whom some good-natured worshiper had charitably provided with a nightlight.

That he ever troubled his head again, without reason, about his rambling challenge to Petersfeld is extremely unlikely. Nevertheless, as we have already seen, these general invitations do sometimes lead to unexpected results, and I would not have you too hastily dismiss Mr. Bunnytail from recollection, at the conclusion of the present chapter.

All Petersfeld's attempts, and they proceeded certainly to the very outmost borders of discretion, to get any farther confidence that evening out of Linda, were perfectly futile. A young lady of the house has her own proper duties to attend to ; and if she has no spare time to devote to comparing notes with an inquisitive gentleman, why so much the worse for him. Without in the least evading Petersfeld, she easily let him feel that, if he wanted farther information, he must ask for it at the proper time, which unquestionably was not then. And so, after having been twice discomfited—once at the tea-table, and afterward beside the piano, there was no help for it but to take leave like other people.

A few moments found us bowling down Bond Street, in a hansom, on our way to his rooms in the Albany.

CHAPTER IX.

THAT dim and jealously-guarded "No Thoroughfare," which runs from Vigo Street to Piccadilly, almost side by side with the Burlington Arcade, and which we now know as the Albany, was a strawberry garden a hundred years ago. It belonged to the mansion in Piccadilly which it now tunnels, then the residence of His Royal Highness the Duke of York, whose second title has since given a name to the whole concern. However, the last strawberry was picked before any of us were born or thought of; and it is now simply a covered avenue, with a range of bachelor apartments on either side ; among the quietest and most severely fashionable in all London.

Paul's sitting-room was a large, low, heavily-wainscoted apartment, upon the ground floor. The chambers had been in his family for an immense number of years, cherished and preserved as forming a sort of *pied à terre*, in the great metropolis. The stiff, black, oaken furniture dated from the day of an equally stiff grandpapa, whose portrait surmounted the mantle-piece. The more modern decorations were Paul's own. And nobody knew his own taste more clearly or gratified it more cleverly than he. Well do I recollect the day when he first came up to Trinity, and I assisted him in making the usual bargain with the college upholsterer.

"Print or two, sir, wouldn't look amiss over that chiffonier. Glass for chimney-piece of course you'll want. Bracket for figure here, sir, would make all the difference. Clock—weather-glass—mahogany book-case. Got a great selection if you'd only call in All Saint's Passage," said the tradesman. "Make your room look very nice."

"Just you knock half a hundred brass-headed hooks into the wall, right and left," replied Petersfeld, "and come and see me to-morrow. Then you'll know what a nice room's like !"

I hope the upholsterer came in the morning, for the result was a thing to be noticed. There was not one hook too many. Foils, boxing-gloves, pipes, daggers, bats, pistols, antlers, alpenstocks, whips, bugles, fox-brushes, skates, fishing-rods, guns, goff-sticks, and Indian clubs, and every conceivable article of similar nature covered the walls in lavish profusion, producing at once, as we all confessed, the most stunning room in college.

Most of these effective decorations had accompanied their master to the Albany, where, with many important additions, they had been arranged with considerable taste. The stuffed animals alone were worth a visit; but in point of fact the connoisseur in any thing, from suits of solid armor down to glowing French ballet scenes (suggesting the motto of our most noble order of knighthood) need not have gone away disappointed. Last, but not least, upon the round table in the middle of the room, sparkled the central glory of the place, a fifty guinea cup of massive silver, fairly won at Wimbledon from a phalanx of nearly one hundred competitors.

To stir the fire—light candles, and produce every proper adjunct of midnight hospitality was the work of a minute. I say "midnight" because I had promised Petersfeld to hear his whole story out before leaving ; as I was obliged to start on the morrow for a distant country château, where I had engaged to spend my Easter vacation. And though my own counsel and experience may not have been very valuable, I knew how intensely he would dislike the being left to stumble on in his adventure as best he might, without having any intimate friend in the secret, with whom he could correspond as to his movements, or consult in a difficulty.

Besides, nothing would have satisfied him short of taking my opinion as to all that he had already heard, done and seen; and, as that could not be learned without listening, I resolved to give audience patiently, and with good grace.

So, seating ourselves in two huge fauteuils, on either side of the comfortably-blazing hearth, Paul began the story of his adventures, which was to the following effect:

We left him, it may be recollected, in a corner of his club library, bent upon following out Kinghorn's canny suggestion, that by searching a file of the *Times* extending over the preceding month or so, he might probably hit upon something which would afford a clue for farther proceedings.

Neither was he disappointed: at least something which seemed not exactly promising, but still possibly to the purpose, soon presented itself. After turning the leaves for some time steadily backward, and wading through a lamentable list of missing husbands, wives, sons, daughters, keys, poodle-dogs, and purses, enough to convince him that we English are among the most reckless and untrustworthy people alive, his eye fell at last upon the following advertisement. It was dated the 17th of April—rather more than a fortnight back.

"ONE HUNDRED AND FIFTY POUNDS REWARD! —Lost, on Wednesday last, supposed upon or near the high road between St. Mark's-on-the-Sea and Riverwood, a RED MOROCCO POCKET-BOOK, containing, among other papers, three Bank of England notes for £1000 each, numbered and dated as below. The said notes are stopped at the Bank of England. Whoever will bring these notes, or any of them to the Branch Bank, St. Mark's-on-the-Sea, or give information leading to their recovery, either at that place, or to Sergeant Wilkinson, Detective Department, Great Scotland Yard, London, shall receive the above reward, or a proportionate part thereof. Bankers and others are cautioned not to take or exchange the above notes April 17th."
[Dates and Numbers.]

Now this advertisement accorded precisely in point of time with the date at which, according to Mr. Bloss, the disappearance of the young lady had taken place. It was, besides, the only advertisement, within some weeks either way, referring to the loss of any sum of money at all worth mentioning. Moreover, toward the conclusion, so at least Paul fancied, it bore some resemblance, in point of style, to the notice which had appeared that morning; and although there was nothing but the very vaguest of conjecture to connect it in the slightest degree with the object of his search, to neglect it altogether was to throw away his only apparent chance. For, after devoting a full hour to the investigation, there was no appeal to be found of any sort or kind which could reasonably be supposed to have emanated from the friends of the lost young lady, or to have any thing to do with the matter. Kinghorn had been too sanguine there. However, nothing could be more simple than to

drop down to St. Mark's, and ascertain by whom the money had been lost. And with that information, it could hardly be difficult, supposing that a young lady answering the description in the *Times* had disappeared from the neighborhood about the same time, to ascertain the fact.

So at least reasoned Paul; who, like most beginners in these matters, fancied that any thing in the world might be found out by dint of asking a sufficient number of questions. And with no more promising base than this to start upon, the next morning found him actually on the rail, steering direct for St. Mark's-on-the-Sea, which is within one hundred and fifty miles of London.

Without taking the trouble to assume any actual disguise, he adopted a well-worn tweed fishing-suit, wide-awake hat, and leathern knapsack, which had done good mountain service, in the Tyrol and elsewhere, as best suited to the expedition. A mere pedestrian wanderer, geologically, botanically, architecturally, or otherwise harmlessly inclined, might, he imagined, loiter and pry a good deal about a country neighborhood; make all manner of acquaintances, and fish out no end of facts, without placing any body upon their guard or good behavior. And, thus appointed, he arrived, about two in the afternoon, at the railway station of St. Mark's-on-the-Sea.

St. Mark's is not one of those towns over which any traveler in search of the picturesque is likely to undergo ecstasy at first sight.

It is a slovenly, ill-built place enough; of which the principal feature is a long straggling Main Street, with woful shops and a deserted air—a street which obviously could hardly do better, if it would. What could be expected, for instance, from those deadly dry auctioneer offices, with faded plans and dreary catalogues, and old prospectuses of sales, which, if they ever took place at all, were over and done with half a year ago? What from that miserable chemist, with all last year's dead flies in his window? What from that fusty little haberdasher, the prices of whose goods, so painfully ticketed, all end with three farthings? What from that stranded Library, which, with useless belief in better things, stubbornly maintains that it "circulates?"

However, in the absence of any personal quarrel with the town itself, one need not make more ado about its demerits, unless to observe that its very name indicates almost as loose a regard for truth, as its inhabitants have for appearances.

St. Mark's-on-the-Sea is not upon the sea at all; in fact more than a mile distant; although it possesses a pretty little suburb in that direction, called St. Mark's Bay, with a beach, a boat, a shrimp-catcher, a bathing machine, and a small hotel—an embryo watering-place—perhaps with a future of its own.

Of course Paul's first business was to look out for some place where he could put up, for a time at least, and relieve himself of his knapsack; and, upon that point, it seemed as if he were likely to be saved all trouble in the way of selection. Boldly conspicuous in the Main Street stands "THE SARACEN, Commercial Hotel and Posting House;" a great, red, hideous building, brandishing its pagan sign-board half across the way.

I don't know that I feel a more rooted repugnance to the shameless blaze of a London gin palace, than I do to the very sight of these commercial caravansaries. There is a bagman, publican aspect about them which suggests the very antipodes of comfort in any decent sense of the word. I know perfectly well what I shall meet with inside, before I cross the threshold. I know that there will be a large lumber-littered hall, with a bar at the end of it, containing a sharp young woman. I know that that hall will be hung with commercial and agricultural placards, three deep, containing information which at all events is not addressed to me. I know that the whole place will reek with spirits, sawdust, and stale smoke.

And as to the rooms, setting aside that uproarious parlor which the children of commerce call their own, and from which the unsuspicious intruder is so promptly ejected, whither shall we turn? The sitting-rooms are all alike. Their very atmosphere is dust and rottenness. They have all horse-hair sofas, naked tables, hard chairs, mythical prints, and a cruet-stand. The windows of each are scratched over, in exactly the same manner, with the names of the several Samuels and Jemimas who, having adopted it as their unsavory bower, invariably append the date of the transaction.

Try the club-room, where the farmers make evening hideous after every market day. There you will indeed find the death's-head without the feast. Perhaps the coffee-room is worst of all:

> "Old boxes larded with the steam
> Of thirty thousand dinners;"

stale newspapers, glass of tooth-picks, and beastly Directory. If you have a fancy to ascend the shallow creaking staircase, you may mount alone. I know too well the mysteries of those airless bedrooms and suspicious beds. And I own to even a more unconquerable distaste for the unclean chambermaid flitting aloof, than I have for her greedy, greasy, thankless brother, the waiter below.

Probably Petersfeld may have been much of my opinion. At all events, after having regarded the house distrustfully for a few moments, he crossed the street, and addressed a hostler-like man, who was loafing about the stable-yard.

"Is this the only hotel in the place, my man?"

"On'y one," replied the hostler, shortly. "Don't it suit you?"

"Can't say till I've tried," returned Petersfeld; and as the question was one which could only be decided by experiment, while the necessity for luncheon admitted of no delay, he entered the hostelry, and without committing himself to any longer stay, ordered bread and cheese and a jug of ale.

Even this rustic refreshment proved a failure. The bread was indifferent, the cheese rank, and the ale villainously hard. The waiter was an apathetic discontented youth, who took refuge from every inquiry in abstract ignorance. Petersfeld paid his half-crown, sat down by the fire to consider, and began by considering that he had made a fool of himself.

It was early times, certainly, to jump to such a conclusion. But there is a strange ebb in the flow of enterprise, which most of us have felt. We press on, for days together, perhaps, toward some coveted end, with scarcely a suspicion of failure, or a cessation of impatience. Suddenly, from some utterly inadequate reason, a chill seems to sweep over our mind. We pause, and with a hesitation which almost amounts to indifference, wonder whether it is really worth while to try on. Something has set the whole matter before us in a changed light. Many a project has failed, simply because its undertaker had not sufficient faith or courage to pull against stream during this mysterious ebb, so that before the tide of resolution again began to flow, irrevocable time and opportunities had passed away forever.

"I was a fool," muttered Paul to himself, with tremendous emphasis upon the noun substantive, "a fool to come down to this confounded place! I wouldn't dine and sleep in this den of thieves a week together for a hundred pounds. As to getting any thing out of these frightful boors, the idea's absurd. In fact, I should never have patience to attempt it. I wonder why on earth I came? By the bye, there's the bank! I forgot that. Of course I'll go there at once, and ask if they know any thing about it. If they don't, I'll go straight to the station, and get back to town by the next train; I can consider there whether there's any thing more to be done; and at worst, it's only a day lost. I wonder what Worsley will say! However, I may succeed at the bank, and if I do, I'll take precious good care not to let him know how near I was shutting up."

And in this unpromising mood, Petersfeld proceeded at once to the branch bank, which he reached without difficulty, although he fancied that the grocer to whom he applied for direction, equivocated strangely, and would have deceived him altogether if he could.

Now to *act*, in any important business, prematurely and without consideration, simply from an impulsive wish to do something, is; as we all know, one of the many recipes for failure. It is almost infallible—as I have noticed again and again.

"Nothing of importance," observes Mr. Thomas Thrifty, in his valuable "Essay upon Early Rising," "ought to be attempted in a hurry. But I except the catching of fleas."

The branch bank at St. Mark's-on-the-Sea, is a small, quiet concern, having the faded ill-to-do look, common to every thing else in the place. Nobody was in the office, except two clerks, one of whom raised his eyes from the desk as Paul entered, and fixed them placidly upon him, as much as to say, that unless time was no object, he was prepared to listen at once.

"I say!" began Paul, in his usual off-hand style, "about those £1000 notes that were lost in this neighborhood some three weeks ago, and advertised in the *Times*. Would you mind telling me who lost them? Not been found yet, I suppose—have they?"

"Sir!" said the placid clerk, "if you have any information to communicate respecting these notes, you had better see our principal, Mr. Crackleton, within."

"Never mind your principal," returned Paul. "Can't you tell me what I want to know?"

"What name, sir?"

"As if my name had any thing to do with it! I only want to know who lost these notes."

This was said with just as much *insouciance* as if the question had been "what's o'clock?" or "how many miles to London?"

"I'll inquire, sir." And the clerk disappeared into an inner office.

"As if he didn't know!" thought Petersfeld. "I never, in all my life, saw a place like this. The whole thing seems like a nightmare. I almost believe it is."

"Now, sir!" exclaimed a little bald, plump, fidgety man, popping suddenly into the bank, and pouncing toward Petersfeld like a spider upon a fly. "You've come about these notes, I understand. What about them? Now, sir! what?"

Anywhere else, the Jack-in-the-box like apparition of Mr. Crackleton might scarcely have been remarkable, but in this weird and sleepy place, it really seemed as if the excitability of a whole town had been bottled up in the testy little gentleman, who had just drawn his own cork, and was enjoying the relief of a fizz over.

"Now, sir! Any information to give? Time's time here, you know."

"None whatever. I just called to ask a simple question, as your clerk has probably told you."

"Oh, yes!—but, you know, I want to know what's your reason for coming here asking simple questions. Now, sir! What do you want to know the name of the person who lost them for? You're to come here, if you've any thing to say—not to go to him. Didn't you see that in the advertisement? Now, sir, from what my clerk tells me—"

"Your clerk be hanged!" retorted Petersfeld, incensed at this additional instance of the malignity of the St. Mark's men. "It'll do him good. What's the use of kicking up a shindy like this? If you don't like to answer my question, let it alone—and take the consequences!"

And so saying, Paul strode loftily out of the bank.

"Mr. Mecklin!" shouted the principal. "I

don't like this. I don't at all. Now, sir! Keep that man in sight! Find Mr. Tobacco, and make him do his duty. I want to know who that man is, and where he goes. That man's got the notes, or else knows where they are. What else should he come here for, asking who they belong to, I should like to know? Only wish I could see my way to detaining that man! Jump, Mr. Mecklin, and tell Tobacco what I say."

And before Petersfeld had proceeded a couple of hundred yards down the street, he was, without being in the least aware of the fact, attended at a respectful distance, by a small prowling man in rusty black, who had been beckoned out of the "Six Bells," an adjacent public-house, and "laid on" by the bank clerk.

If you ask me the why and wherefore of this inquisitorial proceeding, I am obliged to answer that I am in the unfortunate predicament of being only able to deal with one matter at a time. Luckily for you, the explanation is not distant, and you may follow my narrative without the uncomfortable misgiving that you have overlooked a point of importance.

In a peevish and despondent state of mind, Petersfeld took his way toward the railway station, laying the flattering unction to his soul that he had done the very utmost possible for one day, and that to pass the night in such a frowsy town, would be simply Quixotic and absurd. As to giving up his adventure, that, as he was at some pains to assure himself, had never crossed his mind. He wanted time to reflect, before taking his next step. That was all.

Just as he was actually ascending the incline leading to the station, a whistle sounded, and with heavy, deliberate snorts, a train rolled slowly forth in the London direction.

"The up train, by all that's unlucky!" he exclaimed. "What an idiot I was not to look at the time-table. How long shall I have to wait?" continued he, addressing a porter, who was leisurely leaving the premises.

"No train up till 7.15," replied the man. "Run it a leetle too fine this time, haven't you, sir? That's the 3.10 train just gone."

"Good heavens! Then I'm in for four hours more of it. Look here, porter! You know the place. How's a man to get through four hours at St. Mark's-on-the-Sea? What's to be seen? What's to be done? Got any thing to suggest?"

"I know what I should do, if I was you," replied the porter, a jolly-looking, thick-set man, with a pleasant twinkle in his eye. "I should fust of all say to me—'Here, porter; you look after my knapsack for me, and keep me a snug seat, with my back to the engine, by the 7.15 train.' Then, I should just step down to the 'Saracen' yonder, and order a reg'lar fust-rate blow-out. Steak, I should have, and baked potatoes, and fried onions, and a Welsh rabbit, and a pot of the double. I should order all that; and I wouldn't hurry myself over it neither. Then I should smoke my pipe—leastways my cigar, in your case—don't yon see, sir, till 6.45. Then I should have a go of gin-and-water warm, I should ; and get tip-top comfortable. Then I should walk very slowly up here, like a nobleman, and look out for me. That's about what I should do."

"Not a bad idea either," said Petersfeld. "But, I say, is the ' Saracen' the only hotel in the place ?"

" Well—there ain't no other—only publics. The ' Six Bells' ain't much of a place. Not unless you don't mind going a mile on—may be a mile and a quarter—to St. Mark's Bay. There's a nice little house enough there—Mrs. Maldon's. Just on the sea, it is."

"Hang it ; I've been so disgusted with the whole place that I never once thought of the sea ! It's a decent house, is it ?"

"Fust-rate, I should say. If you haven't seen our bay yet, you'd better go there. You've lots of time, haven't you ?"

"Rather too much of it. Well, I won't trouble you with my knapsack ; because, if I like Mrs. Maldon's, I may possibly stay. However, that's for steak and onions, and nothing less, mind," concluded Paul, tossing him a half-crown and striding down the hill.

"Knew he was a gentleman !" chuckled the porter, spinning the coin high into the air. "Won't I just dine upon a dinner of my own ordering ! at four o'clock too—like a director—that's all !"

CHAPTER X.

It was a good half-hour's walk, from the railway station to St. Mark's Bay. Past that ill-favored bank, the way led—past that scowling, unsavory " Saracen"—past rows of alms-houses for decayed shop-keepers, a likely enough complaint in St. Mark's, until at last it emerged in a shaded lane with overarching limes, whose twinkling canopy of transparent green seemed to dally rather than struggle with the westering light. A moment more, and the sea rose broad and blue, folding landward into a rounded nook, with low cliffs and spreading sands. This was St. Mark's Bay.

A few unpretending houses, sprinkled along the sloping down, alone broke the outline. Lower still, almost upon the shingle, a small irregular one-storied building, surrounded by a trim colonnade, announced itself as " The St. Mark's Bay Hotel."

A tiny lawn around was smoothly mown, and the nicely-tended flower-borders were already bright with color, beneath the early break of lilac and laburnum ; for St. Mark's Bay is fortunate in its aspect, and lights up before most places, under the fruitful influence of a strong May sun.

Altogether, there was such a clean, cozy, captivating air about the whole place, that Paul marched in at once, with a feeling of thankfulness that he had been late for the train.

The good-looking, buxom landlady—Mrs. Maldon herself—at once appeared.

Had she any room ?

To be sure, she had. Her season had hardly begun yet. There was only one family in the house. They had the best sitting-room. Nobody at all in the coffee-room at present. Would the gentleman like to be shown up stairs, and choose his apartment ?

Up stairs all seemed as neat as below. Paul selected a bright, airy bedroom which overlooked the sea ; so closely, indeed, that the windows were actually crusted with the salt spray of a late gale. For this, the smart little chambermaid apologized ; observing, with a great deal of truth, that the sea was always a-going on, and praising the room generally, as the loveliest to look out of in the whole house.

Having ordered his dinner at six, for his late performance at the Saracen had been unsatisfactory, Paul strolled forth, a happier man, upon the wide sea-shore. His feelings had undergone a sudden change for the better. Nothing could be more pleasant than his present quarters, or better adapted as a basis for farther operations. What those should be, he now set himself to work to consider.

It was a glorious afternoon ; the sea winking and basking in the sun, as if with an amused recollection of its late misbehavior ; while thousands of birds, hawks, gulls, puffins, razor-bills, curlews and cormorants, whirled incessantly from the grey cliff-side, or swooped and flickered upon the surface of the water.

"Your servant, sir !" said a clear, cheery voice.

The speaker, a slight, good-looking man of forty, or thereabouts, had approached unperceived during the commencement of an interesting reverie, and bringing an Enfield rifle, which he carried at the trail, smartly to " order," touched his cap pleasantly.

"Yours," replied Paul, returning the salute. "Been shooting, I see. Couldn't have a nicer range than these sands, anywhere."

"No, nor better marks, neither. It's a wonderful coast for birds, this is."

"You don't seem to have brought home much of a bag," observed Paul, rather ungraciously.

"Can't hit. That's it," said the stranger.

"Government rifle ?"

"Oh yes. I'm one of the St. Mark's company—only we haven't got to musketry instruction yet. However, as my gun was served out, I sent up to town for a couple of hundred ball cartridges, and blaze away a bit, now and then, along the beach, just to get my hand in. You see we shall have our butt up, and begin target-work this summer ; so I thought I'd just steal a march, as it were. I should like to come out strong in shooting."

"So would a good many of us. Then you're your own instructor for the present ?"

"Can't do any harm, at all events. Can it ?" replied the other, glancing affectionately at his rifle.

"Hum! That rather depends upon your style of teaching. Let's see you take a pot at that gull," said Petersfeld, pointing to a bird which had just settled, about a quarter of a mile from shore.

The stranger at once produced a ball-cartridge from his trowsers pocket, and went through his loading with the patient, clumsy accuracy of a man who has learned his lesson diligently out of a red book, but never seen it reduced to practice.

He then, with equal deliberation, twisted himself into a cruel and complicated posture, intended to represent the Hythe position; and, after taking murderously long aim at the unsuspicious bird, suddenly shut both eyes and discharged his rifle, like a suicide.

"Well done, you!" exclaimed Paul, as a just perceptible fleck of spray, far out to sea, announced the result of the performance. "If he'd been five hundred yards farther off, and a mile or so to the right, you'd have had him, and no mistake. Now, if you wouldn't be offended by a hint or two, I'd engage to improve your shooting straight away, so that, with three days' practice, you wouldn't know it again."

"Offended, indeed, sir! Would you really? I shall be grateful, I can tell you. Perhaps you'll take a shot yourself?"

"By all means," replied Paul, accepting the offered cartridge with a smile. "You are quite right to try what I can do, before you take a lesson. Now, look here."

It is a curious sensation, with which we see a piece of work over which we have been bungling and blundering for some time by the proverbially indifferent light of nature, quietly taken in hand by a real workman. It is vexatiously amusing to watch the rapid, natty way in which all our own difficulties are demolished or evaded, almost before they have time to show their stupid heads. In less time than it takes to write it, Paul's rifle was loaded and capped.

"Now," said he, "this is the way we kneel. Down upon your heel—so! Just you practice that for a week together, and you've a natural camp-stool for life, always handy wherever you go. Now, as to distance. Four hundred and fifty yards is what I give that bird. Look here! I put up my back-sight to five hundred, and, with foresight fine in the notch, I shan't be far wrong. Now I come to the present. Elbow-joint just over the knee; fore-arm well under the barrel. I'm not going to snatch at the trigger, as if I was letting off a shower-bath, I'm not. I'm just going to lay my head rather lazily over the butt. Then, just as I cover that bird, I shall quietly squeeze my trigger, as if it was a young lady's little finger. The gun won't hurt me. I know that. Keep your eye on the mark now."

"Crack!"

For an instant, it seemed as if the bird had exploded bodily, so sharply did a light feathery puff glance in the sunshine, apparently exactly where she floated. Fortunately for herself and her friends, however, she arose uninjured, and flew hastily away, lest the inconsiderate experiment should be repeated.

"Well done you, sir! That was a shot," exclaimed the self-instructing gentleman, opening his eyes to their widest. "I'd give a guinea, any day, to be able to lay my gun on like that. Why the ball went right on to her! How in the world did she ever get out of the water?"

"One hair's breadth more elevation, and she'd have caught it," replied Paul, handing back the rifle. "I suspect I was half a dozen yards short, and rico'd just over her back. The direction was as true as need be."

"Well, if you'd only show me how to do it to-morrow, I should really take it as a kindness. I'm obliged to go up to the house now. Hope you're going to make some stay with us, sir?"

"Stay with you," repeated Paul, puzzled,—"you live hereabouts, do you?"

"Landlord. At your service, sir. Maldon, my name is. St. Mark's Bay Hotel."

"Really! I'm delighted to hear it. Yes, I shall stay a day or so, at all events. How did you know I was at your hotel? You must give me a lesson in clairvoyance, in return for my rifle drill, Mr. Maldon."

"Saw you, from down yonder, sir, go into the house with a knapsack on, and was happy to see you come out without it; which I took to be a good sign," replied the landlord frankly. "Shall I leave you my gun, sir?"

Paul thanked him, but declined the weapon. His resolution, after its late cooling at the Saracen, and dismal experience at the bank, was again beginning to assert itself. Between his volunteer landlord and obliging landlady, it would be odd, indeed, if he didn't obtain information enough to enable him to commence active operations.

There was an air, too, of romance about the very scene around him. The lady, upon his theory, must have resided very near. Had her fair foot ever paced those glossy sands, or perchance stepped out of that little green bathing-machine? Perhaps it had. Perhaps the whole thing was a delusion altogether. Why had he so hastily concluded that she had any connection with those wretched bank notes?

And so, refreshing himself with alternate doses of bright anticipation, and doleful doubt, he strolled about until it was time to think of dinner.

Nothing could possibly have been nicer than that important meal, which Paul had wisely left to the discretion of his landlady. Both in selection and concoction, it showed an amiable care for the comfort and contentment of her guest; a kindness not less appreciable where the repast is to be honestly paid for, than where it is provided gratis in the dining-room of an acquaintance, to which you are only invited for socio-political reasons.

Dinners, however, are fleeting things, which, in their nature, can not last. From the delicately fried whiting to the ripe Stilton, with its attendant glass of port, we proceed buoyantly enough wherever we are. But then, in a lonely sea-side coffee-room, however cosy and hospitable it may contrive to look, there loom before us some three unsatisfactory hours, which insist upon having work provided for them, and refuse, upon any terms, to depart until bed-time.

Luckily for Paul, the coffee-room table was amply provided with a scattered miscellany of light literature; and he got through his time fairly enough until the clock struck nine.

Then the silence of the place became annoying. The respectable family in the best sitting-room were as mute as mice. If they would only have sung, or cheered, or danced, or done any thing to show that they were alive, it would have been a relief. So at last, with a yawn, he rose, filled his pipe, and walked out into the colonnade to enjoy a quiet smoke, and watch the moon rise over the bay.

"I beg your pardon," said his landlord's cheery voice—the speaker suddenly appearing upon the lawn—"but would it be a liberty to ask if you would drink a tumbler of Mrs. Maldon's punch, in our parlor, this evening. Mrs. Maldon is rather famous for her punch. You'll excuse me, I'm sure, if I offend, but I am sorry we have no company for you in the coffee-room."

"My dear sir," replied Petersfeld, "when an invitation like yours needs an apology, we'll talk about it. If you'll only introduce me to Mrs. Maldon as a brother volunteer, it will save me the trouble of making my excuses for intruding. I'll be with you in five minutes—directly I've finished my pipe."

"Why," said the landlord smiling, "you don't suppose Mrs. Maldon would consider we could taste her punch, without a whiff of 'bacco going? Come along with me, sir. Over the step—this way."

Mrs. Maldon's whisky punch did not belie its reputation. A better brew never sent up its fragrant steam from the choice little bowl of real china which had belonged to her grandpapa. Her husband was in the best of good spirits. To have met with such a redoubtable volunteer comrade, who could graze gulls at five hundred yards, and belonged, as he was awed to discover, to the "Devil's Own," was a piece of good fortune to which he was never tired of reverting.

As to Mrs. Maldon, who cared less for ball-practice than for London anecdotes, Paul's information—of which he speedily became very profuse, appeared to border on the miraculous. How things "got into the papers" had always been rather a mystery to her; but she accepted the fact of editorial omniscience just in the same blind way that all women believe in machinery. Tell them that a thing is done by machinery, and difficulties vanish at once. There's nothing left to think about. A machine is a machine, just as a conjuror is a conjuror: and to push the matter farther would be simply to blunder into a world of things which nobody understands.

But in Paul, Mrs. Maldon's admiring eyes beheld a man who had seen and even talked to many of the great people of whom she delight-ed to read:—who had dined in their houses, and knew their ways—who lived in a London Club, and was aware of even more than the newspapers themselves. So she freely accepted more than one tumbler of her own mellow punch, and believed that, in point of fashionable information, she was a made woman for life.

Of course this was just the time for Paul to push his inquiries; and, observing that the more amusingly he talked the more liberally was the silver punch-ladle put in requisition, he lost no time in beginning.

"By the way, what's the story, Mr. Maldon," said he, in his usual blunt way, "about those thousand pound bank notes, lost last month by a neighbor of yours? They were advertised in the Times, and we talked about them in London, I recollect."

"Admiral Mortlake lost them, sir. Lives at Riverwood Lawn—three miles on the London road. Had a mortgage paid off that afternoon. Would insist on having the money in bank notes (that's just his way), and had his pocket picked before night. Serve him right! That's what we all said at market. He was starting for abroad next morning for a longish trip, and I expect he took a nice temper with him. Not much to boast of as far as that goes, any day."

"He's a bad sort of man, I think, is Admiral Mortlake," observed the landlady, "and, if he'd lost twice as much, we should all have said the same—serve him right! By the bye," added she, "that's the business that nasty little man, Tobacco they call him, has been pottering about the town for these last three weeks; isn't it, Maldon?"

"I expect it is," replied her husband. "Don't know what else he's up to. He was round here not two hours ago. I heard somebody say something the other day, I'm sure I forget what, about his being a spy, paid by Admiral Mortlake. Spy, indeed! I'd have no spies in England, if I had my way. I'd shoot 'em — every man jack; that is, if I could hit 'em. Wouldn't you, sir? I'll be bound you would!"

"I should think so! And choose a tender place too. But, about this Admiral Mortlake," continued Paul, pretending to reflect. "Do I know him in London, or not? What family has he?"

"Only his wife, sir. No children. Only Miss Helen Fleetlands, a young lady who lives with him—a ward, I believe. Never a nicer young lady in this world, ever walked through the grass or sat on a saddle!"

"To be sure!" rejoined Petersfeld, quivering with excitement. "Helen Fleetlands is the very name—just about eighteen—very pretty—pale, clear complexion—pleasant girl to talk to—isn't she? Oh, yes. I recollect."

"Ah! I see you know her," interposed Mrs. Maldon, whose belief in Paul's experience had become so extensive, that she would have considered it rather odd than otherwise if he hadn't known Helen. "Yes; she's just that. I'm only sorry they took her away with them ; for I'm sure the poor child has no good time of it, where they are. But they did."

"Took her away? Abroad do you mean ?"

"To be sure, sir. They all went together. They went to France."

Paul was staggered. If she had eloped in France he might as well give in at once, but that was impossible. Bloss had talked about the London detectives, and the sea-ports being watched. There was a mistake somewhere. That Miss Fleetlands was the lady in question, was, however, beyond the shadow of a doubt.

"Ah, I dare say you're right, Mrs. Maldon," he resumed, with pretended carelessness. "Only I hear a good deal of people's movements, you see; and, somehow, I fancied that Miss Fleetlands had not been of the party to the continent."

"But she was, sir," replied the landlady, taking down an account-book, "and I'll tell you how I happen to know. They'd talked about going for some days before ; and, just before they started, Mrs. Mortlake sent to me to come up, about an account I had with her for fish. We supply them with fish and prawns, don't you see. Well, now, here it is, the very day, in my book. April 16th. That was the day I went up with my bill; and Mrs. Mortlake sent me down word that she couldn't see me about business just then, as the carriage was at the door—and so it was—and she'd tell a servant to call on me next day and pay it—which she did. That's why I'm sure, sir."

"I see," said Paul, whose excitement became almost uncontrollable, as he recollected that the 17th of April was the exact date of the advertisement respecting the notes. "So you saw Miss Fleetlands that morning?"

"No, I did not. But I saw the servants, and they all spoke of her as going. She was not well that morning, now I come to recollect. And when the house-maid, Leah, came down here next day, about the bill, she told me they were all off."

In spite of his intense desire to press the matter farther, Paul had sufficient delicacy to forbear.

He was confident that he was upon the right track : but it was equally certain that some mystery existed, of which his hospitable companions had no suspicion.

Under such circumstances, to communicate, or allow them to discover his doubts, seemed scarcely less than dishonorable. He was bound to solve the problem for himself—not to thrust his immature conjectures upon other people ; and so, in all probability, light up a fire of curiosity of which nobody could foresee the end. He must keep his misgivings to himself, for that night, at all events, and try his luck at Riverwood Lawn in the morning.

And so the conversation was allowed to flow back to London town, and proceeded until Mrs. Maldon's news-treasures began to mix as they multiplied, causing the unsatisfactory suspicion that there might be difficult work in the sorting.

There was a famous butcher of Bagdad, once, who, after habitually selling mutton-chops to a Magician for bran-new sequins (which, as the story goes, he hoarded in a bag by themselves), awoke one morning to find these splendid coins a delusion ; and that the pieces which he had so greedily accepted as silver from his regular and ready-money customer, were, for spending purposes, only "leaves cut round."

Probably Mrs. Maldon had never read the story ; but some such experience seemed to be brewing.

However, after a hearty good-night, which his landlord insisted upon enlivening with a tremendous volunteer carol, commencing—

" When the false Foreigner, over the sea,
  Vows to plant foot on old England the free,
  This is the answer we'll make to the Man—
  ' Come if you dare—and go back if you can !' "

Paul took his departure, leaving Mr. Maldon delighted with the assurance that such sentiments were equally business-like and patriotic, and his wife sorely concerned lest they should have been considered unseasonable in the best sitting-room.

CHAPTER XI.

OVERLOOKING a broad plateau of perfectly level turf, studded with mighty clumps of immemorial oak, stands the low, irregular, turreted stone mansion which has, for a couple of centuries at least, borne the name of Riverwood Lawn.

Behind rise the tree-tops of the woodland which fringes, at that spot, the river St. Mark.

On either side, half buried among close-clipped hedges of the densest yew, lie the flower gardens, with their stone stairs, stone seats, stone balls, stone sun-dials, and fish-ponds rimmed with stone. Were our ancestors really so cold, blooded? Did ever man actually sit down to plot and plan one of these rectangular petrified pleasaunces without a quiet chuckle over his diagram? There must be some joke in the matter long since lost forever ; but nothing, to my mind, carries one back to the days which are gone, more than these austere old gardens.

Old houses burn or tumble down ; or, if they stand, have probably been improved and furnished into something quite beyond the expectations of their first inhabitants. Old parks have changed their timber, their boundaries, and their ancient fence ; or towns have sprung up and choked them ; and we can not feel certain in what degree, if at all, they preserve their olden aspect.

But, in these old gardens, substantially nothing is altered. The clipped hedges stand exactly as they stood two hundred years ago. The steps, the seats, the vases, are identical. They also stand where they always stood, and look as they always looked, except for Time's modest livery of rusty green. The Nymphs and Apollos wear exactly the same plump good-natured expression which they wore when there used to be something worth simpering at, in the way of company, around their pedestals. Their faces no doubt are wofully mottled, and they have suffered somewhat from frost-bite or other grievance in the matter of fingers and noses. But they would tell you, if they could, that such as you see the garden now, such it was in the days of the Vandyke'd gallants of the Stuart time, and the periwigged, square-toed, snuff-box-carrying dandies of Queen Anne.

They could tell you a great deal more, too, I suspect, if they chose. I should like to have that bashful Venus in the witness-box for half an hour. I should like to know all she has seen in that secret bower of yew, into which she still persists in prying with inextinguishable curiosity. Unless our elder dramatists drew very strangely upon their imagination, the reminiscences of her early statuehood ought to comprise a great deal that would be well worth hearing.

Of the Lawn itself I am not ready at present to say much. The family are away. The blinds are down, the carpets up, and the furniture smothered in brown-holland. In due time, when it is in a fit state to receive us, we will make ourselves fairly at home. Meanwhile let us accompany Petersfeld thither, upon his first early visit.

After a capital breakfast at the St. Mark's Bay Hotel, and a few cheery words with his landlord, who was counting his cartridges in the bar parlor, Paul set out upon his tour of discovery. An hour's walking brought him to the lodge, the gate at which was opened by a small child who plucked its hair respectfully as he passed in. A long carriage sweep, winding through a well-grown shrubbery, led to the front entrance, near which stood a gardener busily engaged in preparing some flower-beds for his approaching bedding out.

Paul at once broke ground with his accustomed affability. "I'm afraid I shan't have the pleasure of seeing Admiral Mortlake this morning. He's abroad, I hear."

"If you ain't going abroad, I'm afraid you won't," replied the gardener, coolly. "Did you expect to see him?"

"Came from London on some business of his, at all events. Can you give me his address?"

"Can't give you any thing of his. What did the old woman at the gate say?"

"Didn't see her, unfortunately; so I had to walk in."

"Old donkey," muttered the gardener, apostrophizing his absent wife. "If you're a friend of Admiral Mortlake's, sir, why all right. If you ain't, why we've our orders at the Lodge, you see: and those orders are, No Thorough Fair."

"All right! When I asked for the admiral's address, I only meant to inquire where a letter would reach him; and that I suppose I can find out at the house."

"That's the house," said the man with a jerk of his head, as if he washed his hands of the whole affair. "I've nothing to do with the house. If you're going there, that's it."

"I am going to the house," replied Paul, good humoredly; "so you needn't have taken me for a tramp. Have a cigar?" continued he, producing his case. "These are fresh from London. Try one."

For a moment the man looked at him distrustfully. But, after all, the cigar looked less like a bribe than a peace-offering, and he was an amateur in tobacco.

"Thanky, sir," he said. "You'll excuse my mentioning that this was no Thorough Fair; but we've the admiral's orders to mention as much, unless we know the party."

"Quite right, too. And when the admiral gives an order he means it, I've no doubt."

"That he does, and no mistake. What he says has got to be minded: and so it should. If you'll just go round the corner, sir, and ring the front door bell, you'll be attended to."

The front door, to which Petersfeld had been directed, was on the side of the house opposite that which overlooked the lawn. It was covered in with a massive stone portico large enough to admit a carriage, and had altogether an antique, imposing air.

There was no occasion to ring the bell, for the door stood open, and a coquettish-looking housemaid was shaking a mat upon the steps. She stopped in her work on perceiving Paul, and said "fiff!" by way of apology for the dust.

"Good-morning," said Paul. "The gardener has sent me here for Admiral Mortlake's address. Do you happen to know where he is at present?"

"I can tell you where we send his letters to, if that will do," returned the girl, looking for a card upon the hall-table. "This is it. Grand Hotel, Paris."

"All there, are they? Mrs. Mortlake and Miss Fleetlands?"

"Oh yes! They're all there."

"Miss Fleetlands went with them then?"

"Why of course! What do you want to know about Miss Fleetlands for?" suddenly added the house-maid with a saucy twinkle in her eye, as she looked at Paul from head to foot, and noticed his handsome face and dashing *tout ensemble*

"Hum!" said Paul. "That's my lookout. I doubt if you could keep a secret if I told you one."

"Couldn't I?" exclaimed the damsel, who was beginning to feel highly curious. "You try!"

"Well, the fact is, I rather wanted to find out where Miss Fleetlands is at present. However, if she's in Paris, that's enough."

"Oh, I know she's there; because only two days ago she wrote to me to send over some things out of her drawers, and something which she said her dress-maker in the town yonder had forgotten to bring home before she went, and a pretty piece of work we had about it, and one or two things I couldn't find after all. That's how I know she's there. But you said there was a secret, sir, you know."

"Only this—that I asked you any question at all about her. Buy a new ribbon for my sake, and keep that piece of news to yourself," continued Paul, slipping a five shilling piece into her hand.

"Well I'm sure, sir, I'm much obliged; but it's very little of a secret to keep. I'll be bound I won't tell any body."

"And you're sure you've told me every thing —every thing, mind!" added Paul significantly.

"I don't quite understand you, sir—don't see quite what you want to know. Unless," continued she, turning the crown piece over and over in her hand, as if its acceptance pledged her to unlimited gossip, "unless, indeed—but may be what I was going to say, don't concern you in the least, you see."

"How should I know?" cried Paul. "You'd better say it. Then I'll tell you."

"Why," rejoined the girl, simpering, "it just depends upon whether you was a-thinking of keeping company with our Miss Helen. You see I can't tell why you come asking about her, and likely enough you know your own business, but if you had a mind that way, I should say you'd better be more careful than common—that's all."

"More careful than common! Why in the world should I be more careful than common? My good girl, tell me exactly what you mean, and I'll give you a new bonnet, to trim the ribbon on."

"Oh no," said the girl. "I don't mind a ribbon, but I ain't going to tell tales for new bonnets. Only as you have behaved quite the gentleman, sir, I shouldn't like to see you get into the same trouble as others have. Our Miss Helen," continued she, sinking her voice to a whisper, "isn't exactly like other young ladies. Don't you come a-courting of her, sir. She mustn't be married."

"Good gracious — go on!" gasped Paul. "What's the matter with her?"

"Well, we never quite made out the rights of it," replied the house-maid mysteriously, "though we've talked it over often enough, you may be sure. But she mustn't. Not three months ago, or thereabouts, there was a young gentleman came after her, much about your age, I should say, sir; a soldier captain, he was, and she liked him, too, we all said. They used to ride together when the hounds were out, and it was quite pretty, like, her groom used to say, to see the way he'd follow her all across the country; and it took a good one too, to do that, for she's a rare young lady to gallop, is our Miss Helen. And so, of course, we all considered it was a match, and nobody had a word to say against it, for he was every bit like a soldier, he was, and a nice pleasant-spoken gentleman, even fit for our Miss Helen, and that's not saying a little.

"Well, we never heard, any of us, that there

was any difficulty in the way. Our Miss Helen has heaps of money, they say, and he, we found out, had a great estate not many miles off, and was going to be a noble lord viscount some time; and we were just wondering when the wedding was to be, when lo and behold you, just as he was a-walking up to this very door one morning, up steps an officer from London, and 'You're my prisoner, captain!' says he, 'God save the Queen !' "

" 'What now,' says the captain. 'What have I done ?'

" 'Goin' after Miss Fleetlands,' says the officer. 'That's it. So you come along.'

" 'Hands off!' says the captain, and knocks him right through that holly-bush, yonder.

" 'Murder, alive !' shouted the officer. 'Catch him somebody, afore I'm stung to death in this beastly tree !'

"Well, up rushes the officer's man, for there was two of them, and catches up the captain like a baby, and they two goes to work like executioners, and puts handcuffs on his hands, and fetters on his feet, and carries him off—kicking and calling—I believe you, to a cart, and drives him right away to London; and there he is this day, sir, if you'll believe me, in dungeon deep, and won't be let out never no more. Never, no, never! That's why I say our Miss Helen isn't like other young ladies. She mustn't be married. We found that out among ourselves. By talking, sir. Our Miss Helen must be left alone."

Paul stood for a moment like a man in a dream. "Are you quite certain of all this?" he was beginning, when the housekeeper's voice was heard upon the stairs.

"Oh, you must go, please !" exclaimed the girl, "or I shall catch it for talking," and almost before he found himself clear of the portico, the mat was again in such tremendous requisition, that even to look back was at the risk of being smothered.

Not caring again to encounter the surly gardener, Paul took the opposite walk to that by which he had arrived, and which led into a dark suite of yew-surrounded gardens.

Beyond—just where they opened upon a spacious lawn—stood a pretty summer-house, or rustic temple, of unbarked pine. It was a place upon which a good deal of taste and care had evidently been expended. The windows were of colored glass, and the oaken parquet curiously inlaid. The table and chairs were, likewise, all of massive oak. There was a snug little fireplace, large enough to boil the kettle upon tea-drinking occasions, and upon either side of it, large oaken cupboards, which perhaps contained the paraphernalia necessary for such temperate festivity.

Paul walked in and sat down. He was too much bewildered by his own recent discoveries to indulge in romantic conjectures as to whether he might not, at that moment, be smoking his cigar in Helen's own favorite bower.

He was trying in vain to reduce all that he

had learned since his arrival at St. Mark's, into some sort of consistency, and to make it square, if possible, with the contents of the two advertisements, and the information which he had obtained from Bloss.

But the attempt was hopeless. It was like unraveling a tangled skein, in which to untwist one end is only to ensure a tighter knot at the other. That Helen Fleetlands was the person of whom he was in search, he was more than ever certain. His landlady's instant recognition of her as described in the advertisement, was conclusive upon that head. Again Miss Fleetlands had actually left Riverwood Lawn upon the very day, or day after, the loss of the bank notes advertised by Admiral Mortlake. These were clearly the "little fortune" of which Bloss had spoken; in fact, the whole chain of events thus far fitted to a nicety. The detectives had been placed upon her track, and upon their failure, the second advertisement had been inserted in the papers, addressed upon the same authority, to those who had got her.

That so extremely nice a young lady as "our Miss Helen" should have picked her guardian's pocket in such confoundedly good earnest, was of course improbable enough at the first blush. But Paul was in no mood for arguing at that moment. He had got among facts, and motives might take care of themselves. Some such act of "graceful self-possession" had perhaps led to those qualities having been so conspicuously noticed in the advertisement.

Indeed, if there had been reason to conclude that the young lady had then and thereupon decamped with her plunder, Paul would have had a fair start enough. To know more would be to fathom the grand secret itself, for the resolution of which five hundred pounds had just been offered—where had she gone—where was she then? And this he didn't expect to discover without such sustained and arduous exertion as would render his name a household word for indomitable and successful energy through some time to come.

But then arose the calm bewildering fact agreed to upon all hands, that she had left the lawn in company with Admiral Mortlake and his wife, and was at that moment spending her time with them in Paris. Upon this point it seemed scarcely possible that every body should be mistaken, especially the gossiping house-maid, who had clearly told the truth to the best of her belief, and who had actually heard from her at the Grand Hotel.

So the question seemed to resolve itself into this dilemma: was Miss Fleetlands at that moment in Paris, or was she not?

If she was, all was delusion from beginning to end. Never since the world began had a man been so unaccountably and egregiously misled.

If she was not, then indeed matters wore a perplexing aspect. Every body about St. Mark's must have been deliberately and successfully deceived by the admiral, for some purpose of his own, which Paul, at the moment, felt it impossible to conjecture. But taken in connection with Mrs. Maldon's remark, that Helen had no good time of it in his house, it suggested unpleasant misgivings, and made Paul quite flush with excitement, like a champion with a task before him.

As to the wild myth of the chained and captive captain—his unintelligible offense and condign punishment—it seemed rather like a page out of the Arabian Nights than an episode of modern life in England. But it was evidently a romance of the back-stairs—a story which wouldn't bear examination for a moment. The captain had probably been arrested—captains often were; and this was the wise version of the story, with which his own groom, probably, had entertained the servants' hall. Paul knew more of the world than to take his facts from house-maids.

Upon the main question, however, there was only one thing to be done. To rest in his present state of doubt was impossible. To breakfast on the boulevards next morning was easy. It was not in his nature to pause for one moment when any active measure suggested itself.

Great was the disappointment of his hospitable host and hostess when Paul returned about noon, and announced that pressing business compelled him to terminate his visit, and take the next train to London.

Mrs. Maldon was vexed at losing her fashionable and amusing guest. Mr. Maldon had still more cause to be sorry. He had employed the whole morning in polishing up his rifle—until, from nose-cap to heel-plate, it shone like gold and silver. It was too bad that the bloody business of the afternoon, upon which he had counted so securely, should be indefinitely postponed. All had been well enough before Petersfeld came. But to go out again by himself to blaze at the gannets with all his new-born consciousness that rifle-shooting was rather an art, and that his own performance was probably disregarded by the birds themselves, as a mere noisy nuisance, undeserving of the attention of any sensible fowl, was too much for his philosophy.

There was no help for it, however; as Paul was bent upon departing by the mid-day express. So, after a good deal of leave-taking, and a sort of undertaking upon his part to return within a week, and bring his rifle with him, he was allowed to shoulder his knapsack and march off to the station.

His friend, the jolly-looking porter, received him with the greatest deference as he appeared upon the platform.

"So Paul had had a pleasant evening at St. Mark's Bay? To be sure he had! Else he wouldn't have recommended the house—not he! As for himself, hadn't he just taken the change out of that half-crown? Never had any body enjoyed a dinner more—that was his opinion. It was lovely."

And, before the bell rang for starting, Paul had been regaled with a complete *menu* of the most savory and wonderful entertainment that had ever been ordered and devoured by a single glutton regardless of expense, or — which the porter appeared to consider as the same thing—with no necessary limit to extravagance short of two and six.

Just as the train was on the move, after having placed Paul in a compartment to himself, from which, as he assured him, ladies and babies would be rigidly excluded by the guard all the way to London, he suddenly reappeared at the window.

"See that snuffy little chap there, sir?" he said, pointing to a small, ill-conditioned man, who was apparently looking out for a seat. "That chap's name's Tobacco. He's a spy. A London spy, he is. Up to some game, you may depend upon it. Little rascal; he's going to town!"

"A spy, is he? Looks more like an undertaker in difficulties," said Paul, as the individual in question shambled into a third-class carriage. "Get me a Bradshaw, will you, at that book-stall." And the train rolled away.

After the usual display of cheerful perseverance and intellectual dexterity which it seems to have been the main object of the compiler of our national hand-book to elicit, Paul succeeded in ascertaining that he would be in London by 3.30. There was a train for Folkestone at four in connection with the tidal boat, and he might reach Paris soon after midnight. So he resolved to go straight through.

Upon his arrival at London Bridge station, and while taking his ticket for Paris, he was not exactly disconcerted, but certainly surprised, to observe at a little distance no other personage than Mr. Tobacco. Could it be possible that he himself—Paul Petersfeld—was the mark of that hideous little animal? A dim confused suspicion that he had been treading dangerous ground seemed to arise in his mind without any assignable reason. And then the house-maid's concluding warning—"Our Miss Helen must be left alone," came back like an echo. But what had he done?

That was just the question the captain had asked, when, according to her account, he was knocked down to the tune of "God save the Queen," and carried away tied, in a tax-cart.

However, there was no need to pursue the inquiry; since Mr. Tobacco made no attempt to enter the train; although he lingered in view rubbing his nose wistfully through the barrier-railings, until it was fairly under steam for Folkestone.

CHAPTER XII.

It was long past midnight, when Paul found himself at last upon the Boulevard des Capuchins.

This was of little consequence. Nobody ever goes to bed in Paris—nobody, at least, whose presence could be of the slightest interest to a newly-arrived traveler. Paul might have had

C

a "diner à la carte" at ten minutes' notice. But he had dined at Amiens, during that convulsive "vingt minutes d'arrêt," which at once gives individuality to the town, and provides the single reminiscence of it which most Englishmen carry away. So he only went to bed.

By whatsoever token it may please posterity to distinguish this present era, nothing is more certain than that it will be hereafter referred to as the age of hotels. In those palatial edifices which are so fast rising in every direction — which form part of every railway terminus, and overshadow the roofs of every watering-place, and appropriate the best places in our streets and squares, I see something more than the result of a mere joint-stock mania. I see not only a step, but a stride, in the march of comfort and civilization; and heartily wish I could secure to every shareholder a regular dividend of fifteen per cent., with a handsome bonus at frequent intervals. I should like also to be a considerable shareholder myself upon these terms. And, as a fair sample of a comparatively new state of things, I recommend the Grand Hotel, Paris.

A man must indeed be strangely impassive who could walk into that noble Cour d'honneur for the first time, without an agreeable sensation.

It is something to feel that one is going to be so royally lodged and cared for. But the real wonder of the place lies in those interminable furlongs of soft-carpeted corridors—Boulevards, as they are aptly called—rising five stories high, each a swarming hive of guests.

By what mysterious arrangement can the countless wants of this great multitude be provided for? What waiter's sanity would be worth an hour's purchase, exposed to the competitive jangling of five hundred bells? All is easy, nevertheless. There is a bureau de service—one or more—upon each boulevard. Touch the little ivory button of your bedroom telegraph, and you have at once the satisfaction of knowing that you have set a fiery little demon chattering, whose tongue will never rest until your wants have been attended to. You have, as it were, your own particular landlord with all his myrmidons close at hand. And, practically, you find that the requirements of half a thousand people are far more quickly and comfortably provided for, than those of a dozen at the Saracen.

Another advantage, not less noteworthy, is that you can at any moment ascertain the names of all your fellow-guests. There are five mahogany compartments in the grand bureau, on the ground floor, corresponding with the five boulevards above stairs, in which the name and date of each arrival is at once inserted. It seems a simple business enough; but the slovenly way in which this important duty is discharged, or rather neglected, at most old-fashioned hotels, converts into matter of praise what would otherwise only call for simple approval.

Before these gigantic muster-rolls, Paul took his stand early the next morning, in much the same condition of nervous excitement with which, as he well recollected, he had, not many years before, searched for his own name upon the pillar in the Senate House. It is wonderful what a blinding, bewildering affair reading becomes under such circumstances. The very letters seem to be writing themselves over again while you read, and loop, and twist, and dance, and dazzle, until we begin to doubt whether our education has been as complete as it might have been. But there was no mistake at last.

"*L' Amiral et Mme. Mortlake, et Mlle. Fleetlands,*" said the scroll. *Arrivés le 19° Avril.* Their rooms were on the second boulevard.

Paul whistled, and walked away. The crisis had come at last. If that oracular board was to be believed, Miss Fleetlands was probably at that moment dressing within twenty yards of him.

Of course she was: and the people at St. Mark's perfectly in the right. The odd thing would have been to find them all in the wrong. But then what a hideous unintelligible enigma was the whole affair! Who had run away, if she had not? What did the advertisement mean? Lunacy at three-and-twenty was a bad lookout; but that was what matters were coming to. However, under the same roof with her at last, something definite must surely be arrived at.

Even to see her. That in itself would be worth a journey to Paris. To sit next her at the *table d' hôte*. That would be better still, and easily managed. In the meanwhile a question or so at the *bureau de service* of the second boulevard would put him at once in possession of the usual hours and habits of the admiral and his ladies, and enable him without difficulty to identify them. So up stairs he went.

As I have already explained, there is, at the Grand Hotel, a *bureau de service* upon every floor, at which of course, with very little trouble, you may ascertain all the secrets of its inhabitants. Foreign waiters are not apt to be discreet. Their delight is to lay a long forefinger on the top of their nose, and tell you more than you expected.

"Good-morning!" said Paul, marching suddenly into the room. "Admiral Mortlake, an Englishman, lives, I hear, upon this floor. He has two ladies with him, hasn't he?"

"*Nein—nein!*" replied the *gen' de service*, shaking his head, with a smile.

"Nonsense! Nine ladies in two rooms!—that won't do," retorted Paul. "Admiral Mortlake's the man I'm asking about. Fellow from England. Wouldn't think of such a thing."

"*Neun damen habe ich nicht gesagt, mein Herr. Mit der Herr Admiral ist nur eine Dame, die gnädige Frau. Niemand anders.*"

"Come, I say! That's not French, anyhow," exclaimed Paul, impatiently. "Parley Français, my good fellow, if you can't parley Anglais, which would save no end of trouble. You've no idea how easy it is. Try it on!"

"*Ja wohl! Jezt verstehe ich der Herr,*" re-

plied the good-humored Bavarian, who always will start in his own language until driven out of it by main force. "You ask me about your English admiral. Well, he is yonder: in the room at the end of the corridor. Last door on the left. By the stairs. His wife is with him. No one else. He has kept a room engaged these many days for his *fraulein*. But she has not come yet, and will not come now, for they start this morning for Normandie. They and my lady's *kammer-jungfer* — her maid. I am even now making out their note."

"By George, what a rage I should have been in if I'd missed them. Now look here," continued Paul, "I want to know this very particularly. Are you quite sure that Miss did not arrive with them here? Are you certain that she has never been in this house?"

"Quite certain, *mein Herr,*" replied the man confidently. "I know it all the more because two days ago I asked my lady's maid why that expensive room was kept empty so long, when miss did not come. And she said oh, that miss had gone to pay a visit among some friends in the Faubourg St. Germain, and that the admiral wished to keep her room, because it was next his own, and he expected her at the hotel every day. And also, because money was of no consequence. Oh that I were such a lucky lord as that!"

"Seems an odd arrangement, doesn't it?" pursued Petersfeld. "Miss must be very fond of her friends in the Faubourg."

"Ha! Just what I said to the maid," returned the *gen' de service*. "I said to her, *Fraulein,* I begin to think that you've lost this young lady of yours, and that we shall never have the pleasure of seeing her here at all—*hein?* And then she looked at me, all dark and angry, and demanded of me, what business it was of mine? I wonder why your nation are so fond of asking that? No other people do it. I am almost afraid to say to an English fellow-servant '*Wie befinden Sie sich?*' for fear he should enrage himself and make that reply."

"What time do these people start?" inquired Petersfeld, who was in no mood to moralize over insular peculiarities. "You tell me they're going this morning."

"*Ja wohl.* They have ordered a carriage at half-past ten to take them to the railway station —Rue St. Lazare. That is all I know."

"Do they breakfast in their rooms?"

"Oh no. They breakfast daily in the coffee-room restaurant below. Let me see," continued the Bavarian, looking at the clock,—"they will be going down directly I should think. It is now *halb zehn*—nearly half-past nine."

"All right," said Paul, and took his stand upon the great staircase within view of the door of their apartment. Perhaps his notions of what could possibly be done in the way of action under the circumstances were not very definite; but his curiosity to see the admiral, and at least carry away a living image of that man in his mind, was indescribable.

He had not long to wait. In a few moments

the door opened, and Admiral and Mrs. Mortlake passed him as they descended.

Once seen, the admiral was not a man to be easily forgotten. Solid and square built, with a red weather-beaten face, he looked the very impersonation of physical power combined with unconquerable resolve. The stubborn under-jaw—the broad battle-broken nose—the iron forehead, and those self-reliant hempen-shaded eyes, that so seldom and so slowly looked either to the right or left, all told the same story.

Nor was his dress less characteristic. His trousers, cut after a fashion exploded years before most of us were trousered at all, showed that he was not a man to change with the times or ask his tailor's opinion as to the prevailing pattern. An immense bunch of gold seals dangled from his fob. His rough blue coat had flaps, and side pockets, and gilt buttons, and these, with a low-crowned hat and ponderous oaken cudgel, were the prominent points which struck Petersfeld upon his first brief inspection.

Mrs. Mortlake was tall, angular, and frightfully prim. She had a thin aquiline nose, dark uncompromising eyebrows, and no lips. She was dressed entirely in black, and as Paul looked at the couple, he thought that the young lady had exercised a very sound discretion in running away.

Neither she nor her husband took the slightest notice of Paul as they passed him upon the stairs. It didn't seem to be their way. They marched doggedly on into the coffee-room, and took their seats at a table which had been reserved for them; and Paul, whose appetite reminded him that his own breakfast had not yet been accomplished, accepted the services of a waiter, who was bent upon interesting every body with the contents of a little tract, entitled, "*Les plats du jour.*"

The admiral and his wife breakfasted in silence. No domestic confidences, at all events, reached Paul's ear. And, the meal over, Mrs. Mortlake retired to her apartment, while the admiral, lighting his cigar, paced sternly forth into the *Cour d'honneur.*

There Petersfeld had the opportunity of regarding him at leisure. And, to tell the truth, he recognized, in that solid, imperturbable man, a great deal more than his match. He felt positively afraid of him, as his imagination suggested the sudden and picturesque result, if, by any process of divination, his own rash secret could be discovered on the spot. Mere manslaughter would scarcely satisfy the soul of such a tremendous Tartar. However, there was no immediate cause for anxiety.

Punctually, at half-past ten, the carriage rolled into the court-yard. The luggage was brought down, and Mrs. Mortlake appeared in traveling costume, attended by a shrewish-looking maid. Paul resolved to take a fiacre and follow the vehicle to the station. There was just the shadow of a possibility that Miss Fleetlands might join them there; and it was as well to leave no loop-hole whatever open to future doubt.

It often happens, to those whose ears and eyes are alive to every suggestion, that some unexpected clue suddenly presents itself, which to less observant or less practical people, would have no significance whatever. Upon the admiral's portmanteau, as it was being placed upon the coach-box, Paul noticed an old address, which had not been removed. It was "Lord Warden Hotel, Dover." An idea instantly glanced upon his mind. They had come to Paris by that route. He had only to return the same way to ascertain, beyond all possibility of mistake, whether Miss Fleetlands had actually left England with them.

If she had not, then, that the admiral was playing some deep inexplicable game which had hitherto duped every body was decided; and he would never rest until he had penetrated the mystery, and otherwise played the part of a true knight in the adventure. If she had—but his common sense told him that it was otherwise, and that he had only to make assurance doubly sure.

His drive to the railway station simply confirmed his conjecture that Admiral and Mrs. Mortlake would depart alone. There was nothing for it but to return to London viâ Dover. So after ascertaining that the admiral had desired his letters to be forwarded to him at the Hôtel d'Angleterre Quai des paquebots—Rouen, he quitted the Grand Hotel a wiser but far from satisfied man.

At the "Lord Warden" he had little difficulty in ascertaining that the Mortlakes had slept there on the night of the 18th of April, en route for the continent. Miss Fleetlands was not in their company. Her name had not been mentioned. With the exception of Mrs. Mortlake's maid, they had been quite alone.

* * * *

"Now!" exclaimed Paul, giving the fire a tremendous stab, which sent the sparks roaring up the chimney, "that's the end of my travels, Worsley. Tell us what you think of them."

"Anyhow," replied I, "I admit that your character for energy is, from this moment, beyond all possible question. After our conversation of the other morning you ought to be proud of the admission."

"Upon my word, I think I've earned it. But now, Worsley, what's to be made of the whole business?"

"Well," replied I, "taking the story as you state it, just listen to the reply I should make as to the probabilities of the case, if I were counsel on the other side in one of our own courts. In the first place, you fall upon the track of Miss Fleetlands through the medium of these lost bank notes. Do you seriously believe that she ran away with them?"

"Why," replied Paul, looking slightly confused, "I declare, since I first hit off the right scent, I've thought about nothing but herself. Forgot the notes altogether. Probably they were her own."

"Not very likely; if they were those which

the admiral advertised. But, now, look here. Your theory is, that the young lady of the advertisement is your Miss Fleetlands?"

"Of course she is. The description agrees perfectly. So does the time at which she left her home. The whole thing squares exactly."

"No doubt. But the lady whom you and Bloss talked about, was, if you recollect, as he said, pursued by detectives before she was twelve hours over the lawn. Search had been made for her everywhere—the sea-ports watched—and yet she had never been heard of from that time to this. Now your Miss Fleetlands, according to the united testimony of every body most likely to know, both at her own house and in St. Mark's, started quietly for Paris, in pursuance of a long-arranged plan, in the company of her guardian and his wife."

"She never got there, though!"

"Granted. But the admiral and his wife did. Now, I put it to your common sense, is it conceivable that had she eloped upon the road, either with or without a considerable sum of money, they would have complacently pursued their way to the continent, contenting themselves with putting an advertisement in the papers, to the effect that, if found, she was to be packed up and left with Mr. Bloss?"

"Botheration! Of course it isn't probable. But why did they stick her name up at the hotel, and pretend she was in Paris, when she wasn't? You don't half see your way through it yet, Master Worsley."

"Perhaps not. We pass all at once from the improbable to the mysterious."

"That's it, exactly. What right has a guardian to be mysterious about his. ward? Say what you like, I'd lay my head upon it that Miss Fleetlands is the missing girl; and the more perplexing—the more incomprehensible the whole story becomes, the more I am determined to find out whether I'm not right. It's the very charm of the whole affair. You can't make head or tail of it. Neither can I. Wonder whether Kinghorn would! But, when I clear up the whole affair, who'll laugh then? There's a grand discovery to be made; I'm sure. Wrong to be put right, perhaps. By the way, though," suddenly exclaimed Petersfeld, starting upright as he spoke, "I declare, all this time, I've been forgetting the most stunning thing of all! This very night—when we were dining with Buttermere—I declare it seems a week ago already—that little girl Linda, you remember—I sat beside her at dinner—when we were talking about this affair—"

"Of course. What about her?"

"Why, she told me—mark this, Worsley: that she knew all about the matter: knew who the girl was, where she lived, and where she is now. Think of that!"

"Little humbug. Did you believe her?"

"When she gave me names. Not before. I told her she was only chaffing, and then she went to work with those natty little fingers of hers, and spelled out right away 'Helen Fleetlands—Riverwood.' How now, Worsley, hey?"

"I think that you have made a most valuable acquaintance for your purpose," returned I, considerably surprised by the intelligence. "You two should start together, in partnership, in search of Miss Helen and her five hundred. Only that would be next door to bigamy. But you should have stroked her a little and asked for more."

"So I would. Only the ladies, bother them, chose to go just at that moment, and I never got a chance afterward. I'd give something to have another talk with her."

"That you may, easily. She and her sisters are going to the Zoological Gardens to-morrow afternoon. Meet them there, and the thing's done." ·.

"The deuce they are! How do you know? She never told me. I wonder at that."

"It was certainly very inconsiderate. Bunnytail told me. I asked him if he had been to the cattle show, by way of finding some subject in which he might possibly take an interest, and he said, ' no—but he was going to-morrow; while his partner yonder,' pointing to that extraordinary wife of his, 'preferred going, with the Buttermere young ladies, to some shabby show in the Regent's Park of outlandish beasts, that would never pay for their own litter. He gave 'em joy of it, he did.'"

"My dear Worsley, you've done me a signal service! won't I go—that's all! Stay and drink good luck to my chance. At all events, finish your cigar. All may turn upon this. I declare, though, I wouldn't take such a short cut in the matter, if I didn't feel that, knowing what I now know, it might be a sin to lose time."

·."My good fellow, it's past twelve o'clock, and I'm off. I start for the country to-morrow, and have work to arrange before leaving. I can be of no farther use to you, at present. Good-night. Go on upon your own hook—always the best way."

"Good-night, if you must go. I hoped we might have struck out something clear; but I never mind. Let us see what comes of to-morrow. At all events, when we next meet in Lincoln's Inn, you shall find that I have a story to tell. Good-night, and good-bye, for the present!"

And so Petersfeld went to bed, and to sleep, and had rather a remarkable dream.

He found himself walking alone with Linda, in a sequestered part of the Zoological Gardens, into which they had wandered, far away from the rest of the party. And by way of securing a perfectly retired place, in which to converse about Helen, without any rational fear of interruption, they entered an empty crocodile's den, the door of which had propitiously been left unfastened. And as they got into very deep and interesting conversation indeed, and "locked up" for that purpose, closer and closer upon the crocodile's plank, a deaf old janitor of the gardens came by and locked them in.

Naturally they both shouted a good deal, for it was growing desperately dark ; but owing to the peculiar atmosphere of the place, Paul was conscious that he could only crow like a crocodile, while Linda whistled in accompaniment, like some unearthly fowl.

Of course, in the Zoological Gardens, where noises of the kind are only too common, such a proceeding was useless, and they passed the night unpleasantly enough ; Linda insisting that Paul should climb to the very topmost bar of the iron rails, and cling on there until morning—while she arranged her virgin couch amid all the comforts of a crocodile's roost.

And, when morning came, it came attended by Mr. and Mrs. Buttermere ; who, after motioning Petersfeld down, somewhat sternly unbolted the door, and with a few sententious remarks of orthodox purport, led the way to a neighboring church, where he and Linda were married on the spot by a mild-looking gentleman fast asleep.

But this was only a dream.

CHAPTER XIII.

LUNCHEON was over in Harley Street, and the three Buttermere young ladies assembled in the drawing-room in walking array, as the clock upon the chimney-piece chimed two.

"Here's the carriage coming round," observed Lotty, looking out of the window. "I wonder whether those horrid Bunnytails will be punctual. Lucky for them papa's not at home to see the horses kept waiting."

"Well, they haven't begun to wait yet," said Loo. "Country people are always punctual: besides, these wretches dine at twelve, and begged mamma particularly not to be later than two. Imagine any creature, calling itself human, confessing to a regular twelve o'clock dinner. Je le crois parceque c'est incroyable. Only fancy the enormity of the thing."

"After all, what does it signify ?" remarked Linda. "Two hours of wild-beast-land will surely be enough for every body."

"Oh, I should think so !" drawled Lotty—"unless, indeed, they find something more interesting than wild beasts to divert them."

"By the way," exclaimed Linda, starting at the last suggestion, "I quite forgot to ask you before. Which of you told Mr. Petersfeld, last night, that 'we were going to the Zoo to-day ?"

Each of the young ladies to whom this question was addressed looked a little disconcerted. But Lotty, who had most presence of mind, judiciously answered—"Loo did."

"Did you, Loo ?" demanded Linda.

"To be sure I did. Hasn't Lotty just told you so ?" replied Loo, awkwardly trying to divide the fib.

"Well, and what did he say ?" persisted Linda.

"Didn't say any thing. What should he say ?"

"Now, really, Loo, you are too provoking ! Did you make him understand, or not ? You are not answering fairly, and you know it !"

"I know," replied Loo, with useless prevarication, "that I told it to Mr. Goldwin after dinner—here, by the tea-table—and Mr. Petersfeld was standing close by—just where that chair is, and heard every word. I had no chance of telling him otherwise. He scarcely spoke to me once,' all the evening."

"How do you know he heard ?"

"Oh, come, Linda, it's useless going on in this way ! He was quite close enough to hear, and I'll answer for it, he did, for he was doing nothing in the world at the time, except letting you show him those foolish Dutch photographs."

"A likely time to make him hear, wasn't it, when he was talking to me !" exclaimed Linda with perfect naïveté "I didn't hear, I promise you ! I really am ashamed of you both," continued she, with a little stamp of vexation. "When people make wagers, all is supposed to be straightforward and 'pon honor. Ours was not a very wise one, perhaps, and I shouldn't have made it except that I was put out at the moment. But you must both admit that I won it fairly, so far as last night went. And then, that you might have a dishonorable crow over me to-day, you deliberately broke your part of the bargain, while I most faithfully kept mine. However, if you don't feel sufficiently ashamed of yourselves already, nothing that I can say will make you."

"That's quite possible," retorted Lotty dryly, yet with an annoying consciousness that Linda had the best of it. "As you are not satisfied, the wager shall be off."

"To be sure," said Loo. "We don't want to win your gloves. The wager is off !"

"Not at all," replied Linda. "You told me, Loo, not two minutes since, that you had performed your part. You told me that, positively. So did Lotty. I give you the benefit of your assertion. I couldn't allow the wager to be off without accusing you both of direct' untruth. Win the gloves and wear them ! If with a good conscience, so much the better. If not, I give you joy of your spoils."

"As you please," replied Lotty, viciously. "I dare say you'll win yet. You made a famous beginning."

At this moment, Mrs. Buttermere entered the room rather in a fuss. It was twenty minutes past two—and no sign of the Bunnytails.

As there will be some farther demand upon your patience, and I can not expect you to consume the interval in merely watching the clock, I will take the opportunity of explaining how it was that Linda had counted so securely upon her success with Petersfeld. Of course you have already guessed the truth in part.

It happened that, a few evenings before, Mr. Eldon Bloss, barrister-at-law, whose name I have already had occasion to mention, had been her partner in a quadrille at a certain *soirée dansante*.

Now, Mr. Eldon was one of those free and easy, dashing, affable young bucks, whose boast it is, in their own phrase to be able to tell you what's o'clock about every thing, and who are always so anxious to do it. They form such a distinct, well-recognized class in British society, that it is scarcely worth while to define it carefully; but they all dress gayly—converse tremendously—tell funny stories to gentlemen and talk slang to ladies, and otherwise exhibit the hearty exuberance of unembarrassed people who are delighted to find themselves at once ornamental, amusing, and instructive.

And Mr. Eldon was a brilliant specimen of his order. I never yet talked to him for five minutes together without being enriched by a comic anecdote, a conundrum, and a tip for the Derby. And upon standing up with Linda in the quadrille, after having had, as he expressed it, rather more "cham" than commonly fell to his luck, he poured forth a torrent of small-talk with even more than his usual volubility. The fact is, he admired Linda immensely, a distinction of which the young lady was perfectly conscious; and always alluded to her as "a stunner," of which she was also aware. And this, though it did not by any means lead to a return of admiration, made her feel not altogether displeased with his company.

At last, in a rash attempt to establish something like a confidential relation between himself and his partner, the infatuated youth, quite forgetting his papa's solemn injunctions to secrecy, related, during fits of the quadrille, the desperate enterprise upon which Petersfield was bound.

The fact is that Petersfield was a man whom every one in the "Devil's Own," and almost every body in Lincoln's Inn, knew perfectly well by name and sight. And without (at least to my knowledge) being aware that he was at that moment engaged to dinner in Harley Street, Mr. Eldon naturally supposed that Linda would like to hear something diverting of so distinguished a character.

Stories of this description seldom lose in the telling; especially when the narrator happens to be quite reckless of truth—dying to astonish a beauty, and only imperfectly sober.

Petersfield, for, to give zest to his story, the scamp unscrupulously let out his name, was represented as consumed by a devouring passion, all the more intolerable from the fact that he had never yet beheld the object of his devotion. The latter was rapidly pictured as a perfect blaze of youthful loveliness, with half a pound of diamonds in her dress-pocket and her crinoline crackling with bank notes.

Wonderful revelations touching people of high rank might shortly be expected; but whether Petersfield would succeed or not, was, in Mr. Eldon's opinion, a toss-up. His own impression was, that his prospects were decidedly

fishy, and he had good reason for thinking so. "Only pray, my dear Miss Buttermere, keep this entirely between ourselves. The governor, you see, let it out, quite promiscuous, last night —the fact is, it was a great deal too rich not to tell, particularly after I'd seen his name in the advertisement. Only he made me swear so solemnly that I wouldn't allow it to go one inch farther, that—I'm sure you quite understand," concluded the prodigal son with a delicate leer.

"I understand," replied Linda. "You have kept your secret: and I am to keep mine."

Mr. Bloss, junior, would have liked to suggest that he had only been forestalling the day when all his own reservations might be Linda's as of right. It seemed rather premature, however, to allude to that problematical era, and he wisely let it alone, casting about rather hazily for a rejoinder to his partner's last reply.

I wonder whether many people recollect an episode in "Thompson's Seasons," which has just come into my mind. "Thompson's Seasons" was our poetry-book at school; and I once knew the whole four by heart—a dreadful acquisition.

A young lover, Damon by name, wandering absently through a wood, suddenly comes upon his beloved Musidora, who happens to be at the moment enjoying herself in the river.

Even Paul Pry himself, one would think, might under the circumstances have had the grace to retire and hold his tongue. Not so Master Damon, who, after indulging in a good long look, whips out his writing-case and describes his sensations in an amorous ditty, which he carefully commits to the water. The lady, seeing a piece of paper float by, naturally examines it, and finds her curiosity rewarded by a compliment in blank verse.

Upon this she good-naturedly returns to shore, and, after due precaution, let us hope, against catching cold, engraves with a "sylvan pen" (whatever that may mean) a neat inscription upon the trunk of the nearest tree; ending with the encouraging pentameter—

"Dear youth, the time may come you need not fly!"

This, of course, after a decent interval, is perused by the lover, who with due admiration for the maidenly reserve which sheltered itself so vaguely in the future, must have been inquisitive as to what he would, some day or other, be permitted to stay for.

I suspect that, if Mr. Eldon Bloss had ventured upon putting his first idea into English, he would scarcely have been met by so flattering a reply. At all events he contented himself with answering, "Well hang it, Miss Buttermere, what's a man fit for if he can't tell who to trust and who not? If I was wrong just now, you tell me so, and I'll knock under at once!"

"Not wrong at all, Mr. Bloss," replied Linda, laughing, as she recollected that Petersfield was asked to their next dinner-party, when she would in all probability find herself next him at table. It naturally occurred to her what immense fun she might have with that young gentleman, by pretending to know a great deal more than she did, and mystifying him in the most delightful manner. "Not wrong at all. Only you haven't told me her name yet."

"Couldn't, at any price," replied Mr. Eldon Bloss. "Governor would cut me off with nine-pence if he only came to hear of it."

"Oh, very well!" said Linda. "You said something just now about knowing whom you could trust, whom not. But never mind."

"Well, here goes," replied Mr. Eldon, des-perately :

"'In for a penny—in for a pound!
Better be hung for a horse than a hound!'

Miss Helen Fleetlands is her name. Lives at Riverwood Lawn, near St. Mark's-on-the-Sea. Now I've been and gone and done it, by jingo! *Fui—ivi—feci!* as Julius Cæsar used to say. If you go and betray me, Miss Buttermere, you'll effect the ruin of one who—would rather die than do as much for you;" concluded the young gentleman, devoutly wishing that he dared say more.

I am quite sure, and I hope my reader will be of the same opinion, that nothing more than mere childish frolic had in the first instance entered Linda's little head.. It was not until she was provoked beyond endurance by the conduct of her sisters that she ever dreamed of putting her new knowledge to what will, I am afraid, be considered an unscrupulous use.

But we have been absent long enough from the Buttermere drawing-room. Just before three o'clock, when every body's patience was exhaust-ed, and speculations as to what papa would say, when he heard how the horses had been treated, were becoming serious, a tremendous clatter in the street brought every body to the window.

A bright yellow chariot, with a post-boy in pink jacket and shiny white hat, with a satin rosette in his button-hole, came galloping gayly over the stones with Mrs. Bunnytail bawling at the top of her voice from the open window. The vehicle dashed rapidly past the house, and then, as if in obedience to the unceasing vociferations of the pilot in the cabin, wheeled suddenly round, performed a figure of eight in no time, and final-ly pulled up at the door; the horses, for the matter of steam and lather, looking as if they had just come out of a wash-tub.

"Good heavens!" gasped Mrs. Buttermere. "This dreadful woman will ruin us all! Ring the bell, one of you—do! Send her away! Tell her it's the wrong door!—Oh how abominably drunk he is!"

Even the post-boy, at whom this last remark was directed, could hardly have disputed its ac-curacy. Nobody was more sensible of the fact; but as to not being able to see straight, or drive straight, or being ever so thoroughly all right in his life, he would have argued with you as long as he could hiccup.

"Well, dear Carlo," exclaimed the robust lady, as, panting and breathless, she bustled into the drawing-room, "here we are, at last, you see, and goodness only knows what a job we've

had to get here. It was no fault of mine, I do assure you, only all the livery stable's glass coaches had gone to the wedding, and we were to have the first that came home, and come home he didn't till two o'clock, and then as tipsy as you please, saying 'you're another!' when I told him to drive to Harley Street, and then driving right away to Harlesden Green, and wouldn't pull up for all I could screech, till he ran into the baker just by the cemetery, with such a to-do as you never heard. Say good-after-noon to your aunt, my dears," continued she, pre-senting three impish-looking children. "Only I haven't told you one half the man did, Carlo, or how he rode seven times at full gallop round a long church in a gravel square, which of course couldn't be right anyhow; and so I told him, and made him stop and hire a sober man for six-pence to sit upon the dickey-box and call the way till we got to the top of Harley Street. Oh my! what a jaunt we've had."

It took some time to convince Mrs. Bunnytail of the necessity of dismissing her egregious charioteer upon the spot, and still more to induce the latter to depart. In fact, resenting a direc-tion to that effect as simply personal, he was in the act of charging in at the hall door, glass-coach and all, when a policeman interfered, and he accepted his situation.

"Well, if you must send for a cab, send for No. 999, Carlo—do! It's a nice early man that don't charge more than his fare, and brought us from Shoreditch station yesterday sen'night, with a blast in his eye, but quite civil. Send for him, won't you?"

Even this question was adjusted at last, and the whole party deposited at the gate of the Zoological Gardens.

At this juncture the small Bunnytail fry naturally began to be uproarious. Potty, Fly, and Loop seemed to be the calls to which they severally answered, puppy-dog fashion; but what may have been their real names—what their ages—what their genders,—I don't pretend to have the slightest conception. However, the first glimpse of the "Sunday Animals" as, from Noah-Archical associations, probably, they at once christened them, had a sobering effect, and caused them to behave with respectful curi-osity during the greater part of their visit.

Never were two young ladies more deserved-ly surprised and discomfited than were Loo and Lotty, as, just opposite the lion's den, they recognized Petersfeld, evidently got up for the occasion. His glossy new hat—his bright gloves—his whole aspect in short, all told a tale to which they found it most intolerable to listen. And when, after paying his respects to their mamma, he made them each a beautiful bow and then shook hands cordially with Linda, they fairly gasped with vexation—not so much that the gloves were lost, as that Linda was going to be married before them.

Judged by results, this bold experiment of Petersfeld's was little better than a failure. It was in vain that, as Linda had predicted, he followed her about like a showman. Somehow or other, no reasonable opportunity for any thing like private conversation ever presented itself. And although it may be the business of heroes to make opportunities, the manufacture is one which requires a certain amount of leisure, as well as of raw material.

The fact is, that the young lady was not a little afraid of her would-be cavalier. Her conscience told her that she had not only done a foolish thing, but made a serious mistake. What is fun for the evening, may be earnest in the morning, and she was neither inclined to confess the childish joke in which she had permitted herself to indulge, nor to carry it farther in cool blood. So she pretended that the whole care of the children had devolved upon her, and executed her maternal duties with such exasperating fidelity, that she never allowed her little pups to wander beyond ear-shot of their real dam.

Of course this was, literally, nuts for the children, for whose benefit Paul produced shilling after shilling with untiring liberality. Nor was his good-nature allowed to satisfy itself so cheaply, for Mrs. Bunnytail, espying a tempting refreshment counter, availed herself of the opportunity to flop down into a garden seat, and complain of a "sinking," which necessarily induced the offer of some restorative. And her smiling admission, that if she took any thing in that line, she was partial to cherry brandy, was justified by the result, for she took four shillings' worth before confessing to being quite beyond the probability of a relapse.

However, she amply repaid Petersfeld for his kind attentions, by the enthusiastic praises of his manner and appearance, which she poured without ceasing into Mrs. Buttermere's ear.

She never had seen such a real noble-looking young gentleman in all her born days—"And my dear Carlo, what a lucky girl is our Linda, to be sure! Not but what you might have told me what was in the wind before this, considering she's my own niece. But town ways are town ways, and I don't pretend to understand every thing; only you should have seen them talking on their fingers together all dinner-time, last night. Oh it was pretty! But that's nothing to the way he follows her about to-day. That's what I call keeping company in earnest, and no mistake. Bunnytail never courted me like that, I promise you, though never was a man so set upon woman, as he was upon me, if you'll only believe me, Carlo."

Some philosopher goes so far as to suggest that, in this world of ours, no deed is done, nor word spoken, without leaving its individual impress upon the future, and influencing—imperceptibly perhaps, but inevitably—the entire current of time to come. That the chattering of this foolish woman should have had any influence upon a person of Mrs. Buttermere's tact and experience, may seem in the last degree unlikely—but nevertheless, it was so.

She had, of course, observed the very marked attentions which Petersfeld had paid Linda since their first introduction, and had rejoiced over them with considerable pride and pleasure. He was in every respect the very man she wanted—young, handsome, fashionable, and with brilliant prospects. But she knew better than to build too much upon the result of a twenty-four hours' acquaintance. For aught she could tell, he might flirt equally with every girl he met, and to do more than float the pious prayer that the end might be as welcome as the beginning, would have been presumptuous.

But the loudly-expressed confidence of Mrs. Bunnytail, coinciding as it did with her own newly-formed aspirations, gave to the latter a degree of consistency which they would not otherwise have obtained. People, she recollected, made love just as effectually in the grazing counties, as in Grosvenor Square, and her sister might be no bad judge in such matters after all. And so, without being in the least aware of it, she allowed the affair—in her own mind—to take a most important slide in the direction of final consummation.

This, however, was not all. What Mrs. Bunnytail had seen, she had seen; and Mrs. Buttermere knew well enough, that no bribe which London could afford, would induce her to hold her tongue. To assure her that Petersfeld and Linda were not really engaged, would be to waste words. Mrs. Bunnytail had an awkward custom of believing her own eyes. Happen what might, the thing would shortly be as public as if it had been proclaimed in the *Morning Post*.

So she concluded to say as little as possible at the moment, and to discuss the question of settlements with Mr. Buttermere before she went to bed.

I am sorry to say that both Lotty and Loo, who were in the very worst of tempers, owing to their unexpected defeat, displayed a great deal of acrimony, and some want of self-control, before they got back to Harley Street.

Lotty, for instance, upon being accosted by an unfortunate cockatoo with some harmless personality, knocked the bird off its perch with a blow which might have felled a foot-pad, and upon being remonstrated with by the bird-house keeper, whom she at first addressed defiantly as "Man," and afterward deferentially as "Mr.," had to elect in the ignominious alternative of leaving her name and address, or a deposit of one pound fifteen.

Loo made even worse weather of it, for while chastising Fly within range of the Cassowary's cage, the unlucky child was, as Mrs. Bunnytail comprehensively remarked, "pecked into fits," and danced like St. Vitus before it left the Gardens.

As to Paul, he had only one momentary chance of private conversation with Linda, which unluckily occurred in the monkey room.

"My dear Miss Linda," he was just beginning, when a wretched ring-tail made a snatch at the silk tassel of her parasol, with which he went capering away to the top of his cage, to dissect at his leisure, after the careful and deliberate manner with which his brotherhood usually conduct their investigations. Nothing more provoking could possibly have occurred, for to stand by, helpless, in any emergency, makes a man feel seriously ashamed, while to interfere —had such a course been possible—would have been to cover himself with ridicule forever.

Every thing, in short, seemed to have gone wrong, and it was a relief when, after handing the ladies into their carriages, he watched them drive away.

CHAPTER XIV.

When a man is "out of suits with fortune" —unless matters are very serious indeed—he naturally goes to his club. There is a fine bracing atmosphere about these institutions, in which we generally revive.

Paul went to his club, won a game at billiards, dined, and was himself again. His afternoon had been unproductive, but what of that? Great results were not to be obtained by magic, and when one course failed, the obvious expedient was to try another. Except for that miserable monkey, what might he not have known at that moment. No matter. He would know it yet. He had only to write to Linda, and of course she'd reply, with full particulars, by return of post.

It never once occurred to him that such a proceeding would be either unusual or indiscreet, or demand more than the mere semblance of an apology. The only danger which suggested itself was, that his letter might possibly fall into wrong hands. He had a vague idea that the correspondence of young ladies was occasionally used by their mammas, so he resolved to express himself with caution.

He wouldn't trust himself to write from his club. In the quiet of his own rooms he would be better able to concoct a letter, which he fully expected would elicit the grand secret.

Unluckily, just as he sat down to his desk in the Albany, his mental serenity was unpleasantly disturbed. A letter which he had carelessly torn open, as an unmistakable circular, turned out to be of a much less innocent description. It was from his tailor.

Bags was perfectly civil, but at the same time business-like and brief. He reminded Paul that his account had been running considerably over two years. He apologized for troubling him with the well-worn tradesman fib of having a large demand to meet in the course of the following week : and concluded with a formal request for fifty pounds at least on account by Monday.

Nothing could have been more vexatious. Paul's allowance was by no means an illiberal one, but he spent it recklessly, and never had money in hand. One solitary twenty-pound note, with about a dozen stray sovereigns, was all that he could muster at the moment. The former he had set aside, some time before, toward the expense of a Swiss walk in the Long Vacation. It was a fine financial precaution. So long as you regard a twenty-pound note as mere inconvertible paper—not to be touched upon any account until a given day, it is tolerably certain to be forthcoming when wanted. Twenty sovereigns are quite another thing, and may be coaxed out, one at a time, upon the most plausible reasons, until there are no more to coax. Now quarter-day was several weeks off, and to be obliged to enclose this precious note to his tailor was little less than a calamity.

It had already, as we know, been diverted from its original purpose, and dedicated to the persecution of Miss Fleetlands. Indeed, deprived of its assistance, the whole affair seemed likely to end in a dead lock. Traveling and bribery are expensive luxuries, and five hundred pound rewards are not at all to be reckoned upon in one's computation of available cash. Of course, Paul might have borrowed money easily enough ; but, with all his carelessness, he was not donkey enough for that.

Whenever you find yourself dunned in good earnest, and payment quite out of the question, you should meet the matter in a philosophic and comprehensive spirit. Don't be angry with your creditor. "You must think this, look you, that the worm will do his kind," as Cleopatra's clown had the good sense to remind her. You must recollect also, that nothing is more vulgar than to be always flush of money, except the baseness of treating the want of it as an inconvenience, either to yourself or any body else. Try a frank genial course ; with nothing provoking—still less any thing penitential about it. Make the fellow feel that you're all serene yourself about the matter, and ten to one he won't give needless trouble.

Acting upon this view, Paul wrote a very concise reply to Mr. Bags. "He was sorry to hear of his difficulty. He lost no time in enclosing the trifle he happened to have about him, and would look into his bill the first moment he had to spare. He should be very sorry to be dressed by any body but Mr. Bags, who always fitted him so nicely ; but really some of his charges—seven guineas, for instance, for a frock-coat—were more than he had paid, even at Cambridge. He was almost afraid he couldn't afford Mr. Bags."

These latter sentences, he flattered himself, had a particularly solvent sound, and though the sudden apotheosis of his hoarded note was a decided inconvenience, it was useless to send regrets after it, and he set to work upon his letter to Linda.

I should be ashamed to say how many sheets of crested and superfine note paper were destroyed during the composition of this precious document. Nothing within the whole range of his letter-writing experience had approached the difficulty of composing those few lines. Now he seemed to be saying too much. Another sheet was torn to tatters for saying too little. At last a sort of nightmare-like entanglement crept over his mind, and he grew desperate. So, solemnly vowing that the next sheet should be the last, he wrote a cautious note in the best words he could muster, and carried it, with Mr. Bags's answer, to the post. I think I have already observed that Linda had her faults. Among these, and let us hope among the worst, was her custom of never appearing at family prayers—or indeed until farther delay would have involved the loss of her breakfast.

The fact is, that Buttermere always left home at nine precisely, for his early consultations, and was Turk enough to inflict preposterous matins upon an innocent wife and family. Of course he was quite right in so doing, and Linda quite wrong to rebel; but the little sluggard would neither be coaxed nor scolded into submission, and was at last allowed to persevere, as a pet, in what she called "her own comfor' way."

"Who's Linda got a letter from, I wonder," observed Lotty, as the footman distributed the produce of the early post. "Who can she possibly have to direct to her in that great, black, gentleman scrawl, with a seal as big as a tartlet?"

"Let's look!" exclaimed Loo, seizing the letter in her turn. "What a funny crest! Papa, what does this crest mean—a five-barred gate with two great keys across it?"

"Hey?" replied Buttermere, laying down his newspaper. "Why, I seem to recollect that crest too! Oh yes! I'll tell you whose it is. It's the Petersfeld crest. Don't you see the gate with the cross-keys of Saint Peter. Peter's field—that's it. One of those old fashioned heraldic puns. Why? What the deuce—?"

Positively, if the tea-pot had begun to talk, or the French rolls to waltz upon the table, a quiet family could hardly have looked more astounded over their breakfast than did the Buttermeres at this simple information.

A letter from Petersfeld! Why, he hadn't been introduced to Linda forty-eight hours ago. This was bringing her down with a snap shot, and no mistake. Proposing by letter too! Mrs. Buttermere gasped a gasp of mingled thankfulness and bewilderment, while Lotty and Loo scarcely dared to exchange glances, in the depth of their utter discomfiture. •

To be deliberately cut out, in this cool easy way, and probably have to stand up as Linda's brides-maids within a month, was too much for their philosophy.

As to papa, he looked at his wife and daughters with a puzzled and anxious expression, and pushed away his plate.

Just at this moment Linda came fluttering into the room, fresh and buoyant as the morning.

"Good-morning, every body! Good-morning, papa!" accompanying the latter benediction with a kiss. "Late again, am I? Well, this time, I'm sure it wasn't my fault, at all events. Why, good gracious, how dreadfully circumspect you all look! quite guilty, I declare! What on earth is the matter? What is it, mamma?"

"There's a letter for you, Linda," observed Lotty, maliciously.

"A letter, is there?" replied Linda, glancing at the address. "Only a bill, I dare say, and I want my breakfast." Her quick instinct instantly told her that this letter had excited unusual curiosity; which, without having, at the moment, the slightest suspicion as to who her correspondent might be, she quietly determined to disappoint.

Lotty and Loo bit their lips with vexation, as Linda, slipping the mysterious document into her pocket, ate her toast and drank her coffee, all serenity and good nature, and with even more deliberation than usual. At last the time arrived for Buttermere to be off to his clients, and Linda, who, with all her external self-control, was burning with impatience to know what they had all looked so cunning about, soon satisfied her curiosity, upon the music-stool in the back drawing-room.

"My good gracious—a twenty-pound note!" exclaimed she, as she pulled the crisp bank paper out of the envelope. "Well, I never saw a twenty-pound note before, in all my life! Who in the world can have sent it?"

At the sight of Petersfeld's name she started violently. She felt her color go—while every whiff of breath seemed for the moment out of her body. Her fun appeared, indeed, likely to have a serious result. She hastily ran her eye over the following words, and felt stupefied:

"Albany, Saturday.

"MY DEAR MISS BUTTERMERE:—I am most anxious to press for an answer to a question of the very deepest interest to myself personally.

"You can not but be aware of the subject to which I refer, and I most earnestly beg that you will either indulge me with a few moments' private conversation, when and where you please, or set my mind at rest by writing unreservedly. I trust that you will not be offended by my venturing to send you a note; but our conversation yesterday was so vexatiously interrupted that I had no opportunity of saying verbally all I had intended, and accomplishing the purpose for which, in truth, I awaited you at the Gardens. I believe that you will neither misunderstand me nor misconstrue my motives in thus addressing you; and again apologizing for the liberty which I fear I am taking, remain, my dear Miss Buttermere, yours most sincerely,

"PAUL G. PETERSFELD."

Now, considering what had passed between himself and Linda with reference to Miss Fleetlands, not twenty-four hours before he sat down to write the above, I think that Paul was not altogether unreasonable in supposing that his meaning was beyond mistake. Linda had herself told him that he must find some other opportunity of continuing their conversation; and, after having failed at the Zoological Gardens, it was the most natural thing in the world that, to avoid an indefinite loss of time, he should address her in writing. In fact, his letter would have been perfectly intelligible, had he not, with wonted alacrity in blundering, carelessly thrust his twenty pound note into its envelope, instead of that directed to his tailor, previously to sealing them both.

It was exactly the thing which any body who knew his ways as well as I, might almost have counted upon his doing; and yet, considering that an average of many hundred letters, containing notes or money, are annually posted without any direction at all, we must not be too hasty in deciding who is, or is not, fit to be entrusted with pen and ink.*

"I trust you will not be offended at my venturing to send you a note."

Linda read these astonishing words three times over, with perpetually increasing bewilderment.

What could they possibly mean?

At first a confused suspicion that he might be attempting to purchase her supposed knowledge with a twenty pound bribe, entered her puzzled little head. Gentlemen, she was aware, habitually did very odd things, but surely nothing so offensive as that.

Perhaps he was eccentric. Eccentric people went up in balloons—got good-humoredly fined at police courts, and probably forwarded bank-notes gratis to favorite ladies. But this supposition was as absurd as the former.

And then the overwhelming possibility that, after all, the money might actually have been intended for herself, sent the blood flushing and throbbing to her very temples. What did he mean by saying, "I had no opportunity of saying verbally all I intended, and accomplishing the purpose for which, in truth, I awaited you at the Gardens?"

Could it be possible that his presence there had been prompted by feelings of which she was herself the object? Improbable as this might seem, she knew that Petersfeld would never have been invited to dine in Harley Street, unless he had been regarded by her parents as perfectly at liberty to make himself agreeable either to herself or her sisters. Indeed, it might be that he had even received her papa's formal assent to consider himself as her suitor. But the whole business was so wild and unintelligible that she laid the letter down with a sigh of despair, and wished herself several weeks older.

It was most unfortunate for Linda that in so critical a conjuncture she had no trustworthy friend to whom she could appeal for advice.

Her sisters were out of the question. To go to her mamma, without showing the letter and explaining the foolish mystification which she had put upon Petersfeld, would have been useless. To make a clean breast of it would have been simply to ensure herself a sound scolding—all the sounder indeed from the fact that her mamma would, as she was well aware, have been if possible still more puzzled than her daughter. For Mrs. Buttermore's gift was not in the way of expounding parables; which not only perplexed her, but made her very angry and unreasonable.

What would she not have given to have awakened suddenly, and found the whole affair a dream, and the bank note an illusion! But after having convinced herself by experiment that she was so perfectly wide awake that any farther development in that line was out of the question, and recollecting that Petersfeld's communication demanded an immediate reply of some kind, she determined, as the only resource, to place herself at once under the guidance of Mrs. Springletop, a young married lady of her acquaintance who lived in Portland Place, not many hundred yards off.

Mrs. Springletop, whose name has already appeared in these pages, was very young, very fashionable, and very strongly impressed with a conviction of her own profound knowledge of the world and its ways, and consequent ability to give valuable advice.

Nothing could have delighted her more than to see Linda arrive on her early visit, with a letter in her hand and a question to ask.

"Oh my goodness, what a bear! I never saw any thing so delightful—never since I was christened," laughed Mrs. Springletop, handing back Paul's unfortunate missive with its enclosed bank note. "It's the King of the Cannibal Islands all over! Does he mean to buy you right away for twenty pounds—or is it only so much board-wages to begin upon? Why didn't he accomplish his purpose, poor darling, at the Zoological Gardens? and what was the vexatious interruption he makes such a fuss about? Do tell me more about him. I only wish to goodness he'd write to me!"

"My dear Fanny, please be serious. You see I must return this money by the very next post; and I don't know what in the world to say to him about it. I want you to help me. I have no one else to ask."

"Quite right to come to me, my dear," returned Mrs. Springletop, playfully. "Particularly, since after seeing what I couldn't help seeing, at your house the other night, I quite expected that something of this sort would happen in the course of a week. But, as to returning the note, that's fiddlestick! Don't begin by sending young gentlemen to the right-about like that, my dear, or you may die an old maid."

"Never mind what you saw at our house. That was all nonsense. Mr. Petersfeld fancied that I knew a secret about a friend of his, and was trying all the evening to get it out of me.

---

* During two consecutive years ten thousand pounds' worth of property was actually enclosed in blank envelopes, and posted within the United Kingdom. Any one who may be curious to find this astounding fact philosophically accounted for, may, perhaps, like to refer to an article (I believe by the late Sir Francis Head) in the *Quarterly Review*, vol. lxxxvii., p. 80.

That was all. And I'm quite certain, that's what he's writing about now. But why should he send me this wretched bank note, and talk as he does?" continued Linda, ready to cry with vexation. "I'll send it back in a blank envelope and have done with it!"

"You won't do any thing half so foolish, my dear," replied her sagacious adviser. "If you do, he'll have done with *you:* you may depend upon that. I declare I won't have you snub such a nice, affable, generous bear upon any account. Send back twenty-pound notes indeed ! I can assure you they're not always to be had for the asking. I know I've heard my husband say it's a maxim in the city—'Never refuse money ;' and it seems sensible enough. Mr. Petersfeld, who's a barrister, will think you a ninny if you do. Besides, it would just be a simple affront, let alone the cruelty of the thing."

"There could be no cruelty, so far as I am concerned," said Linda ; "but oh how I wish he would only have let me alone !"

"Let you alone, indeed ! I don't advise you to count upon being let alone much, so long as you wear that little face ! I really can't help laughing at the drollery of the thing," continued Mrs. Springletop, "but I declare I quite love him for his simplicity. I'll answer for it he was at his wits' end to know what present to make, so he judiciously sent the money instead, that you might choose for yourself."

"It seems so very unlike him—" began Linda.

"Oh, if you dislike him," returned Mrs. Springletop, pretending to misunderstand, "that's another pair of shoes altogether!"

"I never said that :—I said—"

"Oh, in that case never mind what you said. Don't stand in your own light, my dear Linda. It's only returning presents, you know, if the worst comes to the worst."

"But what must I *do*," persisted Linda, fairly driven to desperation. "See, the morning is passing, and the post will be going, and I must do something, right or wrong !"

"You shall do quite right," replied Mrs. Springletop, ringing the bell, "if you'll only leave it all to me. Do you think I don't understand a little affair of this kind? Trust me, my dear, and don't fidget yourself. The brougham will be round in ten minutes, and then I'll show you exactly what to do."

Linda was by no means satisfied : indeed quite the reverse. But as a skipper blown out of his reckoning into some unknown and reef-sprinkled channel, will take any man on board who declares himself a pilot, and leave him at the wheel so long as he continues to bellow orders with unabated confidence, so she reluctantly, and as an only resource, placed herself unreservedly in Mrs. Springletop's hands.

She did not deceive herself into supposing that she was acting rightly in so doing. But what else could she do ? · She acted just as our forefathers, about whose wisdom we are so fond of moralizing, used to act, when they found themselves engaged in what, by a charitable euphuism, was distinguished as "an affair of honor." So soon as matters took a gunpowder turn, and the question had clearly outgrown the stage of foolscap and armorial seals, they committed themselves, soul and body, into the hands of a second. In the prospect of subsequently getting shot at short notice, it was a grand point to be able to indulge in the school-boy consolation — "It wasn't their lookout." Whatever might be their private likes or otherwise with regard to that contingency, personal responsibility was the one thing intolerable.

Paul sat at breakfast, next morning, alone in his Albanian quarters, waiting impatiently for the post. He was just beginning to wonder whether it could possibly have passed without bringing him a line from Linda, when a twin tap at his door, and a flutter in his letter-box, decided the question. There were two letters —one directed in his tailor's flourishing scrawl, the other a delicate little pink note, addressed to him in a pretty, young-lady-like hand. In the excitement of the moment he felt as if he scarcely dared to open it, and mechanically began to examine the contents of Mr. Bags's dispatch. To his dismay and astonishment it ran as follows:

"SIR :—Your favor of this day's date to hand, stating that you enclose the trifle you have about you on account of bill delivered. Am sorry to say your letter contains no remittance, and not being a jocular party myself, and pressed for money, can't see the pleasantry as you might wish. Must request, therefore, that you will favor me with draft for entire amount of bill delivered, £84 16s., (say eighty-four pounds sixteen shillings) in the course of to-morrow, or shall with great reluctance be obliged to commence usual proceedings, and remain, sir, your obedient servant,   B. BAGS.

"To Paul Petersfeld, Esq., Albany S. W."

Paul read this letter in stupid bewilderment. His note, which he perfectly recollected enclosing, must have been stolen in the post. But what a miserable scrape to be in. Things were bad enough before ; but now it looked as if his grand adventure were ruined altogether. Almost recklessly he tore open Linda's dainty envelope, for let it contain what information it might, this hideous tailor had ruined him for the rest of the quarter.

Twenty pounds gone already, and eighty-four to be raised in the course of the morning, was a financial crash upon which he had not calculated.

But if he was disagreeably astonished at Mr. Bags's letter, he was thunderstruck upon reading as follows—written, as you may suppose, under Mrs. Springletop's dictation :

"DEAR MR. PETERSFELD:—I ought to be very angry with you for sending me a twenty-pound bank note, and my first intention was to

return it to you immediately. But that, I suppose, you would have resented as an affront, so I have lost no time in devoting it to the only purpose for which it could possibly have been intended. Next time we meet I shall have the pleasure of showing you the most beautiful emerald bracelet, and such a love of a lace parasol, to make amends for the one which you allowed the monkey to ruin. I am only sorry that, since you choose to make me such a splendid present, you did not add to its value by choosing it yourself. But, after all, the things could scarcely have been prettier than they are. You talk of an interview in your note, which, I suppose, is to give me the opportunity of thanking you in person. Believe me, yours very truly,
"LINDA BUTTERMERE."

Let us drop the curtain upon Act the First. When it rises again, our prima donna shall at last appear upon the stage.

CHAPTER XV.

HELEN FLEETLANDS first saw the light in a pretty green bungalow, with infinite verandas, which looked out upon the flaming waves of the Bay of Bengal.

Her father's history is briefly told. A soldier of fortune—in other words, a soldier with no fortune at all—he found himself, after a quarter of a century of Indian life, in command of a cavalry regiment in the Company's service. In broken health, he was obliged to relinquish his career, and consoled himself with a late marriage. A child was born—a wife died, and the worn-out soldier simply awaited a fate in Hindostan, which his doctors plainly told him was beyond challenge either in India or elsewhere.

The new house at Cossambazar in which he had intended to live, was the new house in which it only remained for him to die; and, with quiet soldierly fortitude, he resigned himself to his doom.

A brother-officer, whom he could implicitly trust, had promised to take charge of little Helen when the time came, and bring her up among his own children; and Colonel Fleetlands's last and all-absorbing object was so to arrange matters that she should have some sort of independence of her own—enough, at all events, to enable her to live modestly in England, without the necessity either of toiling or marrying for bread, or of drifting miserably through life in that most pitiable of all capacities, a poor relation.

His ambition, in short, was, to secure her a clear annual income of two thousand rupees (two hundred pounds sterling, or thereabouts); and to effect this the dying man denied himself, not only every thing in the shape of indulgence, but many things which, in his condition, were almost among the necessaries of life. He had never saved before; in fact his opportunities in

that direction had not been encouraging; and the freshly awakened impulse took possession of him like a mania. His table was daily littered with papers covered with calculations in rupees, annas, and pice, as to the exact rate of his expenditure, the degree in which his savings were rolling up, and the number of months which he must contrive to live before he could die with his work done.

Neither were these computations quite so simple as might, at first sight, be supposed. His design was to leave the entire amount of his property to the friend who was to be Helen's guardian, in trust to accumulate so much of the interest as should not be required for her maintenance and education, at compound interest for her benefit.

During the earlier years of her life, living as she would among other children, a great deal would of course be saved. Gradually her clothing and education would become more expensive; but still, after allowing for every probable deduction, and reckoning interest at five per cent., the prospect that, at one-and-twenty, she would be mistress of a capital representing two hundred pounds a year, became at last, little short of a certainty. He had only to live a few months longer. Another half-year's pension drawn, and the thing was done.

And Colonel Fleetlands did live, as strong-hearted men, determined to accomplish their work below, sometimes contrive to live, in spite of the soundest medical advice to the contrary. He lived to see the day when, seated in his veranda, with a pile of papers upon the table before him, he could at last exclaim, "Thank God, my task is finished! Helen will not be a pauper. With common economy, and reasonable care of her money during infancy, she will at one-and-twenty have a clear four thousand pounds of her own—two hundred pounds a year, at five per cent. Heaven knows the struggle it has cost me to bring her income up to this. But I would go through it all again—aye, ten times over, rather than die without having done thus much for my darling. I would do more if I could; but I can not now—there is no time. I must rest before I die."

As Colonel Fleetlands sank languidly back in his arm-chair, there was a sharp rattle of buggy-wheels over the gravel in the compound, followed by loud and lively conversation in the same direction. In another moment a visitor was announced.

"Jump is my name, if you'll allow me, colonel," said a smart nattily-dressed little man, flourishing his straw hat with an obsequious wave in the direction of Colonel Fleetlands; "firm of Joy, Jingle & Jump, Calcutta. You know us by name, I dare say—Joy, Jingle & Jump, my dear sir?"

Any body could have seen at once that Mr. Jump had some tremendously interesting intelligence to communicate. It was beaming out of his eyes, fluttering upon his tongue, and tingling to his very finger-ends. But like a child who can never tell a piece of news without first insisting upon one guess at least, Mr. Jump couldn't help coquetting with his secret, and repeating "Joy, Jingle & Jump?" with his head on one side, and a provoking smile. This first step in the riddle had, however, been unluckily chosen.

"I have reason to recollect your firm," returned the sick officer slowly. "Several years ago, I accepted a bill for a friend of mine—a young fellow in our dragoons, and the paper got into your hands. You didn't show me much mercy. It was a rascally transaction, and you know and know it. Don't stand there grinning. I've had quite enough of your firm. Go away and write to me, if you've any thing to say. Do you hear? I have but a few days left, and each moment has its value now."

"Oh, my dear colonel!" exclaimed Mr. Jump—shocked beyond measure at this frightful allusion to an affair which he had long since forgotten—"pray forgive us if any such thing ever occurred! I give you my honor I wasn't in the concern at the time—never even heard of it. I've come now, sir, with the most splendid news for you, and do hope and trust you'll allow me the great satisfaction of delivering it personally. I've come all the way to Cossambazar, colonel, for that very purpose. The idea of my firm having ever sued you upon a trumpery bill! It's the very best joke I ever heard—the very best, indeed!"

"It was a very indifferent one at the time," observed Colonel Fleetlands dryly. "We will not joke again, if you please."

"Certainly not, colonel. Certainly not. My firm—to which I won't allude again for one moment—received, by last mail, from Mr. Bloss, of New Square, Lincoln's Inn, our London correspondent, a letter directed to yourself, together with certain documents which we were instructed to lay before you. The letter," continued Mr. Jump, opening his black leather bag, "is here. The documents are these. And now, my dear colonel, will you allow me the pleasure of communicating the purport of this glorious intelligence myself?"

"Mr. Jump, there can be no glorious intelligence for me, in this world. I have not long to live, and can only attend to business which it may be my duty to transact. Give me the letter which you tell me is addressed to me, and suffer me to read it quietly. My servants will show you every attention, and the house is at your service. But let me read this letter alone."

"Certainly, colonel, certainly," replied his visitor, rising. "Only allow me to fulfill Mr. Bloss's particular desire, that I should wish you, from him, health and long life to enjoy your good fortune, and to do as much upon my own account, colonel."

"You are wasting good wishes, but I am obliged. Is it the Mr. Bloss, I wonder, whom I remember long—long ago, a remarkably stout young man?"

"The same, colonel—the same! Oh dear yes! Sent us his *carte-de-visite* by the mail before last. Not so young now as he was, but an elephant-and-castle to look at. Quite so, colonel."

"Pray, Mr. Jump, call for whatever you require, and use my house as your own. Excuse a dying man; I would rather be alone at present."

And so, while Mr. Jump reveled in pale ale and cigars in an adjoining apartment, Colonel Fleetlands's thin fingers broke the broad black seal, and he read news which for the moment seemed to transfix him to his chair.

The letter was dated from New Square, Lincoln's Inn, and headed

"RE NETTLETON, DECEASED."

Instead of merely copying the document verbatim, I shall take the liberty of giving you its purport, premising a few facts, without which its entire significance could scarcely be understood.

Some five-and-twenty years before the date of which I am now speaking, Colonel Fleetlands, then a frank, fair-haired lad of eighteen, upon the point of embarking for India, had been a great favorite with the dead Nettleton. They were distantly connected, but no more; only just enough to suggest a sort of indistinct family tie. However, Nettleton, a jolly, luxurious bachelor—a wharfinger, I believe he called himself—liked the boy, asked him to dinners, took him to prize-fights, tipped him with sovereigns, and otherwise treated him with great good nature.

One day Mr. Nettleton suddenly took it into his head to make his will. He had found reasons for so doing, which may now be left in peace. Obligations which lawyers distinguish as "moral" are sometimes, by less educated people, called by less edifying names. At all events, to provide a life-income for a certain interesting annuitant, Mr. Nettleton held himself in conscience bound, and sent for Mr. Bloss—then in the first bloom of his attorneyhood—to compose a testament accordingly.

The annuity was provided—a few unimportant legacies given, and then—

"How about the residue? We must have a residuary legatee, my dear sir," suggested Mr. Bloss, suddenly pausing and placing his pen across his mouth.

"What's that?" demanded the testator.

"Somebody to take the balance—pick up the crumbs, as it were, in case the bequests already made should fail to exhaust your entire fortune. It is usual to name somebody."

"I've left all I have. I can't leave more."

"There may be more to come," urged Mr. Bloss. "Better put a name in, in case."

"Name little Ned Fleetlands," replied Mr. Nettleton. "Nice young fellow, that. If there's any thing over, let him have it. Much good may it do him."

To tell the truth, had the will-maker died

then and there, Colonel Fleetlands's residuary expectations would have been dearly purchased at an outlay of eighteen-pence. But Mr. Nettleton did not so die. He lived to coin money for many a long year, and to see his business extend and flourish in a degree of which he had never indulged the faintest anticipation. Moreover, the fair legatee, for whose benefit the whole will had been projected, died in his life-time, so that, in default of any later disposition—which he never made—the provision destined for herself, as well as the entire bulk of his general property, devolved upon his residuary legatee—in other words, passed to Colonel Fleetlands for his own absolute use and benefit.

In fact, the purport of Mr. Bloss's letter was to inform him that he was, at that moment, master of trade property and premises worth some sixty thousand pounds at the least, of ten thousand pounds in stocks and shares, of thirty years' lease of a mansion in Bryanston Square with all its furniture, carriages, horses, and six hundred dozens of wine, of a fishing-box in the neighborhood of Llanfairpwllgwingyll, North Wales, and a shooting-box at Fort George in the Highlands, with sundry little pickings, not yet estimated, but which might be taken as from eight to twelve thousand additional. That was all.

Strangely as it may sound, Colonel Fleetlands's first emotion, upon realizing the extent of this astounding windfall, was one of intense and overwhelming vexation. He had tasted the delights of saving—a passion, by the way, which, once encouraged, will take root and run to seed just as surely as drinking, gambling, debauchery, or any other exceptional human indulgence. He had lived, as it were, with Helen's little hoard before him, enjoying, day by day, its slow but steady increase. He had counted no piece of self-sacrifice too severe which only added a couple of annas to the pile. More than that, he had succeeded. He had made her independent.

And now, as if in mockery of all his toil, came this immense fortune tumbling in, a solid mass of wealth, from which every fragment of his miserable savings—aye, multiplied fifty-fold—might be chipped away without leaving it sensibly less than before. He had worked and suffered for nothing. So, at least, he mistakenly felt at the moment.

Another, and far more bitter feeling, only too naturally crossed his mind. Why had it come so late? Three years ago it might have carried him home to England, with blessed hopes of life and health. Much more. She for whom his heart still silently bled, might have been at that moment in bloom and beauty by his side. Why had it come so late? Again he ground his teeth.

Why had it come at all? Except in so far as little Helen was concerned, it was much as if he had suddenly received commission to divide a great territory in China among the Peacock Mandarins. He could, himself, have neither part nor lot in the inheritance; while, as regarded Helen, there were anxieties almost as vivid under her strangely altered prospects, as those which had tormented him already. If he had dreaded poverty for her, he dreaded friendless wealth still more. He knew no one to whom he could conscientiously entrust the care of a baby heiress, with upward of a hundred thousand for her marriage portion; nobody who would bring her up as she ought to be brought up—watch her as she ought to be watched—and steer her course through the dangerous morning splendor of such a future.

The only man in England to whom his thoughts pointed, at the moment, was Admiral, then Captain Mortlake, of whom we have already heard. But whether he would like, or even accept, so delicate a task, the colonel could not know; and, in any event, there were complicated arrangements to be made, contingencies to be guarded against, and an elaborate will prepared before it could be even suggested. There was no European lawyer at Cossambazar, and Colonel Fleetlands longed to consult Mr. Jump, whose buggy-horse was at that moment panting in the compound before him.

But that hateful bill transaction, of Heaven knows how many years before, still clave to his soul like pitch, and rather than unbosom himself confidentially to one of such a gang of swindlers, as he very naturally considered them, he would, I suspect, have seen Mr. Jump's persuasive countenance revolving in the Hooghly among those of the many native gentlemen who diurnally proceed to sea down that mysterious river.

So he allowed the opportunity to pass unimproved, and dismissed Mr. Jump with a magnificent fee, as became a man who had been so suddenly transformed from a miser into a millionaire.

And then, feeling that his time was short, and that a whole world of responsibility had devolved upon him within the last few hours, he deliberately drew a clean quire of foolscap from his writing-desk, and set to work at once upon his last will and testament.

Perhaps, while he is about it, I may be permitted to offer to the unprofessional reader a suggestion or two, gratis, upon a subject respecting which the most serious errors are unluckily prevalent. He may skip the rest of this chapter and welcome, if he please; and if he can equally contrive to skip the advancing hour, from which, as the law has it, his will must, if he ever make one, "speak," his time will be much better occupied than in pursuing my story.

But to those who like to listen, I would say: Never suppose that any possible amount of common sense (whatever that may mean), or any quantity of trouble which you may be disposed to take in the matter, is sufficient to enable you to make a will, and defy all the world to pick a hole in it. Eschew the weak belief that you can clearly express your meaning, at all events. In a cursory glance among the books upon my shelves at this moment, I have lit upon half a dozen cases, at least, in which the Court has substantially said, "The meaning of the testator is clear enough, but the words which he has used unfortunately oblige us to disregard it." And the reason of this apparent hardship is so well explained in a standard professional work, which I always consult with pleasure, that I have no hesitation in employing the writer's language instead of my own.

"In construing wills," he remarks, "the courts have always borne in mind, that a testator may not have had the same opportunity of legal advice in drawing his will, as he would have had in executing a deed. And the first great maxim of construction accordingly is, that the intention of the testator ought to be observed. The decisions of the courts in pursuing this maxim, have given rise to a number of subsidiary rules, to be applied in making out the testator's intention ; and, when doubts occur, these rules are always made use of to determine the meaning; so that the true legal construction of a will, is occasionally different from that which would occur to the mind of an unprofessional reader. Certainty can not be obtained without uniformity, or uniformity without rule. Rules therefore have been found to be absolutely necessary; and the indefinite maxim of observing the intention is now largely qualified by the numerous decisions which have been made respecting all manner of doubtful points, each of which decisions forms or confirms a rule of construction, to be attended to whenever any similar difficulty occurs. It is indeed very questionable, whether this maxim of observing the intention, reasonable as it may appear, has been of any service to testators ; and it has certainly occasioned a great deal of trouble to the courts. Testators have imagined that the making of wills to be so leniently interpreted, is a matter to which any body is competent ; and the consequence has been an immense amount of litigation. An intention, moreover, expressed clearly enough for ordinary apprehensions, has often been defeated by some technical rule, too stubborn to yield to the general maxim, that the intention ought to be observed."

And our author, in illustration of his last remark, notices a case, in which a father by his will declared his intention to be, that his son should not sell or dispose of his estate for any longer time than his life ; and, *to that intent*, he devised the same to his son, *for life only ;* and after his (the son's) decease, to the heirs of the body of his said son.

Common sense would probably have approved of this disposition, as at once clear and effectual. But common sense and common law are two very different things. The testator had unwarily laid hold of a technical term, and the technical term wouldn't let him go again. And the day of his death beheld his son absolute and irresponsible master of the estate.

Under what inconceivable infatuation, then,

do people, in other respects sound in mind, careful of their own interests, and not inconsiderate of the welfare of others, sit down daily to make their own wills? How do they excuse to their consciences this most cruel and culpable folly? By what right do they dare expose those for whose benefit they ostensibly put pen to paper, to the unspeakable calamity of a Chancery suit, with all its heart-burnings, misery, and waste? And yet, a thousand times over, has this been the penalty of indiscretion in the use of one single drop of ink. Verily, the man who, for the selfish saving of a miserable fee, can leave his family liable to such horrible hazard, ought to be buried in disgrace, and the reason noticed upon his tombstone.

CHAPTER XVI.

A NOTORIOUS criminal was, one morning, proceeding on foot to the place of execution, accompanied by a father confessor, whose efforts to improve the occasion were not altogether well received.

The culprit, unfortunately, chanced to be in what nurses term a "fractious" mood; and evinced his repugnance to the entire proceeding by first of all "stepping short" in the most unconscionable manner, and subsequently subsiding into plain goose-step when fairly within sight of the gallows.

"My good brother," urged his ghostly companion with a persuasive nudge, "if you had the slightest idea how late we are, you would, I am certain, walk a little faster. Do you suppose that, because you have naturally no engagements for the afternoon, we are all equally free? I assure you, for my own part, that I have a great deal upon hand ; and so, probably, have many of the gentlemen yonder. Pray come along! We ought to have been upon the drop by this time. Just look at the crowd!"

"No hurry, governor," replied the penitent, gruffly. "They can't begin without us."

I should scarcely imagine that, under the circumstances, much consolation could have been extracted from this palpable truism. But the words themselves frequently recur to my mind with very salutary effect—"No hurry, governor. They can't begin without us."

Say that to yourself, my friend, as I do, when you fancy you are going to be late for a dinner, a train, a consultation—or possibly for morning church. You will be right nine times out of ten. Either they won't begin without you, or you will pick up your place in a canter, which is practically much the same thing. And the wear and tear of a certain nervous tissue—worn and torn beyond computation by disquieting anxieties upon such matters—will be saved altogether, which is as much as adding two clear years to your life, a consideration not to be lost sight of, as times go. They won't begin without you. Make a note of that.

There is only one contingency in which I can not advise you to rely upon this comfortable assurance. Never write a story under the delusion that your readers can't begin without you. Bless your innocence, why not? They can read you backward, or forward, or skipping-ways, just as they please; and cut altogether those careful passages which you so often smiled over in secret, as the very key-stones and buttresses of your narrative. As to not beginning without you, it is only too certain that they will begin and end exactly where they choose.

The above digression came into my mind as I was finishing my last chapter. I felt a misgiving that the little dissertation in which I had indulged, with a view of preparing the ground for what is immediately to follow, might be accepted by some wary people as a sort of salutary warning, and acted upon accordingly. I fancied I saw them cunningly turning over my leaves until they found themselves quite clear of the shop, and then "beginning without me" some twenty pages down stream, leaving me to trudge after them at my leisure.

It is unpleasant, however, even to moralize upon such possible treachery, and a relief to return to my narrative.

When Colonel Fleetlands deliberately sat down to concoct his own will, he had three objects prominently before his mind.

In the first place, he wished to secure for his little Helen, so far as human foresight could extend, a thoroughly happy and comfortable home, where she should not only be a welcome but a coveted guest. This was easy.

In the second place, he was anxious to protect her effectually, during her girlish inexperience, against those prowling adventurers who were certain to "go in" for so splendid a prize as a maiden with several thousands a year. This appeared a problem equally simple.

Lastly, he desired to restore a large portion of Mr. Nettleton's fortune to the family or relatives of that gentleman. The property had fallen to him through the merest accident, and was far larger than he had even the slightest inclination to retain for his daughter. He had no sentimental scruples about using that which was absolutely his own, but he exercised his right, subject to the self-imposed understanding, that after helping himself and his own liberally, he was not entitled to trifle with the remainder. Here again all seemed plain sailing.

With these objects in view, Colonel Fleetlands's testamentary dispositions ran as follows. I give the will as he wrote it, simply because it is not a technical, but a straightforward, soldier-like document, which in itself explains the manner in which he conceived that his wishes could best be carried into effect:

"THIS IS THE LAST WILL of me, Edward Fleetlands, Lieut.-Col. H. E. I. C. S. I appoint my friend, Hercules Mortlake, of Riverwood Lawn, St. Mark's-on-the-Sea, in England, a captain R.N., guardian of my only daughter, D

Helen, until she attain the age of twenty-three years. Should he decline so to act, or die, then I appoint the Rev. Felix Salterton, rector of Riverwood, aforesaid, guardian of my said daughter. Should they both decline to act, or die, I request the Bishop of London for the time being to name a guardian. I give my said daughter the sum of fifty thousand pounds, which I direct shall be at once invested in consols by my executors. I desire that out of the interest of this sum, five hundred pounds per annum shall be received by my daughter's guardian for the time being, for her maintenance, education, clothing, and pocket-money. The rest of the interest is to be accumulated and added to the principal until she attains the age of twenty-three or marries, when the whole is to be transferred into her name. Should she die under twenty-three, or marry under that age without the consent of her guardian for the time being, her interest is to pass to the persons hereafter named, expect that, in the event of her marriage without such consent, I desire that she may receive two hundred pounds a year for life, and no more, to be strictly settled to her separate use. I give the legacies mentioned in the list below; and, subject as above stated, I give all the residue of my property among the persons who would have been entitled thereto had I not been named in the will of the late Mr. Nettleton. And so I leave my soul to God, appointing Captain Mortlake and Mr. Salterton my executors. Done and dated at Cossambazar, this 13th day of September, etc., etc."   [Schedule of Legacies.]

Now, with one unlucky exception, the above, as every lawyer must admit, was a most creditable specimen of amateur testatorship.

No guardian could help feeling warmly toward a child who brought him substantially an additional income of five hundred pounds a year.

No gay deceiver was likely to entangle the inexperience of a blooming heiress, whose wealth would disappear upon seizure, like the colors of a butterfly under a school-boy's cap.

Up to twenty-three, at all events, her marriage would have to be contracted with the deliberate approval of her guardian for the time being. No great hardship after all. There is no magic in the precise age of one-and-twenty, and many young ladies, who will never be one-and-twenty again, deceive themselves wofully in the estimate of their own worldly wisdom. Indeed I don't understand why we, insular and independent Britons as we are, should vote ourselves mature at an earlier period than people are content to ripen at, anywhere else in the world. In France, Spain, and Germany in general, full majority is not conceded until twenty-five. Under this age no young man can dispose of himself without the consent of his parents or guardians, as the case may be—although young ladies are, here and there, let off more easily. In Spain, for instance, they have only to wait for twenty-three; while, oddly enough, your Burgomaster's daughter is permitted to dive into matrimony upon her own hook the very moment she is out of her teens.

To return, however, to the will, and the unfortunate paragraph just referred to.

Why, in the name of all that is wonderful, was Colonel Fleetlands rash enough to write those lines—"I give all the residue of my property among the persons who would have been entitled thereto, had I not been named in the will of the late Mr. Nettleton?"

Far better to have flung a lighted hand-grenade among the powder barrels of Dum-Dum. The bang would have been big and bad, but soon over. But these few words consigned his estate at once to the mercies of the Court of Chancery in England. These few words let loose at once the spirit of rapine and discord in at least fifty hearts. These few words stirred up envies, hatreds and malices, which may scatter fire and poison among generations yet unborn.

In a will, all is irrevocable. The writer passes away into the land that is very far off, beyond all reach of human question. None can ask him what he meant, if he has failed to express that meaning. If no possible construction can be put upon his words, the law, of necessity, disregards them and distributes the property as if no will had ever been made. But if *any* meaning can be attached to them, however unjust, mischievous, or absurd in the result, the law accepts that meaning, and abides by it through thick and thin. No evidence of intention is, generally speaking, admissible. What the testator has written he has written, and must be accepted as sufficient, and expounded as oracular.

I dare say that, unless you are yourself imbued with the wisdom of the legal serpent, you might read the mischievous few lines above referred to at least twice over without suspecting any particular harm. Perhaps, under similar circumstances, you might even have expressed your own meaning much in the same way. Well, I will not pause now, to explain exactly what was wrong, or what was the exact question to which these words gave birth; but in case you should feel any curiosity upon the subject, or any wish to be wiser, I have transcribed in the note below, and I hope you will read, an opinion written by a brother barrister under the impression (accidental upon my part) that the case I put to him was occurring in my own practice.*

A very few mornings afterward, the long anticipated event occurred. Colonel Fleetlands was found at day-dawn speechless in his bed. And as the boom of sunset-gun from the neighboring cantonments rolled heavily over Cossambazar, the heart of a good man and gallant soldier was quietly hushed forever.

Loving and careful hands tended the little orphan in her unperceived bereavement, and provided for her transplantment to English soil. And, in charge of a magnificent brown Ayah, all turban, teeth, and ear-rings, the child was in due course cleared at the Southampton Docks by Mr. Bloss himself; who, as holding the will under which her splendid fortune had devolved, considered himself bound to do the honors of Old England upon her first arrival. And under his escort, she was safely deposited a few days later with her gallant guardian at Riverwood Lawn, hard by St. Mark's-on-the-Sea.

And this would seem to be the time to give some account of Admiral Mortlake personally. His acquaintance in a casual sort of way we have already had the opportunity of making.

Colonel Fleetlands and he had been schoolboys together, and had contracted one of those early friendships which outlast all others. Mortlake was a brave, willful boy, cock of the school, and deservedly respected all round upon the very sufficient ground that he was going to be midshipman in a frigate before next half. And midshipman, dirk and all, he accordingly became, with as fair a career before him as ever was cut out for a young sailor.

His family were immensely rich, with high admiralty interest; his father chief of one of the greatest county banks in the kingdom, with

---

* "DEAR W.—I have read your note carefully. Of course you will file your bill at once; as no executor would dream of acting upon his own responsibility in such a case. Colonel F. seems to have had £4000 of his own, *plus* say £100,000, bequeathed to him by Mr. N. Out of this fund he leaves £50,000 to his daughter, and the residue 'among the persons who would have been entitled thereto, had he not been named in N.'s will.' What in the world does he mean? The fact that by Nettleson's will the £100,000 became Col. Fleetlands's property, can not be affected by any thing contained in the colonel's will. Consequently it became part of, and passed under the description of, his (Colonel Fleetlands's) residue.

"This residue Colonel Fleetlands attempts to dispose of, by referring to Mr. Nettleton's will.

"But instead of giving it to the person who would have been entitled to the residue of Mr. Nettleton's estate if he (Colonel Fleetlands) had not been named, he gives it to the persons who would have been entitled to *his own residue* if he had not been named!

"The supposed omission of Colonel Fleetlands's name from Mr. Nettleton's will, fails to afford any clue to the persons who would be entitled to Colonel Fleetlands's residue, with reference to that contingency. The description is unintelligible, and the gift must fail.

"I assume that there are no recitals in the early part of the will, such as—'Whereas I desire that, subject to the legacy hereby given to my daughter, so much of my property as I derived under the will of Mr. Nettleton, should revert to his family,' because it is possible that some such recital might connect the bequest so intimately with Mr. Nettleton's will, as to allow the Court to substitute the words 'to the residue of Mr. Nettleton's property,' for the word 'thereto.'

"In short my view is, that the testator has altogether failed to describe the parties whom he intended to take his residue; the description he has given being incapable of being made sense of without introducing a large amount of extrinsic evidence to show his meaning—or probable meaning.

"The bequest therefore fails altogether as a gift, and the residue goes, as a matter of course, to the daughter, as next of kin, unless something in the will prevents it.

"The fact of the testator having given a fixed legacy to his daughter, and the residue to others, renders it morally certain that it was not *his intention* that his daughter should take the residue as well as the legacy. But if, as I hold, he has altogether failed sufficiently to describe the object of the gift of residue, and the gift on that account fails, I do not think that his inferred intention would be considered as any bar to her taking it.

"I can not see how the colonel's next of kin (other than his daughter and only child) could possibly be let in, even if the words of the gift to the daughter went so far as to express a positive prohibition to her taking more than the legacy under any circumstances. If you can not fix upon the *proper* people to take, it must go to the real next of kin, I should think."

the persons who would have been entitled to *his own residue* if he had not been named!

a noble landed estate, upon which young Mort-lake, as an eldest son, might have looked forward to a life of luxurious independence.

But his tastes were not for flocks and kine; while as to sitting behind a desk in pen-and-inky slavery during the best hours of every day, he would far sooner have been mast-headed regularly for the same period—an elevation, by the way, which he subsequently had pretty frequent opportunities of enjoying. In short he seemed, as it were, born for the sea, with every quality, except one, which was requisite to ensure success. A reckless, insubordinate spirit marred all. He could not obey cheerfully. There are men who can not. It is a base failing. "*Imperantur ut imperant*" was not said of such. Not, at least, of one in ten thousand.

And so, after rising to the command of a frigate, Captain Mortlake came suddenly to grief. The version which we landsmen received of the affair may possibly have been even less accurate than the information usually supplied to the marines. But we all believe that one fine afternoon, when a squadron was running down Channel, under all sail, Captain Mortlake received such a series of aggravating and "nagging" signals from his admiral, between whom and himself a private feud existed, that he lost all control over his temper—suddenly beat to quarters, and sent a thundering broadside of blank cartridge right into the spectacles of that fussy old gentleman, who was only half a cable's length to leeward.

Of course, as soon as the latter could be unsuffocated sufficiently to sputter, he signaled Captain Mortlake on board in fury; and though we don't pretend to know precisely what passed in the admiral's cabin, we are quite clear that Captain Mortlake's alternative lay between instantly retiring upon half-pay, or standing a court-martial. And we are morally certain that, but for the tremendous amount of interest which he was fortunately enabled to bring to bear, the result of this unlucky explosion of temper and gunpowder would have had no alternative about it.

Be this as it may, it is beyond all doubt that Captain Mortlake quitted the service entirely against his own inclination, and retired to the life of a country gentleman upon his estate at Riverwood, a morose, dissatisfied man.

Perhaps to an active and domineering spirit, no severer trial can easily be conceived than that of being summarily expelled from a profession. A dark cloud is at once flung down upon the whole stretch of the future, in which it is impossible to discern the "silver lining." In Captain Mortlake's case, the sentence was simply one of civil death. What were a thousand acres of grass and furrow, compared with those few feet of glossy quarter-deck? He resented his fate both upon himself and those about him, and, avoiding society altogether, lived for some time a life of savage seclusion.

No doubt sulking has it pleasures: but unless we have reasonable grounds for supposing

that we are making others at least half as uncomfortable as ourselves, they scarcely outweigh its disadvantages. To some extent Captain Mortlake had the satisfaction of believing that, if he chose to lead the life of a hermit, the neighborhood must have wished it otherwise. With a noble domain, a splendid country house, and every means at his command for the exercise of princely hospitality, it was so much the worse for them when he sternly closed his gates. There is something almost fascinating in such a burial of unbounded wealth. Whereas, let a poor man amuse himself after the same fashion, and we simply say, "Poor devil! The sooner the coroner's wanted the better."

But this gourd of his solitude was destined to dry up as it were in a night. The bank stopped payment. Not a very uncommon occurrence, but, like a railway accident, frightfully astonishing to all concerned, from the directors sitting in dismayed committee, down to the guilty switchman who brought it all about, and the poor third-class passenger whose head is picked out of the ballast. It was a terrible break-down—not quite irremediable as regarded the concern, but involving thousands in the most serious perplexity and distress. To Captain Mortlake it was little less than ruin. Half the Riverwood estate was sold, and the remainder heavily mortgaged, and every sixpence of his stocks and shares confiscated, before he was out of the scrape.

How it all came about, matters little now. No need to talk about that pre-eminently meek and subservient clerk, always clad in Sunday black, who wore gloves, and discountenanced sporting language in the vicinity of his virtuous desk. He is at Portland this morning, suffering from a rather large padlock on the pastern, and in the way, I hope, of being liberally whipped, not once for good, but ever and anon, before he is again entrusted with pen and ink. Pen and ink! that, Captain Mortlake never could abide, and resented his dislike by plucking him bare.

Just at this conjuncture, news arrived in England of Colonel Fleetlands's death, and of Captain Mortlake's appointment as his executor and guardian of little Helen. A few months before, he might have surlily refused to act. But times had changed. In two points of view, the chance was one not to be neglected. In the first place, five hundred a year was just at the moment an immense object. Of course the poor little Indian baby who brought it would be a nuisance; but she might, for the present, at all events, be kept in the nursery and perfectly out of the way; so that there was no substantial drawback upon that head.

Secondly, this very baby might, in a few years become, in another respect, a rather desirable acquisition. Long before the bank smash, Mortlake had begun to discover that he was making a miserable fool of himself by growling through his gates at the world, which he fancied had done him wrong. And the worst of growling is, that when the good wish comes over us to wag our tails and be friendly, the difficulty of getting that said tail into motion, or delivering it at all from our hind legs, without conscious loss of dignity, is a sad obstacle in the way of amendment. But, with a brilliant young heiress to bring forward, all would be easy. She would be an excuse, at once, for entering society again; and the world, as he sullenly admitted, he was no longer in a condition to defy. So he at once accepted his new duties, and, in conjunction with Mr. Salterton, proved his late friend's will in the Principal Registry of Her Majesty's Court of Probate.

That I have been neglecting Mrs. Mortlake all this time, is quite true. In that respect, I am afraid I resemble her husband, who hated counsel of every description, and above all, that of his wife. He was neither in the habit of listening to her reasons, nor of troubling her with his own. And if, for purely financial purposes, he chose to present her with a full-fledged baby instead of the callow little "pledge" which sentimental people so pleasingly describe, and which, in his own case, had never arrived, she had no option, you may depend, but to accept the gift, and make the best of it.

I had no intention, when I began my story, of attempting to entice any body who might do me the honor of perusing it, into the diabolical labyrinth of a Chancery suit. I will not do so now. I will not even explain the construction ultimately put by the Court upon those unfortunate words, "I give all the residue of my property among the persons who would have been entitled thereto, had I not been named in the will of the late Mr. Nettleton."

But the result was, that in the face of the innumerable claimants whom these words called suddenly into legal existence, it was impossible for the executors to act at all, except under the protection of the court. So they filed their bill in Chancery, in which Captain Mortlake and Mr. Salterton were plaintiffs, and Helen, and some score of others, were defendants, and interlocutory and other decrees were made, and costs were ordered out of the estate, and every thing went on as comfortably as need be, and after the fashion in which things constantly go on when testators have been so economical as to make their own wills.

One result of the suit, however, you will perhaps have the goodness to bear in mind. Helen's £50,000 was ordered to be realized and paid into the Bank of England, to the credit of the Accountant-general of the Court of Chancery, to be duly invested in consols; out of the interest of which £500 per annum was directed to be paid to Captain Mortlake, as her guardian, and the remainder accumulated for her benefit until farther order.

It was among the consequences of this considerate proceeding that she thereupon became immediately a Ward of Court.

Over persons in this position, the Court of Chancery, as is well known, exercises a protectorship at once jealous, vigilant, and despotic. To marry a young lady so situated, without the Court's consent, is stigmatized as "Ravishment of Ward," of which, in former times, the Court (succeeding, as it did, the Star Chamber, in cognizance of such offenses) used to mark its disapproval by imprisonment for life, or by enforcing perpetual abjurance of the realm. So that, as was naïvely remarked in an old case, "the grievousness of the punishment showed the greatness of the offense."

Even at the present moment, such a marriage; or indeed any preliminary flirtation with marriage in view, is considered as an aggravated criminal contempt in all parties concerned, which the court will always resent as nearly touching its honor and justice, and severely deal with. The bridegroom goes forthwith to the Queen's prison, and the incautious parson is lucky if he can find any body to listen to his *miserere*.

Ignorance, or want of notice of the fact that the infant was a ward, is an excuse which can not be attended to upon any account, for the plain and satisfactory reason that every suit, or other proceeding, in chancery, is a *lis pendens*, of which all good subjects are bound to take notice.

Neither, in the plenitude of its anxiety to extend protection where protection is needed, will the court withhold its assistance, even where the cause of interference may have arisen in the case of an infant, male or female, not previously a ward.

Not many months ago, for example, a certain affable Miss Richardson contrived to "ravish" a young prodigal aged nineteen, who quitted the paternal roof to enjoy her company unmolested, in the neighborhood of Dorset Square. So far, so bad. But the lady, not content with love, demanded matrimony also, and the feeble youth wrote home to his mamma, bidding her not grieve any more, because he had turned over a new leaf, and was really going to be married.

His papa, however, who looked for consolation from other sources, couldn't stand this, and instantly executed a settlement of one hundred pounds upon the offending simpleton, in whose name, as next friend, he forthwith filed a bill to administer the trusts thereof.

This made the bridegroom intendant at once a ward in Chancery, and the very next morning, Miss Richardson's frail gayety was disturbed by a notice that another interview with her young friend would be purchased at the cost of her liberty.

There now! If any thing in the way of "ravishment" should ever threaten poor Helen, I trust you feel competent to shake your head in good time, and to prophesy that "assuming" this, and "subject to" that, and "apart from" something else (qualifications without which no legal opinion is worth a rush), such and such will be the end of the transgressors.

CHAPTER XVII.

In my last two chapters I have been obliged to ascend for some little distance up the stream of history, in order to explain the circumstances under which Helen passed into the guardianship of the master of Riverwood Lawn. I am now about to square my story, by bringing my account of her down to the exact period at which our friend Petersfeld set out upon his remarkable chase.

It is unfortunate that I should be obliged to leave him so long in the background, especially in such a promising scrape; but he must take his turn like the rest of us, according to the rule of the world, and shall have no cause to complain of his historian before I have done with him.

Admiral Mortlake—for I may as well give him his flag at once, although he did not actually attain it for some dozen years after Colonel Fleetlands's death—was not naturally an avaricious man. Few sailors are—so at least we believe, ashore—though few people, I fancy, are less content with their wages, or cry out more lustily for what they are pleased to call prizemoney, a luxury which we land-lubbers never even expect. But the bank disaster, to which I have just referred, had changed his nature for the worse. It is among the worst results of these mercantile catastrophes that they are apt to damage a man in mind, even more than in purse. The man who limps away out of a railway accident may hope to get his leg put straight again, some day; but ten to one, the man who has been seriously run over in a money smash, will hardly pull through without some crook in his mind which all the doctors in Europe would fail to disentangle.

It was obvious that in accepting Helen and her five hundred a year, he was treading on the very verge of what could strictly be considered honorable. He knew well that her father, in entrusting her to his care, was under the impression that he was possessed of a splendid country seat, with a fortune to correspond; and it might well be that it was in a home of this description, that he wished and expected the little heiress to be brought up. He knew, equally, that the house could now scarcely be considered as his own, while his affairs were so miserably embarrassed, that but for the trifling additional income thus thrown in his way, it was by no means certain that even by the exercise of the most penurious economy, he would be able to continue his establishment at Riverwood at all.

However, he was in no mood to indulge in sentimental scruples, and comforted himself with the resolution that he would take the best possible care of his ward—a precaution clearly desirable under the circumstances.

One point only gave him a little uneasiness. He had a vague suspicion that awkward questions might one day or other be asked by the Court of Chancery, with reference to his expenditure of Helen's money. Trustees, he knew, were considered peculiarly "accountable" people by that intrusive tribunal, and proverbially afforded more sport than almost any other class of individuals when brought in to be badgered. His neighbor and co-executor, Mr. Salterton, had once mooted something upon the subject which rather startled him; but after all, looking at the will as it stood, the case seemed straightforward enough. All he had to do was to feed, clothe, and educate the little lady, and provide her with pocket-money when she was old enough to spend it, and the rest was his plain and proper fee for *quasi* paternal care and responsibility.

Now, although I have undertaken in some degree to furnish a memoir of Miss Fleetlands, from the day of her birth up to that upon which my story commences, I have no idea of wasting useful time and paper in an elaborate chronicle of her nursery days.

She seems, by all accounts, to have been a peculiarly fascinating little creature—the pet of everyone at Riverwood Lawn. Even Mortlake himself found a soft corner in that tough and ancient muscle which he probably talked about as his heart, and suffered the child to follow him all about the house, and to frequent his private sitting-room at her pleasure.

This latter apartment was Helen's especial delight. It was a large, handsome room, with a French window opening upon the lawn, filled with curiosities of all kinds, of which the admiral, it would seem, had in former times been a most fortunate collector. Giant lay-figures were there—copper men of Patagon—fellows who, like the jolly young waterman, renowned in song, "feathered their skulls with such skill and dexterity," that they looked like bad human cockatoos, and were altogether real stumbling-blocks in the way of a self-educating student of natural history. And there were vicious fishes and hulking birds, and serpents which yawned at the little girl, as if she would just have made one delicate mouthful, crackling like a beccafique at Bordeaux. And there were odd corners full of boarding-pikes, cutlasses, tomahawks and working-tools of a like nature, with which man, whether savage or civil, has for various good reasons, let day-light into his brethren from time immemorial.

But perhaps the grand attraction of this wonderful room, was an immense iron safe, or "ark," as the admiral always chose to call it, upon which the little maiden was never tired of gazing. It had once, I believe, held the books and papers of the family bank. On either side, stood one of the plumed Patagonians, with a shocking smile upon his engraved face, looking like its guardian demon.

There was a mystery about the whole affair, which quite fascinated Helen. The tawny sentinels, the huge lock, the clanging bolt, the ponderous doors—that opened with such a reluctant whine, and which the admiral himself could scarcely close. What did it all mean?

It meant simply this : that ever since his grand financial disaster, Admiral Mortlake had distrusted every living soul in England, from his co-partners at the St. Mark's bank, down to the very agent who screwed rents out of the Riverwood tenantry. In this ark he kept deposited all his title deeds—when he had any to keep, most of them being, at the time of which I am speaking, in the hands of various mortgagees — all documents of any value, and not unfrequently, very. large sums in ready money. It amused him to shut the heavy door with a bang, and growl to himself, " Safe bind—safe find ! No clerk there, at all events."

Partly out of pure rough good nature, partly perhaps because the inquisitive interest of the little mite was positively amusing, the portal of this iron cavern was unlocked most days for Helen's private amusement. And nothing pleased her better than to plant herself cross-legged upon the carpet, gaze wistfully into its recess, and wonder, as a child will wonder, what it would feel like to be locked up inside till Christmas, with other profitable speculations of a like nature.

It became an old familiar friend. She knew exactly in what corner of the admiral's writing-desk its bright steel keys were kept, and would have liked above all things to have had a private key of her own, which was plainly not to be thought of. Still, there it stood ; a sturdy acquaintance with a sort of magnetic and mysterious influence, the future of which was altogether inscrutable, and may remain so for the present at all events.

It was lucky for Helen that even this savage boudoir was at her disposal. For Mrs. Mortlake was a formidably good woman, and sternly aware of the fact. When we refer to the doings of somebody else, upon some particular occasion, as "rather too good," we are not commonly supposed to use words in their primary meaning. And whether any lady can by any possibility be too good in reality is a delicate question. But, if such a thing be possible, I should have no hesitation in saying that Mrs. Mortlake must have been very close to the mark.

From the very first moment that Helen could understand a fact, the tale of an immaculate infancy was diligently dinned into her ears. "I never was naughty, all the time I was a little girl," was the pious fib which the child at last began to believe, and to consider what a nice mess she might make of it, if she were weak enough to follow suit.

For, although Mrs. Mortlake in her angelic maturity abundantly fulfilled this early promise, nobody liked her at the Lawn—a fact which, as we all know, children discover just as soon as their elders. Her goodness was the goodness of a good machine which will grind over you, body and limb, before it will go out of its groove, or give you time to get out of the way. So long as you did as she did—thought as she thought—and emitted an equally pungent and persistent odor of sanctity, all was well. You need only discern between Mr. Mulcymist, the curate, who was right, and Mr. Salterton, the rector, who was wrong ; be in your pew ten minutes before eleven in the morning, and ten minutes before three in the afternoon upon every Sunday, fast, and festival, throughout the year —encourage all poor parishioners who read your tracts and said your conversation " did them good," and persecute all who would neither listen to your reproof nor smilingly accept your ready-made flannels—and you took your oar in her boat at once. But the crew, I can tell you, was a picked one ; and there was nothing for it but to keep stroke, or be landed, mud or meadow.

Talking about tracts, by the way, Mrs. Mortlake's mission, you must know, was not only to disseminate, but to create. I dare say you may have sometimes wondered—I have, at all events —whence all the myriad tracts in circulation are actually evolved. It is really a very curious question.

Well then, one flourishing *officina* existed, and may still exist, at Riverwood Lawn. Mrs. Mortlake's themes were drawn from sources wide as life itself, and therefore variegated and various. Sometimes she dealt in hard-headed and argumentative damsels who exchanged logic with the tempter until he modestly admitted his mistake, and disappeared with his hat in his hand. Sometimes in Scipionic policemen, whose rigid and frigid moral philosophy was proof against any temptation at all. Sometimes in serious sailors, who held tobaccoless tea-parties in the forecastle, and whose conversation was seasoned with nothing stronger than "Bless me !" and "Oh, my dear !"

But I intend to take an opportunity before long of offering you a specimen of her composition ; devoting, if necessary, an entire intercalary chapter to that very purpose.

It was no fault of this excellent person that her inherent dislike to children was intense and ineradicable. She detested them so much that she never had any of her own ; and of course the apparition of a little stranger, in the literal sense of the words, for whose care and education she was to be entirely responsible, was any thing but an occasion of rejoicing. Granting, however, that, in this particular, her very failings didn't lean to virtue's side, they at least gave her virtues a famous opportunity of displaying themselves. Many, and probably most of our good deeds derive their principal merit from the amount of self-sacrifice which they involve ; and if the care of the friendless little orphan had happened to have been a pleasure rather than the reverse, there would have been but little scope for self-approbation in undertaking it.

Whether other considerations could have had any possible sway with so austere a moralist as Mrs. Mortlake, is more than I can tell. Be this as it may, little Helen's early experience might have suggested to her that she must have done something naughty in her cradle, and been forthwith consigned to a reformatory for the remainder of her life.

For education by way of reward or persuasion was entirely opposed to Mrs. Mortlake's principles. People ought to obey because obedience was right, and ought to be punished, if they didn't, because disobedience was wrong. Any other system was, according to her creed, a government by lower motives, and unsuited to the case of a reasonable and accountable baby.

Moreover, lest the said baby should by any means entertain the idea that any particular punishment exceeded the offense, or was indeed more than a rather liberal instalment of what might be expected hereafter, the most tremendous threats and texts were always at her service; denunciations which, if they conveyed any meaning at all, produced much the same effect as the invocation of the black sweep, or the wicked old man with the bag—familiars long since cashiered in all decent nurseries.

And so the work of education began—unsatisfactorily enough to both parties; for Miss Helen was not very docile, and her instructress not very patient. Probably she made the pace rather trying on principle, as one who perceived that the high authority for not sparing the rod forbade her to allow any precious opportunity to escape unimproved, which seemed to justify a snug little whipping.

And so things went on for a few uncomfortable years, during which Mrs. Mortlake's patience and trimming tackle were alike exhausted; and Helen's naturally high spirit became so thoroughly chafed and roused, that she disobeyed for disobedience' sake. She even horrified that lady one Sunday, between services, by audaciously announcing that she had broken all the ten commandments that very morning and found herself much as usual.

Of course matters couldn't be allowed to continue upon that footing; and, despite the admiral's dislike to the incumbrance, a governess was the only resource. Firm, good-humored guardianship was all that Helen wanted; and this one would suppose might, by proper exertion, have been readily secured. But with characteristic inaptitude in such matters, Mrs. Mortlake pitched upon Miss Serena Smugg, the *protégée* of one of her clique.

There had been one naughty child in the house before. There were now two; for Serena was as cunning a little humbug as ever stepped in crinoline. Mrs. Mortlake thought her perfection, and, for once in their lives, Helen and she were of the same opinion. Serena didn't mind a little teaching, and she taught rather well; and Helen didn't mind a little learning, and she learned exceedingly fast. But, a very mild amount of daily business once over, and the governess was only too anxious to be quit of her pupil. She had her own correspondence, which was voluminous, to attend to. She had a thrilling "Tale of Fashionable Life" fast approaching completion on the sly, in which all the characters were peers and peeresses, whose graceful badinage was for the most part exchanged in boarding-school French.

She was addicted likewise to siestas, which Helen never ventured to disturb; during which visions of spurred and whiskered counts jingling with jewelry and scented like Mr. Rimmel's shop, passed pleasantly in procession—when ladies lovelier than the morning were followed about their corridors by these peeping Toms, who looked unutterable things, and occasionally said things which would have been much better unuttered — when pages, waiting-women, and satanic valets all did their best to surpass their employers, and when, in short, the whole machinery of modern aristocratic life in England was at last remorselessly unveiled.

All that she insisted upon was, that she was "never to hear of" Helen's being naughty; and the young lady very sincerely promised that, if she could help it, she never should. And so Mrs. Mortlake, having washed her hands of the whole affair, gave herself no farther trouble whatever about the child. She had the greatest possible confidence, so she assured her own conscience, in Miss Smugg, who had been so highly recommended in the best quarters—who was always so demure and unobtrusive, and whose behavior in church was enough to edify any body. Helen was scarcely reasonable yet. When Miss Smugg had once broken her in, and she had fairly arrived at years of some discretion, then would be the time to resume her task, and trim and train this "warped slip of the wilderness" into the faultless model which it would be her pride and pleasure ultimately to present to society.

In the meanwhile, one grand point upon which she insisted, was, that Helen should have no playfellows. It was extremely improbable that she would meet with any child brought up half so religiously as herself; and therefore, while she might possibly be contaminated, she could scarcely be improved, by chance acquaintances. She had her paragon governess for companion, a gloomy old garden to play in, and a shaggy old pony to ride upon, and there was nothing in the world to prevent her from being as happy as Mrs. Mortlake herself. Besides which, it was just as well that she should be kept in ignorance, as long as possible, of her own splendid prospects, a glimpse of which could only tend to unsettle her mind. And so the upshot was that Helen became the pet and companion of all the servants, who felt for her lonely estate, and, as they expressed it, did all they knew toward making her a good time.

One morning in August brought round Helen's ninth birthday. If she had learned to look in her glass to any useful purpose, she might have discovered a wonderful little countenance, which gave promise of unusual beauty long before nine more summers should have passed over her head. Nothing could be more perfect than the pure brown complexion and delicately moulded features, resolute though childish, and stamped with character and originality. But Helen never looked in a glass, nor cared for a reflected fairy face, nor knew by sight her own lithe, graceful figure, nor mused over her pretty hands, unless when exceptionally dirty. And all this bright summer day she had been entirely her own mistress, as was only fit and proper; and had scampered her pony, and wandered in the garden, and climbed the chestnuts, and fished in the pond: while Serena's lords and ladies had an equally busy time of it, for the "assembly" sounded early, and the demure novelist allotted the whole of her idle day to passing them all before her in grand review.

At last Helen's rambles were brought to a disagreeable termination. The little girl managed to tread on a sharp strong thorn of a broken acacia bough, which not only pierced her shoe, but soon stained the white cotton sock with blood.

It was not her way to make the least fuss about so commonplace a casualty. But as she happened to be close to the French window which opened from the admiral's private room upon the lawn, she hopped in there to try the result of the small amount of operative surgery at her command. The admiral was buried in his great arm-chair, devouring the *Times*, which had just arrived from town, and took no notice of her entrance. So, seating herself upon the carpet, between the great oak writing-table and the window, she pulled off shoe and stocking, and, placing the dainty little white foot across her lap, began leisurely to dig for the thorn with a penknife, wishing heartily all the time that she had been operating upon Mrs. Mortlake instead of herself.

So busily was she engaged, that she never noticed the clang of the hall door bell, which announced the arrival of a visitor.

Neither did the admiral. And yet there was a footstep at the door—a footstep bringing something worth attention, both to Guardian and to Ward.

INTERCALARY CHAPTER.

BETWEEN two successive Acts of a serious opera, we occasionally find, what is described in the bill as a ballet divertissement, interposed with the best effect. After the appalling daggerwork, the unfathomable despair, the uproarious chorus in which the last scene culminated, it is charming to find ourselves at once amid the innocent gayety of a happy valley where all the world is dancing. We have really nothing to think about—perhaps the less we think the better—and simply enjoy the spectacle. And, when the ball-music dies away, and the curtain descends upon a sea of smiling eyes and whirling muslin, we are ready to enter with renewed vigor upon the substantial business of the evening.

Well then, let us here interpose the intercalary chapter already promised, with a specimen of Mrs. Mortlake's Tracts served *au naturel* from a

large pile of these compositions upon the table before me.

The fact is, she was in the habit of sending a copy of each, as it appeared, to a maiden aunt of mine, who as regularly passed it on, uncut, to Stone Buildings, Lincoln's Inn. Whether she thought that it was likely to do me more good than she could herself, poor soul, expect from its perusal, or merely got rid of it like a bad shilling which it seemed extravagant to chuck in the fire, I haven't the least idea. Anyhow, here they all are, and to allude to a delicacy in one's own possession without offering a slice or a glass, is a rudeness of which I am not capable. So I have taken "Abraham Brown, Mariner," from the top of the heap, and beg leave to send the dish in your direction—to taste if you like, and by all means to reject, should you find it untempting.

Perhaps it may give you a more favorable impression of their authoress than you have already received. In that case, I beg you, in all sincerity, to judge of her by her writings rather than by mine. Not only have I no possible motive for misrepresenting her, but now that I come to peruse her works myself for the first time, I begin to think that, in some respects at least, hers must have been a simple case of misdirected energy, and that we may not have seen the best of her yet.

RIVERWOOD TRACTS. NO. 41.
SOME PASSAGES FROM THE LIFE OF
ABRAHAM BROWN,
MARINER,
OR
ALWAYS BE FIRM.

H.M.S. Crocodile was a magnificent frigate of fifty guns, with a crew of five hundred and one men, including the Captain.

Among so great a multitude, it would be idle to conceal the fact that there were many whose days were passed in the careless and unthinking merriment too common among sailors—to whom the flowing bowl and the lively hornpipe offered attractions infinitely greater than those of study and serious meditation.

There was one, however, amid that thoughtless crew, whose conduct was a marked exception to that of the generality of his messmates. And yet he was only a common sailor, and his name, Abraham Brown.

From the very commencement of the voyage to which I now refer, it had been Brown's constant habit to devote a considerable portion of each day to the perusal of various works of a moral and elevating tendency. And, in order to pursue his studies with less prospect of interruption, he usually ascended shortly after breakfast to the main-top-gallant-yard, upon which, with sailor-like ingenuity, he had constructed for himself a tolerably commodious seat or cradle, which in fact he rarely quitted, unless for the purpose of partaking of his regular meals.

I need hardly remark that this unusual course of conduct on board a man-of-war drew upon Brown the ridicule and animadversion of his less intellectual companions. But Brown was not a man to be diverted either by jeers or threats from the plain path of duty; and his well-disciplined mind stood him in admirable stead upon these trying occasions, enabling him, in most cases, to refute the charges of his persecutors with so much force and propriety, as to drive them, confused and blushing, from his presence.

It so happened that, as the ship approached the latitude of the Canary Islands, a remarkable change took place in the state of the weather. Instead of the serene and prosperous breezes which they had previously enjoyed, a succession of violent gales from the south-west caused the ship to labor considerably, and rendered Brown's seat upon the main-top-gallant-yard not only inconvenient, but unsafe.

His hat was so frequently blown into the sea, that the Captain at last positively refused to lower a boat again for the purpose of picking it up. The rain wetted his book: the wind curled the pages, and more than once carried away an entire chapter at a time. At last, the yard itself was blown overboard, and Brown only saved by his remarkable dexterity in swimming. Consequently he resolved, if possible, to select a more eligible spot for the pursuit of his studies in future.

Adjoining the large cabin, in which Brown and some two hundred of his comrades were accustomed to repose, was a small but pleasant apartment known as the sail-room. This our hero determined to occupy, after the hour for retiring to rest. To apply his mind in the larger dormitory, amid the boisterous merriment and practical pleasantries, which were too frequently prolonged far into the night, was plainly impossible.

The scheme succeeded perfectly. Appropriating to himself one of the candles which were issued to the men for the purposes of their evening toilet, Brown arranged for himself a most comfortable and even luxurious snuggery among the sails; and, balancing his candle upon a beam overhead, was enabled to read and meditate undisturbed, until warned by his own sensations of the necessity for retiring to his hammock. This was an inexpressible privilege.

I am sorry to say that no sooner did the Captain and First Lieutenant become aware of the plan which Brown had adopted to secure privacy, than they raised every objection in their power to its fulfilment. Not that they were insensible to the perfect propriety of his motives, but they were men of routine, incapable of approving any course of conduct inconsistent with the customs of the service.

"Brown!" the Captain would frequently exclaim, "this will really never do. It is even worse than reading in bed. I beg that I may never again find you in the sail-room at these untimely hours, especially with a candle loose upon the beams. We shall all be on fire some night. I am persuaded that it will be so."

"You should recollect, Brown," added the First Lieutenant, "that, by this reprehensible practice, you not only expose your own life to risk, but the lives of several hundred valuable men, as well as the safety of one of Her Majesty's ships. Is it possible that this consideration should have no weight with one who in point of sobriety and morality is a model to our whole party?"

Brown was firm, but respectful. Study and self-improvement, he assured his officers, were, with him, paramount considerations. In no other part of the ship, and at no other time, could he expect to carry out these objects with equal advantage to himself, and consideration for the prejudices of others. The suggested danger from fire was, he observed, purely imaginary, since no one was habitually more careful with a candle than himself.

"Brown, you are provoking!" exclaimed the Captain. "Mr. Barnacle," addressing the First Lieutenant, "be so good as to see that the door of this room is in future locked at nine o'clock. Brown must be taught obedience at any cost. And Brown was left alone.

Strange as it may seem, upon that very night, a sensation of unusual drowsiness overpowered him. He had had hard work upon deck during the day, and his book was rather hard to understand. Between the two he began to nod—gently at first, and then rather more distinctly, until, at last, he forgot himself altogether, and a sudden dive among the sail-racks brought the candle tumbling down his back.

With a frightful start, amid sparks and smoke, and a universal crackle, Abraham Brown awoke to a sense of his situation. Bounding from the sail-room, on fore-fore and aft, he escaped by the main hatchway ladder, making the ship ring with outcries, prompted, not by any selfish sense of personal discomfort, but by the desire of apprising his shipmates of a common danger.

For one moment, all was confusion on board. There was a general rush upon deck. But then the clarion voice of the Captain rang through the darkness, and the discipline of a Queen's ship was vindicated at once, and effectually.

"Hands, away!" shouted the chief officer. "Afterguard! man the flying-jib-boom! Let go the weather-back-stay, and keep her head to the wind! Up with the helm, Quartermaster! Marines! start cartridges into the quarter gallery, and throw all live shell down the main hold! Master-at-arms—send the ship's band into the fore-chains, and let them play 'Jack's Alive' to encourage the men."

Contrary to what might have been expected, these energetic measures were not in the first instance crowned with success. In a few moments a torrent of flame issued from the hatchway, and, flourishing upward amid the rigging, actually fired the ensign at the fore-truck.

The light flashed far and wide over the sea. It lit up the foaming waters all around. . . . Spectre-like in that ocean-blaze, like a giant amid the darkness, arose, immediately ahead, the towering Peak of Teneriffe.

Another moment, and the Crocodile would have been crashing and grinding upon that magnificent mountain, her timbers splintered and scattered into ten thousand fragments.

"Down with the helm!" shouted the Captain. "That blessed flare has saved us! But for this most opportune conflagration, we should all have been, at this moment, swimming for our lives, amid the insatiable crowd of carnivorous fishes which infest this most unsatisfactory archipelago. What in the world can our helmsman have been thinking of! Was ever such culpable negligence known?

> "'It needeth not that blood bë spilt,
> For folly to amount to guilt,'

as the poet wisely sings. Ah, Brown! how can we sufficiently thank you?"

Torrents of water from exactly five hundred buckets were rapidly poured down the fore-hatchway. Gradually the flames were mastered, and magnificent volumes of smoke, rolling heavily to leeward, left behind them nothing beyond a pungent and rather unpleasant smell.

"Brown," exclaimed the Captain, warmly shaking the hand of the common sailor, whom he had summoned for that purpose upon the quarter-deck, "it is to your firmness and good sense that the Crocodile is indebted for this most extraordinary escape. Adequately to reward your service is impossible. Fortunately the clerkship of the weather gangway is vacant and at my disposal. The emoluments are considerable, including the sole use of a commodious cabin, telescope, thermometer, and well-selected library. From this moment it is your own. May you enjoy it long. Never was patronage better bestowed."

The British navy is not ungrateful. It cherishes the fame of its thousand heroes. From that day to this, wherever the British ensign waves afloat and the strains of our National Anthem resound along the deep, the initials of our humble friend are preserved in every log. When our officers desire to confer the highest mark of approval upon a sailor whose agility, integrity, and general worth appear to entitle him to distinction, they know no higher encomium than that conveyed in these simple words: "Let him be rated as an A.B."

MORAL. [I have felt myself warranted in removing a sententious and rather indigestible moral appended to the above history, before consigning it to the printer. It is with no feeling of disrespect, or doubts as to the original propriety of the appendage, that we pinch off shrimps' tails at breakfast.]

FINIS.

———◆———

CHAPTER XVIII.

I WISH it were possible, by dint of mere pen and ink, to give any sufficient idea of Admiral Mortlake engaging the *Times*.

I have described the man himself, as he appeared to our friend Petersfeld, some few chap-

ters back; but there is all the difference in the world between a bull-dog as he appears in the smooth pages of Bingley, and a live bull-dog over a bone.

Nothing could be more savagely picturesque than the rough old tar, clad in the invariable shooting-suit of iron-grey, with an immense blue choker knotted loosely round his great sandy-whiskered throat. Rolling himself round, in his arm-chair—clutching the paper with both hands—scowling under a pair of enormous eyebrows, that twitched like mice at play, and snorting as he read with that peculiar nasal expletive "Hon!" so characteristic of a Frenchman in a passion, one would have fancied that the editor must have devoted his entire impression to some bitter personal libel, of which he, the reader, was the sole object.

Not a bit of it. Admiral Mortlake read his paper, as he did every thing else, under extravagantly high pressure, and all these growls and gesticulations simply signified assent or the contrary to what he was reading. You had only to listen, to hear an approving "good!" snorted out exactly in the same tone as "fool—rogue—dolt—liar—hammer-headed baboon!" which obviously implied difference of opinion.

As for Helen, she was so perfectly accustomed to these irregular explosions that she considered them just the natural result of reading the newspaper; and took no more notice of them than did the spaniel, who used to be shown in the lion's den at Wombwell's, of the roar of his royal companion.

Upon this particular occasion, the admiral chanced to be deep in the details of a great naval court-martial, and had the misfortune to differ from the majority of the court, as well as from certain views expressed in the paper before him. Consequently, upon him, as well as upon Helen, the door opened unexpectedly, and Mr. Salterton was announced.

The rector of Riverwood, who, it will be recollected, was co-executor with the admiral of the will of the late Colonel Fleetlands, and, as it were, vice-guardian of little Helen, was a tall, dark, handsome man of fifty, reputed to be the only human being of whom Admiral Mortlake stood in the slightest degree of awe. In truth Mr. Salterton was not quite an ordinary character. Upright as a drill-sergeant, with a reserved and rather dry manner, in which people who saw him for the first time detected hauteur and probable cynicism, he was too self-contained to be universally popular. Perhaps he was a little too fastidious in his likes and dislikes. Perhaps he was overweeningly confident in those terse opinions with which he so briefly disposed of every question which it became necessary to dispose of at all. Perhaps a rooted and uncompromising aversion to every thing which he was pleased to stigmatize as trifling or buffoonery made average people find him ascetic. But, be this as it may, there was no one of whom opinions changed more rapidly, when once, which was not difficult, those who

misliked him at first came really to understand
the rector. Then they found a true and kindly heart, with infinitely more practical tolera-
tion than they expected.

Mr. Salterton was a widower. A dire
calamity had overshadowed him in early life.
He had lost his wife within a year of their marriage. An elder sister kept house for him at
the Rectory. She was in delicate health, and
rarely seen abroad; and it was not until long
after the period through which we are now traveling, that Helen became more than vaguely
aware of her existence. Neither will you hear
of her again, until the last hours of my story
are upon the point of striking—its pageant vanishing into empty air.

Naturally, all the naughty folks in his parish
were sorely afraid of him, while those of a
better mind regarded him as a sort of oracle, a
little to be feared, certainly, but not the less
upon that account to be equally loved and respected. Mrs. Mortlake, I am afraid, was an
exception. Two oracles in the same district
were perhaps not likely to agree. At any rate,
Mr. Salterton found himself received with so
little cordiality at the Lawn, that it was not
oftener than once in a year or so, and then almost as a point of ceremony, that he ever entered the gates.

The admiral had no personal objection to
his clergyman, indeed he rather liked him than
otherwise. But that fatal cloud which had
overshadowed his conscience ever since he first
seized upon Helen's money as lawful spoil, had
made him shy and suspicious. He knew that
Salterton himself would have died rather than
divert one sixpence of her income to any purpose not expressly calculated in some way to
promote her welfare. He expected that the
rector would interfere at last, and in many a
moody reverie had mused over the sort of reception with which it would be prudent to encounter the enemy, whenever he advanced to
the attack.

Something in the rector's manner told him
that the hour was come.

"Why, Salterton, is that you? Glad to see
you, indeed. Take the arm-chair, my dear
sir," exclaimed he, in his deep rolling growl,
shaking hands with the clergyman and waving
him to a seat with old-fashioned *empressement.*
"Famous weather this, for the crops. Seen
the paper to-day—ha? Read the court-martial
on John Bonny, master of the Atalanta, for
running his ship into a French brig off the Liz-
ard? Ha, sir! What d'ye think of the egregious land-lubber—the son of a sea-cook, who
wrote this precious letter; a fellow, sir, who
positively signs himself 'AN OLD TAR.' I'd tar
him, sir, and feather him too, till he looked as
old as his grandmother. But, perhaps you
haven't seen the paper."

"I have not," replied Mr. Salterton with a
smile, as he availed himself of the offered arm-
chair. "Perhaps it is as well I did not, or I
might have been innocent enough to believe the

story. By the way, can we have ten minutes'
private conversation? I took my chance of
finding you disengaged, but if it is otherwise,
I will drop in some other day."

"Not at all, my dear sir. I am at your service as long as you please. We are alone, and
not likely to be disturbed—ha!"

Poor Helen literally quivered all over with
excitement. The little blood-bedabbled sock
could not be drawn on in a moment, and even,
had that been possible, the shoe was mislaid on
a chair. To hop out of the window, with the
certainty of being instantly called back in her
dismal pickle, was not to be thought of. So
she scuttled under the table like a lame rabbit,
hoping to goodness-gracious, that nobody would
think it necessary to search the room before this
awful conversation began.

"Admiral," said the rector, after a moment's
pause, "I want to have a few words with you
about your ward, Miss Fleetlands. I should be
the last person, as you may suppose, to intrude
officiously anywhere. But as I stand in a peculiar position with regard to the little girl, and,
next to yourself, am the person most responsible for her, you will pardon me if I speak plainly, and without reserve."

"That's what I do myself," replied the admiral with a slight snort; "and what's more,
stow all palaver before I begin. If you are
anxious to take any responsibility off my shoulders, why, sir, you are heartily welcome. Hitherto, I have been under the impression, right or
wrong, that I was accountable to the High Court
of Chancery, and to that court alone, as regarded all matters connected with the care and custody of my ward. That, sir, subject to correction, was my belief," concluded the master of
Riverwood, working his shoulders and twitching
his brows, preparatory to going into argument
upon the question.

"You are quite right," replied Mr. Salterton,
quietly playing with his riding-whip. "Your discretion can be controlled only by the Court of
Chancery, which of course would not interfere
unless in an extreme case."

"I presume not, sir. And now, if you would
favor me with a little of that plain-speaking which
you were so good as to promise me a moment
ago, I shall probably have the honor of understanding your meaning. Sir, you have my full-
est attention."

"Plainly, then," resumed the rector, in a dry,
decided tone, "it seems to me—speaking merely as a spectator—that you are in some danger
of inviting the interference of this Court of
Chancery. Is it right, admiral, that at her age,
Miss Fleetlands should be allowed to run wild
about the place, with no more suitable companions than your groom and gardener? Of Miss
Smugg, who is, I believe, supposed to have
charge of her, I wish to say nothing. Whatever
her qualifications may be, they have been most
unfortunately applied in this case. I know,
from my own conversations with the child, that
her education, both religious and otherwise, has

been strangely neglected. Positively, I am ashamed of her as a parishioner. There is not a child of six years old in my school, yonder, who is not far better acquainted with her Bible, and at least equally well read in history. And all this with a girl who, in the course of a few short years, will probably be the richest heiress in the county! All this with a girl whose father left the munificent sum of five hundred pounds a year from her very babyhood—for what purpose, in the name of common sense? Surely that she might receive the very best education which money could purchase—that she should have every proper luxury, every elegance and advantage which wealth could bestow—carriage exercise, for example; change of scene, real sea-side pleasures, and most of all, companions and playfellows of her own age and position. I think, admiral, that might be about the view the Court would take, were its attention drawn to the matter."

"My—goodness—gracious—me!" gasped Helen, trying desperately to screw herself up into nothing at all, "only think of my being somebody else all this time, and not knowing it! Oh, this is better than any thing Serena ever invented, and it's true besides. My stars, don't I wish the carriage full of playfellows would drive up! Richest heiress in the county! Why, I shall marry a king's son or somebody. Go on, Mr. Clergyman—go on!"

"Now," pursued the rector, "I have delivered my mind. Not prematurely, at all events, for I have waited long after my conscience bade me interpose, in the hope that such a step would become unnecessary. But Helen is just now at the most critical point of life, and I dared not hesitate longer. There is only one other point," concluded the rector, "to which I will advert while upon the subject. No one, in his senses, will suppose that you would attempt to divert money especially devoted in trust for a particular purpose, to any other use. But let me remind you that to attempt to lay by any portion of your ward's income for her future benefit, is perfectly idle. With her magnificent prospects, any possible present saving would count for nothing at all; while, just now, every sixpence might be laid out to her great advantage, both immediate and prospective. I know you too well, admiral, to doubt your perfect honor as regards motive. If we differ upon a point of expediency, I am sorry."

"Sir," retorted the admiral, who had risen restlessly from his chair, and, with his fists buried two feet deep in his trouser pockets, appeared to be inscribing hieroglyphics with his chin upon some invisible pyramid, "Sir, I am obliged to you. Say no more, sir; say no more, ha!"

"Oh, mercy!" thought Helen, who, crouched in her snug recess, had been devouring every word. "This is much too dreadful. I never heard him in such a rage in all my born days. They'll fight a battle as sure as I'm alive."

"Fortunately, I have no more to say," replied Mr. Salterton. "I have spoken my mind, and,

I believe, discharged my duty, certainly without the remotest intention of giving offense."

"I am willing to take your word for it, sir. But let me tell you that I will be answerable to the Lord Chancellor, and to the Lord Chancellor alone, as regards all that may concern my ward. I do not meddle, sir, in other people's affairs, myself. I do not catechise their children in private; neither do I presume to pass an opinion upon their expenditure or mode of living. I do not insinuate, either directly or indirectly, that they may be making a purse out of moneys entrusted to their care; and, by Heaven, I think that mine's the best way, sir, ha?"

"All right!" returned the rector good-humoredly. "Don't trouble yourself to be civil now. Next time you pass the Rectory, look in and tell us there are no bones broke. Good-day, admiral."

I am afraid that the gruff "good-day" of the latter was supplemented so soon as his visitor was fairly out of hearing, by a thundering roll of maledictions, in which parson, ward, and five hundred a year, were severally consigned *sine die* to Jericho, and several stations beyond. As for poor little Helen, the whole transaction had risen into a hideous tangle of utter bewilderment and terror. Why she was included in the anathema, and what babe-in-the-wood end might be in store for her, were puzzles too terrible to attempt.

"Thank goodness, he's firing off his pipe!" was her first consolation. "Now he'll go out and smoke upon the terrace. That's all right; for I'm tired of being scrunched up here. It's as bad as being in church—only I've heard something worth hearing. Don't I wish Gi had been with me, under the table. Gi would have understood it all in no time. I must talk it all over with Gi."

"Gi," you must know, was the pet name of an elderly young man, who had been groom at Riverwood for something under forty years, and for whom Helen indulged a profound affection. That he could play sphynx upon occasion, seems likely.

The young lady was, however, right in her conjecture. Her guardian, after deliberately lighting his meerschaum, strolled forth upon the terrace, leaving Helen free to shoe herself, and escape undetected. But what the savage old smoker thought of himself, as he paced moodily backward and forward under the statues, is more than I can tell. I suppose he felt as many of us have felt who have been told unwelcome truths, in our time, and made strange fools of ourselves, by way of acknowledgment. I dare say he wondered whether Salterton was really in earnest, and what was after all the law of the matter. That such a comparative trifle as five hundred a year should stand between himself and virtual ruin, was the bitterest part of the business. Yet so it was: while if Helen's accounts were to be overhauled, and he made answerable for the excess of the last seven years' receipts over his expenditure upon her account during the same time, there would be nothing for it but to put the shutters up, and go and live on the Continent.

Whatever course of procedure with reference to his ward might otherwise have been adopted by the admiral, an immediate change, in the way of education, was rendered necessary by the sudden disappearance of Miss Smugg.

That gifted and unfortunate damsel, among other treasures of periodical literature, had unluckily lighted upon one of those detestable publications which profess to afford "a medium of intercommunication" between young ladies and gentlemen capable of committing matrimony in cool blood. "Gustavus Alonzo, dark and aristocratic-looking,"—so ran the precious announcement which one day attracted her attention—"eldest son of a country baronet, and heir to a landed estate of many thousands a year, was in search of a handsome, lively partner, fond of music and dancing, and not over twenty-three." Peculiar domestic difficulties combined with constitutional diffidence, prevented him from making his wishes known among the brilliant circles of his own acquaintance, and drove him with reluctance to advertise in a penny paper. He would gladly exchange *cartes-de-visite* with any young lady who would so far lay aside the conventionalities of rank and fashion as to condescend to answer through the same channel, with a view of adorning what he rather mystically alluded to as his future coronet, and gilding with her constant smile an existence of lonely and luxurious *ennui*.

Serena jumped at the news. The good time, for which she had so long been pining, was come at last; supposing it possible that such a chance should not have been accepted and closed with before the paper which contained it was fairly dry from the press. So her answer was written at once on bright pink note, in a lovely lady-like hand, enclosing a photograph of herself in a low evening dress, reclining in a bower of roses, with a crook and a guitar, and some sheep picking at her petticoats. And, fearing, I suppose, lest her Smugg patronymic should be considered homely among the family of her future lord, she quietly evaded comment by subscribing herself "yours most fervently, Serenissima Southamptontowers."

In her case at least, the course of true love appeared likely to run as smoothly as could be wished. The return post brought an answer from Gustavus Alonzo, expressing the respectful hope that Miss Southamptontowers could make it convenient to be in Rotten Row at six p.m. on the following Friday, when that young gentleman would appear, mounted on a thoroughbred chestnut, and followed by a groom in blue livery with a cockade in his hat. Would Miss Southamptontowers kindly carry a scarlet geranium; at the sight of which Gustavus Alonzo would immediately dismount, and indulge himself with an interview which he fondly trusted was to be the turning-point of his existence?

Alas for poor Serena. She made some frightfully fabulous excuse for a visit to London, and flourished her geranium unsuccessfully before a

great many gentlemen. At last a rakish-looking youth sidled up; and pointing out his father the baronet, an innocent old stock-broker, who was cantering toward Apsley House, announced himself as the Gustavus Alonzo of the advertisement. His horse had unluckily fallen lame, not five minutes before, and had to be led home by his groom, which accounted for his appearance *au pied*. Would Miss Southamptontowers condescend to excuse an accident, and avail herself of apartments at his disposal in Carnaby Street —a sort of family appanage, in charge of an old housekeeper, a pensioner of twenty years' standing. She would do her best to make Miss Southamptontowers comfortable after the fatigue of her journey, until her future mother-in-law could be prepared to receive her in the morning.

By what extraordinary fatuity Serena fell into this open vulgar trap, it would seem at first sight impossible to conjecture. Yet, would to Heaven that it were extraordinary after all! Such things happened yesterday—they are happening even while I write these words, and they will happen to-morrow and to-morrow so long as the world endures. It is a mystery, and a dreadful one. Enough that from that day to this—from thenceforth, from henceforth, and forever, poor Serena's name never was or will be heard of on earth again.

Her disappearance was not perhaps absolutely unwelcome to Admiral Mortlake. It gave him the opportunity of making an entire change in Helen's course of education, without the appearance of having been bullied by his rector. It was quite clear that the best thing he could do with her was to send her to school; a conclusion in which his wife cordially agreed. So in the course of a few weeks Helen found herself transferred to the intensely select and fashionable establishment of the Misses Magnolia, of Luxor Court, Palmyra Stairs, Brighton, where for the modest consideration of some two hundred guineas per annum, she was guaranteed not only the usual education of a young lady, but that last unutterable polish, which, unlike certain other Christian graces, is only to be had for money.

It had seemed better, all things considered, to do the business handsomely, so as not to leave the slightest loop-hole for farther cavil.

CHAPTER XIX.

SEVEN years is a long time—a large slice out of one's existence. Physiologists, I believe, tell us that in seven years we change altogether, body and bones; and that the suit of mortality which we wore at the beginning of the era, is, before its conclusion, replaced by one entirely different. If this be the case, I can only say that I suspect I have either been overlooked altogether, or repaired with second-hand material, and would give a trifle to have my old suit returned in any thing like the condition I once knew it.

Seven years is a long time. So long in fact, that when in the regular course of a narrative it becomes necessary to dispose of it in a sentence, there is always a certain feeling of responsibility and compunction. Nevertheless, seven years and upward have passed away since the date of my last chapter, and the day arrived on which Helen was to take leave of the Misses Magnolia and their fashionable academy forever.

Vividly as, at this moment, I seem to see her before me in all the elastic health and beauty of seventeen, I am perfectly conscious of my inability to transfer to print what I most wish to be understood, or to place before another imagination exactly the image which is present to my own. I had some thoughts of prefixing a photograph to this volume. But that, I am told, would look lazy and eccentric, and were better avoided.

So, to the clearest imaginable olive complexion, with just a fair tinge of color, you may add a straight, pretty nose, and the firmest yet most delicate little mouth and chin which your recollection is able to supply. Dark and glossy and luxuriant was Helen's hair, parted smoothly over her bright brow, and harmonizing with eyes that looked almost melancholy while at rest, and flashed so instantly and wonderfully whenever there was an excuse for flashing at all. A buoyant graceful figure, rather full, I suppose, than the reverse, and charming hands must complete my portrait. I am not sketching, or intending to sketch, a beauty, though in my opinion Helen had a perfect right to the title, but something far better—a form to which one's soul goes rushing forth, because though it may be only clay after all, it is not merely a painted vase. There is light within the porcelain—real living light. Happy the man to whom God has given such a lamp. In the dark and desolate places of this wilderness it is the gift beyond all price.

Seven years had also passed over the admiral, since the day that he growled so famously at his rector for interfering about little Helen. Nor had those years been quite unprofitable. The old fellow had grown decidedly less morose and more sociably disposed. Some of us mellow—some harden with time ; and if Admiral Mortlake's life could only have been prolonged for another half century, he might have grown into an affable and benignant elderly gentleman with a smile and a present for every visitor.

Perhaps this favorable change was partly owing to a good round legacy, which dropped in when least expected, and placed him, all at once, in comparative ease in his possessions. But at any rate, it was so marked as to be a subject of rejoicing to Helen when she at last returned to take up her residence at Riverwood for good.

And how are we to suppose that Admiral Mortlake felt toward the frank, handsome girl, who stood before him, no longer a little toy to be teased or petted according to his humor—but erect in crinoline, ready to ride his horses,

grace his dinner-table, and flirt with his guests whenever he gave her the chance ? I will tell you my own belief upon the subject, which you may take for what it is worth. Only since it has fallen upon me to write the story, you may perhaps as well believe that I am not very far wrong, and accept it as part of the narrative.

I suspect that Admiral Mortlake's feeling with regard to his ward was essentially selfish. I mean, that although he had been amused with her as a child, and glad when her school-holidays came round, he liked her for his own sake, rather than hers. It was pleasant to see her sunny face in the garden, and to hear her voice upon the stairs. She was the life and ornament of that dull old house, and he was well aware of the fact. Still, he never considered her as his own ; he never thought of her as we think of those fledglings, who, if they are not to live with us forever, are never, as we hope, to forget the old birds and the parent nest. Helen must marry, of course, in due time, and so pass away. He would be sorry to lose her, and upon that account alone would, as long as possible, postpone the evil day. But as to any farther regard for her, I don't think it was in his nature. She was his to-day, and would be another's to-morrow—and there the connection would end, so far as he was concerned.

There was, however, one other consideration involved in the contingency of Helen's marriage, which had so deep an influence over his mind, that I must refer to it in this place as the key, in some measure at least, to the remainder of my story.

It was briefly this. So long as Helen continued in his guardianship, and remained unmarried, he received, as we are aware, under her father's will, five hundred a year for her maintenance and education. Now it was a simple matter of arithmetic that, during the seventeen years of her life he had received, at the very lowest estimate, upward of £6000 sterling in excess of what she could by any possibility be supposed to have cost him in money out of pocket. To be called over the coals to the tune of such a balance, was a hideous prospect, and to be by all means averted, if that might be.

Supposing that she remained single up to twenty-one, there would probably be but little difficulty about the matter. She would then be competent to give, and in the ordinary course of events would give, what is technically termed a release in full. In other words, she would sign and place her forefinger upon the wafer of a parchment deed, the concluding paragraph of which would perhaps run as follows:

"And whereas for the satisfaction of the said Hercules Mortlake and in consideration of the premises she the said Helen Fleetlands hath agreed to execute to him the said Hercules Mortlake such a release as is hereinafter contained Now THIS INDENTURE WITNESSETH that in pursuance of the said agreement and in consideration of the premises She the said Helen

Fleetlands hath remised released and forever quit-claimed and by these presents doth remise release and forever quit-claim the said Hercules Mortlake his heirs executors and administrators from all and all manner of action and actions causes of action suits controversies differences debts accounts reckonings sum and sums of money and all other claims and demands whatsoever both at law and in equity for or by reason or on account of the said annual sum of £500 so received by him the said Hercules Mortlake as aforesaid or any part thereof or for or by reason or on account of the payment application or appropriation thereof or of any part thereof by him the said Hercules Mortlake or for or by reason or on account of any other act deed matter or thing by him done committed or permitted in anywise relating to the premises."

This succinct little document, assuming it to be freely given, and after a fair explanation of the state of the case, would operate to silence all possible demands, square all accounts, and spare her guardian all farther trouble in the matter.

But, in the event of her marrying under twenty-one, this smooth and easy course would unfortunately be inappropriate. Until that mystical birthday, we are all infants in the eye of the law—undiscerning babes, unfit to "reckon," or to cast up the mildest sum in compound addition by which our interests may be prejudicially affected. I have, it is true, known one or two infant senior wranglers in my time; but they would have been good-naturedly repressed in the Court of Chancery, had they come there armed with the pence-table, or trusting in the rule of three.

Consequently, in the case just supposed, Helen's accounts would be liable to be overhauled under the direction of the Court itself; while her intended, if of a greedy turn, and given to seeking his own, would be in a position to ask questions which might easily become vexatious. I am not asserting that the admiral, under the circumstances, could actually have been called upon to refund. I volunteer no opinion whatever. He never consulted me; and perhaps felt a difficulty in taking direct legal advice upon so delicate a topic. It was enough to know that the money was most certainly never intended as a mere present to himself, to be tormented with fears of reprisal.

It is not, therefore, much to be wondered at that he had long since resolved to take one short cut toward stopping all nonsense of the above description. Under her father's will he was empowered to withhold consent to his ward's marriage up to twenty-three. Upon marriage without such consent, her whole property became virtually confiscated.

This power he was determined to exercise, and made no secret of the matter. He even, I am sorry to say, gave out that he had the best reasons for believing that Colonel Fleetlands's last and most anxious wish had been, that his daughter should not marry before twenty-three

at earliest, and that he should hold himself bound to respect this desire, so far as his own conduct in the trust was concerned. Of course this was simply a falsehood, and even if true as an assertion, would have carried with it no legal weight whatever; but it gave convenient vantage-ground in the event of his being scouted as an obstinate, impracticable donkey, when he stood upon the letter of his rights.

I don't say that Colonel Fleetlands was wrong in the disposition which he made. Naturally, in the circumstances under which he died, he was anxious to protect his daughter from being run away with, while yet a girl, by any rascal who only coveted her money. A controlling power in this respect must have been vested in somebody, and every controlling power is, in its nature, susceptible of abuse. In all cases of this kind, we must select the most reliable people we know, and after that, "quis custodiet custodem?" is a question more easily asked than answered.

To return to our story. With Helen once again established at Riverwood, the admiral's first desire was to disabuse the neighborhood of the impression that his own conduct toward her bore the slightest trace of mercenary or unworthy motives—in fact, to convince them magnificently of their mistake. Helen was now, as he perceived, too old to be kept in a corner, being indeed the object of curiosity and speculation to half the county. Appearances must be kept up at all costs—even of that priceless convenience, ready money.

Helen's grand passion was riding. The horse to her mind outweighed all that creation ever did in the way of hair, scale, fur or feather. She had been allowed riding lessons at Brighton, as part of the Misses Magnolia's gorgeous curriculum, and of course now hoped for a steed of her own.

To her intense delight and astonishment, her guardian one day presented her with as lovely a blood-mare as could be bought for money—so the dealer had told him, and so I hope he believed—and placed Gigoggin the groom at her disposal, to follow her whither she listed. This was life itself to Helen. To regale her pet with toast and lump sugar after breakfast, to gallop her unmercifully all day, and dream about her religiously at night, made a division of time which was perfectly enchanting. She began to wonder that she had ever reviled Riverwood to her school-fellows as a dismally owlish, mopy old place, and wished she could show them Camilla.

Gigoggin, alias Gi, the fortunate youth who was commissioned as Miss Helen's aide-de-camp and knight-companion in her equestrian expeditions, was a small, brown, taciturn man, who had probably been young in his time, and was still rejoicing in that perennial bloom which, in former days, we used so often to notice among post-boys. He was quite devoted to his young mistress, having, in fact, as we are already aware, been Helen's earliest friend on the premises, and admired her riding as an accomplishment of his own creation. He would have given his ears any day to see her follow the hounds—a performance which, being strictly prohibited, she looked forward to, as the very climax of human enjoyment. And his cautionary "'Ware hounds, Miss Helen!" when Camilla pricked her ears to the distant music, and the girl, who seemed to be pulling so desperately, was away like the wind, before he could even kick Happy-go-lucky into a canter—came from the depths of a sorrowful and sympathizing heart.

By dint of continued badgering, you may make most people admit that you are in the right, or at all events consent to your wishes, which is still more satisfactory. And so it came to pass that the admiral at length gave way in his objection to Helen's taking her gallop in the hunting-field, the more so as the discussion had suggested an idea to his mind, for which he gave himself infinite credit.

It occurred to him that an opportunity now presented itself, by which—without the smallest sacrifice of his own self-complacency—he might at once put himself upon a more cordial footing with people whom he had been foolish enough to estrange. It would, moreover, display his liberality and kindness to Helen, in a picturesque and valuable light, and lastly, would be the correct thing to do by her, if he intended to allow her to hunt at all. He determined that the very next day the hounds met in his neighborhood, he would invite the Master to breakfast at the Lawn, and to bring his field with him.

It was a capital notion, and seemed better and better the more it was reflected upon. The Windmill Turnpike, on the London Road, was in due course announced as next Thursday's meet, and in answer to the admiral's invitation, Sir Philip Chevy replied, that he would with pleasure do himself the honor of bringing his hounds to the Lawn at ten upon that day, and draw the Riverwood spinney into the bargain.

Whatever the admiral undertook, was sure to be executed in good earnest, and the very idea of this jolly *déjeuner à la chasse*, made him ten years younger at once. The "Master's eye," as we all know, is proverbially efficacious, and although—to employ a slang caution—I would advise him to mind it, when engaged in kitchen investigations, it certainly did its duty in the present instance. Nothing was too minute, nothing too palpably beyond its province to be secure from incessant supervision. One moment beheld its owner rearranging the garniture of a ham; the next assuring himself that a due proportion of port wine and oysters were combined in the principal pie. And all this while cross-catechising his footman like a thief, as to the disposable amount of plate, and how it would make out breakfast covers for thirty; and writing to Fortnum & Mason for terrines, caviare and canvas backs, and to Liquorpond Street for a kilderkin of such malt as should rejoice the cockles of the huntsman, and such

of the farmers and yeomen, as could not be provided for in the dining-room. In short, if he had been planning some grand naval "affair," in which details, they say, are half the battle, he couldn't have been expected to do his duty more conscientiously than while plotting this memorable breakfast.

I am glad that I am not a fox. I should hate being cheried, more than tongue can tell. But if I had been born to such experience, and had happened to be the denizen of the Riverwood spinney when that Thursday came round, I must say I should have reckoned upon an easy bargain. I wouldn't be too hard upon any body. But I know an ugly ditch or so, and a few nasty stiles, and a quiet bit of wire in the neighborhood, and I should like to have taken my friends round that way. I think that with the assistance of that kilderkin of XXX, let alone the cider cup upon the high hall-table, I could have emptied a saddle or two, and postponed indefinitely that spasmodic moment which survivors so complacently refer to as "the finish."

If you ask me what Mrs. Mortlake thought of the approaching saturnalia, I am obliged to confess that the subject is altogether beyond me. I suspect that she considered fox-hunting as too shameless a branch of scarlet wickedness to need a verse to itself in the commination service. I dare say that she had delivered her mind to the admiral upon the matter of allowing Helen to take such a palpably short cut to perdition, and I can fancy the grunt she got in reply. I can also fancy the sour odor of sanctity under cover of which she washed her hands of a bad business, and with the rather promiscuous consolation that evil was probably permitted for some useful purpose, allowed the backsliders to slide, and Helen to go to the—dogs.

The important morning arrived at last. Nothing could look more successful than the dining-room at Riverwood, arrayed for a hunting-breakfast. It was a large square room, wainscoted in solid oak, with a handsome panelled ceiling, and hung with time-honored portraits of the dons and heroes of the house of Mortlake. The hearth was ample and old-fashioned, and, with its ponderous log of dry timber, made hospitable music of roar and crackle, lighting up the room with a pleasant glow, and touching the glass, and silver, and holly, upon the breakfast-tables, with good-natured glancing light. The admiral was more than satisfied.

"Ha—hum!" he growled, as, with his hands in his pockets, and Helen at his side, he stood surveying the preparations, an hour before breakfast-time. "This looks about the right thing, Helen. I don't see how it could have been made much better—hey? I wonder how many of these fellows will come. We could manage with forty; and I'll be bound that forty wouldn't get to the bottom of that pie. I wonder if we shall find any body man enough to drink sack of a morning.' That sack, Helen, in those black bottles over yonder, was in Riverwood cellars before I was born—and that's a year or two ago—hum! What says old Sir John Falstaff—ha? 'If I had a thousand sons, the first human principle I would teach them should be to forswear thin potations, and addict themselves to sack.' Hey! There were men in those days, who knew what breakfast ought to be. No slops and decoctions for them, I'll be bound—only fit for old women under physic. Now, look, Helen. You'll sit here, at this table, and pour out coffee. Keep your eye open, and tell me if you see any thing wanting. Call out at once — never mind who hears. There'll be coffee at the sideboard for the people over yonder. Is that vase your filling? Ha! you've made a pretty thing of the holly. Now, I suppose you want to go and sugar your horse. Good for his coat, eh? Well, away with you, and send your groom round if you see him. It'll be all plain sailing enough to-day, I'll be bound; but I may as well give him his course. And take care you're back in the hall by ten exactly—before any body comes. Do you hear? Mind that!"

With this imperative duty twice impressed upon her mind, Helen took her way toward the stables. It was a soft, mild, January morning, with a grey mottled sky, and a delicious air. Outside, as well as within the house, were something more than promises of good cheer. The trebly X'd kilderkin stood trestled upon the terrace, garlanded with holly, and surrounded by tables flashing with bran-new pewters. These, with the mighty loaves of home-made bread, the mill-stone cheeses, the round and the sirloin, the sheaves of tobacco-pipes, and many other good things, were for the benefit of the huntsman and whips, as well as of chance comers, if any, who might be afflicted with Sancho Panza's dislike to feasting in company. It was to be a great day, and nothing could be more promising than its dawn.

Through these preparations Helen passed, wishing, perhaps, that she had learned to drink beer, which seemed so essential a part of a day's enjoyment. She was amused by all she saw. She looked forward to the breakfast as great fun, and to the draw and gallop afterward, as untold pleasure. And yet there was something beyond this in her mind; something that seemed to wander amid those mysterious recesses in which spontaneous thoughts arise and often make themselves distinctly felt, long before they can be grasped and moulded by the mechanism of the brain. What it was, she could not have told us, neither can I. But I do not, and will not, believe that the great events of our lives come down upon us without warning. We know not how the tidings are carried, but I am certain there is a whisper always. Drowned and disregarded at the moment — neglected and forgotten afterward, it may be; but depend upon this, that you never went forth from your house upon the morning

E

when some crowning chance, whether of good or ill was to befall you, without that prophetic whisper.

Is this what you call being superstitious?

What do you mean by the term? I confess to being "stitious," if that will do; but I object to being saddled with a superlative.

CHAPTER XX.

RATHER to Helen's surprise—certainly to her great delight—the very first person whom she encountered upon her way to the stables, was Mr. Salterton.

If he had, as may be recollected, withstood the admiral in former days, upon the question of her own education, all difference upon that score had long since blown over, and he had been specially invited to look in and say grace on that particular morning.

"So you expected me, I see," said he, playfully laying hold of Helen's little sugar-laden fist. "How good of you to bring me such a treat! such beautiful large lumps too!"

"Oh, yes, they are all for you, Mr. Salterton," returned Helen, laughing, "all except one, which you won't be so greedy as not to leave for Camilla. I am on my way to pay her my regular morning visit. Come and see her. There! do you hear that neigh? Yes, we are coming, Camilla, coming, coming! She knows my step perfectly. Look, there's her pretty little nose peeping through the bars of the loose box. Oh, there you are, Gigoggin. Open the door, please, and take off her cloth. Now, isn't she a beauty, Mr. Salterton? No, darling, I have not forgotten your sugar. Here it is! Now arch your neck, and show your handsome crest. Feel it, Mr. Salterton; it is as firm as a racer's, and her coat is as soft as satin. And her color. I do love that rich dark brown. The star on her forehead, and that white hind foot, help to show it off. Did you ever see any thing so soft and gentle as her eye, yet with a wild glance in it, too, like a deer's? You should see it when she is excited by a good gallop. Ah! you may look at her legs and dainty little feet, as much as you please. She has been too well cared for, to show any signs of work there. Are you thinking her rather tall for a lady's horse? Oh, no—only fifteen three, and she measures high. Some people don't like so much fall behind the withers, but I think it charming—it helps to keep the saddle back, and you can guess what easy paces she has, with that good sloping shoulder. She is thoroughbred; you will find her name and lineage in the stud-book; but she was too wise to run well as a racer, and so she came to me to be my darling, and to obey my voice and hand as she will those of nobody else.

"There — that's all!" concluded Helen, as Camilla disposed of the last lump, and eagerly pushed her nose into the bosom of her mistress's riding-habit, having, apparently, some theory of her own upon the subject of pockets. "No more, my pet: no more! What an affectionate creature a horse is, Mr. Salterton. I don't know any animal that shows its love for one in so expressive a way. Just look at her eye, now.",

"To judge from what I have just seen," replied the rector, "your mare has very good reasons for being affectionate. If I got so much petting and coaxing myself, you've no idea how nice I should look in return. Don't laugh, but try me."

"Ah, that reminds me of one of Leech's sketches that I was looking at last night. A lady is leading an immensely fat pampered spaniel by a ribbon. A coster monger passing by, observes to his companion, 'Now, I dare say, Bill, that 'ere beast of a dawg is a good deal more petted than you or I should be!'"

"Thank you! That is a compliment and no mistake. I remember it, however. It is one of Leech's many bits of genuine humor. Can you tell me what it is exactly in the costermonger's remark that makes one smile? I will give you another instance from the same pencil. It is headed 'Disagreeable Truth.' A sentry, on duty at Buckingham Palace, says to a couple of little street urchins, 'Now then, you must move away from here.' 'Ah, but you mustn't, old fellow!' reply the young scamps. Now these designs are both admirable. Both are in the highest degree diverting; but analyze them, and you will find that they are so for perfectly distinct reasons. The coster-monger need not have been far wrong in his premises, although lamentably unlucky in the conclusion which produced his remark. The little boy simply employed a false antithesis which resulted in a lucky jingle, embodying an unexpected home thrust. You may get no bad lesson in logic out of the pages of Leech."

They had turned away from the stables and were strolling along the broad walk at the back of the house. Mr. Salterton had seen Helen frequently since her return, but something in her bright fresh look of youth and loveliness struck him particularly that morning. Perhaps the riding-habit set off her beautiful figure to more advantage than usual. Perhaps the excitement of the coming breakfast, and of the glorious gallop which was to follow—her first day of riding to hounds, lit up her countenance with more than ordinary animation. He was not a man given to compliments, but he could not for the life of him help saying, "Do you know, Helen, I can't take my eyes off you, this morning. I think I never saw you looking so well and charming. I hope you are as happy as you look."

"Indeed, I am, Mr. Salterton. I have no reason to be otherwise. Do you know I was dreadfully sorry, at first, to leave Brighton for good. I cried right out when it came to the kissing at last. I thought I should be so frightfully lonely here; and there were many girls that I cared about a great deal. I knew the admiral would never ask them here, you see, and that

made it worse. But he has been very kind to me ever since I came back, and, now that I've got Camilla, I don't feel in the least forlorn. I hope you don't think it's wrong to hunt, Mr. Salterton?"

"Not in the least, my dear, or I shouldn't have been at Riverwood this morning. I should be heartily sorry to see hunting abolished in this country. Of course many people hunt who have no business to do so—but that is all beside the question. To take my own case for example, I should be just as much out of my place in following Sir Philip as he would be in mounting my pulpit. If the admiral has no objection to your hunting, do so by all means. He seems anxious to give you every indulgence, and I sincerely hope that you may continue happy in his house. You ought to be a great blessing to him; and I believe he is aware of it. He has a rough manner, and you don't expect much petting I suppose. But if you only choose to go to work with him the right way, which you'll discover much more easily than I should, I'll answer for your making him a great deal fonder of you than even Camilla—rather a triumph I should say in the way of domestication."

"Mr. Salterton," said Helen, after a moment's silence, "would you mind my asking you a question? There is something on my mind about the admiral which I can not shake off. You will not be displeased at any thing I may tell you—will you?"

"My dear child," replied the rector, noticing her doubtful and puzzled look, "ask any question you like; and tell me any thing in the world. Nothing would delight me more than to have your confidence. Talk to me just as if you were talking to yourself—that's to say if you think I'm discreet enough to be trusted."

"Well then," continued Helen, speaking very slowly, "a long time ago—quite seven years it must be, Mr. Salterton, do you recollect having a conversation with the admiral about me in his study yonder?"

"Perfectly. Stay, let me think what it was all about. Yes; I believe I remember every thing that passed. But, surely, the admiral never mentioned to you what I then said, Helen. How do you know we talked about you?"

"I was under the table all the time."

"The deuce you were!" was the commentary which I am afraid rose to the rector's lips. Luckily it was suppressed before publication, and he simply said—

"What a good little girl!"

"It was an accident, Mr. Salterton. I had hurt my foot, and lost my shoe. But I heard every thing."

"Well, you had better remind me of what was said."

"I think it came to this. I was to have a great deal of money some day; and in the mean time all the allowance my poor papa left me was paid to the admiral. I understood that—and that, instead of doing what you thought he ought with the money, he was spending every thing he could upon himself. You told him he had no right to do so, and made him frightfully angry. Now, from that day to this, Mr. Salterton, I have never felt toward him exactly as I did before. I have never been able to feel quite cordial. And, now that I know more, the gulf appears to grow infinitely wider, and I have a miserable feeling of doubt and distrust. I wish I hadn't, but I can't help it. I want you to put me right, Mr. Salterton," concluded Helen, rather piteously.

"Were there any children of eight years old at the Misses Magnolias when you left, Helen?"

"Oh yes,—two or three little chits. Why do you ask?"

"Suppose one of these little chits had repeated to you the import—or what she imagined to have been the import—of a business conversation which she had accidentally underheard. Should you have been inclined to take her version exactly for gospel? 'Little miss from under the table *loquitur*.' What would Leech have made her say?"

"Oh, Mr. Salterton, this is not fair! I can trust myself; and I am trusting you, now."

"I beg your pardon," returned the rector, feeling, I suspect, a little abashed; "I will answer you as plainly as I would a solicitor. But you said something just this moment about knowing more now. Tell me exactly what you mean, and depend upon it I will be as plain with you."

"Why, just this. Of course, at a girl's school we tell each other all about home, you know."

"I dare say, Helen: although, not having been brought up at one myself, I don't speak from experience."

"Well, then, we do. And I told Sophy Hunter, who was my particular friend, all I had discovered; and we had a good deal of talk about it. In short we talked so much that Sophy Hunter, who has an old brother, a barrister, or something of the sort, in London, said she would ask him to find out the real truth."

"Capital! That was business and no mistake. And pray did Sophy Hunter's old brother enlighten your minds?"

"Oh, dear, yes. You must know, Mr. Salterton, that there's a place near London called 'The Doctor's Common,' where every body goes to make their wills, and where you may see every will that ever was made by paying a shilling and asking. Well, Sophy Hunter's old brother paid his shilling, and saw my poor papa's will with his own eyes."

"Well?"

"Why, it's just as you told the admiral, the day I was under the table. I ought to have had five hundred a year ever since I was born, to begin with. And I am to have a whole heap of money when I'm twenty-one, or twenty-three, or if ever I marry; only there's some jumble which I don't quite understand, and, if certain things happen, why it seems the admiral has the right of giving all my fortune to somebody else, and what Sophy Hunter's old brother was

very particular about telling was that 'I had better keep a bright lookout or the old bloke was cock-sure to chisel me out of my tin.' I wrote the very words down on the back of a French exercise at the time, that I might be certain there was no mistake. It's only slang, of course, Mr. Salterton, but still you see what he means."

"I congratulate you upon the possession of such a valuable legal opinion. You said just now that you wanted to ask me a question. Was it as to whether I was of the same mind with this learned old brother, or only as to my advice in general?"

"I only want your advice, Mr. Salterton. I want to be put right upon the whole subject. It is so very miserable to distrust those with whom one has to live. And there can be no helplessness like that of feeling that those who ought to help one are interested the other way."

"My dear Helen, I have not the slightest hesitation in offering you my advice, which I earnestly entreat you to follow. When I thought it right, some years ago, to interfere in the manner which you so unfortunately overheard, it was for a twofold reason. In the first place, I was distressed at the manner in which your education was being neglected under the auspices of Miss Smugg, and at the idle uncivilized life which you were then permitted to lead. In the second place, I certainly felt it my duty to point out to the admiral that he was receiving a very large sum annually for your care and maintenance, and that it was incumbent upon him to give you corresponding advantages. I think that my interference was not unsuccessful. You have had the benefit, ever since, of one of the first—at all events one of the most expensive—schools in the kingdom. You now appear to have every indulgence which could be wished; indeed, to judge from to-day's proceedings, your guardian has only waited for your return home to make an entire change in his mode of living. As to what Sophy Hunter's old brother told her —forget it altogether. What do you know of him? What reason have you for supposing that he is even competent to divide a biscuit between two puppy-dogs? Can you suppose that I, as one of your father's executors, would stand by if I suspected that injustice was being done you, or ever will, so long as I have the power to prevent it, permit it to be done? Leave your interests entirely in my hands, Helen, and forget them altogether for the present. And above all things, never, my dear girl, allow any thing in the shape of suspicion to rankle in your mind. Make yourself unhappy, if you must, in any other way you please, but send this sort of feeling to the winds forever! Upon my honor, Helen, to discover that, at your age, you were indulging a morbid distrust of your guardian, and wondering whether he stole your money, would give me almost the same sensation as being told that you drank whisky on the sly."

"Oh, Mr. Salterton," exclaimed Helen, in rather an unsteady voice, "I didn't quite mean all I said just now.. But thank you so much for all your kindness. I would give any thing that the subject had never got into my head. Why can't we pull these things out of our brains, and trample upon them, and walk away ?" she concluded, with a half petulant stamp.

"Ah, there you have touched upon a terrible question, which we have no time to discuss now. It is awful to think how things take root in our minds, never to be dislodged again. Sometimes we sow them ourselves—sometimes they seem to be chance-sown, or sown by the enemy. Helen, these weeds are the very bitterness of life. For God's sake guard your own garden while you may! But it is getting late. You will be wanted within doors."

"A quarter to ten, still, Mr. Salterton," replied Helen, not unwilling perhaps to change the subject. "Come and see my country house. It is close by. The admiral has just had it done up for me, and you can't think how fresh it looks. It will be charming in summer; and do you know, there is actually a fire-place for cold weather—poker, tongs, and every thing! Come and stay with me some day, Mr. Salterton, and I'll order a fire!"

I believe I have already described this rustic lodge in the wilderness, while speaking of Petersfeld's surreptitious visit to Riverwood. A pretty little haunt it looked, and the rector was amused at Helen's girlish enjoyment of the triumph of possession.

"Now this is my own—my very own, Mr. Salterton, given to me out and out. This is where I intend to entertain my friends from Brighton school, whenever they are allowed to visit me. Here we shall smoke our pipes and talk politics, and nobody in the world will be allowed to come in except yourself. We have just time for one peep at the inside, which I never allow any body to see, except people for whom I feel the most particular regard—"

Probably Helen would, not unwillingly, have recalled these last few words, for scarcely had they passed her lips before a young gentleman, in full hunting costume, appeared at the summer-house door.

He could scarcely have been more than two-and-twenty, and might even have been younger, for his was one of those joyous, sunshiny, reckless faces which we can scarcely believe have seen much of this rough world in earnest. His fair complexion was just weather-tanned enough to set off to the best advantage a pair of pleasant blue-grey eyes, and harmonized well with his bright brown hair. Slenderly, almost slightly built, and perhaps not above what is usually described as the middle height, so firm, quick, and graceful was every movement, that you perceived at once that his training had been athletic, and that of a good school.

And if Nature had been kind in the first instance, it was quite obvious that his tailor had been careful. His pink and cords were the most perfect you ever saw; new, spotless, and fitting like a pair of gloves. His boots were so pretty that they looked like those one sometimes sees under glass shades in very superior shops, and glittered with a polish which seemed nearly supernatural. All this Helen took in at a glance, with the neat spurs, and little sparkling watch-guard trinkets into the bargain.

Her first impression was one of unqualified admiration. But at the same moment a suspicion flashed across her mind that he was a fop. She had read about fops frequently, but never seen a clear case for certain—not at all events close enough to talk to: so she listened with eager ears. "He will lisp, I'll be bound," she thought, "and that will settle the matter. What makes him smile like that? Can't he speak?"

All this took place in a single instant, and Helen had not perhaps observed that the smile was directed not at herself, but at her companion, who received the supposed fop with a face of wonder which was amusing.

"Good Heavens, Ferdinand! who'd have thought of seeing you here to-day?" he exclaimed in a tone which struck the young lady as remarkable.

"Not you, evidently, Mr. Salterton," replied the youngster gayly, as he grasped the rector's hand. "I beg your pardon for offering a bridle arm, but the doctors won't allow me to shake the other myself, yet; so I musn't ask you to do it for me."

"You are not going to hunt, to-day, surely?"

"Oh, yes. Why not? I am not going to try any thing difficult, you know. I shall make up to some cautious party who opens gates, and we shall get along nicely. I shall explain to him that, in my opinion, going 'cross country is quite dangerous enough to be wicked. We shall agree that every rational enjoyment of hunting can be had by jogging away like a couple of undertakers, without risking our necks among a parcel of lunatics and mad dogs."

"Well, but the arm?—how's the arm going on?"

"Oh, as right as possible, thank you. It was nothing to signify, after all."

His arm was in a sling, as Helen had noticed, when, after shaking hands with the rector, he had turned to raise his cap to herself.

"Nothing! God bless the boy! Why, I thought the ball went through it?"

"Well, what would you have had, Mr. Salterton? Just about the best thing it could do. But I'm afraid," continued he, "that I ought to apologize for being found where I was. Do you know I tore up Sir Philip's note last night to light a cigar, and forgot the hour for to-day, which I fancied had been half-past nine—and so—"

"Good gracious, I beg your pardon, Helen!" exclaimed the rector, as if suddenly aroused from a reverie. "What upon earth can I have been thinking about? Let me introduce Captain Ferdinand Hunsdon, of the Victoria Cross—Miss Fleetlands."

Helen started at the words, as if she had been shot like the captain.

Hero-worship is, as we all know, one of the essential elements of the girlish mind. The frightful error of judgment which she had so narrowly escaped committing confused her altogether, and she stood perfectly breathless, with open eyes and lips apart, looking interesting enough certainly, if not unusually wise. Could it be possible that this bright boy, who seemed at first sight the fit Adonis of a fancy-ball, tricked out for an evening in hunting-array, had really won the glorious and all-coveted jewel upon a blood-stained field, amid the thunder and tumult of a great battle?

She had a vague impulsive longing to ask him questions; but, without knowing exactly why, she felt frightened and unable to count upon her own self-control.

Luckily the rector continued:

"Captain Hunsdon, Helen, I hope you are aware, is an old pupil of mine. So I feel a little excusable pride in announcing him."

"Were you one of the last made?" inquired Helen, with a sudden courage. "I mean, I saw an account in the newspaper some weeks ago of a grand distribution of the Cross—at Southsea, I think."

"One of the very last," replied the young officer, thinking how nice it was to be looked at after that fashion. "I am glad to see that Miss Fleetlands intends to hunt to-day."

"Were you really there?" persisted Helen with glistening eyes. "I mean when all the troops were drawn up on Southsea Common, and the whole line presented arms, and the drums rolled, and the Victory fired? Was that when—"

"That was it, Miss Fleetlands. Do you know that your question reminds me of an odd sort of sensation which came over me at the moment. It was all jolly enough till the old ship joined in; but when, just as we were called to the front, her first heavy 'bang!' went sweeping over the ground, it was regularly too much for some of us. I declare I'd have given a pound to have been allowed to use my pocket-handkerchief, which is contrary to Queen's regulations, you know. Can't say how it was. How should you account for it, Mr. Salterton?"

"I should so like to hear," interposed Helen, grown quite reckless in her curiosity, "how it was you won the Cross. Do you mind my asking?"

"Oh, there is very little to tell, I assure you. Besides, I only wear it as representing many better fellows who did more and fared worse. I shouldn't be here at this moment, but for one of them, who had a far better right to it than I—a fellow who stood over me and got cut to pieces, while I escaped with this scratch. . I only wish he had lived to wear it."

"Come, come," interrupted Mr. Salterton, "if there was to be nothing of this sort, there would be no crosses to wear. And if you expect a civil answer, Helen, don't ask Captain Hunsdon to tell you what all the world knows, except yourself. But, hark!—what's that?"

It was the clear, ringing tantara of Sir Philip's horn, blown by way of announcement, as he entered the Lawn gates.

Far away, through the shrubbery, they could distinguish the pack, trailing in like a snake, and a scattering and scampering of pink-coated horsemen.

"My gracious!" exclaimed Helen, "I must run home directly, or I *shall* be in a scrape."

CHAPTER XXI.

THE hunting-breakfast was a complete success; and Helen got credit for the manner in which she behaved as hostess, and conducted the business of her own table. Every body left the Lawn in good humor; and, what was more to the purpose, the run which followed proved the most brilliant of the season. A magnificent dog-fox ran his last race, and fulfilled his destiny on that eventful morning. His brush was of course secured for Helen. Sir Philip carried it off to be mounted, and returned it with an ivory handle, bearing her name and the date, engraved upon a tiny silver shield.

But, after all, what do you care—so I hope at least—for these huntsmen and their glorious appetites, or for the fox dead and docked? You are aware that a story-teller never brings two eligible young people together for purposes purely Platonic. You are satisfied that, after a certain amount of variegated experience, a few ups and downs, and an entanglement more or less amusing, Captain Hunsdon and Helen Fleetlands will at last "fall out" (in a military, not matrimonial sense), in order to enjoy the large family and prosperous future which are always given away gratis when the play comes to an end. Quite right; and I will not only make you a present of your conjecture, but tell you plainly what were the exact difficulties which stood in the captain's way.

You may imagine possibly, as I dare say you do, that Helen, with her youth, health, and beauty, to say nothing of her many thousands and good social position, would have been a *partie* to whom no demur could possibly have been raised: more probably the object of a general scramble when once fairly in the market. You may suppose, reasonably enough, that if Captain Hunsdon chose to press his suit, and Helen was not willful enough to say "no," the admiral was the only rock ahead likely to cause trouble. Unfortunately we live in a state of society which philosophers complain of as "highly complicated," and the working of which is unquestionably mysterious to outsiders. How it came to work unfavorably in the present instance, I will explain at once.

Lord St. Margarets was a widower, with only one surviving child—the youth whose acquaintance we have just made. He was in popular estimation a very proud man; and if a vast territory, immense wealth, an historic name, and ancient coronet—things which no amount of intellect or ability can ever command for any body —gave any good reason for pride, he was not much to blame. Perhaps, however, we sometimes suppose such people proud from a confused suspicion as to what our own feelings might be, could we be suddenly placed in their shoes. Sometimes from a natural wish that they would abase themselves to our level, and not walk about as if they were, in fact, what the catechism aggravatingly describes as "our betters."

Be this as it may, one would have fancied that pride itself could scarcely have desired to perpetuate a fairer lot than that which apparently awaited Ferdinand Hunsdon.

Half a million of money, a fair slice of a southern county, with a title into the bargain, ought to have satisfied Methuselah. One need scarcely be overfrugal to wonder how it was all to be enjoyed in a modern life-time.

Lord St. Margarets had all these things, and was not discontented with his lot. And probably he was the happier for having the one grand wish of his heart still to be satisfied—that of seeing Ferdinand a greater man than himself. The anxious and eventful period at which his boy would naturally look out for a wife, was now coming on. Upon its result all depended. Money he did not care about. A few thousands more or less, could make no sort of difference in his son's position, but the alliance—for which he hoped and prayed—with one of the oldest and noblest families of the empire, was another thing altogether. That was his object.

But the event of the last few months had brought with it higher aspirations even than these. Ferdinand had been encouraged to enter the army rather in accordance with an old family tradition, and as the best possible finish to his education, than with any idea of treating it as a profession. The signal distinction which had so suddenly fallen to his lot, had never entered the calculations of Lord St. Margarets. He woke up one morning to find that his son was a soldier in earnest. Young as he was, he had done a deed of more than mere dash and daring. He had shown a cool judgment, a resolute will, and a power of self-sacrifice which commanded others, in one of the most critical conjunctures which ever tested the mettle of an unfledged subaltern. He had "done the state some service, and they knew it;" a service which, for the hour, at least, was talked about at head-quarters, in every capital of Europe.

The letters of congratulation which Lord St. Margarets received upon the occasion, would probably have papered a study, and brought him more pride and pleasure than he had ever known to arrive through the post. His son's path to the very highest destinies of his profession seemed fairly cut out. A dazzling and triumphant career, with an ultimate earldom of his own winning—this would indeed be to add lustre to an already illustrious house! And the old peer, who was an inveterate day-dreamer, made up his mind that, for some years to come, it was plainly expedient that his son should not marry at all. He was still very young, and for the present, at all events, would be far better occupied with his regiment—then on foreign service. The happy combination of chances in his favor, were such as did not occur to one in ten thousand, and it would be inexcusable not to make the most of them.

It was an odd conclusion, certainly, all things considered. One would have thought that he might have been shy of exposing his coronet a second time to the chance of being sent down a collateral line, by some wretched ounce of lead; and one might naturally have supposed that Ferdinand must be wanted at home. But Lord St. Margarets was an odd man, and didn't see things always in a regular light. His real home was in his London club, among a clique of gossiping old cronies, who babbled of Talleyrand and Waterloo. Of course, in this society, his son's late exploit had created a prodigious sensation, and Lord St. Margarets found the excitement agreeable. At any rate, having made the above reflections, he remarked to himself that his mind was quite clear upon the subject.

Its crystallization, however, was destined to be abruptly disturbed. A few days after the hunt-breakfast at Riverwood, Captain Hunsdon surprised rather than delighted his papa by the announcement that he had found him a daughter-in-law; in other words, that he had seen the girl whom, of all others, he would like to make his wife, provided his father saw no objection.

Lord St. Margarets prided himself upon his savoir faire. He had been ambassador at the court of one of the great powers, and knew how to handle matters. He wouldn't even allow himself to be ruffled by the intelligence. It simply demanded an exercise of tact. Nothing could have been more frank and honorable than the way in which his son had spoken his mind in the very first instance. Knowing that Helen was no match for him, according to his father's views, he had come, as was right, for a "permit" to fall in love. The only question was—how to act? As to that, his mind was quite clear.

In the first place, to run the risk of estranging his son, was out of the question. Rather than that, he would have seen him turned off with the "Ratcatcher's Daughter" herself. They must be friends always, whatever happened. In the second place, he knew that suddenly to thwart a lad in an affair of this description, was absurd in the light of all experience, and would be simply to send the last chance overboard. Finally, his diplomatic education had taught him, that if you wish to divert any body from a darling project, you must never allow your objections to appear in the first instance, when they are certain to be considered as mere prejudice, and treated very shortly.

However, instead of pursuing this inductive process further, let us invite ourselves for a few minutes to the pleasant dining-room at Saintswood, with father and son beside us, in snug after-dinner *tête-à-tête*.

Lord St. Margarets had, according to promise, given the matter every consideration, before finally clearing his mind, and committing himself upon a point of so much importance.

"Fill your glass, my boy, and give the fire a stir," he exclaimed, with easy gayety. "Well, Ferdinand, are we to drink Miss Fleetlands's good health, and may she soon be a lawful prize of war—hey?"

"You have not yet given me your opinion, sir," replied the captain, laughing. "I took the liberty of giving you mine pretty freely the other morning."

"You did; and I was most pleased at your doing so. You see, Ferdinand, that if it had been one of the Strawberryleaf girls, or any body from Hainault Towers, for instance, I should have been ready for an agreeable surprise. But as Miss Fleetlands is, as yet, a stranger, I am glad that you gave me your confidence in the first instance. As yet, I suppose, you are only feeling your way?"

"Just so, sir. Salterton introduced me to her, at old Mortlake's breakfast, last week. It was love made easy upon my part, I can assure you. I was lucky enough to sit next her at breakfast, and I've seen her twice since, and hope to find her to-morrow morning at coverside. We meet at Bunnytail End."

"Well done, you," remarked his father, unable to repress a smile at this liberal instalment of candor. "Try how you like her, by all means, Ferdinand. I only wish you to please yourself. Only don't get out of your depth before you know where you are. There are people about that young lady who will bring you to book if you do. I'm quite clear about that."

"That trying how you like young ladies, is awkward work," observed the captain musingly. "You see, directly you begin, they're down upon you with just the same game. 'No trial allowed,' is nearer the mark."

"Much nearer. But I leave you to manage all that for yourself. It's a pity she should be in troublesome hands. She has money, they say."

"A great deal, I'm told, sir. Fortunately my conscience is quite clear upon that head. I really know nothing about her being an heiress until long after I was in for it. However, that I hope is no objection. One can put up with a little money."

"Do you know, Ferdinand," replied his father quietly, straightening his legs against the fender, and holding up his glass to the firelight as he spoke, "this money would be about my greatest objection, supposing I were inclined to make any, as I certainly am not. The idea of your marrying any girl for money, is of course absurd. Nevertheless, people will talk. Somebody is always ready to explain every

thing. This money annoys me, and I will tell you why: Miss Fleetlands—of whom every one speaks well—is, as I dare say you know, the daughter of an Indian officer, who was the son of a Glamorganshire parson. Of course, since you spoke to me, I have made it my business to ascertain her antecedents."

"Well, sir?" inquired his son, not altogether satisfied with the last word.

"Well; her father was an officer in the Company's service—nothing more: and the fortune of which we are speaking fell to him quite suddenly, under the will of an old relation—Nettleton, I think he was called, who was, I am told, a monger of some sort."

"A what, sir?"

"A monger," repeated Lord St. Margarets, as if employing the word for the first time, and undecided as to its proper pronunciation.

"Not a coster-monger, I hope?"

"No. But I am not sure as to the exact prefix. Stay. I believe it was a wharfmonger. Oh, no. Wharfinger—that was it! At all events he managed to hoard up a great deal of money, which I would not have pass into our family upon any consideration. It would be a mistake, Ferdinand, and a serious one. I would rather lay it out in founding a house for decayed people of that sort—or get rid of it in any way—and even then we should be laughed at for our trouble. But let that pass. Miss Fleetlands, I hear, is fresh from a boarding-school at Brighton, where she has spent the last seven years. All very charming. I only wish I were her age. Of course we don't send our own daughters to boarding-schools; but, as to that matter, she was probably better there than living with that cracked old admiral, and his muffin of a wife. I really have now told you all that has passed my mind upon the subject. I don't pretend to see exactly the person I should have chosen for you, Ferdinand; but you are to choose, not I. You ask my advice. I advise you to please yourself. With your prospects here, and the position which you have won with your own hand, I don't believe you stand second to any man in the kingdom in the way of a splendid marriage. You might probably wait at least a year or two with advantage. You are not tired of your profession yet, I suppose, with a staff appointment waiting for you. But, as I said before, please yourself. Isn't that quite clear?"

"I should like to ask one question. You spoke just now of Helen's being in troublesome hands. Of course I know that old Mortlake has locked himself up a good deal, and behaved altogether in an odd way. Is that all? I declare I took rather a liking to the old fellow the other morning. I could have fancied myself talking to Admiral Benbow!"

"I am glad that you have asked the question. When I said that this young lady was in troublesome hands, I meant, of course, as his ward. He is her guardian in Chancery. I call him troublesome for this reason. Some years ago—before he locked himself up, as you say—he got into a shocking mess when the St. Mark's Bank stopped payment—in fact he lost the best part of his property. He had to sell a good deal of land; and I happened to know that a few hundred acres in our direction were actually in the market. I wanted them, to square our map on the north-west, and wrote to him about them. I declare I had no idea that I was doing him otherwise than a friendly turn; in fact, I offered to take his title without inquiry, and named a round sum for the land. However, he chose to fancy that I was riding the high horse, and about to amuse myself by buying him up, and referred me at once to his solicitor. Since then, we have scarcely spoken. Therefore, in the present case, I must not be expected to open the ball. I am rather sorry that I did not know you were going to his breakfast the other day; or I should have mentioned all this. That, however, is of little consequence. Only recollect, that no correspondence, between myself and the admiral, should such ever become necessary, can begin from this house. I will answer any communication, the other way, most willingly. It is more than likely that in your case he may find himself inclined to show temper. Now, only one word more, my boy. A few weeks ago you caused the whole land to ring with your name, by making up your mind in a moment, when the lives of hundreds depended upon your decision—in fact upon the next words which fell from your lips. That was well done—that was glorious! But depend upon it, Ferdinand, that whenever you hear a man boast that his rule is, never to hesitate, but to decide instantly in important affairs, that man is either a charlatan or an imbecile. Fellows of this kind are either simply reckless, or too nervous for the regular game of life. They would rather toss up for the stakes and have done with it, than play the rubber fairly out. Take your time and mind your moves while you can; and never trust to luck what you may make by play. Now, ring the bell, and let us have coffee."

The test of diplomacy is success. Young Hunsdon went to his room that night in a restless and undecided state of mind. If his father had spoken of his lady-love with open scorn, or pronounced himself decidedly against the match, he would at least have had the consolation of feeling himself unfortunate, if not ill-used. But he had no such solace. Not one single word indicative of the slightest disrespect for Helen herself had Lord St. Margarets let fall. All that he had said was true enough, and infinitely less than most fathers would have said, in a case in which such interests were at stake, and the descent of a noble and ancient house immediately involved.

What more could a fellow, in his position, ask than to be told to please himself? What more do any of us desire? And yet, after all, isn't it generally the most aggravating permission which it is in the nature of words to convey? When your groom or gardener retires from ar-

gument with a stolid shrug and misbelieving eye, and remarks, " Well, sir; of course you will please yourself!" how do you feel toward the rascal? Of course we want to please ourselves, and intend to manage it if we can. No need to tell us that! But we want to be helped to do so in our own way; and not dismissed to the endeavor with a suppression which is an abuse of language.

Again and again, Ferdinand thought over the whole conversation. The more he did so, the more was he impressed with the conviction that his father had been most kind and self-denying in the business. That an union between himself and Helen would be a disappointment, he felt keenly enough, and infinitely the more so from the light easy way in which certain topics had been touched upon. He admitted to himself that marriage at his age might be a bad beginning, if his father's ambitious views for him as a soldier were to be at all regarded. He perceived also, what had naturally never occurred to him before, that, in point of worldly position, Helen was a mere nobody in Lord St. Margarets's eyes; and that her money was, in his own case, by no means a desirable part of her belongings. The idea of his proposal being made the subject of an unworthy squabble upon the admiral's part was highly annoying—and the expression "brought to book" rested unpleasantly in his mind. Upon each and all of these topics his father might easily have enlarged; and he could not help feeling the delicacy and good nature with which they had been allowed to pass, as mere hints for his consideration.

Then he set himself to work deliberately to consider all that had taken place between himself and Helen. He had, after all, only seen her thrice, and he had to confess that even her attractive presence and engaging ways would perhaps hardly have produced the effect they did, but for the flattery of their first interview. The curiosity and admiration with which the young girl had regarded him, as the living wearer of a Victoria Cross, had been more than repaid upon his part. His passion for her had begun with vanity. Was it, after all, real or not? He had not yet committed himself. Did he know himself? Another meeting might render these questions superfluous.

Lord St. Margarets had known his son's mind thoroughly. Ferdinand Hunsdon had his own good, and even great gifts, from nature; but they were of a kind which are conspicuous rather in the field and the drawing-room, than in the chamber of meditation or debate. To the most perfect amount of nerve and physical courage consistent with penetrable flesh and blood, he added a singular degree of out-of-doors judgment. This last is rather a rare, and, to those who have it not, a very inscrutable instinct. Its characteristics almost defy description, and fortunately, scarcely require it.

There are two very different sorts of people in this world. I am not thinking of the good and the wicked—among one of which classes every body is supposed to sit—but of two prominent sets: people who always know *how* a thing is to be done, and people who always know (or rather, want to know) *why* it is to be done. Ferdinand Hunsdon was one of the former. When he troubled himself about whys and becauses, he was out of his depth directly. He had no turn for argument, and gave way under the feeblest pressure of "pro" and "con." Action was his forte. Action whether in the football-field at Eton, in the happy hunting-ground around Riverwood, or in a sterner arena where life and death are laid in balance, and every faculty of mind and body strung to quivering tension amid the "dreadful revelry" of battle. It was then that he knew how to trust himself. And, young as he was, he was wonderfully trusted by others. The men of his company thoroughly believed in him. Not one of them but looked upon young Hunsdon as an inspired soldier—a chief to be followed through thick and thin—an officer for whom it would be worth while to sacrifice one's light of day. There wasn't his equal in the regiment, from the colonel down to the small boy in the band—such was the creed of rank and file; and I don't know that they were much out in their estimate.

And yet, with all this, nobody could be more easily led by those whom he was accustomed to regard with affection and esteem. Nobody was more ready to take advice, in cool blood, upon points as to which he felt that others were better qualified than himself. In short, he had all the weaknesses of a trusting and sensitive nature, and, accordingly, not only took his papa's diplomacy greatly to heart, but tormented himself through a night of sleeplessness, by wondering what the deuce he had better do about Helen.

At last it occurred to him, that obviously the best plan would be to call upon Mr. Salterton the next day, after hunting, and ask his advice. He had known Helen from her infancy; and was, besides, a man whose opinion was really worth having. And this seemed such a good resolution, that he slept upon it for a whole hour before it was time to rise.

There was, in Lord St. Margarets's dining-room, a picture, upon which he had once set the greatest value, and held the pride and gem of his whole collection. He had purchased it, many years ago, at Florence, and a check of four figures had paid the price, a reflection which, so far from being disagreeable, only added to his enjoyment as its possessor. "Diana Venatrix," was the subject; and certainly, if buxom beauty, in its lustiest and least embarrassed form, gorgeous coloring, and wondrous power of animal painting, could justify implicit belief, the gilded scroll beneath, which bore the name of "P. P. RUBENS," was rightly worn by that magnificent canvas.

Day after day, Lord St. Margarets was never tired of feasting his eyes upon its breadth of splendor, and congratulating himself upon the possession of a work which might even bear his own name down to posterity. It was already known, in the leading hand-books of art, as "The Saintswood Rubens," and report said that the town counsel of Antwerp had sent a special envoy to this country, for the purpose of ascertaining whether it was to be reclaimed for money.

One day, a foreigner called, as many foreigners did, for permission to view the Rubens. Lord St. Margarets chanced to be at home, and good-naturedly received the visitor himself. Nothing flattered him more than these little pilgrimages; while, to stand beside the shrine, and enjoy an occasional whiff of incense in person, was doubly pleasant.

The foreigner in question chanced to be a dried elderly man, of particularly small stature, with high shoulders and wide spectacles, who looked as if he had been littered in a dust-bin, and brought up upon rusks and snuff. His card bore the name of "Ant Krinkel," and he received Lord St. Margarets's attentions with a business-like air, observing that he was pressed for time, and alluding to an appointment at Amsterdam.

This might easily have been excused; but, not so the way in which he inspected "the Rubens." Instead of looking at it from the best light in the room, to which he was courteously invited, or looking at it from under his hand, or through a roll of paper, or in fact, as it seemed, to any useful purpose whatever, this abominable little cinder of humanity began to peer into corners of the drapery, and ferret about the frame, in a manner which appeared to Lord St. Margarets scarcely less than impious.

"Confound the fellow, does he think there's a rat behind the arras!" he growled to himself. "Come here, sir! Did you never see a picture before? Come and look at one now!"

"I have looked at a great many pictures, milord," replied Ant Krinkel, hitching himself together, and readjusting his spectacles in a complicated fashion. "And I have looked at a great many pictures by Rubens, milord—a great many indeed. *But this is not one.* Excuse me. But I am right."

"What the devil do you mean, sir! and who are *you?* Go to Amsterdam, and—" I declare I mustn't finish the sentence; Lord St. Margarets was so outrageously angry.

"One moment, milord!" implored the intruder, with the air of a man who had been kicked aforetime, and deprecated the practice. "One moment. Will you listen to me? Yah?

Lord St. Margarets did listen; and this was what he heard.

Unrolling as he spoke a dirty paper, and twisting his spectacles more ominously than ever, the fawning Low Countryman reminded him of every circumstance connected with the purchase of his picture. He gave him names and dates; and even went to the unnecessary length of producing for his edification a copy of the draft on Coutts, to which the money had been paid. With equal circumstantiality, he detailed the exact story of the work, and of the sublime and patient ingenuity by which it had been worked into the market as an accredited original of the great master.

All this, he explained, was practically known to no man in Europe but himself. Milord had been imposed upon, no doubt. But by men who were dupes themselves. The greatest critics had been deceived, and were at that moment without suspicion. He ventured to place with his lordship a paper embodying every word which he had just uttered. He had no concealments. He requested none. Would his lordship condescend to inquire into the matter. Would he farther, at his high leisure, command that the picture should be reversed, and observe the monogram at the left hand lower corner. A fac-simile would be found in the paper which he had the honor to present.

And was that all?

Not quite; as you may suppose. In a slimy shuffling manner, which drove Lord St. Margarets to the verge of criticide, the rogue explained that he was at the moment engaged upon a great work—"The Painters of the Low Countries." He had the patronage of many crowned heads—of the principal Universities in Europe. Lord St. Margarets's Rubens was a work of mark. To pass it over without notice was impossible. His lordship could judge, from proofs now in his own possession, as to the speaker's qualifications as a critic. Should he call again? In a month? In six weeks? Time was of no consequence. His work was for all time. As regarded *that* picture, he concluded with a frightful shrug, he was at his lordship's service.

I have no occasion to pursue the subject. I don't know what happened next. That Lord St. Margarets had been the victim of a masterly swindle, which had entrapped people much better able to judge of pictures than himself, is certain. I only know that, ever after this interview, he hated the very name of Rubens, and would gladly have consigned the Saintswood specimen to the billiard-room, or the backstairs. But to have confessed the extent of his victimization was more than his diplomatic philosophy could abide. The secret, however, secured, remained his own, and the chaste goddess was allowed still to smile from his dining-room wall, silently preaching to his lordship an useful lesson upon the mysterious unrealities of life. The picture had not changed. The sky still shone—the wind blew, the floating canopy of cloud sailed on; the hounds bayed and bounded around their mistress, and the gallant Flemish steed, with foaming curb, snuffed lovingly among her flying tresses. But a loathsome little Dutchman had crawled in like a toad, and fire and wind and radiant air and the music of exultant life had departed at his whisper, and given place to naked vulgarity and tawdry glare.

Lord St. Margarets paused that evening before the picture, on his way to bed, and surveyed it steadily by the light of his flat candlestick.

He was very deep in thought; and, as he looked, a dry compressed smile passed slowly over his lips. It was the smile of a statesman who had made a *coup;* of a man whose mind is quite clear upon one point. But I am not in the confidence of ex-embassadors, and have only my own private guess as to the nature of his meditations.

So I shall follow the example of the editor of the *Daily Courant,* the first daily paper ever published in England, who in his opening number announced that he should not be at the pains to write leaders upon his news—"supposing other people to have wit enough to make reflections for themselves."

I have read a few essays, and heard a few speeches, and undergone a good many sermons in my time, wishing earnestly that the expounders had been of the same mind as honest "Edward Mallet, over against the Ditch at Fleet Bridge," Anno Domini 1702.

CHAPTER XXII.

It was a splendid winter morning. A pearly vaporous haze was drifting over lake and lawn and clustering woods, as the sun went slowly up into an unclouded sky. Scarcely a breath of air was stirring, yet there was a living freshness in the atmosphere which felt like a promise of the far-off spring.

Ferdinand's dressing-room was at the top of a large and lofty pile of building, known as the East Tower. Its quaint octagonal shape, deeply recessed windows, and vaulted ceiling, were picturesque; but the great glory of the room was its lookout. It was a thoroughly English landscape such as you never find abroad, and not very often, it must be confessed, at home. People who ought to know, pronounced it one of the most perfect in the kingdom.

It would be difficult to imagine a more commanding eminence, with forest, park, and water stretching far into the lower distance, down to where, miles away, appeared the smoke of a small sea-town. Beyond, and high over all, piled as it were against the horizon, stood the broad, unbroken circle of ocean-rim.

The perfect stillness was only broken by an occasional measured boom from the sea. An iron-clad was trying her new guns at a target laid out in the offing, and each sullen reverberation came shuddering through the morning air as if marking another interval of time.

One hates to be reminded of its passage when one has a nervous business coming on; and Ferdinand, to tell the truth, felt desperately nervous that morning. It could scarcely have been otherwise. His heart misgave him that under the influence of his first fascination he had permitted himself to show more of the state of his own feelings than was either prudent, or generous by Helen. Now, he had to see her in a new light, and look at her, for one morning at least, with his father's eyes. He could not dare to trust himself as he had done before. Perhaps she was, at that moment, looking forward with pleasure to seeing him in the field. He knew she liked to meet him—indeed she had never been at any pains to conceal the fact. And now he had to atone for his own previous indiscretion by a behavior which could scarcely fail to occasion her both vexation and surprise. However, there was no help for it,.and he proceeded uncomfortably with his toilet.

Ferdinand, as we know, took a good deal of thought about his raiment, and was indescribably careful of his personal appearance. To some men this is natural, and they would like to go smart, even if their days were to be as those of Robinson Crusoe, before he caught Friday to look at him. With others it is a pure matter of vanity; and some people are tidy on principle. I am thinking of an anecdote which a brother-officer of his happened to tell me only a few nights ago. He had been observing that Hunsdon used to come in for no small amount of chaff upon the score of his dandy habits while on service, and more especially for the exceeding care with which he always attended to every nicety of dress and person in the immediate prospect of action.

One day, on the morning of an assault, my friend chanced to overhear a couple of privates exchanging their own comments upon Ferdinand's appearance.

"William," said one, "see little Hunsdon walk down the ranks just now, with new gloves and a pocket-handkercher, and his hair curled for fightin'? Blessed if there's such another little game-cock in the whole brigade!"

"Not of my knowledge," replied William. "Where man or officer can go, he'll go—and stand who won't, he will."

"Aye, that's what's at the bottom of it, no doubt," returned the other. "But, mind you, William, that to see that little chap looking just as if he was fresh out of England at a go-in like this, is as good as ten files to.the strength of the company."

This conclusion, William did not gainsay, and my friend seemed to think that there might have been something in the remark. But, while I have been digressing, Ferdinand has been dressing; and his horse is already pawing the gravel in front of the coffee-room window.

This coffee-room was quite an institution at Saintswood. It was a very modest apartment upon the ground-floor, with a great oaken table in the middle, which had a mission of its own.

Every morning, during the winter months, breakfast was laid upon that table, for the benefit as well of any guests staying in the house who might choose to patronize it, as of the many people in the neighborhood who had the privilege of entrée. It was a convenient arrangement. There was no fuss, no waiting, no ceremony, and you might light your cigar in the room. There was one particular bell labeled

"Breakfast," a single pull at which, at any hour of the morning, was answered by the apparition of coffee and toast for one, with something appropriate in the way of hors d'œuvres chaudes. You took your chance of what came up, like children round a bran-tub. Every man for himself, and wait for nobody, was the greedy rule of the room.

There were only three men at breakfast when Ferdinand entered, by whom he was of course received with acclamation, and a chorus of inquiries as to the state of his wounded arm.

"All right, thank you. Hard as ever, I hope, in another week's time! All breakfasting, I see. That's right. Getting late, isn't it? Half-past nine, I declare, by the clock!"

"You've just come in time for.a bet, Hunsdon," exclaimed Mr. Scatterley, a loud boisterous youth fresh from Oxford. "Andrew has just offered.to lay Kingston and me a pound apiece, even, that he rides off with Miss Fleetlands, of Riverwood, within a fortnight. He'll give you a chance too, I'll be bound."

"Ha, ha! Now, that's too bad," laughed Captain Andrew, "What I said was, I'd bet a pound any body might do it, and I was just considering, ha, ha, whether I would go,in for her myself or not ;—that's what I said."

Captain Andrew, who claimed military rank as an ornament of the county yeomanry, was also a very young man, with weak eyes, and a weak laugh, and the face of a debauched doll. He was reported to be the richest man, next to Lord St. Margarets, for a great many miles round.

"Would you mind touching the bell behind you, Kingston?" said Ferdinand, horrified at the conversation which he perceived had been going on.

Few young ladies, I suppose, are sanguine enough to imagine that the gentlemen of their acquaintance always talk of them, among themselves, with exactly the same agreeable empressement which they display in their presence. Many a pair of innocent eyes, however, would open considerably, could the owners only overhear their own points, action, temper, and market-value candidly discussed in free-and-easy conclave around a smoking-room fire. I am not sure but that many a young lady might be allowed to listen with considerable advantage. And yet I don't know. Without a certain amount of illusion, reservation, and conventional insincerity, life would become insupportable. The little girl who spoiled her scissors in opening Matilda Jane, to find her filled with sawdust, fell a victim to indiscreet curiosity, and left a warning to her elder sisters. But, if punishment were in question, and I were at liberty to devise the sorest I could think of for a damsel who had affronted me, I should assuredly condemn her to hear herself talked about for half an hour by a fool in high spirits.

"Well, but, I say, Hunsdon," continued Captain Andrew, still gobbling away as he spoke, "what's your opinion of this new star of the hunt? What do you say to her, now, as a fine animal, sir, hey?"

"I have not as yet formed any opinion whatever," returned Ferdinand, dryly. "I say, Kingston, what are we to do about that row with old Rogers? Are we to pay, or not?"

"By Jove! you've had the best chance of any of us," interposed Scatterley. "I envied you, I'm sure, the other day, at the Riverwood hang-out. As if you weren't next her all the time, and all the fellows said she couldn't keep her eyes off you; and was seen cracking away ever so long at her coffee-cup instead of an egg —through being what the ladies call *preoccupée.*"

"Nonsense! However, since I was so fortunate as to find myself next her, I'm glad to hear I was supposed to make myself pleasant."

"It strikes me as a deuced odd thing—I don't know how you see it—Hunsdon," observed Sir Edward Kingston, "that old Mortlake should allow this young lady, who I understand to be his ward, to ride, as she does, with no better escort than her groom. I'm told she's entitled to a whole heap of money under some strange will or other, and loses it all if she marries under twenty-three. Did you ever hear the real story?"

"As to riding," interrupted Scatterley, before Ferdinand could reply, "I don't know a girl in the county better able to take care of herself with hounds. She's not likely to ask you to show her the way, nor to want anybody's help either. I'd give something, if she'd show me how to ride 'my horse as she does hers. And, by Jove, sir, talk about escort, just you notice that fellow, Gigoggin, always at her heels. He's got his orders to range within half a stable's length of her all day; and, if any body hails, to lay alongside, with his bow on the engaged quarter—bring his starboard daddle to the peak, like a marine, and hold on till they cease firing. Those are the admiral's orders, sir, and, by Jove, you may see them carried out to the letter, any day of the week. No tricks with Gigoggin, I can tell you, or you'll find him as great a cherub as his master!"

"Pawn my soul, that's true, now," remarked Captain Andrew. "The beggar has the most diabolical countenance. He almost rode into me last Friday, when I ventured to wave my hand and cry 'bravo!' to his lady, as she came after me over a rail. I begin to think that I shall have to whip him, before very long, do you know, in the natural course of events."

"I recommend you to do so, most decidedly," remarked Sir Edward, gravely. "You won't be too rough with the young man, I dare say? Very likely he thinks he is only doing his duty."

"Ha, ha! No—I'll pity him a little for his mistress's sake. I'll bet the story about the money is all moonshine. I can see plain enough how the land lies. The old admiral is trotting her out, horse and all. Riding them

to sell; that's my opinion. Only wish he'd let me take them both upon trial, for a month or six weeks!"

"I tell you what, Andrew," observed Ferdinand, in a careless tone, which nevertheless had something not quite natural about it, "I strongly advise you, when you get home, to ask your mamma to rummage out the family birch! By Jove, you'd be the better for it."

"Ha, ha, capital! No more birch-rods for me, brother-soldier!" sniggled the miserable youth. "Nimrod, ramrod, and fishing-rod, are my rods now."

"Oh come, Andrew, we've heard that before! Shut up and show us your new nag. Hunsdon, we'll wait for you at the west lodge. Come along, you little rake, or, by jingo, I'll tell Miss Fleetlands that you're given to gluttony."

"That fellow ought to have been drowned young," muttered Ferdinand, as the pair quitted the room. "Pity his friends ever let him grow up. What do you say, Kingston?"

"Ah, it was one of those mistakes parents make. Lucky for him, as you say, that they didn't weed the kennel. I don't know whether you are at all acquainted with the young lady, but I saw you look annoyed."

"I only wish I were sufficiently acquainted, to give Master Andrew something else to chatter about. He shan't breakfast here again, if I know it. Try one of these cigars. They have a history. It is about time to be off."

Nothing, to my mind, is more unsatisfactory than to have to do any thing I don't like. But to be watched in doing it is to undergo the difficulty and annoyance doubled. Under certain circumstances the intrusion becomes insupportable, and although heroes are popularly supposed to be less susceptible of the *pudor in oculis*, than other people, I suspect we are all pretty much alike in that particular.

It was not till toward the middle of the day that Ferdinand chanced to encounter Helen. There had been a brisk run, and a fox killed, and the people had pulled up, and were walking their horses about in groups, talking of what was to happen next.

The first glance warned him that, if he was to look at her with his father's eyes, he ought to have brought his papa's tinted spectacles in his pocket. Nothing so lovely as she looked at that moment, flushed and happy with excitement, and scarcely able to rein the impatient Camilla, quivering for another gallop, had ever crossed his imagination. He thought he had known her face well enough—and yet, for an instant, it seemed as if he had scarcely grasped it at all. A confused suspicion, moreover, that, if all secrets were told, he had himself something to do with that radiant overflow of beauty—that the pleasure of that particular minute was told in those colored cheeks and sparkling eyes, made the meeting still more embarrassing. Not to dwell upon the fact that he felt that many were watching, and that in all probability the dirty green peepers of the scandalous little Andrew might be blinking maliciously in his direction.

It was very unlike Ferdinand to lose his presence of mind, or fail, either in deed or word, to do justice to himself in any emergency. Unluckily upon this particular occasion he contrived to blunder and break down altogether. He was confused and spoke awkwardly; and, worse still, made a miserable mess of a matter of common politeness. He didn't perceive, as he raised his cap to Helen, that she not only expected him to shake hands, but had passed her whip into her bridle-hand for that purpose. And, when he did perceive it, the young lady had withdrawn her offer, looking a little disconcerted. It was a trifle—but trifles of this sort drive a sensitive man to the verge of distraction. They are recollected, long after they happen, with a stinging bitterness of self-accusation which ought to be reserved for nothing less than one of the seven sins. In short, after having contrived, in the course of a couple of minutes, to impress Helen with the conviction that some extraordinary change had come over him, and that, for some inscrutable reason, he intended to drop her acquaintance, he fairly turned his horse and rode off the field, desperate with vexation and self-disgust.

Luckily Mr. Salterton's rectory was within a mile, so he rode there for luncheon. He determined to lay his whole mind, so far as he knew it, open to the rector, with his father's views into the bargain, and to be guided by his advice. It was a wise resolution, for there was no man in the county better capable of advising him.

I am certain that every young lady who may do me the honor to peruse these pages, is confidently trusting that Captain Andrew may not be forgotten altogether, or dismissed without some appropriate casualty. Fortunately I have one to record.

Gigoggin was not to be trifled with. He was a man of wrath, and easily roused to vengeance. He looked upon Helen very much as his own child, and was careful as to her acquaintance. To tell the truth, I believe he had already awarded her in marriage to Captain Hunsdon, who was his *beau ideal* of what a gentleman ought to be. Captain Andrew he could not abide. And when that young simpleton came cantering and capering in front of his mistress, foolishly trying to attract her notice with puppy smiles and impertinent "bravyos," the cauldron of Gigoggin's indignation boiled hotter and higher, till it boiled over at last, to some purpose.

That groom of iron saw his chance and seized it. The hounds were running, the field was riding, when the audacious yeomanry officer, in trying to display his horsemanship and adoration at the same time, blundered stupidly under the nose of Camilla. In an instant Gigoggin was upon him, not upon Happy-go-lucky, for, when Helen had been allowed to enter the hunting-field, her esquire had been provided with a mount

to match the man. Over he went—fifteen or sixteen times, according to his own subsequent calculation—amid a perfect kaleidoscope of squibs and horse-shoes, which only settled into intelligible pattern when he found himself spread-eagled in a furrow, like a turned turtle, and ridden over by every body who had a horse.

It was a serious lesson; for so strongly was he impressed with the conviction that the shock had "done harm to his wits," that I believe to this day he seldom speaks three words consecutively without whimpering. I wonder if Gigoggin will ever come to be tried for manslaughter. It will go hard with him, I am afraid, unless he has a very honest judge, and a jury composed chiefly of dragoons.

But it is time to think a little more of Helen herself, to whom I am not quite sure that I have as yet done author's justice.

It may seem a bold assertion to make, but I believe it to be true nevertheless, that Helen had passed through the ordeal of seven years' noviate at a fashionable boarding-school without sensible damage to her character. There are some minds whose native purity and freshness seem to preserve them against the mischief of unwholesome contact, just as gold is able to retain its lustre in an atmosphere which would be tarnish and destruction to baser metal. Whatever she may have heard or learned in the playground, she was still, at heart, thoroughly young, simple and unspoiled. The wildness and self-will of her childhood had moulded themselves into a quiet, resolute, and independent spirit—a little enthusiastic perhaps, but still, for every-day purposes, under the control of no small amount of judgment and good sense. Even her own singular position and prospects, which would have turned the heads of most girls, were in her case disarmed of half their danger. She thought about them, certainly; and was pleased, so far as she could realize their meaning. But, except in the unfortunate instance, when a painful, and perhaps inevitable, suspicion had been forced upon a mind which was frankness and sincerity itself, she had scarcely wasted one serious reflection upon the subject. She had not yet learned to "give thought to the morrow," and "the evil of the day" was yet to come.

The change was near at hand. Feelings that had never yet been awakened, were now to bloom and break, and dart their living tendrils through and through her nature, and overshadow her very being with a sudden canopy of tropic growth.

That she should have been quite insensible to Captain Hunsdon's marked attentions, was impossible; but it is not less true that she had hitherto never ventured to accept them as her own. Her first impressions of Ferdinand had been those of wonder and admiration. She regarded him as a bright young hero, whom to see and converse with, was pleasure enough in itself. She noticed the way in which he was flattered, and courted by every body in the hunting-field, and innocently wondered that he should ever find time for a word with her, or even remember her name. And when the conviction grew stronger and stronger, that he not only found time to talk to her, but talked to her more and more eagerly than to any body else ; and when she remembered that, whenever he appeared, Gigoggin always broke a stirrup-leather, or cast a shoe, or met with some other calamity, and went off to a gate, or got behind a tree to examine damages—a sort of dream-like illusion seemed to be settling over every thing.

And perhaps as a dream it might have continued for some time longer, but for the sudden awakening brought about upon the morning of which we have just been speaking.

Ferdinand's behavior had been to Helen a perfect mystery. Her first impression naturally was that she must unconsciously have said or done something to annoy him, and she puzzled her head accordingly to very little purpose. People who never take offense themselves, are slow in comprehending how that unwholesome process evolves in the minds of others, and make odd mistakes when they attempt to pick out the veritable point of discord. One thing, however, she did discover in the course of her self-examination, and what that was, no young lady will be at loss to imagine. It was her turn to look forward to the next meeting, whenever that might be, with a troubled and anxious heart.

I do not know exactly what passed between Ferdinand and the rector. Perhaps even if I did, I should be bound to consider it confidential, seeing that the latter, in giving any advice at all, must have found himself upon delicate ground. But it is certain that, at the very next meeting, ample amends were made for the mistakes of the last, and that for many days and nights afterward, the secret chambers of Helen's heart were warm and glorious with that "purple light," which, alas, for many of us—perhaps not for you, oh, fortunate reader—is kindled but once in a life-time.

It may strike you as grotesque, to say the least of it, to picture the heir of Saintswood, with its baronial towers and forest miles, on the one hand, and a wealthy and beautiful heiress like Helen, on the other, exchanging amiabilities from their respective saddles, simply because they had no other place in the world to transact business in. Polly and her baker, at yonder area railing, are not more obviously at sea for a bower.

It was, however, one of the necessities of their situation, and what you may probably call upon me more seriously to explain, is how the flirtation could possibly have been carried on, without at once coming to the ears of Admiral Mortlake.

That point became also a puzzle to the admiral himself in due season, but then he was not as alive as he might have been to the fact that he was an unpopular character, and that it would have been difficult to find any one base enough to carry tales of Helen—especially in connection with an universal favorite like Ferdinand Hunsdon—to such an unsentimental old crocodile.

But, not to mince matters, Gigoggin was the real go-between, and scandalously betrayed his trust. He had been sworn by all that he held holy, whatever that might be, to keep strict watch and ward over his young mistress ; to allow her to speak to no one, except in his immediate presence, and to report all that he had heard, seen, or suspected, to the admiral, in the evening, like the spy of a private inquiry office. And the old henchman was really so ugly and uncivil to people in general, that one would have fancied he would have enjoyed the task.

It so happened, however, that, like Desdemona, Gigoggin perceived before him " a divided duty," and while he conscientiously fulfilled his mission as Helen's aide-de-camp, and would have tolerated nothing which might have struck him as an impropriety, he deliberately declined to bring her to grief about matters which he considered as not only natural, but very much to her credit. So he shut his eyes to a good deal that passed in the field, and lied like a dentist whenever he was, what he called, kicked into it, in cross-examination.

Some people assert that he was bribed by the captain, but this is a mistake. It is true that upon one occasion a gentleman, who wished to be well with Helen, offered him a ham sandwich with a sovereign in it, but the result only proved in what perfect simplicity this expensive refreshment was accepted. For Gigoggin, after the most unearthly chuckling that ever proceeded from human glottis, suddenly exploded like a horse-pistol, and fired the unlucky coin into a farmer's garden, two fields off.

As for Helen, she fortunately had no occasion to tell one single fib in the matter. It was not her guardian's policy to make her feel herself mistrusted, and he never pressed her with questions of an awkward nature. On the other hand, he entered into her amusements with a sort of growling good humor, and began to talk about people she must visit, and dinners that he must give, until she was reminded of her old fairy-tale reading, and of how Orson came at last to be endowed with reason.

All this was very well, but it could not last forever. Never count your secret safely kept, merely because you do not hear it told. The bird of the air may have carried the matter, and you none the wiser. And one day that same spiteful fowl explained the whole story to the admiral.

CHAPTER XXIII.

THREE weeks of fine open weather, which had made every body happy in England who deserved to be so, broke up suddenly at last. A good honest frost with bracing breath, and shooting, skating, and the like, to employ and console the frozen-out fox-hunter, would scarcely have been unwelcome, but it was not so written in the calendar. The weather had broken in bad earnest, and for days together there was a howling north wind, and skies that streamed with sleet, and roads that offered nothing to man or beast but cold abominable mire.

Luckily for all parties concerned, the guest-chambers at Saintswood chanced to be at the moment tolerably well filled. It was a famous house to be weather-bound in, for more reasons than one. In the first place, you were always certain to find there people whom you liked to meet. In the second, it was one of those grand old buildings in which there is room enough for every thing and every body. And then, there was no formality. Lord St. Margarets had seen a little of embroidery and etiquette, sticks and chamberlains, at one or two places where he had spent the greater portion of his diplomatic career, and perhaps had no objection to a rather rigid ritual when at home in Grosvenor Square. But at his country house, he liked nothing so well as to surround himself with holiday life, and to see his guests assemble, like folks at a picnic, with the undissembled intention of enjoying themselves.

And, to people thus disposed, even the villainous weather which had set in, presented no insurmountable difficulty. The great dining-room was cleared for croquet, and a famous lawn it made, upon which all the main fascinations of that pleasant game came out rather heightened than otherwise. And, at luncheon-time, it was voted, that to have the tables and chairs replaced, would be grievous waste of time, and give a vast amount of useless trouble into the bargain. So it was ordered to be laid upon the carpet, and to be considered as taking place in the Forest of Arden.

I am told that the face of the reverend butler, when he entered the gallery, and announced with lofty composure—"Luncheon is upon the floor," was a study in itself.

However, the plan succeeded; and when somebody proposed to change the scene, next day, to the Gemmi Pass, and have it upon the great staircase, the suggestion was unanimously applauded, and ordered to be carried into effect. After luncheon, there was a grand *tir au pistolet* for prizes, in the hall; and an important billiard match between Captain Hunsdon and Flora Richmond, one hundred up—twenty points given—for a pair of gloves.

"Now," exclaimed that young lady, as the game grew warm, "that was something like a break, Captain Hunsdon! Two cannons and a winning hazard! You in hand, and both balls in baulk! Well done me, I declare! It is you to play. Fifteen to thirty-one is the game. The striker fifteen."

"A cannon on the balls," observed Ferdinand.

"No!—is there? I should like to see you make it," returned Flora, chalking her cue. "Only tell me how, first, or it shall be called a fluke."

"Right hand cushion, six inches from top

corner pocket—side to the left—come down just below left middle pocket, and cannon, mademoiselle! Now, then."

Click—click.

"Well, I declare, that's too bad. And look what's left! Really, Captain Hunsdon, if I had known that you were such a disreputably good player, I shouldn't have put my gloves on at those odds, I assure you!"

"Chalk away, Flo!" exclaimed her sister, as Flora, after the custom of people with a game going against them, applied dose after dose of the carbonate to her idle cue.

"Miss Richmond has the best of the game yet," said a young guardsman, who was marking. "I say, Hunsdon, I should like to give you two to one about that last stroke, and go on as long as you like. Will you have it?"

"A letter for you, sir," interrupted a servant, entering the room. "Admiral Mortlake's groom is below, sir, with directions to take your pleasure as to his waiting for an answer."

"Put it down. Tell him I am engaged at this moment, and will let him know presently. It is you to play, Miss Richmond, I believe."

"Oh, please don't mind me, if you want to write an answer," cried Flora. "I can wait as long as you like, you know, so long as there's plenty of chalk. Won't you read it?

"'It does seem so shocking
To keep people knocking,'

as somebody says."

"I beg your pardon a thousand times, Ferdinand, for asking questions about a letter," exclaimed a young cousin, peering inquisitively at the envelope, "but, really, I have such a great curiosity about Admiral Mortlake—I mean Admiral Mortlake of Riverwood—that you won't mind my looking at the outside, will you?"

"Look as long as you like, my dear Constance; you would be perfectly welcome to open and read it, only that, I suppose, would be scarcely fair by the admiral, since he has chosen to favor me with his correspondence."

"Fair! No, of course it wouldn't. Only fancy my writing you a letter, and your letting Flora read it first, for instance! Catch me writing to you again!" laughed Lady Constance. "But, Ferdinand, do tell me; is it true that he really keeps that beautiful Miss Fleetlands locked up in a strong-room, and fed upon sugar-plums; and only lets her out on hunting mornings with a keeper disguised as a groom?—and what's that dreadful story about her papa's being buried, and the will, and all the money?"

"Oh," exclaimed Janet Richmond, "is that the man? Do you know we're dying to hear all about it. Every body talks of her, you know, and somebody is always sure of something; but the worst of it is that nobody is ever able to understand more than any body else; and there are no more bodies in the world than that, are there? Perhaps he tells you in his letter?"

"If he does, I'll let you know," replied Ferdinand, smiling. "But I should almost doubt his pitching upon me, as a proper person to know the facts, and suddenly sending full particulars. I had heard of her papa's having been buried; but it struck me as the regular thing."

"I'm just as curious as my sister," began Flora, but a famous cannon presented itself, and the well-chalked cue was brought into requisition.

"Game!" called the marker, at last. "Miss Richmond, one hundred; Captain Hunsdon, ninety-six.".

"Fairly beaten," confessed the latter. "Miss Richmond, I owe you a pair of gloves. You must let me measure you for them very carefully this evening, or there will certainly be some mistake. And, now that you have defeated the line, I advise you to demolish the Guards, while your hand is in. Come, Heston! let Miss Richmond polish you off, while I send this unlucky groom away with his answer."

Coolly as Ferdinand had passed off the matter, it is not to be supposed that he retired to read his letter in either a tranquil or comfortable state of mind. Like Bob Acre's memorable epistle, which had a designing and malicious look about it, and, to honest David's apprehension, "smelt of gunpowder like a soldier's pouch," there was something positively formidable in the large envelope—the scrawling, yet tremendously legible address—and the great broad scarlet seal. It was, in fact, "a dispatch"—nothing less. The contents were as follows:

Riverwood Lawn, *January 18th.*

" Sir :—Circumstances have occurred, which, while rendering it necessary that I should place myself at once in communication with you, seem to suggest personal explanations, rather than a written correspondence.

"I am debarred by considerations which no one can lament more than myself, from waiting upon you at your father's house.

"I take the liberty, therefore, of requesting that you will either name some place where I may do myself that honor, or favor me with an intimation that you will visit me at Riverwood; in which event I shall await your pleasure at any hour you may think fit to appoint. I have, etc., HERCULES MORTLAKE,

"Rear Admiral.

" The Hon. Captain Hunsdon, V.C.,
"Saintswood."

Whatever might have been the meaning of this gracious summons, one thing was certain —that it would have to be attended to sooner or later; and, that being so, Ferdinand wisely determined to get the business out of hand at once. There is no more miserable mistake in life, than the postponing of that which is unpleasant. It is like keeping something objectionable in your pocket, to molest and poison you the whole day long, instead of instantly getting rid of the nuisance. Therefore, having ascertained from the messenger that his master was certain to be found at home during the remainder of the evening, he dismissed him with a brief note, to the effect that Captain Hunsdon would lose no time in affording the desired interview, and might be looked for at Riverwood toward four o'clock. And he ordered his horse accordingly.

It would be difficult to imagine a more perfectly detestable afternoon. Torrents of sleet were still spattering down through the discolored air; there was a vicious wind blowing, and the roads were as bad as a bog. But the rider felt that go he must. He did not like the tone of the note which he had just received; and, knowing that it could only relate to one possible subject, felt that there was no rest for him until that business was settled.

Perhaps you may have expected that I should have said rather more than I have, about his own private feelings with regard to Helen, since the day when he broke down so unfortunately in the attempt to admire her at arm's length. Very young ladies, at least, would like to hear how his heart turned to her, and her alone, amid all the gayeties of Saintswood; and to be supplied with copies of sonnets composed in his airy tower, and repeated to the family owls, by the comfortable light of a January moon.

Well, if I leave something unsaid, in this part of my story, it is partly because I do not pretend to know every thing, and partly because the process of falling in love is one which must be described by a very clever hand; or else, beyond all question, let alone altogether. Neither you nor I, probably, would like to have all the thoughts, feelings, and doings of that golden morning retailed to courteous readers; or wouldn't walk in the middle of the street for the rest of our lives, if any one were cunning and cruel enough to put us to such open shame.

But if I may at all guess at Ferdinand's meditations during the rough half hour which carried him to Riverwood, I suspect that they were much to this purport:

Come what might, the die was cast and his choice made. Nobody but Helen should be the next mistress of his old halls, so far as he was concerned. The impression of that first meeting, when he might have remarked with the Moor—

" She loved me for the dangers I had passed;
And I loved her that she did pity them!"

had grown and strengthened with every succeeding interview, until it had ripened into that wild hungry longing, which it is easier to remember than to describe. Could he have helped himself with precipitation? Scarcely. Had he not boldly explained to his father what was likely to happen in the very first instance, and received permission to please himself? Had he not fairly talked the matter over with Mr. Salterton, and learned nothing which he could have wished otherwise? True, his acquaintance could hardly be said to be a very deep one; but what matter for that, if it had taught him all he cared to know? Nine people out of ten know little more of their wives, when they propose, than he did of Helen. Old women tell us that "marriages are made in Heaven;" and certainly, unless these arrangements are, in fact, the objects of a peculiar providence, there are few important affairs in this life which are managed more religiously at random. An accidental meeting —a chance conversation—a glance—a word, have done the work fifty times over in every week since the Conquest, and lit the flame which was to weld two lives inseparably as one, and leave a lasting impress upon the development of the human race.

There was a touch of mystery, too, about Helen, which had an interest of its own. Every body knew that she was under some strict control in the way of marriage, and that the destinies of a great fortune were involved in her choice. That obstacles would be interposed appeared quite likely, but Ferdinand was ready to wait. He had all but satisfied himself that his own feelings were returned—indeed, to tell the truth, he knew that there was no doubt about the matter; and, that being so, he was content to bide his time. The prospect of a couple of years' delay would, as he well knew, make all the difference in the world to his father. Lord St. Margarets never started difficulties two years in advance. Give him but that space of time to turn about in—to bring his diplomatic spiriting to bear—and to await the flux and change of all things terrestrial, and you might make your own bargain. And by the time that two years or so had run out (any change of mind upon the part of an enamored couple being, of course, out of the question), he would have become so far acclimatized to the project, and so much in love with Helen himself, that she would be received with open arms.

In the mean time, while his papa was being thus gracefully relegated to self-delusion, Ferdinand, as he was well aware, would be remorselessly marched off to the wars, to take his chance of coming back with a cork leg or a glass eye, or, more serious still, no skull for his future coronet. All families have their traditions, and those of the St. Margarets's were feudatory and warlike.

"Adsum!" was their motto, centuries old. The heir was bound to serve. And Ferdinand had begun to think how nice it would be to receive letters from Helen, in camp, and to compose most interesting replies, for her benefit, when a vivid piece of descriptive writing was suddenly demolished by finding his horse's nose at the gates of Riverwood.

He had only once before entered the place, and if any thing had been wanting to convince him of the true state of his feelings, he might have found it in the strange and inexplicable interest which every thing around him seemed to awaken. Nothing, though ever so commonplace and trivial—whether tree, post, or gate, old woman at the lodge-entrance, or handle of the hall door bell, but seemed hallowed by her look or touch. And she was there herself! Somewhere

F

up in those snow-beaten caves, perhaps. More probably in that warm-looking, lamp-lit drawing-room, whose glimmer went out upon the lawn between the shutters which a servant was, at the very instant, employed in closing. But just as far removed from him that evening, for all useful purposes, as if she had been ten thousand miles away, and down in the Valley of Diamonds.

However, it is in the nature of business to supplant romance, and Ferdinand found himself at once ushered into the admiral's study.

We know the room already, with its clubs, canoes, and cocoa-nut men, its towering iron chest, and other belongings.

A great log was slowly consuming itself upon the hearth, and the lamp, just lighted, threw mysterious glimpses around the dark apartment. Admiral Mortlake rose hastily from his arm-chair, and received his visitor with even more than customary ceremony. But it was plain that some strong constraint was upon him, and that he had a matter in hand which he would have given a good deal to know how to get rid of, or to transact.

"Captain Hunsdon, I am perfectly confounded at seeing you here on such a frightful evening. Sir, I hope and trust that there was nothing in my note which could have been so far misunderstood as to lead you to take this ride upon my account. Sir, you should have allowed me the honor of waiting upon you, rather than have driven me to apologies which I am at a loss for words to convey. Can I say more, sir—ha?"

"I beg you will say nothing more, admiral. I was rather glad of an excuse for a ride; that was all. And, as to the weather, I've seen rather too much of this sort of thing to care a button about it."

"Ha! You are young, and a soldier. At all events draw your chair to the fire, Captain Hunsdon, and let us try another log—so! If I had had the slightest idea that I should have the pleasure of a call from you this evening, I would have taken care to be better prepared—ha!

"Captain Hunsdon," resumed the admiral, after a pause which threatened to become awkward, "in making the communication which I have to make, and to which my note of this morning refers, I will be brief and straightforward. I was not aware, sir, until last evening, that your acquaintance with my ward, Miss Fleetlands, had extended—without either information or inquiry directed to myself—into a degree of intimacy which has become the subject of general conversation. I learned so much, sir, last evening. It is for you to say whether I have been misinformed."

"I don't know who your informant may be, admiral; however, I dare say you may trust him. My hope is that the acquaintance may ripen into something considerably more satisfactory; and, as her guardian, I take the liberty of telling you so."

"But you should have told me before, sir— you should have told me before," muttered the admiral, rising from his chair, and displaying his broad coat-skirts to the chimney-blaze. "Captain Hunsdon, I entertain the very highest respect for you personally, both as a gallant soldier, and one of the leading men in this county. Still, sir, you will permit me to remind you, that a young lady's position in society is injured by marked and public attentions, from any one, no matter how distinguished, which may ultimately come to nothing; and that it is the duty of those about her to preserve her, so far as possible, from expectations which can only end in disappointment and useless pain."

"Had you not better proceed, admiral?" said Ferdinand, leaning back in his chair. "Your last remarks require a conclusion."

"Ha, sir, very true! And the conclusion is this. It is a conclusion, sir, which would have been at your service in the first instance, had you condescended to inquire it. Miss Fleetlands, as you may probably be aware, is heiress to a very large fortune. That fortune, sir, her father, under views with which I have no concern, chose to preserve to her own use thus far —namely, that he exerted all legal means in his power to restrain her marriage up to the age of three-and-twenty. I have a copy of his will in a safe yonder, which you will perhaps accept, to read at your leisure. Now, sir, Miss Fleetlands will, in exactly five years from Wednesday last, attain the age of three-and-twenty. Until that day, I, as her guardian, must decline to promise my assent to her marriage. You may think that my late friend, Colonel Fleetlands, was unreasonable in what he did. I do not. We grow cautious as we grow older, Captain Hunsdon; and though I may regret the course which I feel obliged to take in this particular instance, I am pledged to fulfill his last wish to the uttermost. I am sorry, as I said before, that mere casual information, volunteered by a stranger, should have led me, as it were, to obtrude this information upon you—rather than it should have been supplied at an earlier period in answer to some direct application from yourself."

"Three-and-twenty! Is it possible that I can have understood you, admiral?"

"It is the fact, sir. My control over my ward's actual marriage may or may not extend beyond the age of twenty-one. But should she marry without my consent, previously to attaining that of twenty-three, the whole of her large fortune, with the exception of an insignificant annuity secured to her own use, passes, without any act of mine, into other hands. That is the actual state of the case, sir—ha!"

"As you may suppose, admiral," replied Ferdinand, "Miss Fleetlands's fortune is not my object. Let it pass, sir. I would rather that it did."

"Humph!" broke in the admiral, upon whom this last piece of information appeared to produce a most exasperating effect. "You are very generous, sir, of what, I may remind you, is not, and can never be yours to give away. With a little more knowledge of the world, sir, you would have been aware that upon my ward's marriage, whenever that event may take place, it will be my duty as her guardian to see, and in fact the Court of Chancery will insist, that her property is settled upon herself in the customary manner. And when you speak of Miss Fleetlands's fortune not being your object, and of allowing it, as you say, to pass, the observation may be a romantic one, and made in good faith into the bargain—but it necessarily leads to questions which we should scarcely discuss in good temper."

"I am quite at a loss to understand your meaning, admiral."

"My meaning, sir, is this!" retorted the other, almost fiercely. "You are heir, as all the world knows, to a viscount's coronet. Probably to an immense estate. As to the latter point, I know nothing whatever. My Lord St. Margarets's lands may be entailed, or they may not; and he may live thirty years yet, and I hope he will. Sir, I have not the honor to enjoy your father's friendship, and circumstances have occurred—circumstances to which I need not advert at present—which seem to have placed a bar between us. And now, sir, do you come from Lord St. Margarets, without one word of courtesy from him, haughtily to ask for my ward, and fling her money to the winds like dirt? Or do you come, sir, simply upon your own account, unprepared to inform me whether Miss Fleetlands would be received at Saintswood at all?—as ignorant as I am myself of the aspect in which your father would regard such alliance upon your part, and of the prospects which you would be able to offer her, could every thing be arranged as you wish? You propose, as I understand, to throw her fortune, overboard. And you expect me to fold my arms and allow this to be done, without the slightest opportunity of judging as to whether or no you are in a position to replace that which in the whim of the moment you boast of being ready to scatter. Sir, could you marry her to-morrow, regardless of my consent, you might certainly show that money was not at present your object—not, however, by sacrificing any thing to which you have or can ever have lawful claim, but by virtually sweeping away from Miss Fleetlands every sixpence of her private and independent patrimony. That would be liberal indeed! Sir, if I have rendered myself thus far intelligible, I will merely add that had the negotiation which I understand you to propose been fairly and formally opened in the first instance, my only answer could have been, that, for these three years to come, it would be inconsistent with my duty as guardian for me to allow it to be entertained at all. Under present circumstances, I must distinctly, upon my ward's account and my own, finally decline the honor which you propose to do her."

"In that case, I need trespass no farther upon your time," remarked Captain Hunsdon, gravely, as he rose to take leave.

"After what I have felt it my duty to say, sir," rejoined the admiral, "you will not think it strange, if, for obvious reasons, I request your word that all intercourse whatever between yourself and Miss Fleetlands will be at once and henceforward totally discontinued."

"If you are serious in requesting that at your instance I should pledge myself to any particular course of conduct with respect to any person alive, you must be aware that there is only one answer," returned the young officer, buttoning his cloak. . "We had better part without farther words."

"Not quite so, sir; not quite so!" interposed the admiral. "It is my duty, sir, to protect my ward against, I will not say solicitation, but against any which could only tend to unsettle and disturb her mind, and place her in a false and most improper position. Sir, unless you tender me the pledge which I require before we part this night, Miss Fleetlands does not quit these grounds again, so long as you remain in the county. Make it necessary, sir, and she does not pass yonder hall door. One step more, and her room becomes her prison! The power is in my hands; and it is you, sir, and not me, that she will have to thank, should it at once be put in exercise."

Ferdinand's face grew suddenly quite pale. His eyes looked as if a light were slowly passing behind them, and his lips assumed a slight yet peculiar curve. Perhaps it was after some such look that in a desperate hour, not many months before, he had "called upon" his men!

"Admiral Mortlake," he said, "I know what is due to a man in his own house. I am sorry that you did not take my advice just now. You should have permitted our conversation to close as it stood. Allow me to pass you. It is time."

And the admiral was alone.

CHAPTER XXIV.

I AM going to take the liberty of hazarding a guess as to the true explanation of Admiral Mortlake's conduct in the interview which I have just described.

For many years previously his views, with regard to Helen, seem to have been little better than selfish and mercenary. He was receiving a considerable sum annually upon her account; and between the natural desire to retain so easy a source of income, and the dread of being dragged into Chancery upon the score of past receipts, he had come to regard her marriage as a day of evil, to be postponed as long as possible, and awaited at last as one of the inevitable misfortunes of life. Still, since it was morally certain that Helen would marry somebody, one might have supposed that he would not only have seen in the heir of the St. Margarets's a husband who would do credit to his choice and care, but rejoiced in the absolute certainty that the whole question of arrears, if such really existed, would be settled at once :—dismissed, in fact, as an idle topic.

And so it might have been, but for the affront which he conceived that Lord St. Margarets had put upon him, in the matter of that wretched bargain and sale. That he could not forgive. And that, coupled with what he was pleased to stigmatize as stolen interviews, and love on the sly, roused up in him the dogged spirit of resistance, until, dismissing all prudential considerations, he made up his mind to fight, and allowed temper to clear the deck.

Whether or not, had Ferdinand only inherited a portion of his father's diplomatic wisdom, and condescended to coax and be cunning, instead of marching out like a man who had been defrauded and did well to be angry, is not now a very important question. It is even possible that you may think that the admiral had some show of reason in his view of the case. At all events he thought he had; for, next morning, he sent for his lawyer.

Mr. Clover, attorney - at - law, the leading practitioner in that direction at St. Mark's-on-the-Sea, was a little, sturdy, middle-aged man, whose maxim was, "bonne guerre—bon paix !" In other words, he always liked to see his clients fight first, and shake hands afterward. By this means, a great deal of unworthy haggling was avoided; and the parties, instead of hating each other, as people always do who imagine that they have been overreached in a compromise, retired with feelings of mutual respect. And, lastly, Mr. Clover's reward was written upon blue-ruled foolscap, tied up with green ferret, instead of being limited to the territorial recompense ultimately in store for the peacemakers.

You would never have supposed from his conversation, however, that Mr. Clover was the man to draw you into a needless quarrel. Quite the reverse. He was so particularly dry and guarded in the matter of giving advice, and discountenanced so gravely all that seemed to savor of precipitation, and took such a responsible amount of snuff, that your only doubt was, whether he would ever get the coach started at all—never, whether he would rattle the ribbons, flick the leaders, and upset the whole concern into the ditch.

"We must not be too precipitate, admiral, indeed we must not," he remarked, after half an hour's conference. "An application to the Court in a matter of this description is not to be lightly risked, nor, generally speaking, without some more distinctly overt act upon the part of the individual sought to be affected. Still, sir,"—he proceeded, after an infamously large pinch—"still, sir; while we must by all means avoid precipitation, we must not, on the other hand, lay ourselves open to the charge of negligence. Our course, should we feel it right to adopt an active one, is plain. It is to restrain Captain Hansdon from all intercourse, whether written or verbal, with your ward. In these cases the affidavit is half the battle. The affidavit is every thing. And it seems to me that we are in a position to swear as good an affidavit as ever was put upon the file. Miss Fleetlands under age by these three years—her property diverted upon marriage without consent—clandestine interviews—suitor barely one-and-twenty—no proposal for settlements upon the part of his father, who to best of deponent's knowledge, information, and belief, is either unaware of or opposed to the conduct of the respondent—unsuitable match altogether. Hang it, admiral, what could one want more? I'm afraid we must go on."

"Go on, then," growled the admiral. "Sir, you precisely expressed the reasons upon which I desire to put an end to this absurd and most objectionable flirtation. Am I to understand that you see your way to doing so at once and effectually?"

"Certainly, admiral. God bless me, yes! I shall write up by to-night's post to have affidavit settled by counsel, and sent down at once to be sworn."

"And then, sir—ha?"

"Then, sir, we obtain an *ex parte* injunction, as a matter of course, and serve the captain forthwith. And, after that, sir, he'd better mind his moves. You see there's the Sergeant-at-Arms and the Queen's prison, and commitment during pleasure, all upon the cards if he doesn't. Famous!" concluded Mr. Clover, smacking his lips and tapping his box, like a man who has just produced a very particular bottle, and is confident as to flavor.

"Good!" snorted the client. "Hope they'll clap him in irons, with a sentry over him!" And so the conversation ended.

Without the slightest ill-feeling in the world toward Ferdinand, for whom indeed he really felt a sincere respect, the opportunity of inflicting a marked and mortal snub upon his haughty neighbor at Saintswood, was temptation too strong for the admiral. Such a chance might not occur again in a life-time, and he determined to make the most of it. That it might be unwise to invite the direct attention of the Court of Chancery to his conduct in the guardianship, was a reflection which of course had not escaped him. But it also occurred to his mind that a bold stroke might, after all, be the safest in the end. It would at least have the effect of scaring inferior intruders out of the field. And since, unless, contrary to all probability, Lord St. Margarets should take up the affair in earnest upon his son's behalf, which he could scarcely do without absolutely tendering him as Helen's suitor, the game was in his own hands.

There are two mistakes so universally committed by people, upon falling in love for the first time, that they seem rather part of the diagnosis of the complaint than mere instances of casual weakness upon the part of individuals. In the first place, they never see any difficulties at starting: none at least which, in their early ardor, appear of more account than the

hurdles in a steeple-chase. Without these, there would be no sport—no excitement—no triumph in ultimate success. In the second place, directly a difficulty is really reached, it presents itself as a hurdle ten feet high, with a ditchful of spikes and pitchforks on either side. And unlucky Strephon at once discovers that nobody, since love was invented, ever ran his head against such a barbarous and insurmountable *chevaux de frise*; and would like to make the world ring with lamentations, and complaints of a measure of ill-luck, heaped as measure never was heaped before.

Perhaps, to say the truth, Ferdinand's first hurdle was rather a stiff one, and might well have cost him a little uneasiness.

It was with infinite difficulty that he managed, as in duty bound, to carry on his duties as host, and give no outward token of the volcano that was burning within. It was too frightful, so he felt at least, not only to have awakened in Helen's young mind expectations which, to use the admiral's own words, seemed likely to end in disappointment and useless pain, but to have actually roused feelings in the heart of that old curmudgeon which would assuredly be vented upon herself. And that coward threat, "Make it necessary, sir, and her room becomes her prison," rang and reverberated in his ears with such intolerable and insulting violence, that he thought of the Chamber of Horrors in Baker Street, and felt his pulse.

The worst of it was, that there was no human being to whom he could apply for sympathy, advice, or assistance. He had spoken manfully to his father when he first found himself touched, and had no reason to repent of having done so: but to go to him again would be simply idle. A few empty expressions of profound condolence—a mist of insincere hopes that something might yet supervene, and a sprinkling of polite regrets that his lordship's own relations with the admiral were such as necessarily to preclude his own personal interference—even if such interference could, by any possibility, have been of use—were, he knew, all that he had to expect.

He did not know, and we will not tell him, that his profound papa, not altogether confident as to the success of his previous diplomacy, had already taken the most effective steps toward having him forthwith recalled to his regiment; and had written letter after letter to know if there was not some non-combatant capacity in which his lately-wounded son could be immediately required to serve. Neither was he aware, which we will also consider confidential, that Lord St. Margarets had carefully arranged that his bailiff should pick a little perverse quarrel with the admiral's people upon some trumpery question of trespass over adjoining lands, and thereby incensed that irascible old gentleman against the whole house of Hunsdon to a degree which threatened apoplexy. So smooth, silent, and unsuspected is the under-current of affairs when guided by the discretion of ex-embassadors.

There was Mr. Salterton certainly—his own former tutor—to whom he had already appealed in a difficulty, but to whom, whether wisely or not, he felt it in that conjuncture impossible to resort. The rector, as we know, was associated with the admiral in the trusteeship created by Colonel Fleetlands's will. Still, he was not Helen's guardian; and Ferdinand felt a natural delicacy in, as it were, inviting him to intermeddle. Besides his interference could work no possible good, and nothing but additional humiliation could spring from it. So the young soldier found himself alone, with no other counselor than his own resolute heart. Then was the time to think. Then was the time to decide; without one gainsaying word! Swift was the thought—stern the resolution. The council-chamber was closed: the doors locked; and the word passed for war!

His first impulse, and one upon which he immediately acted, was to write to Helen herself. I shall resist the temptation to give the letter verbatim, because love effusions, however worthy of the occasion, appear, generally, either insipid or ridiculous to outsiders who read in cold blood. But I will take upon myself to say that it was a brave, manly letter, which told his own feelings in as few words as could be expected, and challenged her own in terms equally plain. He mentioned, as he was bound to mention, something of what had passed between her guardian and himself, carefully avoiding whatever might, even in the slightest degree, have conveyed an impression of petulance or ill-will. And then, if she felt toward him at all as he to her, he begged one single interview; and as it was his place to make things as easy as possible, and to name a rendezvous, he inquired if there was any time, either by day or night, at which he might hope to find her, even for a few moments, in the little summer-house where their eyes had first met. If she ever found an opportunity of answering, and would only name an hour, he would be there.

This letter he entrusted to his own groom, Ailsa, a smart, intelligent ex-sergeant of dragoons, who had a wonderful way with people, male or female, and always succeeded in his errands. Tell him what was to be done, and he did it, without even asking a question, which was marvelous.

"Ailsa, my lad, this note is for Miss Fleetlands, at Riverwood—prisoner with enemy. Do you understand?"

"I will see to it, captain," replied Ailsa pleasantly, touching, as he spoke, the peak of a supposed cap.

And when Ailsa said that he would "see to a thing," that thing was as good as done. Nobody knew exactly how he managed his missions —least of all, people whom he absorbed into unsuspecting complicity. Why, indeed, should we know, or want to know? When your doctor sets you upon two legs again, after a week on your back, you don't ask him why he wrote the prescriptions which did the business, in cunci-

form symbols and Gower Street Latin, instead of Queen's English. Bull's-eyes are the real thing in life, and the world in general has nothing to do but to look to the score. Helen's letter was in safe hands, and reached her own before dinner-time.

To picture the delighted surprise with which it was received, would probably be impossible in print. Who has not dreamed some splendid dream, and woke up with a sigh, that the glimpse of happiness, just seen and lost, belonged to another world—a living, vivid realm into which, in this mysterious helpless way, we are sometimes permitted to peep—a world from which, alas, we can bring nothing back to this. But, oh, to be told, on waking, just as we had dismissed the magic story as a baseless fancy of the night—a vision to be rubbed away from morning eyes—"It is all true! Dreamer, you have not dreamed in vain! Wake up; for it is real! Wake up; amid the lights and the music and the love of Fairy-land!" Why, then, we might probably scratch our eyes to some purpose, and feel very much like Miss Helen.

Ferdinand's note was not an easy one to answer, nor was the swift and delightful emotion which it produced, altogether favorable to business.

I hope you will not at once set Helen down as a young lady of ill-regulated mind, if I confess that the idea of a clandestine interview was eagerly welcomed, as something particularly delightful. Such meetings formed an essential item in every romance which she had ever read; indeed, without some such adventure, the story of her own life would be as tame as a tract. Besides, Ferdinand's letter had revived old feelings in her mind. Not, indeed, in their girlish bitterness; but not the less dangerous for all that. It was quite clear that her guardian was playing some deep game, of which she was herself the subject; and that her future was, in some mysterious manner, concealed in mist and labyrinth, which was obviously unfair. Ferdinand, she found, had actually asked for her, and had been sternly repulsed, with orders to think of her no more—to address her again at his peril. How was this? Why was she dangerous? What had she done to be thus treated? Upon this footing, she might next hear that Captain Andrew had made a similar application, and be called in to kiss him. This would never do. Sooner or later, she would learn her own position, and there could be no chance like the present.

It was Monday. On Thursday, she knew that her guardian was to attend a meeting at St. Mark's, which would occupy him the entire afternoon. Mrs. Mortlake, after four o'clock, always locked herself up in her own room with a tea-pot, and devoted the time, till dinner, to literary composition. Tracts, as you are aware, were her strength, or weakness, in that department; and they were regularly read to Helen upon completion, much upon the same principle as that which made Molière recite comic scenes to his housekeeper. Not, of course, to see whether the young lady would laugh, but to try whether she could be induced to look edified, and ask intelligent questions. Perhaps this was one of the reasons which made Helen resolve that her own career should be very different—not, indeed, from those of "Abraham Brown, Mariner," or the "Blasphemous Boy.of Brighton," who was scarified by forked lightning on the spot, which were altogether out of her line—but from the deadly dull experience of the staid and sententious damsels who prosed for her benefit.

So she settled that half-past four o'clock on Thursday would be a nice time to name; and after spoiling several sheets of note-paper in trying to frame a reply which should be exactly what it ought to be, gave up the attempt, for the moment, in despair. Miss Smugg would have rattled off an answer in no time. But, then, Serena's notions of maidenly reserve were gleaned from the frank pages of Paul de Kock.

So she locked the new treasure up in her desk, reflecting that there would be plenty of time to write, especially since there was no chance of her being able to post her letter until the following afternoon.

That desk had been a present of the admiral's, when she first returned from school. It was a beautiful gilt steel-bound affair, with a real Brahma lock; and Helen had been quite touched by the kindness of an act which possessed her of so charming a depository for all her little valuables. She did not know—and how should she have suspected—what I blush to write. That desk came home from the maker's with two keys, only one of which found its way into Helen's hand. Mrs. Mortlake took charge of the other.

By what conceivable self-imposture the donor palliated, or supposed that he could palliate, such infamous treachery, I do not care to inquire. I am not, thank goodness, holding a brief for such a rogue, and leave him undefended to his own conscience, and any amount of infamy you may choose to smother him under.

Of course, Admiral Mortlake's long experience of mankind was sufficient to assure him that Ferdinand, after his late rebuff, would lose no time in writing to Helen. Unfortunately, he had better evidence still to work upon.

The dashing ex-sergeant of dragoons had done his part so well, that no human being in the house, except Helen, knew how or when the letter had been delivered. But Crimp was on the admiral's side, and received secret-service pay. Crimp was Mrs. Mortlake's maid, and acted in the same capacity for Helen. Every woman knows when another has received a love-letter. That is a fact; argue over it as long as you like. So Crimp knew, and told the admiral.

You now know as much as I, and can understand how it came to pass, that even before poor Helen's manuscript was fairly transcribed and posted, Mr. Clover was again in requisition. The interview was business-like and brief.

Admiral Mortlake was in a position to inform his legal adviser, without confessing to the subsidiary and shameful source of information, which, however, he had freely used, that he had been informed, and had the best reason to believe, that Captain Hunsdon's attentions had reached the stage of written correspondence. That was an important count in the indictment.

"Capital!" replied Mr. Clover, tapping his snuff-box. "Clearly, we must proceed at once. I'll write by to-night's post to my London agents, Talbot & Castle, and beg them not to lose an hour. You shall hear from me directly we serve the injunction; and then it's for you, you know, to keep a bright lookout."

The eventful Thursday arrived at last. Lord St. Margarets had been obliged, unexpectedly, to return to town, and the party at Saintswood had broken up. It was a relief to Ferdinand to find himself comparatively alone. Distraction is sometimes a safe and soothing medicine to the self-devouring mind, but like other empiric remedies, if it doesn't happen to hit the particular case, it only aggravates what it was intended to allay.

"Get along with you into society, and forget your troubles in merry-making and parlor dancing, right and left," is a favorite nostrum with old women. It may succeed now and then, with those who are lucky enough to know where to go for the remedy, and young enough to dance back again. But, in serious cases, the theory is that of the lunatic, who got into the casualty-ward at Guy's Hospital and tickled the patients all round.

Ferdinand sat at breakfast alone in the coffee-room, in that delicious state of mental exaltation which is just consistent with practical sanity.

"A young man from London, sir, would be glad of a few minutes' conversation, on particular business," said a servant, presenting a card, with this inscription, the address being added in pencil:

MR. JACOBS.

From Talbot & Castle, Lincoln's Inn.

"What does he want? I don't know the fellow. Never heard of such a name. Let him mention his business, if he has any."

This was just what the young man from London had overwhelmingly declined to do. It was with Captain Hunsdon alone, and couldn't possibly be mentioned in the hall.

"Send him in," at last said Ferdinand. In came the young man from London, with brisk step, free-and-easy wave of his hat, general air of a man accustomed to castles.

"Got a nice place of it, indeed, captain," he

began, running his fingers through shocks of well-buttered black hair, and throwing open his overcoat to display the thunder-and-lightning scarf, brimstone buttons, and general dandy-flash make-up of a Chancery Lane swell. "Nice place, indeed! You are Captain Hunsdon, I presume?"

"We will not ask questions. Be so good as to mention your business."

"Ah, business, of course! Well, just this," replied the visitor, rummaging in his pockets. "Got my name, you know? Talbot & Castle, Lincoln's Inn, are my governors. And this is a paper, captain, which you'll have the goodness to look at, perhaps? This one; thank ye. Now, Captain Hunsdon, you'll take notice that you're served with the injunction of the Court of Chancery against holding any farther intercourse whatsoever, whether written, verbal, or oral (if that's any thing else), with Miss Helen Fleetlands of Riverwood Lawn, upon pain of commitment—and so forth; and 'pon my word, do you know, captain, if you'll allow me, being here, to offer advice as a friend, I should say that, as things go, the sooner you're off with that little party the better. My governors won't stand any nonsense, you may take your oath of that. So if you was just to drop her a line, as much as to say she'd better look out for some other gent in the way of company, you understand, and not get you quodded for nothing; why," concluded Mr. Jacobs, with a cool wink, "that would be about the c'rect move, in the eye of the law. Nice place you've got here. Very nice place indeed, captain."

"*What* do you call this?" demanded Ferdinand, holding up, as if by the nape, the document which had just been placed in his hands.

It was a closely-written sheet of foolscap-paper, bearing a peculiar purple adhesive stamp. I have a copy before me at this moment, but to transcribe it verbatim, would be useless trouble, and savor too much of the shop.

"Office copy of order on motion for injunction, captain—that's what it is. Like me to go through it with you? Come alo..g!" exclaimed Mr. Jacobs, preparing to draw a chair to the table, with a wistful glance at the fish and coffee, for he had traveled all the way from London upon a very early breakfast.

"Go through it, indeed!" returned Ferdinand contemptuously, crumpling, as he spoke, the piece of paper that had just come a hundred miles for his benefit, and tossing it into the fire. "Now, Mr. Jacobs, you may have simply done your duty, for all I know to the contrary, and if so, you had better begone at once; but if you venture to offer me another syllable of advice—as you are pleased to call it—or take that young lady's name into your mouth again in my presence, by George, sir, I will have you tumbled into a large pond by gamekeepers, before you are ten minutes older. There! I have rung for them. Don't wait, if you care about going home dry."

"Oh, I say though!" exclaimed Mr. Jacobs, combing his hair rapidly with his fingers, as he edged away in the direction of the door, "this won't do, you know, captain, at any price! This is contempt, you know—gross contempt. You'll find you've put your foot in it, captain, as sure as you stand there!"

"Send a couple of under-keepers here, directly," said Ferdinand to the servant who answered the bell. "Contempt, indeed!" taking the words in their social, rather than professional meaning.

"No, don't!" cried the young man from London. "Hi! show us out, somebody! Which is the way through these horrid long halls? I say, who let me in? Don't send the couple, footman! I'm going, captain—I'm going—gone ever so long ago!" And Mr. Jacobs was forthwith seen diving down the approach, with his heels clicking his shoulder-blades, at a pace which would be very insufficiently described as a "double."

The being tumbled in a horse-pond upon an empty stomach, is a process which, without being over-particular, most of us would wish to evade, even if certain that the aggressor would be never so quickly visited and chastised. This was just Mr. Jacobs's reflection. He had done his work, and even gone out of his way in supplementing it with gratuitous advice. But some people never know how to be grateful. Supposing that he had stood upon his rights, and defied Ferdinand to touch him at his peril; not all the men of Saintswood could have saved their young master from prison before the week was out, had he ruffled so much as one anointed hair of the Chancery-protected puppy.

However, as I said before, he had done his work. That foul scrap of foolscap placed in Ferdinand's hand, had laid a bar between himself and Helen. They were fellow-creatures still, if that was any comfort. But their lots had been shorn asunder by an edict. They were never to meet again without permission, on pain of imprisonment—upon his part, at least. By neither word or sign, look or line, must any communication take place. The Court of Chancery, which can marry nobody, had unmarried them by anticipation, and warned them thenceforth to walk apart, and with averted eyes.

Of course the apparition of this Lincoln's Inn gorilla had no influence whatever upon Captain Hunsdon's conduct. Helen and he met in the summer-house at the appointed hour, and had it all their own way. I am neither going to peep nor listen upon such an occasion. Earnestly, happily, daringly they talked, and laughed—I have no doubt—merrily over the episode of the young man from London, and at the ridiculous imbecility of guardians, Lord High Chancellors, and other meddlesome people in general. Nothing could be definitively settled just then, except that they must meet again, and that very often. And they parted at last, and how Helen got back to her room she never knew, but there seemed a rich and radiant mist around her pathway, and a band played a march in the air, or somewhere among the glooming yews; and the statues, as she hurried by, were all alive and excited; and she reached her own room at last, unobserved, and flung herself upon the bed in an ecstasy of joyous tears.

And how came it to pass that the admiral, knowing all he did, did not take, as it was his duty to take, due steps to render impossible this most undesirable meeting? The truth is, that Ferdinand's letter, which had been perused by his wife, in Helen's desk, had misled him altogether. It had never entered his mind that "the summer-house where their eyes first had met," referred to the little pavilion in his own grounds. Not having the slightest idea that his ward and Captain Hunsdon had ever met there, he naturally enough concluded that the words had reference to some spot at which, upon riding occasions, they might have indulged in an impromptu *tête-à-tête.* Thus it was that all his precautions turned out quite inadequate to prevent the interview; although he was not so ill served as to remain unaware of its accomplishment. In short, Captain Hunsdon had been observed leaving the grounds, and thenceforth his doom was sealed.

An attachment was issued, at the instance of the industrious Mr. Clover, and executed a few days later, when, as it happened, Ferdinand was wandering in the neighborhood of the bower, like a gentleman Peri who had lost his latch-key.

In case you should like to peruse a true copy of this ugly but influential document, here it is. Travelers, as we all know, when pursued by bears, are ready to fling overboard, for the examination of these animals, any thing which seems likely to attract their attention, and divert it, however transiently, from themselves. You must not be offended at the allusion. I am upon an unpleasant topic, and wish to close the present chapter as speedily as may be. Therefore, if you will good-naturedly snuff at the Writ, instead of pursuing me with a demand for minute particulars of an arrest which ought never to have become possible, I shall consider it a particular favor.

ATTACHMENT—(**Chancery.**)

VICTORIA, by the Grace of God of the United Kingdom of Great Britain and Ireland Queen, Defender of the Faith, to the Sheriff of Southernshire, GREETING. We command you to attach CAPTAIN FERDINAND HUNSDON of Saintswood in your county aforesaid, so as to have him before us in our Court of Chancery on the first day of March next, wheresoever the said Court shall then be, there to answer to us as well touching a Contempt which he, as it is alleged, hath committed against us, and also such other matters as shall be then and there laid to his Charge, and farther to perform and abide such Order as our said Court shall make in this behalf. And hereof fail not, and Bring this Writ with you. Witness Ourself at Westminster, etc., etc.

Such was the writ. The house-maid's story, already reported, was necessarily rubbish; but nevertheless Captain Hunsdon was in fact not only caught, but carried off to London; and conveyed in a cab to the Queen's Prison without superfluous ceremony, and with a certain business-like promptitude in the highest degree exasperating.

He was, however, neither lowered into a dungeon nor loaded with chains, nor even left all night with a lamp out of reach, a pitcher of water, and a crusty loaf, like the bad young man in the wood-cut. He was only marshaled into a tight little room, asked what he would like for dinner, and advised to send for his solicitor.

It was rather a scrape certainly; and might have been an ugly one for you or me. But, bah! The Chancery Lion must blink now and then—if only to keep himself wide awake for chance comers. And what came of it all you shall learn in due time.

A furious explosion followed, between Helen and the admiral. How it began is not so certain; but she reproached him with treachery, cowardice, and cruelty. And he, not being quick at repartee, and stung by unpalatable truisms, replied in terms of clumsy banter, and told her, with prolonged guffaws over his own delicate humor, that the captain had been arrested for poaching. That was all!

CHAPTER XXV.

A GREAT many years ago—more indeed than I find any satisfaction in reckoning—I used to sleep in a little white bed, in a well-filled nursery, at the top of a tall house in Wimpole Street.

Well, once it so happened that long after we children were asleep, and the place quiet for the night, the nurse and the nursery-maid took advantage of the mysterious stillness of the hour to set about the concoction of some elaborate cosmetic wherewith to sleek their soft ambrosial locks in the morning. I do not know the exact recipe which they had been fortunate enough to secure; and am almost reluctant to name the only two ingredients as to which I am morally certain. Gin and pig-suet are homely items, but great is the power of alchemy, and wonderful results are sometimes achieved out of very unpromising materials.

In this instance the process went on with unusual rapidity, for the gallipot, boiled over. There was a fizz and a gush of solid flame which licked the ceiling. There were shrill screams from the fair Rosecrucians, who expected nothing less than to go down alive and blazing into the cellarage.

The whole household was instantly in commotion. Every body came jumping up stairs, like moths to a candle; and the alarm was upon the point of being given up and down the street. Luckily there stood a large tub in the corner, wherein I was regularly soused at break of day; and it occurred to somebody, whose presence of mind must have been remarkable, to send the contents bodily into the immediate centre of danger. Under this hydropathic treatment the conflagration was soon subdued; and, barring a suffocating atmosphere of steam and hot rags, a few odd sparks wandering like flies, and a din which might have come from the Tower of Babel on fire, all immediate reason for disquietude was at an end.

"Jane—Jane! what's the matter?" exclaimed I, sitting up like a little white scarecrow in bed. "What makes the room full of smoke, and why are they throwing all the slops up the chimney, and what's every body up stairs for?"

"You lie down and go to sleep again, 'this very minute," replied the nursery-maid. "There isn't nothing at all the matter. It was the leg of our table came off. That's all."

I have always considered this as about the finest instance of a ready fib within the limit of my own personal experience. And I never hear an absurdly and palpably untrue reason given for any phenomenon without thinking of the leg of our nursery-table.

Of course the explanation with which the admiral had pretended to account for Ferdinand's abrupt disappearance, did not for one moment impose upon Helen. Indeed, it was never intended to do so. It was simply an intimation that if she chose to cry for her lover she would be treated like a baby, and must be content with a child's answer.

As you may suppose, she was desperately angry. She lost no time in hurrying to Mr. Salterton for sympathy and advice; and with eager lips and lighted eyes poured her whole peck of troubles into his indulgent ear. She went to him as a child to a parent, and told him all that had happened. No one knows what the confession cost her, but she wanted absolution for the past, and counsel for the future, and wisely began by making a clean breast.

I think that we are very often unfair toward people whom we consult in our difficulties. You, for instance, have been ill used, suppose, by A, and have resented it more or less becomingly. You bring me your version of the story, and expect my friendly sympathy, my entire acquiescence in your own conduct, and unqualified condemnation of A. And you are disappointed, because I give an opinion with some reserve, and don't express myself with indignant enthusiasm in your favor.

But remember: in the first place I may have my doubts about the merits of the case; and yet, without insincerity, decline informing you of my suspicions. If I think you unreasonably angry with A, I reflect, with some justice, that you may probably be still more so with me, should I take his part. Again, I have no personal quarrel myself with your antagonist; and though I may think that he has not behaved to you quite as well as he might, I don't intend to give you the opportunity of telling him so from me. Moreover, it may so happen that should I confess how exceedingly ill I think you have been used, I should stand pledged, in your opinion at least, to some active course of conduct, of which I can not expect you to perceive the disad-

vantage. Possibly too, in blaming A, I might be indirectly blaming myself. So that, if you choose to force your confidence upon me, you should recollect that there may be excellent reasons which prevent me, in spite of our friendship, from mixing myself up, with too much alacrity, in the quarrel, and perhaps turning your little duel with A into a triangular battle.

Could Helen only have known what was passing in the rector's mind, she would have had no cause to be dissatisfied. Rumor, of course, had been busy with the gross and extraordinary affront which had been put upon a person in Captain Hunsdon's position; and the most exciting accounts of the whole transaction were in free circulation. All this had caused him the deepest uneasiness, and Helen's unreserved confidence was received with a feeling of thankfulness and relief. He was aware of the feud which existed between the admiral and Lord St. Margarets, and rightly guessed the leading motive which had induced the former to act as he had done. He considered the admiral's conduct base, ungenerous, and unkind; and his indignation—for he could be famously indignant when he saw reason—blazed hot and high upon Helen's behalf.

Yet, what was he to say her? To speak his own thoughts—to set ward against guardian—would be simply breach of duty, both as a clergyman and a gentleman. He could only, in the kindest and most considerate manner, set before her the leading points of her position. During the next three years, at all events, the admiral had an unqualified right to her obedience. He stood in her father's place; and her father's will was explicit upon one subject at least—that of discouraging an early marriage. She and Ferdinand wouldn't be the battered old couple they might possibly imagine, even were her bridal morning postponed till twenty-one. Even an additional two years would be nothing very serious. In the mean time she must wait and be patient.

"I know all that, Mr. Salterton," interrupted Helen. "I could be as patient, I suppose, as most people, if there were nothing but misfortune the matter; but you must see that, in a thousand ways, I have been cruelly ill used. One word would have been enough at the beginning—but to leave things to go on by themselves, and to keep spies peeping without warning, and then to do this at last, is enough to break one's heart. I only know that he has forfeited all my respect; while, as to any sort of confidence in his honor, that's gone and done for, long ago!"

"I see," observed the rector. "And if he should, by any possibility, wish to be heard upon his own account, you would rather that he held his tongue?"

"Certainly. I should wish to have nothing more to say to him. I wouldn't sleep another night in his house, if I could help it."

"And you would punish him, I suppose, if you had the power?"

"I should send him to jail directly," replied Helen, apparently surprised at the question.

"And show him neither justice nor mercy?"

"Lots of justice, and very little mercy," returned the young lady. "I see what you mean, Mr. Salterton. You want to show me what might be said upon his account. No use at all! When a person does me a plain downright wrong, and says, 'beg pardon,' I'll shake hands and forgive him, any day. When he's been mean and malicious I'll forgive him, without shaking hands. But when he's been both mean and malicious, and wants to palaver afterward, and talk about good intentions and all that sort of thing, why that party goes to jail, quick, when I'm Queen, and doesn't come out till long after he's shockingly sorry. Do you think me very wicked?"

"Not in the least, my dear. I don't doubt but that you have cause to be angry. Turn the matter over coolly, and we'll talk again. Perhaps I am rather too much of your mood to be an useful guide at present. Only let us recollect two things—first, that to condemn a person unheard, even if we could march him to the tread-mill at once, is an incomplete and savage sort of satisfaction; secondly, that to give ourselves the trouble of inquiring whether his conduct, looking at it in all possible lights, may not admit of some sort of excuse, is to assume a much worthier position than to sit scolding from below, like somebody who has been stepped upon. Isn't it so, Helen?".

"Perhaps. I dare say you are right. Only, you see, Mr. Salterton, I do so wish that all this trouble had happened to somebody else!"

"So do I, with all my heart! What business have you with any trouble at all? Only, since things are so ordered, you will have to show how somebody else ought to behave. Let us talk of this again another day."

I have preserved the above scraps of conversation entire, partly, perhaps, as being in some degree characteristic of the parties—partly, because, to a certain extent, it may have done good in its way. People of Helen's temperament are much more easily guided than driven, and it might not have been wise to challenge her to argue the matter fairly out. A quiet course of sympathy, without prejudice, as lawyers say, to what might possibly be advanced on the other side, was best calculated to calm her mind, and allow it to work for good. Any appeal to higher motives might probably, at the moment, have been unsuccessful and mischievous. Unless religion be the ruling and habitual guide of life—and alas! how few among us dare suppose that it is so in their own case!—it is dragged into play at an immense disadvantage when its precepts are suggested as a consolation to the spirit smarting under a direct sense of injury and injustice. Passions must calm, and reason in some degree regain her balance before we can accept a divine arbitration, and patiently regard the oppressor, safe under its eternal shield.

With Helen, a very long time, I am sorry to say, was occupied in this cooling process. She broke her whip, and vowed that she would never mount Camilla again. All the admiral's advances were repelled with supreme disdain; and his wife's daily invitations to tracts and tea disrespectfully declined. She wandered all day about the place in moody despair, wishing almost that she could only see her way out of the dreadful labyrinth of life. That last, one passionate hour with Ferdinand burned like wild-fire within her brain: but he was gone—she knew not whither: she was controlled—she scarcely knew by what invisible power: her future, her fortune, and her freedom were in the hands of one whom she deliberately regarded as a tyrant and a villain. Existence had become insupportable.

This could not last forever. One morning she surprised the admiral and his wife by suddenly assuming much of her old demeanor. She actually volunteered conversation at breakfast; caught perch before luncheon, and quoted one of her own tracts to Mrs. Mortlake, which so delighted that lady, that Helen was in no small danger of figuring, herself, in some future page, as an instance of the efficacy of good advice laid on thick. More than this, she confessed to her instructress that she stood self-convicted of an indolent and selfish life, and would like nothing better than to be put in the way of doing needle-work for charitable purposes. This was adding fruit to flower; and, though she was no great hand at thread and thimble, her industry was rewarded with all praise, and stimulated by unlimited supplies of raw material.

Probably you may have already suspected the secret of this mysterious change in Helen's behavior. If not, without expressing any opinion whatever as to your perspicacity, I will proceed to inform you. She had resolved to run away.

It was a wild, sudden determination, the result at first of a momentary and wayward impulse; but the idea throve and strengthened the more it was reflected upon. Her life at Riverwood had become simply intolerable, and the prospect of liberty, excitement and adventure, even to the very limited extent in which a self-emancipated young lady could expect to revel in such forbidden luxuries, had an intoxicating charm for Helen. This, however, was not all. If she could only get clear away for a fortnight or three weeks, she knew that the consternation produced by her disappearance would be feebly described by the admiral's favorite simile of "The Devil to Pay." Something was certain to turn up. Very probably, as her limited experience of Chancery procedure suggested, her guardian would find himself in preciously hot water upon her account. Serve him right for not taking better care of her. Nothing would be more likely to set the Court going again than the news that its ward was upon her travels with nobody's leave—least of all, her appointed guardian's. Why, it might even end in her being removed from his custody altogether, and handed over to Mr. Salterton, whom Sophy Hunter's old brother had acutely indicated as the next card in the pack. Perhaps it might result in something better still—who knew? The Court of Chancery, as she was aware from the newspapers, is perpetually reversing its own decrees. Suppose it did so in the present instance, when the whole story came before it again. Wouldn't Ferdinand be required to marry her at once, or go back to prison? How was that, she wondered, as a dry point of law? At all events, the oppressive mystery by which she felt surrounded would, somehow or another, be infallibly cleared up. Questions would be asked and answered; and, come what might, any thing was preferable to the hopeless, helpless present.

I don't mean, in my capacity as a Chancery barrister, to commit myself entirely to this view of the case. But the scheme certainly had one or two possible advantages; always provided that it could successfully be carried into effect.

How to get away, in the first place, and how to dispose of herself when this was done, in the second, were the chief points to be settled; and it is only doing Helen justice to say that these problems were deliberately and skillfully worked out.

Merely to escape from the Lawn was an operation which presented no great difficulty. Beyond a prohibition against leaving the grounds unattended, and a pretty strict amount of surveillance undertaken by Miss Crimp, she was at liberty to do much as she pleased; and there were plenty of places where she could slip out upon the high road whenever she thought proper. This, however, although a step certainly, was only a step in the direction of freedom. Her only means of actual escape lay in availing herself of the railway; and this was not quite so easy. There were two stations within reach; one, as we are already aware, at St. Mark's-on-the-Sea, the other some four miles from the Lawn, at Bunnytail Bottom.

But at both of these stations she was perfectly well known to the authorities; and she suspected, probably not without reason, that they might have received hints from the admiral which would lead to highly disagreeable results if she walked in alone for a ticket.

A disguise was the obvious resource, and it was with this end in view that she fell in so amiably with Mrs. Mortlake's schemes, and stitched clothes for poor people like a regular seamstress. In a few weeks she had managed to provide herself, on the sly, with a print-gown, a colored petticoat, a plain check shawl, and close straw bonnet; partly her own handiwork, partly purloined from the charity-stores of her preceptress, to which her diligence had obtained for her free admission. All these, together with a covered basket containing sundry little matters, neither necessarily nor unnecessarily to be mentioned, she quietly smuggled away, and hid piecemeal in one of the great cupboards of her house in the garden, of which she carefully kept the key.

This was the secret of her whole scheme. When the materials for disguise were complete, nothing could be easier than to stroll out some afternoon—change her clothes in the summer-house, leaving her usual dress snugly locked up, and march off whither she listed. She determined, farther, to carry away nothing whatever from her dressing-room which could possibly be missed, so that the real meaning of her absence should remain unsuspected as long as possible; and that, when search came to be made for her, it should be assumed as certain that she had departed wearing the identical costume in which she had been last seen. This would of course throw every body upon a wrong scent, and was a conception for which she naturally gave herself credit.

As to how she should dispose of herself when fairly launched upon the world, like a parlor-maid unattached, her projects were perhaps a little in the air. This part of the programme, naturally, did not admit of being arranged quite so artistically as the other. Indeed, if one could map out every thing in the shape of adventure beforehand, the "going in quest" would be clear waste of traveling and time. Nevertheless, Helen had a scheme of her own, to begin with; but, as I suppose you will not close these pages without accompanying her to the end of her rambles, I shall not lose ground at present by anticipating what you may, in due time, discover for yourself.

I ought to mention, perhaps, that out of her last instalment of pocket-money, Helen had nearly twenty pounds at her command, which seemed amply sufficient for her purpose. It is true that she owed the greater part of this sum to her milliner and other similar claimants; but they would have to wait for their money. It was an unlucky necessity.—part of the fortune of war.

<hr />

CHAPTER XXVI.

LORD ST. MARGARETS's diplomacy had been really a success. He had had a difficult game to play, and had played it thoroughly to his liking. In the first place, with all his aversion to the alliance which his son was so anxious to thrust upon him, he had never allowed one syllable to escape his lips which Ferdinand could by any possibility construe as exacting obedience, or indicating any unwillingness to let him follow up the object of his own choice. Lord St. Margarets had known perfectly well, from the beginning, that the match, for the time being, was out of the question. The admiral, he was persuaded, would refuse his assent to any arrangement of the kind, so long as his pleasure required to be consulted at all. But that piece of information he had been careful to allow his son to acquire for himself. It was quite needless to urge what was absolute matter-of-fact, just as the sagacious engineer leaves the enemy to blunder upon a bona fide battery without warning, while he makes every possible parade of works which he would rather should not be attempted at all.

In the next place, his off-hand disparagement of Helen and her possessions, so careless and indirect as to appear like mere good-natured criticism, had its own time and purpose. That it would have no immediate effect he was well aware. But it would rest in his son's mind, nevertheless. And when he found himself suddenly and rudely thwarted at Riverwood, then was the hour when it might be expected to bear its fruit.

A man in the first bitterness of disappointment—one who has beheld his darling object in life either vanishing altogether, beyond reach and hope, or drifting silently ahead into the shadowy and uncertain future, hates to be comforted by those who would tell him that the prize, after all, was nothing worth. Why should people insult his judgment and mock his misery at the same time? But, let him alone, and that is, probably, the very consolation which will ultimately spring up in his own mind. All this had been foreseen by the thoughtful father, who had scattered just sufficient encouragement for the soothing growth, whenever it spontaneously took place.

He was a little startled, certainly, shortly after his arrival in Grosvenor Square, by receiving a letter from Ferdinand dated "The Queen's Prison," and informing him of all that had occurred. Not but that it tickled him extremely, in one sense; but he felt vexed with his son for making such a fool of himself, and considered that the Court had been hasty, and taken a great liberty into the bargain. However, he wrote a very kind note in reply, informing Ferdinand that he would take immediate steps to procure his release, in order to get into any fresh scrapes he thought proper.

What these "immediate steps" were, you will probably never know. Lord Chancellor Bacon, they say, was open to arguments more tangible than those employed in our "windy war," and his wink was as good as his bond. No writer in a penny paper, nowadays, would hazard such imputation upon even an imaginary judge—at least when deciding between conflicting parties. But Ferdinand's transgression might, in an indulgent point of view, be looked upon as a mere question of violated etiquette, and disposed of without vindictive displeasure. And if his father couldn't arrange thus much, why where would have been the use of being Lord St. Margarets at all, and as good a Conservative as the chancellor?.

In the mean time, having—in disregard of Mr. Jacobs's friendly caution—so rapidly succeeded in getting himself "quodded for nothing," or rather for love, which in popular phraseology means much the same thing, Ferdinand had ample leisure to review his own conduct, and find excuses, if he could, for what, considered in calmer moments, looked far too much like rash and reckless folly.

He would have given a great deal to have been able to undo much of the past, both upon Helen's account and his own. His father's solicitor could only inform him that his position was not one to be trifled with. He stood committed to prison in downright earnest, and during the pleasure of the Court. Beyond question, all intercourse with Miss Fleetlands must be suspended until that young lady attained twenty-one; and since it could serve no possible purpose to remain where he was, merely to indulge in the reflection that she was daily growing older, the sooner he made his submission, and took leave of the Borough Road, the better. The necessary steps should at once be taken. Probably the chancellor might be disposed to view the case indulgently. It was just one of those matters which nobody could prophesy about.

Shortly afterward, an intimation was received from the Lord Chancellor, directing that Ferdinand should attend at his private room in Lincoln's Inn, the following afternoon, at three o'clock. Thither he was escorted in a cab. Business was encroaching upon romance.

He was received with a degree of distant and freezing gravity, which might have chilled even the courage of a Victoria Cross. It was not until after some moments of saturnine silence, that his lordship condescended to appear aware of his presence, and ultimately to address him; and when he did, it was in a low, icy tone, and in syllables so far apart, that you might have counted them easily.

He was grieved, he said, and surprised, to see a person in Captain Hunsdon's high position, wantonly encountering the displeasure of the Court. For his conduct there could be no excuse. He had been warned, and had slighted the warning. He had disobeyed, and it was for the Court to weigh the circumstances of that act of disobedience, and inflict commensurate punishment. One consideration alone, induced him to stay his hand. Upon perusing certain papers before him, he perceived a statement to the effect that, in the event of his being discharged from custody, it was intended that Captain Hunsdon should at once leave England to join his regiment, then on foreign service. With a proper assurance to that effect, with a sufficient undertaking upon the part of Captain Hunsdon that he would thenceforth hold no communication whatever with the ward, until she should attain the age of twenty-one years—and upon Captain Hunsdon's making due submission, and paying all costs of his commitment, he was disposed to direct his discharge from custody. His lordship trusted that a warning so lenient would neither be misconstrued nor forgotten. Captain Hunsdon might be removed.

There was nothing for it but to grin and knock under. Ferdinand would perhaps have been pleased to hear that, just before he entered the chancellor's room, Admiral Mortlake had quitted it, after a "wigging" which would have astonished a midshipman, and for which he had been expressly summoned up to town.

The Lord Chancellor in fact had told him, in those peculiarly reassuring accents for which he was famous, that he considered his conduct in allowing Helen to appear in the hunting-field so insufficiently attended and escorted, was a breach of his duty, grave and scandalous; that out of regard for her, whom the Court would presume to be innocent, he had directed the present proceedings to take place in his private room; but that, had it been otherwise, he should have visited him with marked censure at the bar of the Court. He warned him against supposing that he was himself the judge as to who might be a proper match for his ward—which it was for a higher intelligence alone to determine; observed that he intended to consider at his leisure, whether or not it was fit and proper that further inquiries in the matter should be directed, and concluded by pointedly desiring the admiral to observe, that what had already befallen Helen was nothing less than a marked calamity, the result of most grievous negligence—and to pay all his own costs of the application.

After this benediction, the admiral jumped into his cab, firing broadsides right and left all the way to the station. Even the ticket-porters themselves, those dreamy sentinels of the virgin apron and the pewter badge, who see a little of this sort of thing occasionally at the Court door, roused up sufficiently to nudge one another, as he drove away.

Selfish people have at least one considerable pull over others, which need not be grudged them, considering that in most respects they are at no small disadvantage. Your thoroughly selfish man generally has the credit—to which most of us aspire—of knowing his own mind. Nothing conduces more to this sort of self-acquaintance than the caring very little what other people may feel, and not a bit in the world what they may think or say. It was Admiral Mortlake's custom to make up his own mind, and then act upon his resolution as inflexibly as if he had only his late ship's company to deal with.

And it so happened that, just as Helen's little preparations were upon the point of completion, her guardian, one morning at breakfast, announced a plan which drove her either to put her project into execution without delay, or to consign it to indefinite postponement.

It had occurred to him, while smoking his afternoon pipe in the grim yew avenue, and meditating upon his late encounter with the keeper of Her Majesty's conscience, that a trip to the Continent would be the very thing under existing circumstances. Helen had latterly begun to behave so very much better, that she deserved some reward. A month abroad—so, in his abysmal ignorance of the female heart, he imagined—would be quite sufficient to change the whole current of her thoughts, to fill her mind with new ideas, and cause all recent trouble to be regarded as a dream of the past. Paris cured most people, and a round home, through the pleasant roads of Normandy and Maine, would settle the business.

To tell the truth, he rather wanted to get out of the way himself. He couldn't think of Lincoln's Inn without choking. He had revenged himself, after his fashion, upon Lord St. Margarets, and found himself cut by the county. People who had previously tolerated him as eccentric, now avoided him as cracked. Lord St. Margarets, indeed, secretly chuckling over the whole affair, lost no opportunity of referring to it as an excellent joke, and declaring that it served Ferdinand perfectly right, and would be the best possible lesson to him against making promiscuous acquaintance in future. But this was not the popular view. Mortlake could not even walk through the village without being saluted by shrill cries of "Cotched another capting, guv'nor?" and similar specimens of juvenile wit. Rough allusions to himself and his behavior were chalked upon his park fence. Mr. Salterton's studied silence upon the subject was a reproach in itself, while Sir Philip Chevy, and young fellows of the Scatterley stamp, threw all delicacy to the winds, and chaffed him in a free-and-easy manner, which he felt plainly enough was intended to be insulting. In short, he was in a very bad position.

The proposition was a startling one to Helen. The idea of the admiral, of all people, talking of going to France was almost too extraordinary to be credible. Under happier auspices, she might have been delighted with such a change; but the prospect of traveling in such company was not amusing, and she felt an irrepressible misgiving that the proposal was intended to cover some deep-laid scheme of which she herself was the object. A vague sense of insecurity tormented her. She felt that, once across the Channel, she would be perfectly in her guardian's power, and the story of a month's trip might be really only a blind. Young ladies, who had been even less imprudent than herself, had been coaxed into convents, and expiated their incaution by life-long imprisonment in a human menagerie. Was it possible that the admiral had some intention of this kind, and proposed to return and take possession of her fortune, leaving her to the uncovenanted mercies of a Lady Superior? Vague and childish as were these alarms, they were sufficient to induce her, at any risk, to put her scheme of escape into immediate execution.

This was Monday. On Thursday the admiral had proposed to leave Riverwood, and take the early train from St. Mark's to London. "Wednesday must be my day," thought Helen, and proceeded to remark how very pleasant it all would be, and to wonder when they might expect to find themselves in Paris.

Upon the whole this sudden arrangement seemed rather in her favor. Her plans were already matured; her summer-house-hidden disguise complete; and the bustle of preparation would probably render her task all the more easy.

Nor was it without a sensation of mischievous delight that she reflected upon the strange consternation which would follow her sudden and inexplicable disappearance at such an unlucky moment; and upon the fine unpacking which would have to take place in the morning.

Wednesday arrived at last; and although, to do Helen justice, she had never for one moment wavered in her determination, or allowed her mind to flinch from the enterprise, it must be confessed that, as the hour drew near, her excitement became almost uncontrollable. She had determined to get away, if possible, about half-past five o'clock, which would enable her to reach the railway station shortly after sunset; but, as the story of her travels belongs to another department of these pages, I shall at present say no more of her movements than is absolutely necessary. Fortunately for her, the house was in that outrageous state of bustle and disorder which commonly precedes a journey upon the part of people altogether new to road and rail, and which is so highly amusing to seasoned old stagers like ourselves. Still more fortunately, Mr. Salterton happened to be just then absent, upon a month's holiday. To have taken leave of him under the circumstances would have been more than embarrassing to Helen. It would have been impossible.

She had, as you may imagine, been at Mrs. Mortlake's beck and call during the whole of the forenoon. The good lady hated the projected journey more than can be told; and what with providing against every possible contingency, and anticipating every conceivable disaster, gave one the idea of a person booked for the moon, and laying in traveling-stock at short notice by the light of nature. In fact Helen was called away from an agonizing discussion as to the best method of economizing space, as presented in the empty skull of a huge imperial, by a summons from her guardian to his study below.

She had been sent for to rummage among the book-shelves for an old road-book, or "itinerary," of Northern France, which he had some idea would be of use to them in their expedition. But while spending a good deal of time upon her knees to no purpose, the front door bell suddenly rang, and "Mr. Clover and Mr. Twick" were announced as visitors.

"Don't go," said the admiral sharply, as Helen rose to leave the room. "Find the book first, at all events, or we shall start without it to a certainty. Ha! Good-evening, Clover. I am happy to see you, Mr. Twick."

It was evident that business of some sort was about to be transacted, for a broad new parchment deed, crackling like a bonfire, was unfolded by Mr. Twick, and the admiral produced a bundle of brown documents upon his part from the recesses of the iron Ark. And then, biscuits and sherry were rung for, and an animated conversation took place, the purport of which was not clear to Helen.

"Three thousand pounds, we make the mort-

gage debt," began Mr. Twick, a jolly-looking, chestnut-colored man of five-and-forty, with a curly head. "And half a year's interest, less income-tax, is seventy-three, two, six. You had a fancy, sir, Clover tells me, for the money in cash—so I've brought you three thousand-pounders. Not every day one has the chance of handling a thousand-pound note. Pretty paper, isn't it?"

"Ha, ha!" growled the admiral. "You've had your laugh against me as you came along, I'll be bound. But money is money, Mr. Twick, and if you'd lost what I've lost by trusting to banks and clerks and all that sort of humbug, you'd do as I do—keep a strong box of your own. Give you a week to see your way through *that* door," added he, glancing over his shoulder at the Ark. "Now you want a receipt, I suppose, ha?"

"And your execution of this reconveyance, please," replied Mr. Twick, spreading his deed upon the table; "and then Clover and I will look over my client's documents together. This is the parcel?"

"Those are the deeds, sir, as I received them. Probably you will attest my signature. I deliver this as my act and deed. Is all square, sir, ha?"

"All right, sir." And the admiral, after having carefully scanned the three thousand-pound notes, and compared their numbers with a list handed to him by Mr. Twick, enclosed them in a great red leather pocket-book; and placing it upon one of the iron shelves of the Ark, shut the door with a bang which made the room shake.

"Safe investment," observed Mr. Clover with a slimy smile.

"So I fancy, at all events," returned the admiral dryly. "For the present, at least. I have been advised to give matters a few weeks' turn before making the reinvestment which I purpose. Things are going down in the city."

"There was a wonderful safe, shown at the exhibition of '62, by a man from Cork," remarked Mr. Twick, sorting his papers. "You should have seen it, admiral. You locked the door, and then dropped the keys into a little slit in the lid, which shut up of itself—snap! and there you were, safe as a church."

"How the devil did you get it open again?" inquired Mr. Clover, without taking his eyes off the table. Mr. Clover was a stubborn man of business, and beyond a joke.

"Ah! that's just what lost him a medal. The jury asked the very same question. Unlucky, wasn't it?"

"Can you and Clover stay and drink a bottle of port?" interposed the admiral. "We dine at seven."

"Thank you, impossible! I have to be in London again to-night. Directly I've looked over these deeds of my client's with Clover, I must be off to St. Marks, and catch the six o'clock up train, if I can."

"Sorry for it. You shall give me a cast to

St. Marks in your carriage, if you will. I have a matter to attend to there, which I quite forgot this morning. We are off to the Continent, all of us, to-morrow. Helen, tell Mrs. Mortlake where I've gone, and ask her to put off dinner. I shall be back by half-past seven to a second."

This was all in Helen's favor. Her guardian would be out of the way, which was one good thing; while, by suppressing the message to his wife, a great deal of bewilderment and mystification would be introduced at the critical moment, which was still better. For the admiral was a rigidly punctual man in the matter of his meals. All sailors are so by habit. And to find him missing at dinner-time, would be almost enough to throw her own disappearance into the shade, and make his wife believe that chaos was come again.

The examination of the papers lasted some quarter of an hour, during which the admiral retired into an adjoining dressing-room to change his coat. At last the documents were pronounced satisfactory, and stuffed by Mr. Twick into his great black leather bag. Another glass of sherry was filled all round to clench the business, and in two minutes more the post-chaise was clattering through the lodge gates.

Helen looked at her watch. It was twenty minutes past five. "Now or never!" thought she, and was just leaving the room, when a sudden idea struck her. It was one of those presentient impulses which have occurred to most of us at some period of our lives, and of which it is impossible to give any reasonable account. She walked straight into her guardian's dressing-room, and examined the coat which he had just taken off. A jingle in the breast-pocket, in which she had observed him deposit the keys of the Ark, rewarded her curiosity. They were actually there! clean forgotten, and left behind! Oh, man of Cork, you should have had this tale to tell, when the jurors waxed so foolishly funny over your invincible strong box.

With light, deliberate step, Helen proceeded to the Ark, unlocked it, and put the red leather book into her dress-pocket. She then refastened the door, replaced the keys exactly where she had found them, gave one glance round the room, and was gone.

I don't know that I am bound to account for every action which I may happen to have to record. What on earth could have possessed her, if I may be allowed the vulgarism, to carry off these bank notes, passes my comprehension altogether. Whether it was a mild access of kleptomania—which, however, is commonly supposed to molest ladies under circumstances to which she had no pretension; whether she indistinctly fancied that she was securing a "material guarantee" for the restoration of thus much of her fortune, at all events; whether it was sheer mischief, such as prompts the Gazza Ladra to make away with silver spoons, which are useless and out of place in her rubbishy nest, I have not the smallest idea. My conjecture, were I bound to conjecture at all, would be, that

she was simply bent upon making the greatest row possible, and forcing on, at all hazards, a general explanation. Felony was certainly a strong measure; but a young lady who has been wronged, and is bent upon righting herself, is not apt to stick at trifles.

Certainly, if she could only have been invisibly present at Riverwood that evening, her satisfaction ought to have been unbounded.

She had been missed, almost immediately after her departure, by the ever-watchful Crimp, who lost no time in informing Mrs. Mortlake of her suspicions.

For a long time that lady was perfectly incredulous, and stubbornly refused to see any thing remarkable in the story. Miss Fleetlands was somewhere about the place, she was certain—perhaps in the shrubbery, the garden, or the stables, and would re-appear in due time. Crimp was talking nonsense!

But when another half hour had passed away, and Helen was still unaccounted for, she was obliged to confess that it was a strange business altogether. A rigid examination of her bedroom only made matters more perplexing than ever. There was her trunk, half packed, just as Crimp had left it in the morning. Her toilet-table was exactly as usual. Not one single article—even so much as a brush or comb—had been removed. Not one iota of wearing apparel was missing from its proper place. That she had run away, seemed out of the question. Run away, without any thing but what she actually carried upon her back! But where in the world could she be?

"May have made away with herself, you see, mum," suggested Crimp, adopting an explanation of absence which always suggests itself to waiting-maids. "My aunt's mother, mum, drowned herself, fourteen years come Michaelmas, with nothing on but a strong calico chemise; and she having to walk four miles, too, to get to the water; and, what's more, was carried eleven miles down stream before she was swallowed up—leastways, it was that distance before she was hooked out of the river by a strange gentleman in a morning punt, if you'll believe me, mum, and she not able to swim no more than me, which is the most amazing and fabulous part of it all."

"Nonsense!" replied her mistress. "Ladies don't make away with themselves."

"Then she may be pursuing of her captain, mum, in a po-chay and pair, which, to my mind, she is morally doing at this solemn moment."

As Captain Hunsdon happened to be just then in the very middle of the Bay of Biscay, this supplementary suggestion was repressed with equal brevity.

"I wish your master were at home," groaned Mrs. Mortlake. "I wonder what keeps him out on this particular evening!"

"Lassy me, mum! Well, I thought of course you knew. The admiral, mum, set out of his own accord, an hour ago or more, in a glass coach with two lawyers—Lawyer Clover and another, and drove right away down the St. Mark's Road. Quite fearful fast they went, mum."

Mrs. Mortlake started at the news. Not of course that she supposed he had eloped himself, and smuggled off Helen, disguised as a couple of solicitors; but his going without leaving word appeared exceedingly strange, and things seemed to be tumbling into confusion around her, like the difficulties of a dream.

"I can not understand it," she gasped at last, subsiding into an arm-chair. "Crimp, let nobody in the house suppose that Miss Helen is not in her room. Go about exactly as usual. The admiral will certainly be home by dinnertime. He will know what to do. At least I hope so!"

But when dinner-time arrived and passed, and the admiral was as scarce as his ward, she really felt that if the floor were to open under her it would be more vexatious than surprising in such a bewildering *bouleversement*.

Her husband returned at last, and entered his study alone, by the garden door. He had already missed his precious keys, and was annoyed to the last degree at his own carelessness. Hastily lighting a candle, he plunged into his dressingroom, and was gratified by hearing their clink in his coat pocket. To unlock the Ark, and ascertain that all was secure, was the work of a second. Imagine, if you can, his blast of rage and execration at the sight of the empty shelf! It was something too terrible for description. His face turned absolute indigo; and if he hadn't torn open his necktie, to let the oaths out, he would certainly have burst upon the spot. Who the thief could have been he couldn't form the slightest conjecture; but oh, my goodness, if he could only have caught him, then and there!

"Gone—gone, ma'am!" he shouted, as his wife came hurrying into the room. "Gone, since I left home, not two hours ago!"

"Isn't it dreadful?" exclaimed Mrs. Mortlake, thinking, of course, that he referred to Helen. "What in the world will become of us? Where did you see her last?"

"In this confounded safe, ma'am; locked up with this infernal key! I left it in my pocket, like a fool as I am, when I went across to St. Mark's—and look there!" pointing to the empty shelf.

"Why, surely you never locked her up there when you went out!" cried the lady, looking horrified in her turn. "What an awful thing to do!"

"Of course I did! What else do you suppose safes are made for? And why the plague do you keep on calling it 'her,' like a Welsh woman?" retorted the admiral, thundering with rage.

"I'm talking of Helen!" shrieked the lady.

"And I'm talking of a red leather pocketbook, with three thousand-pound notes in it! What about Helen? She's not gone too—is she?"

A vigorous explanation followed, during which each party endeavored to throw the blame of the young lady's disappearance upon the other, with

the result usual in such cases. The mystery of the pocket-book was however cleared up at once. It was morally certain that Helen must have taken it, and almost equally so that it would some day or other be accounted for. Indeed the admiral leaned to the belief that she had only removed it out of sheer mischief, and hidden it somewhere about the place,—not a very welcome piece of pleasantry, by the bye, considering its contents.

As regarded Helen herself, he at once formed a conjecture which, although incorrect in fact, was plausible enough at the time. He fancied that some deep-laid scheme, at the instigation of Captain Hunsdon, was at the bottom of the whole affair. Somebody had driven by in a carriage, according to previous arrangement, and picked Helen up; while, probably through some misunderstanding as to the time, or in the confusion of the moment, she had been unable to make the slightest preparation for her journey. That, he fancied, would account for what was otherwise inexplicable, and instantly addressed himself to active measures.

Applauding Mrs. Mortlake for her previous discretion, and desiring her upon no account to allow the truth to be known in the house, but to say that Miss Fleetlands had gone to bed with a severe headache, and was to be kept quiet, as the only chance of being able to start in the morning, he sent a servant off at once, to procure the immediate re-attendance of Mr. Clover. In his note to that gentleman, he desired him to telegraph to London for a couple of detectives from Scotland Yard. In the mean time slops and dry toast were ordered up stairs for Helen, and the secret was kept with entire success.

As may well be supposed, the conference between the admiral and his solicitor, when the latter arrived about ten, was long and anxious.

The predicament of the Chancery guardian of a runaway ward is never a nice one; for the Court is apt to be horribly inquisitive in such cases, and to overhaul the unlucky custodian with a degree of acrimony which it would be difficult to exaggerate. In the present instance the admiral, who had no mind for another excursion to Lincoln's Inn, had determined upon one desperate course of proceeding—not, as his legal adviser warned him, free from very serious risk, but still offering some chance of preserving Helen's name from the greatest possible scandal, and allowing her guardian, at the same time, to creep undetected out of a most awkward scrape.

If, by any ingenuity, the servants could be so far imposed upon as to believe that the morrow's journey took place with Helen in company, the story of her indiscretion might possibly be concealed altogether. The detectives and Mr. Clover could obviously do their work just as well, during the admiral's absence, as if he were present at Riverwood; while to break off the journey at the last moment, would be simply to invite every body's curiosity, and probably ensure the discovery of the truth within twenty-four hours. In the mean time, should Helen be recaptured, she could be quietly conveyed to London, and her guardian telegraphed for at any moment. Nothing compromising need ever transpire; and they must all take better care for the future.

Such was the plan of operations which it was ultimately determined to adopt. The two advertisements, which you may recollect already to have read, were at the same time sketched out by the admiral, and " settled" by Mr. Clover.

The first, you will remember, had reference to the bank notes. The amount represented by these securities was far too large to be trifled with. Whatever might have become of the pocket-book, its restoration was well worth the one hundred and fifty pounds offered, irrespective of the fact that, if recovered at all, it might not improbably lead to some trace of Helen herself. The story of its having been lost upon the high road was merely a fable, intended to make matters easy, should it ever happen to turn up.

The second, and descriptive, advertisement, which had so serious an effect upon poor Petersfeld, it was arranged should be suppressed until the detectives had had a fair run. Guarded as its terms intentionally were, they could scarcely fail to excite an undesirable amount of general curiosity. Besides, although the admiral would at the moment readily have paid down five hundred pounds, were that the only condition of having his ward safely back again, he winced exceedingly at the notion of handing over such a sum, so long as there was the faintest hope of obtaining his object at a less ruinous rate.

Nothing at present remains but to describe the device by which the household were to be deluded into the belief that Helen was actually of the party next morning. It was the joint invention of Mrs. Mortlake and her maid, and as a specimen of what very superfine people might stigmatize as low cunning, may be recorded.

Crimp, for her own part, undertook to leave Helen's room in such a state that no house-maid alive would suspect that she had not slept and bathed as usual. And in the mean time she carried so many messages down stairs from Miss Helen, that although to serve her was the delight of the servants' hall, people began to think her exacting.

In the next place, a half-length figure, composed of air cushions, traveling wraps, and the like, was dressed up in Helen's hat and burnous in the admiral's room.

When the carriage was at the door, and after Helen's trunk had been ostentatiously corded in the hall, it was easy enough to get the servants out of the way, while her bedroom door was thrown open, and the figure handed by Mrs. Mortlake and her maid into the farther corner of the carriage, instantly followed by the lady; the admiral engaging the coachman's attention upon the opposite side. The transaction, taking place under the carriage portico, could not be criticised from the windows, which was an advantage. In short, nothing could have been more successful.

G

Nobody had the slightest suspicion—as how should they ? Tricks like these are easily played when no one is upon the alert, or concerned in detecting them. Otherwise, you may deceive children and white mice, but not the fellow-creatures who live under your dining-room. What you know, they know : make up your mind to that.

During the drive to St. Mark's, Helen's effigy was quietly dismantled ; and, while the admiral talked to the driver, Mrs. Mortlake and Crimp walked into the station.

That coachman, honest fellow, could and would have sworn, had need been, that he had driven a gentleman, two ladies, and a maid to the railway station upon that especial Thursday. Every servant at Riverwood would have abetted him in his involuntary perjury, and not only pledged his or her oath to the effect that Helen accompanied their master and mistress, but sworn that they saw her in the carriage. So much for human testimony.

It had been arranged that they should arrive at St. Mark's a little before the train started, in order to give the admiral time for a flying interview with Mr. Clover. In that gentleman's office he found the two detectives, just arrived from London, looking as like conjurers as they could, and asking questions with rich gravity —like medical men. And here let me assure you that you will hear no more of these worthies. I never yet encountered a detective in a story who was not about as much like the original as an average Englishman is to the John Bull of a Paris novelist. I declare that sooner than meet with such a character in a friend's book, I would find one under my own bed.

It was then settled, for reasons hinted at in the outset, that instead of inserting the names of Mr. Clover's London agents—Messrs. Talbot & Castle—in the advertisement, Mr. Bloss should be the person to receive applications, and pay the reward, if claimed.

It was Mr. Bloss, if you remember, who, a great many years ago, prepared the will which made Colonel Fleetlands a millionaire ;—who wrote, upon old Nettleton's death, to apprise him of his good fortune ; and who had actually received Helen herself at Southampton, upon her first landing in England. Naturally, as Nettleton's solicitor, he had been concerned with Talbot & Castle in the administration of the estate, and seemed the fittest person to fix upon for the above purpose.

It was hastily arranged, at the same time, that the Mortlakes should, by every means in their power, while abroad, keep up the delusion that Helen was in their company. It would be as well, for instance, always to keep a room in her name at hotels—write messages home in which she should be mentioned, etc., etc. But there was then no leisure for details.

And so, while the flag waves, and the whistle screams, and the train glides from the platform, let us allow the curtain to descend upon the Second Act of our drama.

CHAPTER XXVII.

I DON'T mind telling that this is the first time I ever found myself in the thick of a big story, like the present. It has grown, in the telling, to a length which I never intended, and, like certain unruly plants, may not have grown quite as straight as I could wish.. When I undertook, some chapters back, to make all square, by bringing my account of Helen down to the time at which Petersfeld thought fit to set out in pursuit of her, I little expected to drift away down stream, till our friend, and all belonging to him, dropped clean out of sight. No matter now. What is writ is writ : and critics must live. Let us, however, return for one moment to the Albany.

We left Petersfeld, if you recollect, in about the most dismal pickle in which a man could well find himself. Dunned by his tailor, without a penny to pay, and accepted by a young lady to whom he had never proposed, there was only one thing to be done.

Tearing Mr. Bags's letter and Linda's delicate little note severally into a thousand pieces, and confounding the writers with fierce impartiality, he hastily packed his portmanteau, sent for a hansom, and set off at once for St. Mark's-on-the-Sea. It was a pleasant place to stay at. Mr. Maldon and his wife were civil and sociable ; and, now that it was clear that Miss Fleetlands had not traveled with her friends to the Continent, there was no reason why he should not resume his search in good earnest. The inveterate dislike which all young Englishmen feel to being baffled, awoke with fresh force in his mind ; and he vowed that, this time, it should go hard, but he would succeed.

You may have forgotten, and are forgiven if you have, that I myself, John Worsley, so far from being a mere narrator of other people's deeds, am an actor upon the boards. Indeed, now I think of it, I don't see why I should not have made a good deal more of my own part from the very beginning. There is, however, no help for it now.

On my return from the country house where I had been spending my Easter vacation, I lost no time in calling at Paul's chambers in the Albany, to hear, if possible, the latest news of his adventures.

But I found his outer door closed, and at the entrance-lodge I got no farther information than that Mr. Petersfeld had left some days previously, in a hansom, saying that he was going abroad. ·

Returning to Lincoln's Inn, the first person I chanced to encounter, in crossing New Square, was Mr. Buttermere himself, in his wig and gown. Directly he saw me, he shouted rather than called, "Worsley—Worsley ! I want to see you at my chambers, immediately, if "you please !"

He had just come out of court, and was evidently desperately busy, with more than one consultation-party waiting for him in his anteroom.

But he snubbed his clerk for reminding him of the fact, with a fiery *brusquerie* which was quite alarming, and bidding him get the gentlemen to wait, led the way into his own room, and desired me to take a seat.

"Now, Worsley," he began, flinging his wig upon the table, "I want to know what has become of your friend Petersfeld."

"Unfortunately, that is ·just .the question which I am unable to answer. I have this moment called at his rooms in the Albany, and found them closed. The porters tell me that he left, saying he was going abroad, some days ago. Beyond that, I know nothing whatever of his movements. As to where he may be at present I have not even a conjecture."

"Went abroad !" exclaimed Mr. Buttermere, who was fast losing his temper. "That's exactly what I was told myself. Worsley, do you mean to pledge me your honor, as a gentleman, that you don't know where he is ?"

"I have already told you all I know on the subject," returned I. "I suppose you do not require me to pledge my honor to 'that statement ?"

"But, confound you !—I beg your pardon, I mean confound him—I thought you lived together. At all events, you told me so, and you came to my house one night to dinner together. Worsley, you see that I am annoyed, very seriously annoyed, indeed. Here's this young fellow been making all sorts of love to my youngest daughter—Linda, you know—and sent her all manner of letters and presents besides ; and now, in one moment, I'm to be told he's gone abroad ! Gone abroad, indeed ! without a word to her· or to me, or to any of us. Of course the poor child is terribly cut up. That infernal Mrs. Springletop has been spreading the news of her engagement all over London, and boasting that she managed it all. I only wish to Heaven that something unholy would fly away with her ! Gone abroad, indeed ! This won't do, you know !"

I had never suspected that the smooth, creamy tones peculiar to Mr. Buttermere, could have been exchanged for accents so ferocious, or capable of a clinching malediction, which it would be irregular to produce in print.

"I am quite certain," I replied, after a moment's pause, "that my friend Petersfeld is perfectly incapable of trifling with the affections of any young lady. That he should have done so in the case of your daughter, whom he met·at your own table, is, to me, simply incredible. Of course I am not going to suggest an explanation in his absence. But that you have mistaken his conduct altogether, and are bringing a very needless charge against him, I would stake my existence. I am satisfied that when he turns up—as he is certain to do before long—he will be able to justify himself."

"Satisfied, indeed ! It is I who have to be satisfied ; and as to justification, he shall justify himself, by George ! or I'll know the reason why ! Worsley, I now give you a message for him personally, and I call upon you to deliver it."

"Mr. Buttermere, nothing has ever passed between us to warrant you in making me your messenger in this peremptory manner. If you like to entrust any communication to me, I will convey it to Petersfeld, next time I see him. If not, you will probably allow me to withdraw from an unpleasant conversation, respecting matters with which I have nothing whatever to do."

For a minute at least Buttermere looked at me with a steady mistrustful gaze, drawing his hand slowly over his chin. Then he took a sheet of note-paper from the stand before him, and began to write. Then he suddenly stopped short, and offering his hand, said:

"Worsley, you must excuse me. I have behaved confoundedly ill. But Linda was my pet—my darling. Worsley, what I have to say can equally well go by the post. Good-bye. I am sorry that you should have seen me make such a fool of myself."

There was something to me inexpressibly touching in the emotion of my old friend, whom I had always regarded as the very impersonation of easy and unchangeable good humor. Alas, there is in this world—as Lambro, that famous sea-solicitor discovered in his day—many

"A deep grief,
Beyond a single gentleman's belief."

Especially among people who have daughters to marry.

"If you will send your letter to our chambers, Mr. Buttermere," I rejoined, "you may depend upon it that Petersfeld shall receive it within an hour after I meet him in town. In any event, the moment I ascertain his whereabouts, he shall be informed that it is awaiting him, and demands his instant attention. Goodbye, sir."

"Good-bye, Worsley, Will you tell my clerk as you pass, that I am disengaged, and desire him to show in the first consultation? Good-bye."

It occurred to me, before I reached Stone Buildings, that there was at least a possibility of Paul's beating up his old quarters, at the St. Mark's Bay Hotel. In short, it seemed so far from unlikely, that I wrote him a short note there, mentioning in a few words, the subject of the interview which I had just held, as well as the letter which awaited him, and strongly advising him to return to London at once.

In point of fact, as you already know, Petersfeld, so far from having gone abroad, was all this time indulging himself in economical retirement at that sequestered watering-place, little suspecting the trouble which he was giving his friends.

He found his good-natured host and hostess, Mr. and Mrs. Maldon, in excellent health and spirits. The weather was fine, and the season had opened well. There was more than one visitor in the coffee-room, and business was going on, and the private apartments going off, at a rate of which nobody could complain.

Paul had a grand scheme in his head for recommencing his search after Helen, and the very day after his arrival took the precaution of dropping a line to Mr. Bloss, to inquire if he was quite sure that she was still at large. An answer by return of post, brought him Mr. Bloss's compliments, and an assurance that the five hundred pounds still remained unclaimed.

It began to strike him, however, before he had been more than a day or two in the hotel, that although nobody could be more civil or attentive than were Mr. Maldon and his wife, there was something in their manner not altogether as cordial as before. Nothing is more difficult to analyze than the conduct of our acquaintance, when, for some undiscoverable reason, we are obliged to suspect that they like us less than formerly. In Paul's case, the change in their behavior, although utterly indescribable in words, was sufficiently marked to occasion him both annoyance and surprise.

His landlord, however, was not a man to keep things to himself, or to expend needless curiosity upon his customers for want of asking questions. So, a few days after Paul's arrival, during a conversation respecting rifle-practice and volunteering in general, he suddenly broke ground.

"Seen Mr. Tobacco to-day, sir?" he inquired mysteriously.

"Seen whom?" retorted Paul, puzzled.

"Oh, I recollect. The dirty little rascal you told me was a spy. Not I! By the way, it's odd enough, but, do you know, the day I left your house last, he got into the train after me—followed me all the way to London Bridge Station—and saw me off to Paris!"

"I know he did," remarked Mr. Maldon gravely, and with an oracular nod.

"Come, come, my good friend, what the deuce is the matter with you? Tell us what you mean, and have done with it. Only don't cock your head, and say 'I knew it,' like a bully at the Old Bailey."

"Beg your pardon, sir, I'm sure," replied Mr. Maldon, with the air of a man unwilling to give offense—"but the trouble seems to be about those notes, sir; as you must surely know."

"Trouble! What trouble? What notes? My good friend, pray don't equivocate, but speak your mind at once, if you've got one."

"Well then, sir; as we were saying in this very parlor—you and me and Mrs. Maldon together, not so many evenings back—there were three Thousand Pound notes lost by Admiral Mortlake of Riverwood over yonder, in a red leather pocket-book. Well, those notes were not only advertised, of course, to be brought to the bank here, but two chaps—inspectives, detectors, or whatever one should call them—were sent down from London, just to rout out, as we understood, all about these bank notes, and make plain, as it were, why they didn't turn up. And a precious lot of questions they asked, to be sure; as much about Miss Helen as the notes, so I hear—as if she was likely to have found them, poor young lady. Well, at last they went away, leaving word that it was all most uncommonly odd. ' No need to come all the way from London to tell us that,' says we. Well, and when they went away, they left that little prowling chap behind them, what for I don't know. Always drinking at the ' Six Bells,' close by the bank, he is. Well, sir, and when you went into the bank t'other morning, and asked Mr. Crackleton, the manager, quite sudden, and as it were sagacious, about these very notes ; and told him to take the consequences, and all that sort of thing, if he didn't let out all he knew before you left the counter, why Mr. Crackleton, very naturally, I mean for him, took it into his head that he should like to know a little who you might be—thinking you wouldn't likely have asked the question just for the mere fun of the thing. I'm only telling you, sir, simply what I hear, you know, and, what with being church-warden, and all that, I naturally do hear a good deal of what goes on up at St. Mark's. And so, as I couldn't and shouldn't have thought of giving Mr. Crackleton any information about you, sir, even if, in fact, I'd had any to give, and wouldn't hear him mention the matter twice over, what does he do but set this chap, Tobacco, to dodge about here, and track you all the way right up to London, till he could lay the regulars on, don't you see ? That's what he was up to. Only you gave him the slip. That you did! They never expected you were going foreign, not they, and didn't find him money enough for that sort of travel. Besides, he can't talk French, of course, or any thing over the way ; not even if he kept sober on purpose to try. So you got away, don't you see ? I'm told he cried like a pump, all over the platform, directly the train started."

" Go on," retorted Paul, severely.

" Well sir—ever since you've been back here, I've noticed him as it were snuffing about after you. He ain't a pleasant follower to have about one, is he ? He asked me a question or two, only last night ; and said it might be worth a ten-pound note to him yet, to keep his eye on you."

" I don't know what he values his eye at. Under ten pounds, I hope. Go on."

" Well, that's about all, sir. I'm sure I've meant no offence. I'm sure it's all quite right. I've made Mrs. Maldon quite clear as to that, sir. She's of the same mind as I am. I know it's all right, sir. I'll take my oath to that, as soon as you like. Pray, sir, name something that I can have the pleasure of doing for you."

" If you will have the goodness to let my bill be made out within ten minutes, I shall be obliged."

Poor Mr. Maldon ! He was absolutely unconscious of having done wrong. He had been a little inquisitive to be sure ; and had told Paul, unasked, what other people had said of him. And yet he fancied that he was either very roughly treated, or that Paul must be a perfect Claude Duval. So little was he versed in mankind.

Still, it is only justice to Paul to observe that, great as the provocation may have been, it was aggravated in the sudden overthrow of his grand scheme, which was thenceforth out of the question. To go gossiping and ferreting about, with Mr. Tobacco at his heels doing as much for him, would be too ridiculous. Besides, it could end in nothing less than homicide. It occurred to him, to be sure, that he might go to the bank and explain, once for all, who he was, and what little good could come of dogging him. But the obvious retort would be—"You may be, as you say, Mr. Petersfeld of the Albany, and we are quite willing to believe you respectable : but what made you ask that extraordinary question about the bank notes ? What business was it of yours ? You must have had some reason. Satisfy us as to that, and we will let you alone and welcome."

And what answer was it possible for him to give ? To tell the truth was out of the question, while to invent an excuse, even if such ingenuity could have been justifiable, was altogether beyond his power.

It was a severe blow. Was this to be the end of all his vaunted energy and resolution, of which we heard so much at first starting ? Shouldering his knapsack, and informing his conscience-stricken host that, under the circumstances of the case, it was impossible that he should prolong his sojourn at St. Mark's Bay, he marched straight for the railway station. What he meant to do—whether to return to town at once, and send for the tailor and Linda to divide him between them, or how otherwise to dispose of himself, he had not made up his mind. In short, he not only didn't know where he was going, but, what is more remarkable, it is quite certain that the fact never will be known.

For, on his way up the long straggling street already described, and when just opposite the " Six Bells," there came a loud cheery shout from a small, stout man, who had just mounted a copper-colored pony before the door.

" Hoy ! I say, sir, how d'ye do—how d'ye do ?".

" Well, much as usual, thank ye !" replied Paul, taking the friendly inquiry for market chaff. " Remember me kindly when you get home !"

" No, but, hoy ! hang it ! Stop, won't you, Mr.—I forget your name ?"

" Why, you, Mr. Bunnytail !"

Paul was one of those lucky people who never seem to confuse names or faces, and have the former always handy for use.

" Thank ye, sir, I'm sure, for recollecting me. It was at Master Buttermere's we met last, wasn't it ? Something like a blow out, that was ! Will you come across and see us, sir, now that you're close by ? Make my good lady as happy as a Princess Royal, that would. You'll do it, won't you ?".

Mr. Bunnytail called his fat wife his good lady, and revered her as a bloated aristocrat, in consequence of her connection with the Buttermeres. To be redolent of Harley Street, was rank and precedence at Bunnytail Bottom.

There was no reason in the world why Paul should not accept the good-natured invitation. His time was his own, and Bunnytail Bottom as good a base of operations as St. Mark's-on-the-Sea. Better, in fact. Indeed, this meeting seemed a piece of unusual good luck.

"Do you really mean, Mr. Bunnytail, that you would offer me a night's lodging? I was just on my way to catch the next train for London; at least, that would have been the end of it, for I've had about enough of St. Mark's. But I'll leave London alone for to-day, and pay you and Mrs. Bunnytail a visit with the greatest possible pleasure."

"Come, that's kind now! Lodging for the night, indeed!" exclaimed the farmer, who absorbed ideas gradually, and to whom a moderately long sentence was worse traveling than a ploughed field. "Lodging for the night? that's good! That would be a joke, indeed, wouldn't it? Say three weeks, Master Petersfeld—say a month. The longer the better. That's to say if you should be spared so long; as it's hardly reasonable to hope you will."

"Spared so long!" echoed Petersfeld. "I hope I'm not on my last legs yet! Not got any thing infectious down your way, I hope. No cholera?"

"Lord love you, no! 'Twasn't that sort of sparing I meant. But if somebody that I mustn't name, I suppose—leastways, only as Venus, as my good lady would say—could only spare you, I'll be bound we won't quarrel about any thing till you come to speak about starting. My good lady, down yonder, has talked of nothing but you for the last two days and more; nothing whatever."

"Talked of me! Very kind of her, I'm sure. Why she should have taken the trouble to recollect my name at all, is more than I can imagine."

"Eh?" exclaimed the farmer, with a tremendous wink. "Quite fair, sir, quite fair; ha, ha, ha! But now let's see. Out with the filly directly, Joe, and clap the new saddle on. Dust her down, Joe, and look alive. And then, Joe, you step over to the Bottom with this gent's knapsack. That's about the time of day, sir! Won't my good lady be proud and happy," continued he, looking at Petersfeld with the sort of honest pride which comes over anglers when they regard a twenty-four pound salmon fairly landed on the grass.

Just at that moment the postman passed, and handed my letter to Petersfeld. "For you, I think, sir? It's directed to the St. Mark's Bay Hotel. I believe you were staying there."

"Quite right, thank you. Oh, from Worsley, I see. Wonder what the old boy's found to write about!" And Paul thrust the note, unopened, into his breast-pocket, for he was extremely curious to know what Mr. Bunnytail meant.

"Aye, she's talked of you, off and on," resumed the farmer, as they jogged along down a by-street, "ever since that day she met you at the Zoological Gardens, you recollect, and you sent her home half-seas over with cherry bounce. Ever since that famous dinner at Master Buttermere's, when we spoke, I remember, about that handsome young woman as had run away, and was going to be rewarded if any body could find her. I'm not much of a reader, myself, and I never saw the story in print. Not found yet, sir, I suppose, is she?"

"Not that I'm aware of. By the way, Mr. Bunnytail, you told me, if I was lucky enough to find her myself, to bring her to Bunnytail Bottom."

"So I did, sure enough, and so I do. What I mean, I say, Mr. Petersfeld, and what I say, I mean. And welcome you are to do it any day. Ah, yes: now I recollect the whole story. She ran away because she didn't want to stay at home—wasn't that it? And they offered a reward for her persecution. More shame for them, I say. Oh, yes. You bring her to Bunnytail Bottom, and let's see if they'll persecute her there. Not while I've a cart-whip and a horse-pond on the premises. She'll be quite company for you, Mr. Petersfeld, won't she? Oh, no! Bless me—I forgot. That would never do now, would it?"

"Really, Mr. Bunnytail, you are determined to puzzle me. Come, that's no use! You might wink your eye out without making me any the wiser. And, if your're bent upon poking me off my horse with that big whip of yours—why, do it at once, and get it over."

"Eh?" chuckled the farmer, who was manifestly laboring under that tremendous amount of internal pressure characteristic of pastoral badinage. "Quite fair, sir, quite fair! ha, ha, ha!"

As there is nothing to which even the most good-natured people, who have not been brought up to it, feel a more wholesome aversion than waggery of this description, Paul changed the subject as soon as possible, and their talk ran upon bullocks and barley, all the way to Bunnytail Bottom.

CHAPTER XXVIII.

I AM not going to put your patience to the test by any labored description of the agricultural retreat, which for little less than a century had been the modest castle of Clan Bunnytail. I will only say that the first *coup d'œil* presented a large, comfortable, rambling farm-house of the olden style. Around and behind rose out-buildings, barns, granaries, stables, cow-sheds, and piggywiggeries, upon the most extensive scale; and a grand rookery, too, from which the birds hoorayed in airy chorus, as if celebrating the new arrival.

This was all that Petersfield was able to take in at the moment, for he was immediately ushered into the parlor. Much as Mr. Bunnytail would have liked to have had the drawing-room arrayed for reception, and his good lady adorned to match, it was clearly out of the question. It would never have done to keep Petersfield waiting; while to postpone the triumph of presenting him, was simply impossible.

Accordingly, with buoyant alacrity, Mr. Bunnytail danced into the room, hustling Paul before him as if he had been caught stealing eggs. "Mr. Petersfield, madam! Madam, Mr. Petersfeld!" he exclaimed, with eager voice and sparkling eyes; and then, tucking his riding-whip under his coat-tail, straightened himself up into an attitude of profound yet respectful curiosity, waiting to see how the "nobs" would behave.

Mrs. Bunnytail looked, strange to say, several layers larger in her own house than she had appeared at the Buttermere dinner. Perhaps the smallness of the parlor caused an apparent difference. Perhaps the fact that instead of being tightly girthed in, and properly saddled and bridled, she was dressed in the loosest possible costume, out of which nevertheless she was, in the most unmistakable manner, bursting at every seam. Perhaps she was still growing. She reminded Paul, indeed, of the lobster at the Zoological Gardens, when in the act of splitting up his old shell, preparatory to starting a new suit.

The three impish children sat at play on the carpet, diverting themselves with sheep's knuckle bones. There is a base mediæval game, which it appears can be played with no nicer materials. I fancy I remember it at school, under the name of "dibs."

Whatever Mrs. Bunnytail may have been doing when Paul entered the room, she seemed heartily ashamed of detection; and tumbled a large basket hastily into the corner before she could collect herself sufficiently to recognize her visitor.

"Mr.—Petersfeld—?" she exclaimed at last, as she arose amazed from her sofa with the air of a person who gradually becomes aware of an apparition. "Mr. Petersfeld? Is it possible? Oh, how truly kind to come all the way from London, and bring us the good news yourself!"

And, before Paul had leisure even to imagine a reply, the good lady, sailing across the floor, had clasped him to her bosom, and imprinted upon his expostulating lips half a dozen of such smacking kisses as made the room ring again.

"And all in such a moment, too!" continued the lady. "Oh, I was happy to get Carlo's letter! Not but that I knew well enough what was in the wind; only it seemed almost too good to be true. Jump up, you little rogues, and kiss your new cousin; and thank him for coming here to day."

"Mrs. Bunnytail!!" exclaimed Paul, as soon as he could find breath to speak, "what is the meaning of all this? You must be dreaming!"

A dreadful suspicion—and then a certainty had flashed upon his mind almost at the same moment; and a dream of the night, long since forgotten, was remembered with intolerable accuracy.

"Dreaming, indeed! Well done you, Paul. Why, when you're Linda's husband, and that's as good as done, shan't I be your aunt, and Bunnytail there, your uncle? and won't these precious pets be all your own cousins? Oh, what a blessed thing relationship is—isn't it, Paul, my dear?"

"Seems about the right way to take it, don't it, nephey?" struck in Mr. Bunnytail, respectfully; observing the blank look of utter and indignant astonishment with which this rapid sketch of a new position was accepted.

"But I have no sort of intention of marrying Miss Linda Buttermere, or any body else," retorted Paul. "The whole thing's a delusion; and I wish to Heaven you'd let it alone!"

"Not marry my niece!" screamed Mrs. Bunnytail. "What are you going to do to her then, Paul? What have I got ears to hear for—and eyes to read writing for—and Carlo's letter in my pocket for, if you ain't going to marry her? Oh, Petersfeld, you astonish me now, indeed."

"Hoity, toity!" chimed in her husband; not so much for the value of the remark, as from fear of being twitted with "want of spirit," if he said nothing at all.

"You will rue the day, and rue the hour, when you did this, you know," continued the lady, portentously.

"Damages, nephey," commented the farmer, with a grave roll of his head.

"Yes, you will indeed, Paul. This night shall my sister Carlo learn what it is most meet that she should know. But, Paul—if I may still call you Paul—you're not in earnest, are you, really? You're only playing off your fun upon us, as I do hope and believe. Oh, Paul, if you was to turn out a scoundrel, it would break the whole set of hearts in our family."

"Mine, anyhow," came from Mr. Bunnytail, with a profound sniff.

What to do with our nerves when we don't want them, is one of the grandest secrets in the world. How to keep cool under red-hot pressure, and leisurely "take occasion by the hand" instead of being run away with by ourselves, is a problem very deep. Paul had gone through his course at Hythe, and perhaps had picked it up there. At any rate, with all his tendency to impulsive and immediate action, he could sometimes be cool where coolness was indispensable, and think in a critical moment. Just then, he certainly had need of all his *savoir faire*. To have stubbornly withstood this overwhelming woman and her husband would have ended in his being turned out of the house. Not that this would have been any such irreparable calamity; but goodness only knew what was in store for him in Harley Street, or how far Mrs. Bunnytail might contrive to complicate matters.

"If you would only allow me one moment to explain, Mrs. Bunnytail," he said, "I feel confident that we should understand each other. You will listen to me, will you not?"

"Oh, if you want to explain," remarked Mrs. Bunnytail, bridling loftily, "go on, Mr. Petersfeld, as long as you please."

To a certain order of minds, the idea of an explanation is associated with a contrite attitude, and a miserable hope of being forgiven.

"As long as you please, nephey," repeated Mr. Bunnytail. "You shall speak the truth, and the whole truth, and nothing but the truth, mind; because, so help you, that's the law. Will you take a nip of something, nephey, before you confess? Beer—brandy—or gooseberry wine? Only put a name to it, nephey. It may be a help, don't you see?"

"Thank you," replied Petersfeld, feeling very much as if he were in the custody of a couple of orang-outangs, at their private residence in Java, "I think I can get through it without assistance. Of course, Mrs. Bunnytail, your sister, Mrs. Buttermere, is in the habit of giving you the very earliest information upon all points of family interest?"

"That she is, Peter—I mean Paul," replied the lady. "You may depend upon that. For I say to her always, Carlo, say I—Do you tell me all that is right and proper I should know, and behave true and handsome to me, as I to you, and then all's fair and square between us. But don't you think to play hide-and-seek with me, because I don't stand that at any price; and if I haven't news from you, to tell the Shankers, and the Greens, and the Beestleys, and the Swabstalls, and the rest of my neighbors, why I'll invent for my credit sake. I ain't going to have it whispered about that my sister in Harley Street looks down upon me from the top windows of her haughty mansion, and that I don't know more of what goes on inside than the scullion in her kitchen."

"My good lady has the soul of a noblewoman, and well she may," remarked Mr. Bunnytail, admiringly.

"To be sure. But do you know, Mrs. Bunnytail, that what you have just told me seems to afford a simple explanation of the whole matter."

"Not to me," interrupted the lady sharply. "Not one bit of good your explaining, if I ain't made happy and satisfied."

"Of course not. But I am sure you must have observed that engagements of this kind, always supposing them to exist at all, invariably occupy some considerable time among the higher circles—"

"Oh, yes! That may be. But they always come to the same thing in the end."

"Not always, Mrs. Bunnytail, as your experience of society will remind you. Now, my dear madam," continued Petersfeld, "the fact, I am confident, is this: Your sister, Mrs. Buttermere, in her anxiety to afford you the earliest possible information upon an interesting subject,

has been slightly premature. She has told you what she no doubt believed was, or would turn out to be, the truth; but before it was at all wise to mention it even among relations. You would not have done so by her, had the case been reversed. Your better judgment would have induced you to withhold all information upon so delicate a subject—even to a sister—until there could be no longer the possibility of mistake."

"Mistake, indeed!" cried Mrs. Bunnytail, who was rapidly getting out of her depth. "Why, as I said just now, what had I got eyes to see for, and ears to hear for, in Harley Street, let alone the Zoological Gardens, which was a sight in itself? Ah, you won't get out of that, Paul, my man, in a hurry! And what have I got Carlo's letter in my pocket for at this very moment? What's the meaning of this?" continued she, producing the document referred to from some extraordinary marsupial cavity. "How about half a dozen chemises trimmed with Valenciennes lace, and as many with worked edges? How about six white petticoats, all with rich flouncing, and colored skirts embroidered and braided? How about silk stockings and pocket-handkerchiefs, and all the rest of it? What's Linda to be trussed for if she ain't going to be married? Answer me that, Paul!"

Petersfeld grew desperate. The foolish mamma had evidently made up her mind that he was safely hooked; and had not only imparted the fact to her sister, but—for fear of being suspected of suppressing a material fact—had regaled her with the description of a possible trousseau, for the edification of her country friends.

"I tell you what, Mrs. Bunnytail," he exclaimed, without farther care or caution, "this is going a little too far! Linda and I have only met twice in our lives, and all the rest is mistake and delusion. If you don't choose to believe me, all I can say is that this moment I leave your house. I'll go up in a balloon, or down a mine, or right away to the end of Egypt, and never come back till I hear Linda's married and done for! You're enough to drive a man mad among you. Yes—you may look as you like, but I'll stand no more of this idiotic nonsense; and so good-bye to you both."

"Good-bye, indeed! Not if B. does his duty. B., do it like a man! Don't let him go. Stand up for your own niece. Fight for her, B.!"

Fighting for any body was entirely out of Mr. Bunnytail's line; but standing as he did in ghostly and bodily fear of his wife, especially when invoked as a simple consonant, he prepared for the worst. Hoping something, perhaps, from a little experimental demonstration, he began by backing against his parlor door, and saying "Wo—ho!" like a carter.

"Come, come, my good friends, all this is foolish. You don't think you are going to arrest me, I suppose. Why not part without quarrelling, if we can? Mr. Bunnytail, you appear to be trying to sit down, which is impossible upon a perpendicular surface., Hadn't you better come back to your chair?"

"B.! why don't you seize him, before he escapes?" cried the good lady, at the top of her voice.

"Madam, because I'm not so sure he'd let me loose again," replied her husband, brushing the wall behind him in all directions, with his eyes fixed on Petersfeld, like a comet with tail turned away from the sun. "My nephew's blood's up. I can see that. Now, look here, you two! Can't we see a cool and kindly way out of all this? So long as nephew likes to stay with us here, and the longer the better say we both, why not promise to say nothing to nobody? Why should we? So long as he's safe to hand, where's the good of driving on matters? They'll come all right in the end, I'll be bound. He's not up to the mark at present, madam, our nephew ain't. That's clear as the day. Look at him. Lean as a tree, with no red about him anyhow. Let me feed him up here for a fortnight, and he'll take off his hat to himself in a glass, that he will! He's pining now: nothing else. Won't be fit for trussing for ever so long. Come, madam, what do you say?"

After considerable discussion, Mrs. Bunnytail was induced to promise that, so long as Paul chose to consider himself as one of the family at Bunnytail Bottom, and made no attempt to elope without warning, she would refrain from denouncing him to her sister in Harley Street.

Not that she gave her consent without misgivings of the most complicated description, which were all volubly reviewed for Paul's benefit. But her husband, who, to do him justice, was animated by all good feeling, and actuated by considerable good sense, ultimately carried his point.

As for Paul, he certainly was to be pitied. The humiliation of being pounced upon by a farmer's wife, and finding himself after capture a sort of prisoner on parole, was a horrible absurdity, But what was he to do? Was he to allow himself to be driven out of the house, as he had been out of the St. Mark's Bay Hotel, by his own over-sensitiveness, and roam the country like a wandering Jew? Was he to permit this disastrous woman to write what she liked of him to the Buttermeres, and not only keep the dreadful question alive, but perhaps render any satisfactory solution impossible? Was he to give up his pursuit altogether, and return to Stone Buildings a beaten man, with his character for energy disposed of altogether, in exchange for the consequences of a painful and deplorable blunder?

He resolved to sacrifice every thing for a little breathing-time, and with very bad grace—it must be confessed—reaccepted the farmer's hospitality, and consented to make himself at home at Bunnytail Bottom.

The preliminaries of peace thus settled, were ratified by the high contracting parties over a tea of tremendous proportions. Story-tellers

are fond of making ill-natured fun of these rustic hospitalities, and describing the amount of home-made bread, reeking toast, and pig in all its phases, forced upon the distended and perspiring guest. However, I can safely say that all descriptions which I ever read, fall short of a reality in which I was myself an actor. Probably I have got hold of the wrong word. I don't imagine that the Dean of Canterbury would allow a man to be an actor (active) who only sat impatiently still to be stuffed (passive). But I declare that I left the table with some thoughts of having myself stamped "proof," like a gun-barrel, since, after that, whatever may happen to me, I am certain never to burst.

Next morning Petersfeld was called out of bed at cock-crow to behold the milking, and the whole forenoon was devoted to a grand inspection of the farm and its belongings. Bunnytail was delighted with his visitor, and made no secret of his contempt for the policy which had cut up the making of a first-rate farmer, to manufacture nothing better than a limb of the law.

Solomon, the bull, was first visited, praised and patted, and his various points of excellence, and noble pedigree, enlarged upon with unsparing eloquence. And once set going, Bunnytail took care that Paul should know no rest, until he was almost as well acquainted with the stock and premises as he was himself. Like Farmer Philip in the idyl, taking our young friend remorselessly in tow,

"He led him through the short sweet-smelling lanes
Of his wheat suburb, babbling as he went.
He praised his land, his horses, his machines;
He praised his ploughs, his cows, his hogs, his dogs;
He praised his hens, his geese, his guinea-hens;
His pigeons, who, in session on their roofs,
Approved him, bowing at their own deserts.
Then from the plaintive mother's teat he took
Her blind and shuddering puppies, naming each."

And so on, until another gluttonous bell announced the hour of noon, and that the board was again covered, for more serious work than ever.

Dinner over, Petersfeld was pleased to find his host and hostess retire to their respective arm-chairs, and begin to snore like a couple of old-fashioned giants.

Availing himself of the welcome opportunity, he lost no time in turning out for a quiet stroll. "Oh, solitude, where are thy charms?" may have been the song of Alexander Selkirk. To any person undergoing a course of penal education upon the "separate system," the absolute immunity from interruption, and the liberty of pursuing, in consequence, any desirable train of thought to its utmost limit, may savor of what gormands deprecate as toujours perdrix. But as clothes to the cold, food to the famishing, sleep to the weary, and balm to broken heads, so is perfect loneliness to one who has been bored to extinction, and escaped as by a miracle. We seem to drift idly on, through sheets of delicious calm, and the very sensation of existence becomes, in itself, enjoyable.

But Petersfeld had a great deal to think about. Now or never was the time to put into execution the grand scheme of which we have already heard. What this scheme was, I need hardly be at the trouble of telling you, for reasons which you will discover for yourself, before you have read five pages farther. I will only say that it was based upon the fact that, by his recent journey to Paris, he had ascertained, beyond all possibility of doubt, that Helen had *not* left home with her friends, and that consequently he felt himself released from all obligation to conduct his inquiries with the care and reticence which he had scrupulously observed while that question remained open. He knew, now, that something was wrong somewhere, and that people had been deliberately deceived. He therefore .considered himself at liberty to act upon his own discretion, and cut, if he could, the knot which appeared so difficult to untie, without farther ceremony.

Just at that moment, while rummaging for his cigar-case, he pulled out my still unopened letter. Its contents horrified him. Matters had been black enough before, but he had always trusted that the misconception, as between himself and Linda, was one which would right itself easily enough, and that he might at least count upon Buttermere's practical good sense to view the matter in its proper light, should it ever become sufficiently serious to call for his attention. But to find that the latter had already taken it up in such uncompromising earnest, was a frightful fact, and seemed for the moment to paralyze his energies altogether. So this was the result of that fatal advertisement!

Angry, irresolute, and in utter despair, he wandered for hours about the country, wondering what was the best thing to be done. To rush off instantly to London, and ask my own advice, was his first impulse. To be sure, Mrs. Bunnytail would consider him a deserter, and send hue and cry after him by the evening post. But that was of little consequence, as matters stood. It might be more gracious, after all, to go back for his knapsack, and wish his late entertainers a proper good-bye. He had still plenty of time. It was but little after three o'clock, and it might be better not to arrive in London before dark.

His meditations were interrupted, or rather his attention distracted, by finding that he had quite inadvertently arrived at the boundary of the Riverwood estate. He had approached it, in fact, from a direction contrary to that which he had previously taken, and his proximity was altogether a surprise. A low stone wall was all that separated him from the pleasure-grounds, and within little more than a hundred yards from the road he could distinguish the tiny weather-cock which surmounted Helen's summer-house, veering and twinkling in the sun.

Nothing could have been more disconcerting at the moment. "It is well," he growled, "that I should own myself a fool and an im-

postor, upon this particular spot. I have thrown away both time and money in a pursuit which none but a lunatic would have undertaken, and I am justly punished by finding myself in a scrape of which goodness only knows the end. No matter! I am awake at last. I will clear my mind of the whole of this egregious business while I can. In that arbor I will stand and swear the most solemn oath I can think of to abandon this accursed chase forever, and try to be wiser through time to come. Energy, indeed! I hate the word. Mine has been the energy of Milo—if the comparison isn't too preposterously in his favor. Let me only find my hands loose again, and Worsley may thrash me like a donkey before I give another kick without reason. As to this Miss Fleetlands," continued he, striding leisurely over the fence, "from this moment I wash my hands of her rights and wrongs. I only wish I had never heard of her. Positively, if I found her at this moment, sewn up in a sack, and labeled 'Constantinople,' I wouldn't interfere—unless I saw them going to hang her upside down. So now, then!"

As Paul reached the summer-house, the door was quietly unlocked, and a young lady descended the steps.

She was dressed in brown silk, with a purple cloth jacket; and her white straw hat, trimmed with black velvet, was ornamented with a grey grebe feather.

Paul staggered and started back.

He knew at once that it was Helen.

A sudden thrill shot through every fibre.

A sensation, such as few experience more than once in a life-time, held him planted where he stood.

As for Helen, she sprang forward, with a half-uttered exclamation of delight; and then, violently trembling, drew back, cold and pale.

In the bewilderment of sudden meeting, and amid the shadow of the yews, she had mistaken Paul for Ferdinand.

CHAPTER XXIX.

AND how came Helen there?

Fortunately for you, if you are disposed to put the question, it is one which in due course of story-telling must at once receive a solution.

We left her hurrying from her guardian's room, toward that precious depository in the garden, whither all materials for, as she hoped, complete and impenetrable disguise had already been so carefully transported. Once there, the work of disfigurement was rapid enough. Her usual dress was thrown off in a moment, and as quickly locked up in a cupboard. And the slops, which came out in exchange, not only made her look seriously old at once, but, having been padded after the light of nature, gave her a buxom aspect in the way of waist and shoulders which at once rendered identification impossible.

A touch or so of color, rubbed on at random, produced a result which was quite reassuring, as examined in her pocket-mirror. To attach a small bit of black sticking-plaster to one of her front teeth was the next process; but the result was so hideously successful that feminine philosophy gave way, and the experiment was abandoned. However, when her bonnet was at last tied tight under chin—her shawl adjusted house-maid fashion—her basket on her arm, and a pair of fat worsted gloves, which were a feature in themselves, assumed, to make all complete, she would have liked nothing better than to drop a courtesy to the admiral himself.

Whatever may have been her sensations as she stepped lightly over the stile which bounded the Riverwood property, and marched for the first time in her life an independent traveler upon the Queen's highway, she started with unwavering pluck and resolution. It was too late to look back; and there was not much use in looking forward, for that matter. Events would have to shape themselves; and so she trudged straight to the Bunnytail Station, certain admonitory lines ringing warning as she walked.

"'Tis said that the Lion will turn and flee
From a maid in the pride of her purity,
But, anyhow, if she's a wise little thing,
She'll steer quite clear of the Beastly King!"

Luckily for her, the Lion happened not to be abroad that evening, and she arrived within view of the station without the necessity of exchanging a word with any one.

"Come along, Jess!" exclaimed a young woman, in a weary tone, who was walking in the same direction, upon the opposite side of the road. "You keep up with me or you'll be left behind."

"Can't, mother," replied Jess, with a shrill sob. "It's the bundle won't come—not me!"

"Well, you must make it. I've got the child to carry, and ever so much besides. You'll hear the train-bell ring next; and then we shall be lost, and no mistake."

"Ain't much farther, mother, is it?"

"No. Not a step, scarcely. Can't you see those lights yonder?"

"Can't see nothing over the bundle," gasped the unfortunate mite, hugging the unwieldy affair to her bosom, as if it had been the dearest friend she had in the world.

"Poor little thing," exclaimed Helen, good-naturedly crossing the road. "You carry my bag for me, and I'll carry the bundle. That will be fair enough, won't it?"

"Yes, thanky!" gasped Jess, delighted. "I'll carry the bag for you, and no mistake."

"Don't do no such thing, ma'am," interposed the mother. "It's not for the like of you to be carrying our baggage. We'll do well enough, and thank you all the same. It's not far to go, now."

"Nonsense!" said Helen. "Who do you take me for, I wonder. Poor people must help one another."

"Well, it's very kind of you, I'm sure, ma'am, but I'm afraid you'll find the bundle over-heavy."

"What makes you call me ma'am?" demanded Helen, impatiently. "Can't you see that I'm not a lady? You are going by train, I suppose. So am I.". It was rather too bad to be detected by the first tramp she met.

Perhaps had her new acquaintance been better up in poetry than she probably was, she might have retorted, with the Seneschal of Artornish:

"Worship and birth to me are known
By look—by bearing, and by tone:
Not by furred robe, or broidered zone."

But, having no such resource at command, she merely murmured—"No offense, miss, and thank you kindly. Jess, little maid, mind and carry careful. Don't you drop the bag whatever you do. Hush, baby darling, we're almost home now."

"And we'll see daddy again there, won't we, mother?" cried Jess, skipping along with the bag. "You know you said we should see him again, didn't you?"

There was no answer to this question. The baby was only rolled round and smothered with kisses. It was not until they reached the bridge over the line, that a quiet husky voice said—"Yes, we are going by the train. We have a long way to travel."

"So have I," observed Helen, gently. "How far do you go to-night?"

"All the way to Izzleworth town."

"Just where I'm going myself."

"Is it, indeed!" exclaimed the young woman. "But I dare say you'll travel—not with us. You go third-class too, though, perhaps," she added, nervously; trusting that in this daring attempt to get right, she was not blundering beyond all possibility of forgiveness.

"Third-class! yes, I'm going third-class, like you," replied Helen, clutching eagerly at any thing like companionship. "I've no money to throw away, I assure you. Do you know what the fare comes to?"

"Twelve shillings, ma'am, the full-sized ticket, and six shillings for Jess. Eighteen shillings, with nothing in the world to show for it at the other end. It's like flinging money all about in the dirt, isn't it? It's all the same to them, I should say, whether I get in or not. If I don't, where's their eighteen shillings? If I do, what odds does it make to the train? If I'd got another eighteen shillings, I shouldn't mind so much. But I haven't."

"Well, take a ticket for me," said Helen, producing her money. "I'll mind Jess and the traps. Say you want another ticket for your sister, then they'll be sure to put us all together, and it's lonely traveling without some one to talk to."

Unhesitatingly committing herself to this very shallow piece of strategy, the woman soon returned with the tickets; and, almost at the same moment, a pair of calm expanding eyes, devouring the dusk, appeared in the distance. Helen held Jess tight by the hand, so that neither could run away. Then the bell rang; the train pulled up with a crash and a grind, looking weird and large as train never looked before, with lamps burning, and people smoking. "Any one for Bunnytail? Third-class, behind! Now then, young woman, look alive!" And the guard hustled Helen and her companions into a third-class compartment, and blew his whistle, before he shut the door with a bang.

"That's a nice steady man, and I should like to give him a shilling," thought Helen. "He can trust his own eyes. People like that give no trouble."

I may as well notice here, by way of parenthesis, that it was to this fortunate encounter upon the road that Helen was indebted for the chief element of mystery which surrounded her disappearance—perhaps for making a successful business of it at all.

The station-master at Bunnytail, in answer to close and persistent interrogatories, was so confident that nobody had left his station by that particular train, which happened to be the latest of the day, except two females with babies and bundles, who took third-class tickets, that the detectives gave up the rail theory altogether. Oddly enough, at the St. Mark's Station they fancied that they had got hold of a clue, which they followed with profound sagacity as far as St. Bees, where they overhauled the wrong lady, and re-appeared in disgrace.

The journey passed quietly enough. There were several people in the compartment, and the only thing which struck Helen as remarkable, was a sort of honest spontaneous friendliness which is not cultivated in coupés and first-class carriages. Nobody seemed to feel that a remark needed an apology, or that the commonest act of civility might be construed as an affront. On the contrary, an old lady, who at once addressed the mother as "my dear," overflowed with valuable advice as to the nurture and admonition of the baby; while a workingman, after offering Jess tobacco by way of introduction, took her upon his lap and conjured lollipops out of his trousers pocket. Indeed, he seemed to have quite a quantity of these delicacies binned away somewhere about him, for he gave them away right and left, and one which he presented to Helen was speckled all over with sawdust, and tasted of timber.

The story which the poor woman had to tell, and which it seemed to be a relief to her to tell again and again, was sad, not strange. Her husband, a carpenter at St. Mark's, had died suddenly a few weeks before. In an instant the blight and the shadow of death fell upon all that he had left behind. Her home was broken up, her furniture sold, and that "daily bread" for which, I am afraid, too many of us pray like parrots every morning, with about as much earnestness as if asking that the sun may continue to shine, and the earth to revolve as usual, was no longer forthcoming for her children's meals.

In despair, she was making her way to her late husband's father in Izzleworth — not hoping much, poor soul; for "the more the merrier," is a welcome only heard in first-class company. And three new mouths to be fed, fresh from a third-class van, could only, as she was aware, come down like a calamity upon a household in which daily bread had not only to be prayed for, but watched and worked for in good earnest.

It was just as well for Helen that she caught this glimpse of real trouble to compare with her own dissatisfaction. Rarely in early life do we make acquaintance with pain, mental or bodily. And when the truth breaks upon us like a surprise, and we learn the conditions under which we actually live, we are ashamed of the fuss which we used to make in our ignorance, and understand that we have still an education to complete.

"I suppose you'll go to your clergyman when you get settled, shan't you?" said Helen. "What's his name? How old is he? Perhaps he'll give you a lift."

"Doctor Orchard was our clergyman, ma'am, when I left Izzleworth—but that's six years ago. I hope he's not dead too. He was a nice kind old gentleman as ever lived."

"I think clergymen ought always to be old. I've no patience with young ones. They are always conceited, and a great deal too fond of their own opinion."

"Well, we must all have a beginning, ma'am, mustn't we? I'm sure I heard Dr. Orchard's curate preach a wonderful sermon once about Daniel in the lion's den. You should have heard him, ma'am, when he come to the lions!"

"Very likely. I hope he did you good. Curates are all very well in their way; but as to making a beginning, the worst of it is that they make it at our expense. However," continued Helen, much relieved by certain information which she had just obtained, "that's a matter which is no business of mine. Poor little Jess! you look as if you had had quite enough of the train. How old is she?"

"Five, ma'am. That is, she will be five next Monday as ever is. Poor thing! we used to keep her birthday."

"I wish you would give her this from me on Monday, will you? I've rolled it up in this piece of paper. Don't open it till then. It's only a trifle, and you can spend it for her."

"Surely, ma'am; and thank you kindly."

It was three sovereigns, which Helen, in generous disregard of the value of money, had privately extracted from her purse, and folded in a neat little packet.

"Do you know, ma'am, I think this must be Izzleworth. That's the factory, where all those lights are. Yes, I should know the place anywhere."

It is not likely that she will ever recognize it anywhere else. But it is a strange sensation, that of hurrying into a new town for the first time by lamp-light. Nothing seems absolutely real. The shadowy buildings—the changing streets, the vague window-lights, the smouldering fires and outlying lantern-pickets on the line side, as the train pulls up, whirl past like pictures in a dream, from which we suddenly recover ourselves bright awake in time for the too practical rush and tussle upon the platform.

As Helen had no luggage to look after, she lost no time in walking courageously into the street. It had always been her project to apply in the first instance to the clergyman of the place at which she might happen to arrive, with a story which, when it came to be subsequently sifted, she hoped would be considered as a natural and excusable fib. A clergyman, as she innocently supposed, would hardly dismiss a friendless young woman into the streets the last thing at night. It would be almost his duty to see that she was decently taken care of; and, if so, something might turn up in the morning. Moreover, should she find his ecclesiastical hospitality unsatisfactory, what could be easier than to slip off a hundred miles or so without notice, and try the same experiment elsewhere. This seemed quite a promising programme, combining all the amusement of traveling with the advantages of orthodox society. And, so long as her funds lasted, there seemed no reason against its being continued until her friends at Riverwood had received a lesson which they would never forget. It was delightful to think of the consternation which must have already begun at the Lawn; but a certain nervous wish to find a roof over her head left her no time to make the most of the reflection.

Asking her way at the first baker's, she paced rapidly along the street, for the shops were being closed, and there was no time to be lost. The red leather note-case began to be a dreadful weight upon her mind. She was heartily vexed with herself for having been willful enough to take it, for not only did it seem certain that it would either crawl out of her pocket upon its own hook or lead to her being robbed and murdered at the first dark corner, but she had a vague impression that people were sometimes stopped and questioned by constables when found abroad at irregular hours, and searched in case they failed to give a fluent account of themselves. And since it was morally impossible that any piece of autobiology which she could offer at short notice would be considered satisfactory in the presence of these overwhelming documents, there was nothing for it but to hope very heartily that she might be left alone.

Fortunately such was the case. She only fell in with one policeman, to whom she appealed at once, by way of throwing him off his guard. And when the youth pointed carelessly with his thumb, and replied, "Orchard's? Two doors down there—left hand side," she experienced an indescribable sensation of relief.

Izzleworth Vicarage, as seen in the dusk, was a large, roomy, red-brick building, standing well back from the road, and protected in that direction by a broad belt of shrubbery. There

was a handsome glass porch before the door, with a large bell-pull, which produced an unexpectedly loud noise in answer to Helen's modest appeal.

A dreadful contingency at once flashed upon her mind. It might be opened by a footman! That was a casualty upon which she had never counted. To stand confronted with a footman in her absurd disguise; to be obliged to bandy question and answer, and to be made the butt of his hideous pleasantries, would be no common scrape. But she was in for it now, whatever might happen, since to retreat was out of the question.

To her great joy the door was opened by a florid old lady with a flat candlestick. All that could be seen at the first glimpse was a handsome cap, a little nose, a complexion which reminded you of apples not gathered yesterday, and a pair of twinkling eyes of the quick inquisitive order, which at once began playing upon Helen from head to foot.

"Well. Now then. Who's this?"

"Is this Doctor Orchard's, ma'am?"

"Why, you've rung the bell. What made you ring it for, if you didn't know that? Yes, it is Doctor Orchard's! Now then. What is it?"

"I should like to see Doctor Orchard, if you please."

"If I please! Suppose he's not at home."

Helen's heart sunk within her, if that solution of a deplorable sensation be anatomically admissible.

"I am very anxious indeed to see him. I am in this town by mistake, and have nowhere to turn. I only wish to ask if he could put me in the way of obtaining shelter for the night. I don't want money, or any thing of that sort."

"And how comes it that you are in this town by mistake, and have nowhere to turn?" demanded the janitrix, allowing Helen to enter the hall, but surveying her by such close candle-light that it was just as well she had no whiskers to singe. "What shall I tell the doctor? He's busy you see, now, and don't like being disturbed. Only just look at the clock. You couldn't possibly, I suppose, walk back to the station, and take the train for where you was going, and where you ought, of course, to be by rights before this; and then we should have no bother here, don't you see? They're civil people at the station, and you'll get a ticket for almost anywhere, with nothing to pay, if you only say that they've carried you wrong. That's about what you'd better do, to my mind."

"Couldn't possibly," replied Helen. "Don't know my way back in the dark, to begin with."

"Dark, indeed! You'd have been more welcome if you'd come by day-light," snapped the old lady. "Funny time to call, this is. Well, wait there," she added, closing the door. "I must talk to the doctor, I suppose. What he'll say, I'm sure I don't know."

Whatever the doctor may have said, the library door was presently reopened, and Helen found herself in the presence of a burly, curly, elderly gentleman with a rosy face and a benevolent eye, who looked up from the charity sermon which he was in the act of preparing with the air of one to whom interruptions come as matters of course, and are disposed of as fast as they happen.

"Well! What's the matter? Lost your way on the rail—is that it?"

"Yes, sir, if you please, I have lost my way. And I ventured to call here in hopes that you might be able to direct me to some proper lodging for the night. I was never here before, and I am alone. I really do not know what to do."

"Mrs. Nosegay," said the doctor.

"Sir," said the lady.

"Leave us for a few minutes, if you please."

Mrs. Nosegay, by turning one ear to her master, and steadying the opposite eye upon Helen, seemed anxious to afford either party the opportunity of providing her with some crumb of information to carry down stairs. But perceiving that nothing whatever would be said while she remained in the room, she shook eye and ear into their regular places, and retired in displeasure.

Doctor Orchard looked Helen rather hard in the face—much harder and longer, indeed, than she thought either necessary or gracious. Not, of course, that upon calling at a strange house at half-past ten at night you are to expect to be bowed up stairs at once to the best bedroom, but still the look was one of something more than mere ordinary curiosity. There was, however, nothing for it but to confront it as best she might, and wonder to herself whether they could ever possibly have met before, and if she was going to hear her own name pronounced directly.

At last, with a good-natured blink which was not exactly a smile, but the cheerful arrangement of countenance which comes over people who have solved a riddle, or made a good speculation, or otherwise brought intellect to bear to some purpose, he laid aside his pen, drew his arm-chair toward the fire, and said gravely and gently:

"Tell me in two words why you are here. That is, if you can—if you please, in short. Don't be afraid. We will take care of you. Just give me something to say to Mrs. Orchard. Sit down, if you are tired. You shall have tea directly."

Helen could have burst into tears upon the spot. It was not the words themselves, but the kind, deliberate, powerful manner in which they were spoken, that upset her. She felt it impossible to prevaricate, and yet to condense a satisfactory answer into a few words was impossible.

"I had to quit my last place on a sudden," she answered, almost unconsciously. "Things happened which obliged me to leave. It was no fault of mine, I assure you. I have a very good character."

"Let's look at it," said the doctor, holding out his hand.

"Oh, I didn't mean a written one," cried Helen, growing utterly bewildered; conscious that the fatigue and excitement of the day had been too much for her, and that she was betraying herself as fast as possible—"I meant—"

"I see! You meant a good conscience! Come, that's a better thing still. Well, we will take care of you for the night at all events. It happens luckily that we have a room vacant next Mrs. Nosegay's, and she shall look after you. Mrs. Nosegay," continued he, as that lady re-appeared with marvelous rapidity in answer to the bell, "this young person is under your protection for the night. You will have the goodness to make her very comfortable. I have special reasons for these orders. She will explain to me to-morrow enough to enable me to forward her to her destination. In the mean time, I have forbidden her to explain any thing. She requires rest now." And, with a courteous wave of his hand, Helen found herself dismissed.

It is not to be supposed that any amount of precept or exhortation would have bound Mrs. Nosegay's tongue, or that under ordinary circumstances she would have gone to rest without such an account of Helen's previous life and belongings as would have done credit to the perseverance of a grand inquisitor. Luckily, however, Helen was no sooner in the housekeeper's room, than Mrs. Nosegay made the startling discovery that she was "a real lady." Her hands betrayed her at once. Indeed she was no longer in the mood for masquerade, even if she had been enough of an actress to play out her assumed character with success. And this discovery, while it infinitely inflamed Mrs. Nosegay's curiosity, not only paralyzed all attempt to gratify it in the usual manner, but made her so shy and obsequious that it was a relief to both parties when bed-time put an end to their conversation.

In short, Helen was shown into a tidy little servant's room adjoining Mrs. Nosegay's own dormitory, and, after all possible wants had been most kindly and carefully provided for, was left at last in peace and silence, to muse over the events of the day.

And the more she thought about them, the more unreal did the whole affair begin to seem. It appeared a week, at least, since she had changed her dress in the summer-house. The railway journey seemed an episode of very distant date; and the strangely considerate and even cordial reception which, in spite of her disfiguring disguise, had been so readily accorded, grew into an actual mystery before she fell asleep. Something in his manner toward her seemed to suggest that Doctor Orchard was influenced by other motives than those of mere charitable good nature—but the elimination of that something was a task beyond her power.

As a last precaution, she fastened the red leather pocket-book by a ribbon just below her knee, a little extra-careful device which perhaps I have no business to mention, but the wisdom of which appeared by its being found perfectly safe in the morning.

CHAPTER XXX.

"Sir," said Doctor Johnson, one day, "what a man has no right to ask, you may refuse to communicate; and there is no other means of preserving a secret but a flat denial. For, if you are silent, or hesitate, or evade, it will be held equivalent to confession."

A nice lot of liars we should all make, if we gave in to this cool philosophy. But that some speculation of the kind ran through Helen's brain when she awoke next morning, and reflected upon the account which she would probably be expected to give of herself, is perhaps not the less probable. A change, however, in one respect seemed to be passing over her mind. Doctor Orchard's kindness had made a deep impression. A sense of the uselessness of all efforts at concealment was gradually growing up, as well as a sort of undefined consciousness that results were being taken out of her own hands.

So she dressed; and, after carefully securing the pocket-book about her bosom, went down to Mrs. Nosegay's breakfast.

It was ten by the chime of the hall-clock before she received a summons to the library. Thither Mrs. Nosegay attended her, all civility, and with as much pride at having improved her costume into something presentable, as if she had been Helen's own waiting-maid.

The doctor was there in his arm-chair by the fire, in just the same attitude, loose coat and slippers as she had left him in the night before. The same papers seemed littered upon the desk, and he was playing with the pen which she had last seen in his hand. It looked almost as if he might have forgotten to go to bed.

"Good-morning!" he said, as Helen entered the room, fixing upon her as he spoke the same grave penetrating gaze which had disconcerted her the evening before. "I hope you have slept well and been properly cared for. Let us see now what we can do for you. There is no hurry at all; remember that. Remain here as long as you please. But, if you wish to leave us, let me know where you would like to be sent, and I will see to your being properly packed up and directed, at all events."

"I couldn't think of trespassing upon your kindness any longer, sir. Now that it's daylight, I can find my own way."

"Aye, but where? You came here last night lost on the rail. Where do your father and mother live?"

"I never spoke to a father or mother in my life," replied Helen. "I am alone. I told you so."

"But your friends? Don't resent questions. I must help you, you know. It is my duty."

"My friends obliged me to leave them; and that is my whole story. I am not going back to them at present. I choose to remain away."

"You choose to remain away! And you only eighteen last birthday," resumed the doctor, with a more puzzled look than before.

"Eighteen," replied Helen, mechanically.

It seemed almost superfluous to acquiesce. Doctor Orchard evidently knew all about her, if he only chose to say so.

"This is a sad business—very sad. I am not quite unprepared for what you tell me; but we must consider what is best to be done. Excuse me if I leave you for ten minutes. I wish to consult Mrs. Orchard in the next room."

Thus left to herself, Helen had leisure to look about her. It was a handsome and almost luxuriously furnished study, opening into a small conservatory. All around were massive bookcases, filled with evidently costly volumes, and what was particularly noticeable at first sight, quite an array of busts and heads—some of marble, some of plaster, which stared you out of countenance on all sides. The tops of the bookcases were crowded with these silent effigies. Others, more honored, were accommodated with private brackets; while little knots of heads appeared to be conversing in all corners; and two or three, less favored still, were evidently hatching mischief under the table. Some of them attracted Helen's girlish curiosity at once. They seemed to be faces which she had seen somewhere, and ought to remember. The sensation was not entirely pleasant.

It was upward of ten—more than twenty minutes before the doctor returned. "Come!" he said, reinstating himself in his arm-chair, "all is arranged. Nothing could suit better. Sit down now, and listen to me."

The same indefinable sense of power which had struck her the evening before, compelled Helen to obey like a child. She was to be told what to do. In fact, she had found a new master.

"You have a secret—a reservation," continued the doctor, "which you probably wish to keep. I don't ask it. I should not listen to it at this moment. Whenever you deliberately wish for my advice, it shall be yours. In the mean time, observe this. I am a father myself, and indeed have daughters much about your own age. Whatever I should wish a man to do by my own daughter, did she ever appeal to him for aid in a difficulty, I will do by you. You will be inquired after before long, I have no doubt. In that case, I give you fair warning that I shall exercise my own discretion. I shall do just as I should wish the man to do. Until then I intend to place you in a situation of safety, where you will be perfectly unmolested, and absolutely out of the way of inquisitive people. Mrs. Orchard will explain all particulars, and convey you thither. To invite you to remain here would be against your own interest. We should only excite the curiosity of all Izzleworth. Tell me simply, that you trust yourself in my hands until farther notice, and I shall be satisfied."

"I do, indeed, sir!" replied Helen. "I don't know how to thank you enough for all your kindness. As to my secret—that I will tell you with pleasure, at any moment. I would rather do so, I assure you."

"Tell it me when you find yourself perfectly free. Now let me take you to Mrs. Orchard."

"But—" began Helen, not knowing exactly what she was going to say, yet overwhelmed with irrepressible curiosity.

"But what?"

"I beg your pardon, sir! But it is impossible to receive all this care and kindness without a sensation which I don't know how to express. I have had a feeling too, ever since I came into your house, that you knew all about me—every single thing. Do you really? You have not treated me like a stranger; and I can't understand it at all. It is like a dream to find myself received as if I had actually come by invitation. You won't mind my asking, will you? And how did you know that I was eighteen last birthday?"

"One must be a conjurer indeed, to guess that—mustn't one?" returned the doctor, rubbing his hands and looking pleased all over. "Ha, ha! Your question delights me more than I can tell. Know all about you indeed! I wouldn't have had you miss this house for twenty pounds. No, my dear young lady! Seriously, I am not only at this moment in perfect ignorance of your name, but I have not the slightest conception as to what part of the kingdom you may come from. And, what is more, I know for certain that, until last evening, I never saw your face before."

"You know that!" exclaimed Helen, amazed.

"Certainly."

This made matters worse than ever. Doctors of Divinity are not supposed to dabble in any thing very deep—still less to entertain familiars that "peep and mutter;" and this negative assurance, so confidently given, sounded more like necromancy than any thing else.

"Now you puzzle me quite. I could not say that myself of any face in the world."

"Neither could I, if you mean that you could not speak so positively with reference to each and every face which might come before you. But you're wrong, I'll answer for it, in saying that you couldn't do so with regard to any face. Look at me, now. Did you ever see me before? Don't think; but answer, yes or no."

Helen looked for a moment at that round plump rosy countenance, that keen twinkling eye, bold forehead, and firm good-natured mouth, and replied, "No. Not at least since I was a child."

"Very well answered. I don't suppose you ever did. But if I wore the face of Frederic the Great, for instance, the question would have seemed ridiculous. You would have answered that to have seen such a face and forgotten it would be quite impossible. There would be nothing to consider about—nothing at all. Did you ever hear of the great Philosopher of Zurich?"

"No, sir, never."

"What! Not of Jean Caspar Lavater?"

"Oh, yes. Of course I've heard of Lavater. He was a great phrenologist, wasn't he?"

"He was the father of Physiognomy, the sister science. I am one of his disciples. Physiognomy has been my hobby, and I hope an innocent one, for the last thirty years. I am at last beginning to walk alone. All round the room you see my teachers. Lavater was right when he recommended above all things the study of moulded busts. You can handle them, turn them, examine and measure them, entirely at your ease. That is your true education. Of course in this, as in every other science, infallibility is beyond our reach. We aim high, it is true, but at a point which fools only actually expect to strike. Nevertheless, I can safely say that, during the last dozen years, I have been deceived in my first estimate of character from countenance very slightly and very rarely—never altogether."

"That does not make the matter less of a mystery to me," replied Helen, smiling.

"There is no mystery about it! When one considers the astounding fact, that among the countless millions who swarm upon this earth, there are as many bodies as minds; that there are no two human organizations precisely alike—certainly no two minds—and when we add to this that in our present stage of existence the mind can only act through the agency of the body, it is surely no extravagant conjecture that external difference of face and figure may have a certain relation—a necessary analogy to the internal difference of heart and mind. Is not this much more reasonable than to suppose that minds and bodies were distributed chance-medley? But we know that they are not. 'What treatment would that man deserve,' asks Lavater himself, with indignation, 'who presumed to assert that Leibnitz might have conceived the Theodicea in a brain like that of a Laplander; or that Newton might have balanced the planets and divided the rays of the sun, in a head resembling that of an Esquimau, who can reckon no farther than six, and calls all beyond it innumerable?' This, you will answer, is merely a question of power. Granted: but it is part of a principle. Come with me to Hanwell, and I will show you heads which never could have held a responsible brain. Come to Dartmoor or Portland, and I will point out skulls which couldn't possibly hold an honest one. These are simple facts, which all experience not only warrants us in accepting, but forces upon us, whether we will or no. Is there then any clue to the nicer shades of character, as printed upon the outward face? Unhesitatingly we answer, yes. Every day's experience convinces us that there is such a correspondence. Every day, consciously or unconsciously, we pass judgment accordingly. We speak of a good and of a bad countenance. We say that such a face expresses pride; of another that its owner must be morose and peevish. A third we declare looks sly, and a fourth benevolent. One face talks to us of cheerful activity, another only of brutal indolence. We could trust one face: we doubt and detest the next. And we are usually pretty much in the right, at least in the more marked cases. Now, with this clue in his hand, who would sit down contented? What should we think of the man who, having discovered that there was sense to be extracted from a hieroglyphic, and having actually deciphered some half dozen lines, gave up all farther attempts as useless, and declared that the rest was either unintelligible altogether, or a mere blind string of casual crooks and dots? The physiognomist does not stop. He is not content with perceiving that one particular face unmistakably announces some special endowment —say sincerity, for instance—without demanding why, and tracing the same quality in others which to a casual observer would indicate nothing of the kind. Neither is he content to deal alone with those qualities which are in general more boldly proclaimed upon the face. He reverses the process, and dissects the lineaments of men remarkable for some especial gift—wit, judgment, eloquence, fortitude, or what not. He traces at last some line, some curve, some peculiarity of formation in lip or nose, eye or forehead, common to these men in their several classes. He recognizes the same mark in a stranger, and spares no pains to discover whether, in his case, it announces a like possession; if so, he continues his investigation, until what was originally only conjecture, assumes the place of an established fact, and he can congratulate himself upon having added one link, at least, to the noblest knowledge of mankind. This is a most vague, imperfect sketch of what we physiognomists venture to attempt. To indicate even the bounds and borders of our science, would be impossible in mere conversation. Even Lavater avowedly wrote only in fragments, and confessed himself incompetent for the finished task."

"I can't conceive how you could have formed any opinion about me, in such a moment," persisted Helen.

"The true physiognomist—the man who has learned to grasp a face at all—decides always by first impressions. That is one of Lavater's golden rules. If I decide wrongly, it is not because I have been precipitate, but because I didn't understand my business. Never mind what I saw in your own case; I saw enough to justify me in acting as I did, and as I am doing. I told you just now that I had never seen your face before. I could safely say so, because if I had I should have considered it with interest—made a mental note of it, in fact. I should have liked to touch your head, too. Allow me to do so now. Will you look toward the window?"

"Ah, just as I should have expected," continued the doctor, dropping his fingers upon Helen's brow, as if he had been striking chords upon a piano. "All firm and sound, and balanced well. Hey? what have we here? Acquisitiveness, I declare—and a little marked. Not run away with the family spoons, I hope?"

Helen felt herself blush and tremble. The red leather pocket-book which weighed upon her bosom, in more senses than one, might be inquired about after the next pat.

"No. I was just able to resist that temptation," she said, trying to evade farther scrutiny.

"Ha, ha! Combativeness, I declare. I had not traveled quite so far down the parietal, but I'll be bound there's no mistake about it. Don't be affronted. Acquisitiveness is no bad point in itself; without it, no one can take care of their own, or even enjoy their property. You'll ask me next, why I didn't find out this by physiognomy. Well, we have two weapons: physiognomy, like the rifle, which strikes at a distance. Phrenology, like the bayonet, which we play with at close quarters, when we get the chance. I should like to give you my views upon the whole matter, but that is impossible while Mrs. Orchard is waiting. Come along with me, and in the mean time, allow me to thank you for the pleasantest ride on my hobby I've had for I don't know how long! Stay, I forgot. You have not told me your name, yet. Will you do so?"

Helen looked him in the face. Neither could avoid laughing, as their eyes met.

"Yes; that must be part of the bargain. It is necessary that I should know it."

"I am Helen Fleetlands, sir."

"Thank you. The name is new to me. If you like to call yourself Miss Brown for the present, do so by all means. No one shall know who you are through me, unless with your own permission. Now, come along."

Mrs. Orchard, a nice, bright, bustling little woman, received Helen with genuine good nature, mixed with some slight shyness at the irregular nature of the introduction.

"You've had a good lecture on physiognomy, I'll answer for it, by this time! I don't know when I've seen my husband so pleased as when he came up stairs last night and announced the discovery he had made. Well, he has made me promise to ask no questions, and you may be sure I don't want to ask any; but he is satisfied that you have reasons for wishing to remain *cachée* at present, and has himself arranged a plan which I should hope would suit you perfectly. When the doctor is satisfied, I am, of course; but indeed, there's no need to be a physiognomist in your case; at least, if there is, I'm one myself!"

"You are very kind," said Helen. "I have told Doctor Orchard that I am ready to explain to him at any moment who I am, and how I come to be here—"

"Oh yes! But you mustn't explain to me! It would be as much as my place is worth to listen. You have no other clothes with you, I presume? I am obliged to ask the question."

"None at all. These are a disguise. I made them myself."

"Hadn't you better employ somebody else, next time?" asked the lady, laughing. "I am afraid we must change them for you. But I am forgetting what I was told to propose. Doctor Orchard, you must know, has a sister who lives some five miles from this — a sad invalid, poor thing. Her late companion was obliged to leave her suddenly, only last week, and she is miserable without one, and not yet suited. Now, Doctor Orchard thought that if you liked to go and stay with her for a week or so—in short until things took the right turn in your case, as I dare say they will before long, it might be pleasant for both parties. Any one whom her brother sends, Miss Orchard will welcome gladly. You will have no duties, except the attentions which one naturally pays to the afflicted. As to salary, you would of course resent the offer, so that the favor will be upon your side. There you will be perfectly safe and quiet, you see. Will you go ?"

"That I will, most gladly. It is the very thing, above all others, that I should have wished for, had such a chance ever come into my head."

"Then we will lose no time. I could drive you over there; but that wouldn't do. Mrs. Nosegay is too provoking; and if she had the least idea that you weren't sent home again directly, we should never hear the end of it. What a pity it is that such chatter-boxes were ever invented. Every chatter-box should have a regular lock, and some steady person to keep the key. That would be a capital plan, wouldn't it ? No, I must take you in the carriage to the station. Then she'll think you've gone right away by train, and forget all about you. I'll send the carriage home, and go on with you to Fell's Road, the first station out of Izzleworth, and we'll take a fly across to King's Woodlands; not much more than a mile. That will do famously. And as to dress, why we must borrow one from my eldest daughter, which will fit you to a nicety. Not that it matters much as regards Miss Orchard, for she's almost blind, poor thing; but the servants would talk, you know. And I must lend you a box, mustn't I, or people would wonder. When you get to King's Woodlands you can make your own arrangements. By the bye, Doctor Orchard specially charged me to ask you whether you had brought any money with you. You see his physiognomy couldn't tell him that!"

"Plenty, thank you. Enough for all possible purposes."

"That is well. Then suppose we start in half an hour."

I have no occasion to lengthen my story by giving you an account of the house in which before luncheon-time Helen found herself fairly installed. It was simply a neat, quiet cottage standing in its own grounds, just within sight of the smoke and spires of Izzleworth. Miss Orchard, several years older than her brother, was, as Helen had been prepared to find, a sad invalid; almost helpless, and all but blind. From Helen she required little, except the sensation of her presence; but the voice and manner of her new companion struck her instantly,

and she sent word back to her brother that he had found her a real treasure. He must have been pleased, I should think, with this additional testimony to the value of first impressions.

And now in comparative solitude, and relieved from the fret and worry of Riverwood, Helen had time to turn her thoughts inward, and reflect upon what her life had been—upon the strange position into which she had so unexpectedly stumbled—upon all that might be going on elsewhere, and upon the future that was to be. Gradually, and to her own infinite confusion, she recognized the stupendous folly of which she had been guilty in plunging unprotected and alone amid the eddies of this extraordinary world. Vague glimpses haunted her of what might have happened had her drifting been less providentially directed. And the very sensation of safety became so vivid and delightful, that when poor Miss Orchard wanted her to promise to remain with her so long as she lived, and offered to settle two hundred pounds a year upon her for life if she would strike the bargain, she almost felt that in devotion to this lone and ailing woman, it would be pleasant to repay the great debt of gratitude which she owed to her brother. And then she thought of Riverwood Lawn, and her grim old guardian and his wife. It never crossed her mind that they would have left England in her absence—indeed the journey (I suppose for financial reasons) had always been talked of as projected for her especial benefit. There was a keen, malicious pleasure in picturing the extravagant amount of wonder and confusion which her disappearance must have created; but, as days passed on, this reflection was indulged in subject to one serious qualification.

When young ladies are lost, people usually think it worth while to advertise. Helen was quite aware of this, and fully prepared to be advertised for. Moreover, she guessed, and correctly, that Doctor Orchard would feel it his duty to watch the papers upon her account. Every morning she expected to see him appear with the *Times* in his hand, and to be obliged to recount her whole story, in the hope that perchance he might be induced to regard matters from her own point of view, and not insist on packing her off instanter. But as day after day went over her head, and to all appearance no more notice was taken of her departure than would have been vouchsafed in the case of the kitchen cat, she became puzzled, impatient, and at last quite angry. It had cost her a great deal of trouble to manage her successful escape. And now it positively seemed that if she had ordered a post-chaise, and driven away in broad day-light, nobody would have taken the trouble to remonstrate. This was very provoking : but furnished another reason for not going back in a hurry.

Long and earnestly too she thought of Ferdinand, with the calm and happy trustfulness of a young and ardent mind which has never known the pangs of doubt, or the blight of disappointed love. She knew that, for the time, correspondence was impossible. But what of that? She was as confident as of her own existence, that his heart turned to her as faithfully as her own to him. A few weeks more, and, come what might, a grand revolution in her prospects must necessarily take place, and their next meeting might not be so very far distant after all. All was vague indeed and uncertain, but there was a rosy dawn in the distance, and she must bravely await its breaking.

Doctor Orchard, however, as time rolled on began to wonder seriously. He could make neither head nor tail of the business. There was not the slightest doubt upon his mind but that Helen was a young lady of birth and position; and that her absence should apparently be treated with perfect indifference by those whose duty it was to care for her, was to him most unaccountable. The motive from which, as we know, the advertisement respecting her had been delayed, very naturally never occurred to him. He searched files of all the London papers from a date a week at least antecedent to that of Helen's arrival, and continued his unsuccessful investigations day by day for a fortnight afterward, when he gave up the attempt in despair. For some inscrutable reason she had been permitted to depart in peace. He was ten times upon the point of calling upon her to explain every thing; but then the reflection occurred to him that after all he had no right to force her to gratify her own private curiosity. If her friends didn't choose to inquire after her through the ordinary channels, it was they who were alone to blame. She was perfectly safe where she was. He should be able to account for every moment of her time. Moreover, and irregular considerations of this kind will present themselves to the best constituted minds, it was quite evident that her presence was now life to his afflicted sister. No hireling either would or could have done for her all that Helen did so cheerfully and gracefully every day. So Doctor Orchard at last resolved that, unless something were heard of Helen by a time which he fixed in his own mind, he would allow matters to remain as they were. When that period arrived, he intended to point out to her the necessity, for her own sake, of a full explanation.

In the mean time, having given up his daily search in the papers, the advertisement which gives its title to this volume never attracted his attention; and, but for an accident, the whole affair would have remained as great a mystery as ever until the young lady herself thought proper to solve the riddle.

CHAPTER XXXI.

One morning, while looking out of the breakfast-room window at King's Woodlands, Helen was surprised to see the doctor's great glittering black spatterdashes striding hastily toward the door. The doctor himself was evidently plunged in thought, and carried a newspaper. There was no need to guess at what had happened. "Found, at last," thought Helen; "and a precious time they've been about it!"

"Well, my dear young lady," he said, taking Helen's hand between both of his own; "I dare say you have your suspicions as to what brings me here this morning."

"Well—yes;" replied Helen frankly, as she glanced at the paper in his hand. A sort of nervous sensation came over her for the moment; for, do you know that to read an advertisement respecting yourself is one of the most trying things in life. People really should think twice before they advertise for one another.

"Ah, bother that paper! It's almost a fortnight old. I'm a dolt and a dunce—not fit for regular business of any sort or kind, I verily believe. But, come now, tell me this. You didn't happen to leave any thing behind you at Bunnytail Station, did you? No trunk, parcel, bonnet-box, or any thing else?"

"Certainly not, Doctor Orchard; and for a very good reason."

"Ha, ha! Well, now I'll tell you how the whole thing came about. I chanced to be visiting among some of the small houses in Izzleworth yesterday, when a poor woman, Mrs. Feltham I think she calls herself, asked me who the young lady might be whom she had seen in my wife's carriage a week or so since. At last I made out that she meant you, and then it all came out. She met you—that's her story—walking alone to Bunnytail Station. You traveled here together; and you gave her three pounds when you parted, like a princess in disguise, which naturally made her wonder why you chose to cross the country third-class, instead of staying at home to ride your camel. Of course, I couldn't enlighten her upon that point, and I was at first really perplexed as to what I ought to do. I had neglected looking in the paper of late, because, to tell the truth, I fancied that for some strange reason or other your friends didn't intend to inquire after you in that way. However, upon going again to our reading-room to consult the file, this was the very first paper I chanced to lay my hand on. Will you tell me whether that paragraph concerns you or not?"

We have read the advertisement ourselves already. Here it is once more:

"FIVE HUNDRED POUNDS REWARD!—Disappeared lately, a YOUNG LADY, aged eighteen, of very distinguished appearance. She is slender and of middle height—dark hair and eyes—pale clear complexion, and is in manner peculiarly graceful and self-possessed. She had with her a very considerable sum of money; but, it is believed, no personal luggage whatever. She was dressed, on leaving home, in a brown silk dress, purple cloth jacket, white straw hat, trimmed with black velvet, and grebe feather. Wore a curious oriental gold bracelet, plain gold guard-chain, and watch by Rosenthal, Paris. Whoever will bring her to Mr. Bloss, solicitor, No. 14 New Square, Lincoln's Inn, or give information leading to her recovery, shall receive the above reward. Thursday, May 1."

Helen read the passage from end to end, her color heightening all the time.

"It must mean me, I suppose," she said at last. "That was the dress I wore. I know Mr. Bloss by name. I think he was my papa's solicitor, or had something to do with the property. But this is painful, Doctor Orchard—dreadfully painful."

"Not so pleasant as might be, I am afraid. Nevertheless, since I, who never had the good fortune to see you in a brown silk dress and purple cloth jacket, or white straw hat trimmed with black velvet, contrived to recognize the portrait at once, we must not quarrel with your description. Now, you know, I have only one course open. As a clergyman, a gentleman, and a father, I am bound to take the matter out of your hands. I do so from this moment. Mr. Bloss, whose name I see here, is, I suppose, a mere man of business. You have no fancy for being carried to his office, I presume?"

"Certainly not. Admiral Mortlake, of Riverwood, is my guardian. I left his house the very day upon which I arrived at yours. It is no use talking about reasons now, but I fancied that I had very good ones for acting as I did. I am perfectly ready to go back."

"Good," replied the doctor, making a note in his pocket-book. "This, then, is the course which I propose. I shall write to the admiral by to-night's post to apprise him of your safety, and accompany you myself to Riverwood to-morrow by the ten o'clock train. I do not ask your acquiescence; because, as I have already told you, I mean to relieve you of all farther responsibility. But if you have any objections, let me hear them."

"I couldn't think of allowing you to take such a journey upon my account," replied Helen. "I found my way here alone, and I can easily take myself back."

"But it is my duty not to permit it. Your having done a foolish thing once, is no reason for doing it over again. Besides, you said something to me, when you first came, about your friends having obliged you to leave them. A regular misunderstanding, I suppose?"

"I had better tell you the whole story, hadn't I?" said Helen. "I have often wished to do so, and I shouldn't be happy in leaving without letting you know all about me. I have sometimes wondered that you should never have asked."

"Hum! Perhaps not from want of curiosity. Tell me now, however. I shall be delighted to listen."

In as few words as possible, Helen told her tale; sufficiently, at least, to show what had been her leading motive in running away. "And now, Doctor Orchard," she exclaimed, as she concluded, "I am quite satisfied! Five hundred pounds! My goodness, what a sum to offer. Oh, I'll answer for it the admiral must have been in the most dreadful fidget, before he thought of giving that much. Somebody must have made him do it; for he's a great deal too stingy to have offered it out of his own head. I really am quite delighted. There must have

been the most famous to-do, and the whole thing will be cleared up now. Don't you think it will?"

"I hope that every thing may turn out as you wish; but I am no lawyer, and do not sufficiently understand your position to offer any opinion. But, as regards your returning home alone, you must recollect one thing. This advertisement has been read, as you may suppose, by thousands upon thousands of people. Every body in your neighborhood must be on the qui vive, with such an immense reward in the air. You will be stopped before you reach Riverwood Lawn, as surely as you stand upon that rug."

"I see you are determined to claim the reward yourself," laughed Helen.

"Upon my honor, I think I deserve it a great deal better than the first clown you may meet; who will pounce upon you with a great whoop, and scamper away with you like a sack, making the whole parish ring with the noise of his good luck!"

"My good gracious me! What a dreadful position to be in—to be liable to be taken up by any body!"

"I am afraid it is exactly the position in which you have placed yourself. However, upon second thoughts, and after hearing your story, I believe it may be as well that I should not accompany you personally. I don't suppose I should be over-welcome, and it might almost look as if I came to have the pleasure of magnanimously declining the reward. No, I won't go; but I will do what will answer equally well. I'll send my gardener, David, along with you. He'll travel second-class, so that you'll know nothing about him; but, in any emergency, recollect that you're in his custody by my written orders. When you reach home, send him to the right-about without ceremony. I think that will do."

"Dear Doctor Orchard, how very kind and clever you are! But, is it absolutely necessary that you should write beforehand? I would so much rather return unexpectedly if I might."

And then came out all Helen's little plan. She had set her heart upon reaching the summer-house unobserved, and there quietly arraying herself in the identical dress which she had worn on leaving Riverwood, and which had been so graphically described in the advertisement. Then she proposed to walk boldly into the house, as if she had never been away at all, and take her chance of what might happen. She had no fears as to the result. She intended to be a helpless ward no longer. "Defiance, not Defense!" was to be the watch-word of the coming day.

The doctor good-naturedly yielded. "You shall carry my letter yourself," he said. "A letter must be written. You have no idea of the care which is required in matters of this kind. You have no conception of the awful forfeit which this prank of yours might have demanded. Don't think of that now; but submit to any thing rather than run such a risk again. By the way, I quite forgot to ask—how about this 'very considerable sum of money,' which I see mentioned in the paper?"

"Ah, that was my folly. I did carry away some bank notes, and they have been the plague of my life ever since. I really did so out of the merest mischief. My guardian I felt had been wronging me for ever so long, and I thought it only fair play to frighten him out of his wits. Besides, I wanted my disappearance to make a great row; and I thought that every little would help. But the notes are quite safe. They are in my pocket at this moment."

"Oh dear me. The family spoons after all! Well, this only makes it the more imperative that no time should be lost, and no risks run. Remember that these notes are really a dangerous possession. I don't know that it ought to alter arrangements," continued the doctor thoughtfully. "I don't know that it is my business to inquire farther. But, for Heaven's sake, be very careful. You might be arrested at any moment upon a warrant for having them about you. I almost wish you hadn't told me this. Don't let us say any more about them. Get them out of your own hands at the first possible moment, whatever you do."

And the next morning saw Helen in the train. There had been quite a sorrowful parting all round. Miss Orchard was in despair, and would have doubled her late generous offer, if there had been any use in doing that. The doctor felt as if he had been taking leave of a daughter; and Helen herself was conscious of a sense of dislocation such as she could never have imagined would have attended the severance of so short an acquaintance. But partings are the rule of this life; although we only notice them when they are painful.

"Write to me when you get home," said the doctor. "Write at all events when you get married. I must send you a souvenir. I think it shall be myself in white wax. You didn't notice me, I dare say, among the much better company upon my book-shelves?"

"Do send me your face, Doctor Orchard! It shall have the very best place in my room."

"You shall have it. Physiognomy forever! People laugh at us physiognomists—at us who see them through and through! Don't forget David. He is in the next carriage. Give me your hand once more. Let us hope that we may meet again."

"We'll manage that much, some day, which is better than hoping. You shall have a good long letter before long. I am only sorry I can not stay upon Miss Orchard's account."

In due time the train arrived at the Bunnytail Station. Followed by David, who slouched after her at a respectful distance, ready however to do any amount of combat on her behalf at the shortest notice, Helen reached the outskirts of her guardian's territory, which she re-entered exactly at the same spot by which she had quitted it, more than three weeks before.

"Thank you, David," she said. "You see

I am safe at last. You can tell the doctor that you left me upon my own ground. I am vexed that I can't ask you to the house. But you'll find a little inn close to the station; and you'll have time to get some dinner before the next train." And dropping five shillings into his hand, she disappeared among the trees.

The cupboards were exactly as she had left them. Nobody had thought of searching the place, and the doors had never been unlocked. In ten minutes' time her clothes were slipped off, and she stood dressed in exactly the same attire which she had worn on that memorable Thursday afternoon. Had Paul arrived a trifle earlier, he would have been too soon to catch her in that costume—perhaps too late to find her in the other.

Agitated as she was at the moment, his sudden appearance upset her altogether. A mist came over her eyes, and for an instant she fancied that Ferdinand himself stood before her. As she recognized a stranger, her heart after one sharp bound seemed to waver and then stand still. She did not speak.

"Miss Fleetlands!" exclaimed Paul, unable to contain himself in his astonishment.

"You know me?" replied Helen, after an embarrassing pause. "Perhaps you were looking for me," she added, with returning composure.

"I have read an advertisement relating to you, Miss Fleetlands; and of course recognized you at once. I know perhaps more than I have any business to know," continued he, stammering and blushing like a school-boy, "but I hope that you will believe that I am entirely at your disposal, and that you may implicitly count upon my services, should there be any which I can possibly render."

"You have been amusing yourself with trying to discover me, I suppose, ever since you saw the advertisement," retorted Helen, with sudden displeasure.

"Not with any sordid motive, I assure you, upon my honor. I am a gentleman—a barrister of Lincoln's Inn. I certainly amused myself, as you say, by following up the announcement which appeared in the *Times*, just as one might try to solve a riddle. Your name was then utterly unknown to me; and I had not even the remotest idea where you lived. It has so happened, however, that information has fallen in my way which leads me most earnestly to wish that I could serve you. My folly has already cost me dear," concluded Petersfeld, with a dismal recollection of the calamities of the past fortnight, "and if you tell me that I have now arrived too late, I not only take my leave at once, but with the solemn assurance that I will never mention your name again to any human being."

No one could possibly doubt the perfect candor and sincerity with which these words were spoken. In fact, Paul's face was one which it was impossible to distrust, even without the practice and penetration of Doctor Orchard.

"Thank you," replied Helen, more graciously. "But I am upon my guardian's own grounds at this moment, In a few minutes all this will be over."

"You are aware, I presume, that the admiral and Mrs. Mortlake are both abroad—"

"Abroad!" echoed Helen. "Is it possible that they should have gone without me? Are you perfectly certain of this? You must be mistaken."

"Perfectly certain," replied Petersfeld, delighted to find that there was some prospect of his being of use, after all. "They went abroad on the 17th of last month—the day after you left Riverwood, and have not yet returned. Some servants remain. Otherwise the house is empty."

"Good gracious, this is a nice business!" gasped Helen in dismay. "I'm really very glad that I met you. I wouldn't go home for all the world in their absence. I must go to Mr. Salterton at once. And yet that's just what I don't want to do. It would spoil the whole thing, and look as if I flinched at the last moment. Besides, it would not be right by him."

Naturally enough, she concluded that the servants left at home had, in all probability, received orders to detain her should she ever venture to return. That would be humiliating enough; but the unlucky pocket-book made matters a thousand-fold worse. To have walked into the drawing-room, triumphant at her successful escape—triumphant at having fulfilled her own time, and returned of her own free-will, for all that Scotland Yard and the *Times* newspaper could do to the contrary; and finally, to have flung the unopened pocket-book upon the table, a splendid trophy of ingenuity and magnanimity combined, would have been a grand beginning. But to be seized and searched, and have it taken from her as if she had been a thief—perhaps even to be treated as one, was a terrible contingency.

"Oh, by the bye, I quite forgot to mention one thing," suddenly exclaimed Petersfeld. "You'll think it very strange, but the servants in the house yonder are all under the impression that you are with the admiral and his wife on the Continent. I am perfectly certain that none of them have the least suspicion that you are missing."

"Impossible!" cried Helen, opening her eyes. "Why, they must all have known of it directly I left home. There could have been no starting in the morning, and I not missed."

"I assure you, however, that it is the fact. I have not a conception as to how the business was managed, but managed it undoubtedly was. You know the St. Mark's Bay Hotel, I dare say. Mr. and Mrs. Maldon's."

"Perfectly."

"Well, I was staying there lately, and we talked about the admiral, and the people at Riverwood, and both Mr. Maldon and his wife were confident that you had been of the party. From what I have heard, I have no doubt whatever but that by some clever ruse, effected for some particular purpose, a complete mystification was accomplished. Indeed, that was what first made me suspect that something or other must be wrong, and ten times more anxious than ever to get at the bottom of the whole affair. I saw your guardian myself in Paris at the Grand Hotel; and what do you think—he had not only engaged a room for you, but had actually procured your name to be posted up in the bureau, as if you were staying in the house. It's all part of some regular plan, you may depend upon it."

Helen looked utterly bewildered. "I think," she said at last, passing her hand slowly over her brow, "I have some guess as to what his motive may have been. I fancy he may have been liable to get into some shocking scrape with the Court of Chancery, if it had been known that he had lost me. If so, I'll answer for it, the fright has done him good. At all events, I've had traveling enough; though, most assuredly, I didn't get as far as Paris. If you are right in thinking that the servants suppose that all is as it should be, and that I am upon the Continent at this moment, I shall have the pleasure of undeceiving them. I shall go to the house at once. But one favor I will ask you to do me."

"Name it, my dear Miss Fleetlands!" exclaimed Paul, delighted beyond measure. "You can not imagine the pleasure I shall have in being of service to you."

"It is an important service," rejoined Helen, half hesitating, "and you will see the perfect trust which I repose in your honor, directly I name it. I took with me, when I left Riverwood, a very large sum of money in bank notes—"

"Three thousand-pound notes," interrupted Paul. "They were advertised for. I have the advertisement in my cigar-case. It appeared immediately after you left home. £150 was offered for their recovery."

"My goodness me!" exclaimed the young lady, "what a hopeless tangle the whole thing is, to be sure. However, since the notes were all the time in my pocket, the one advertisement was of about as much use as the other."

"Just as much."

"Well, then, what I want to say, is this. I have the notes about me at this moment. Now it may be quite true that the servants at Riverwood have been deceived, as you say; but I'm confident that there must be some one or other about here who knows the whole story. Depend upon it, there is some one on the lookout for me upon the admiral's account. It is inconceivable that it should be otherwise. Well, I wouldn't for the whole world have these notes found upon me, and taken away, as it were, by force. That would be too ignominious. Nobody shall hand them over to the admiral except myself, or some one by my authority. Would you mind taking charge of them for me for the present? Then I shall feel quite safe, and ready to brave and bear any thing. Will you do it?" continued Helen, producing the pocket-book. "I feel that I can trust you, although I do not even know your name."

"I will do any thing in the world you please," replied Petersfeld. "But this is indeed a great piece of confidence to repose in a perfect stranger."

"I must trust somebody," returned Helen, impatiently. "I can't have this thing about me any longer, and I won't carry it into that house, as matters stand. Take it — please do! and give me your address to write to, when I want it again."

Paul produced his card. "There is my name," he said, smiling. "You see the Albany is my London address, but I am staying in this neighborhood for the present. I will write down the name of the place."

"What! Are you staying with the Bunny-tails?" asked Helen, surprised.

"You know them, do you?"

"I know the farmer as a neighbor. I know his wife by sight. How do you come to be there?"

There was evidently a compliment conveyed in the question, and Paul congratulated himself that he had not been indiscreet enough to trust to the farmer's promised hospitality, and offer Helen a shelter at the Bottom.

"I am there quite promiscuously at present. Mrs. Bunnytail has a sister who married Mr. Buttermere, a member of our bar. I chanced to meet them one night at dinner at his house, and only yesterday I encountered the farmer at St. Mark's, who induced me to pay them a visit. Mrs. Bunnytail is not fascinating."

"A fat, odious woman. Insupportable, I should think. But you will take this pocket-book, will you not? Don't think me very rash and foolish. I have been studying physiognomy of late."

"It is very good of you to accept mine. Fortunately, as perhaps you are aware, these notes are stopped at the bank, and owing to their amount, mere waste paper in my hands for all practical purposes, so that I shan't be tempted to run away with them."

"Ah! I remember hearing my guardian ask for their numbers, and all that sort of thing, when he received them. Thank you very much. They can, I think, cause you no trouble, since no one except myself can possibly know that you hold them. How long do you remain with the Bunnytails?"

"Until I hear from you," replied Petersfeld gallantly. "My time is at my own disposal. Will you send me a line at any moment when I can possibly be of use? I don't know whether I could help you as a lawyer. To tell the truth, it's just about the only capacity in which I don't think I could. But at any rate, do let me have the satisfaction of thinking that you would send for me in any emergency, as some atonement for my folly in pursuing an enterprise with which I had nothing whatever to do."

"If I find myself in distress, I will send for you, Mr. Petersfeld!" replied Helen, gayly. "But I shan't be killed and eaten up, at any rate, until the notes are forthcoming. Now we must part," and she held out her little hand.

As Paul grasped it with all the earnestness necessary to explain his complete devotion to her interests, there was a low rustle among the neighboring yews. Some one was passing close by; in fact, the back of a black coat was indistinctly visible.

"What's that, Mr. Petersfeld? That was not a dog."

"No," said Petersfeld, and started in pursuit. He was much quicker than the intruder, whoever he was, but the latter knew the ground, and dived through clipped hedges, and dodged round statues, in a way which gave his pursuer no chance.

"I have lost him," said Paul, returning discomfited. "But I am sure I know the man. You were quite right, Miss Fleetlands, in suspecting that there was some one on the lookout for you, upon the admiral's account. I have seen that fellow lurking about for ever so long. His name is Tobacco. He has gone in the direction of the house. Will you go there now?"

"Yes. I am in for it, and can take care of myself, now that my pockets are empty. But I shouldn't mind if you would be good enough to see me safe in-doors."

Gladly Petersfeld accompanied her within sight of the garden entrance, and was rewarded by the display of unfeigned astonishment with which the house-maid who opened it, recognized the apparition of her young mistress.

He had been right in his conjecture. It was Mr. Tobacco himself who had vanished so concisely. From the tap-room of the "Six Bells" he had observed Petersfeld leave St. Mark's the evening before, in company with Farmer Bunnytail, and thought there could be no harm in looking him up on the following day. And when Paul set out upon his afternoon stroll, Mr. Tobacco accompanied him at a wary distance, delighted to find that his progress, although capricious and irregular, and enlivened with an occasional pipe, tended steadily in the direction of Riverwood Lawn. He watched him enter the grounds, and to his intense amazement, beheld the meeting which took place, and which he naturally considered must have been deliberately planned and preconcerted. He could not manage to creep sufficiently within earshot to discover all that passed, but he ascertained enough for his own private purposes. To have attempted to arrest Helen under such formidable escort, would have been downright madness. To have been detected among the bushes might have led to a thrashing. So he crawled off at a critical moment, in hopes of getting away unnoticed altogether.

How Petersfeld got back to Bunnytail's I don't suppose will ever be explained. His brain seemed absolutely on fire. He had found the lady of the advertisement. He had touched her hand, looked in her hazel eyes, and been rewarded by her unbounded confidence. What would he not have given for another interview, to have heard from her own lips the whole strange story! Whither had she been? Where had she passed

universal blaze of sunshine, the crisp waves leaped and glittered. The water was alive with craft of all descriptions, and as we neared the Jura, towering over all, the joyous roll of her band, playing

"In the days we went a-gipsying,
A long time ago!"

made the whole thing seem like some grand party of pleasure. But there were bursting hearts and weeping eyes on board the Jura, for all that. The crowd and confusion was something wonderful. Shore-going people were being seriously admonished of their boats alongside. Leave-takings were going on in all directions. Sheep and pigs, ducks, and cocks and hens, were more plentiful than even at Bunnytail Bottom.

I walked forward at once, knowing it to be a matter of conscience with all young Englishmen, the moment they find themselves on board a steamer, to hurry to the bowsprit and fill their pipes. As I expected, there was Petersfeld, seated on a hen-coop, and offering biscuit to a chicken opposite, with as much composure as if he had been bound for Greenwich, with nothing more serious than champagne and whitebait in prospect at the end of his trip.

"Hollo, Worsley!" he exclaimed, starting up. "My good fellow, what upon earth brings you here? Did you get my letter?"

"Of course I did. Were you in hopes that the postman would make a mistake?"

"What a fool I was to post it last night! I didn't mean you to have had this trouble. I thought we should have been off hours ago. My good fellow, I hope you haven't come down upon my account?"

"But I have come upon your account, and, what's more, I have a boat to take you back again. This ship sails in ten minutes. I tell you candidly that I shall write you down a fool if you sail in her. What business have you here? Do you mean to throw away all chances of work, annoy your people at home, and get yourself called 'eccentric' into the bargain — about the most damaging adjective a man can have tacked to his name? Nonsense! Come down the side with me. I've read your letter. I understand your feelings perfectly. And I'll undertake to satisfy you that I am right in what I now call upon you to do. Recollect the success you have just achieved. I declare, when you first started, I should have liked to give a hundred to one against your doing what you actually did. It would be a real disappointment to me now, to see you throw away your chances, without giving yourself fair play. Come along. By Jove, here's the mail-steamer actually alongside."

"My dear Worsley," replied Paul, grasping my hand, "I dare say you're quite right. I'd take your advice with pleasure if I possibly could. But I can't. I can't face Buttermere. I can't face the men at Lincoln's Inn. I can't indeed, after all that has happened. Besides, look here. That's my ticket for Alexandria—

just cost me thirty pounds down. Can't afford to throw that into the sea, you know," concluded he, with a forced laugh. "Thank you a hundred times for coming. I shall always recollect it. But, I say, you'll be too late. Hark!"

A clear hearty voice, distinct above all the bustle, suddenly shouted—

"Gun!"

There was a flash and a bang. A cloud of silver smoke went whirling overhead in the sunshine. Fluttering down from the mast-head came a small blue and white flag. The band stopped dead in the middle of a polka; and, after a moment's pause, struck up the National Anthem.

The voyage had begun.

"Hullo, governor, we thought you'd given us the slip," said my boatmen. "Another half jiffy, and we should have had to cast off without you."

CHAPTER XXXIII.

WHEN a castle of cards four stories high comes tumbling flat upon the nursery-table, there is something in the suddenness and completeness of the disaster which makes even a good child ready to cry. A great deal of pains has been taken—a great deal of ingenuity exerted. Little fingers have been anxiously moistened—lips compressed—and eyes curiously peeped through, as the bright pagoda rose up square and tall. In one moment, all is over. Time and pains and trouble have all been thrown away. The tower is a thing of the past. There is nothing to show for it — absolutely nothing. Buttress, wall, and pinnacle, all are gone. Not a trace of their existence, not a vestige of identity need be looked for in the fallen pack.

I felt much in a child's mood myself as I returned from Southampton. I had taken a good deal of trouble, and put myself to no slight amount of professional inconvenience, in order to make the journey. Ten minutes on board the Jura had been sufficient to send me home again. And what had I done? Absolutely nothing. I might just as well have been in court. Petersfeld was gone, and to attempt expostulation upon paper was—as I well knew—perfectly useless. A confused feeling that I had some share of personal responsibility in the matter of his going, already annoyed me. An idea, however, occurred while in the train, which I put in execution directly I reached Stone Buildings. I wrote a note to Buttermere, and sent it across by my clerk. This was what I said:

"MY DEAR SIR:—Petersfeld left England for Alexandria by P. & O. Steamer to-day. I knew nothing of his intention until I received a letter from him this morning, when I immediately started for Southampton, in hopes of bringing him back. Unfortunately, my journey was unsuccessful. I now venture to ask if you will allow me to have an interview with your daughter, upon the subject which we discussed the other day at your chambers. I should not make this request without good grounds, and I believe you know me well enough to trust to my discretion.

Yours faithfully,   JOHN WORSLEY."

The reply was immediate.

" DEAR WORSLEY :—I was hasty and inconsiderate upon the occasion to which you refer, and you have a right to every amends in my power. Linda shall be prepared to receive you in my study in Harley Street to-morrow after-noon at five. Will that hour do? I have the most perfect confidence in your honor and discretion, and shall not expect her to communicate one syllable of what may pass. Should she wish to do so, it is understood that I am at liberty to hear every thing. Yours truly,

"F. BUTTERMERE."

I was, of course, punctual. My visit had evidently been arranged for, as I was ushered at once, and without a word, into a small untidy room upon the ground-floor, furnished with two chairs, and an immense table littered with books and papers. A pair of great shaded lamps, like genii of the apartment, stood sentinels over the green-baize. Rakes of lamps they looked, accustomed to sad hours, and to wink and blink, and pledge one another in cannakins of midnight oil, long after all the household, except its laborious master, were warm in bed. In a few moments Mrs. Buttermere, accompanied by Linda, entered the room. I will not do the former the injustice of saying that she seemed very doubtful as to the propriety of my visit, and perfectly certain that I had acted most audaciously in proposing it. I had only a general perception that such was the case; perhaps as intuitive upon my part as it was politely veiled upon hers.

"Mr. Buttermere tells me that you wish to see Linda alone," she remarked, after the usual commonplace observations. "Shall I leave you together? You will not be disturbed here, and you will find tea in the drawing-room when you have had your say. Linda, you must bring Mr. Worsley up stairs."

"Mr. Buttermere was good enough to allow me a moment's interview with Miss Buttermere," I replied, "and with her permission, I will avail myself of your kindness, before joining you in the drawing-room."

"Oh, by all means. I understand nothing of the matter, but Mr. Buttermere's wish is quite sufficient." And with these words, rather dryly spoken, the lady quitted the room.

I have seldom felt more keenly shocked than when I looked at the poor child before me. Oh that this should have been the little sparkling coquette of but a few evenings ago. The pretty form—the delicate features—the rich auburn hair impatient of its tiny bonnet—these were all there ; but there was pain and misery written all over her countenance ; there was

nervousness and almost terror in every quick movement of her gloved hands.

"We have just come in from driving," she said ; "I hope you have not been kept waiting?"

I perceived that she spoke because she could not help saying something. The excitement of the moment was unendurable. I would have given any thing to have known how best to soothe it. I could only do my best.

"I have not waited a moment. I have only just strolled down from Lincoln's Inn. I believe, Miss Buttermere, that I am here to take a great weight off your mind ; at least, I sincerely hope so. I am here, at all events, upon the part of a friend of mine, to offer you the most submissive apology which man can make for having made your papa very angry, and yourself, I fear, very unhappy, by one unfortunate act of incaution. If he were not at this moment probably somewhere off Finisterre, I would bring him here to plead for himself."

"Oh, no, no, no, Mr. Worsley. It is I who have done wrong. It is I who have made myself unhappy. It is I who have spoiled my whole life, and learned what real misery is at once and forever. It is I who ought to ask his forgiveness ;—it is, indeed. You don't know all, I am sure."

"Pretty nearly so, I believe. It began with a conversation about a certain Miss Fleetlands, at your papa's dinner-table."

"Yes—yes. At least not exactly. I had made a most foolish wager with my sisters—I did not know how very wrong it was—and I led him to suppose that I knew something about that young lady. In reality I knew nothing—only her name. I had happened to learn that by the merest chance. I have never ventured to say a word about this either to papa or mamma; it would have made them so dreadfully angry. And a day or two afterward he wrote me a letter, and sent me a bank note. I could not quite understand the letter; but I felt certain that the money was never intended for me."

"You were quite right. The twenty pounds was intended for his tailor. He put it into your envelope by mistake. It is just the sort of thing he is always doing."

Linda fairly sobbed. "I see it all now. I see at last what I have done. Oh, why did I ever go to Mrs. Springletop! She is a friend of mine, you must know, Mr. Worsley; and as misfortune would have it, I went to her to talk about the letter. I wanted advice, in short. Well, she persuaded me that it could only have one meaning, and made me lay out the money on an emerald snake-bracelet, and write and thank him for it, and so on ; and so it all came about. Oh, how dreadful it seems now. Is there any hope—any help for me, do you think?"

"My dear Miss Buttermere, these little contretemps happen every day. We will put yours to rights at once. Your acquaintance with our friend Petersfeld was, at all events, a very short one."

"There was no acquaintance at all! That was what made the whole thing seem so frightfully shocking. But, say what I would, I was always met by the same answer, that I was only a child, and that it was lucky I had people about me who knew how to manage affairs. I am so thankful to think it is all over. Will you take back the bracelet? Pray do. I will fetch it directly."

"You shall give it me presently. He would of course wish you to keep it; but I agree with you that it had better be returned. That is the right course. And now, one word upon my friend's behalf. He is in such perfect despair at the annoyance which he has inflicted upon you, that he has actually left the country, and is at this moment upon his way to Egypt. He has thrown up his chances at the bar—probably incensed his relations; and will most certainly never come back until he feels that you have forgiven him."

"Forgiven him, indeed! He must forgive me first; or, rather, let me forgive and forget myself, which I can never do."

"Upon my word, I never had such an impracticable pair of penitents to deal with in all my life! You're just as bad as he is. You both tell me you can't forgive yourselves, so I advise you to try what happens after forgiving each other. However, I shall now know what to say to him when I write by the next mail. Now, my dear Miss Buttermere, I took the liberty of asking for this interview in order that this foolish entanglement might be cleared up to yourself in the first instance. I was quite right you see. If Mr. or Mrs. Buttermere had known of the very innocent little trick which brought it all about, a good deal of trouble might have been saved. Everything must now be explained to them, and you may take my word for it that they will be intensely relieved upon learning the whole truth. There really is nothing to be angry about, which is rather a pity, after all the fuss that has been made. Have I your permission to tell the whole story to your father?"

"Papa has just come in," gasped Linda, in a choking voice. "I heard his footstep in the hall."

"Capital. Then we will get the business over in no time. Allow me for one moment to assume the freedom of an elder brother, and beg you to ask him to join us."

"Well, Worsley," he said in his old cordial tone, yet looking fagged and worn to the last degree, "is the consultation over already, or am I called in to assist? Can you give us any new light upon the subject—hey?"

"I hope so, at all events. You will scarcely believe what a ridiculous little blunder lies at the bottom of the whole affair. Your daughter will explain it all; but, before she does so, let me say one word. You remember, doubtless, an evening when I had the pleasure of dining with you, not very long ago. We talked, if you recollect, of a young lady whose mysterious disappearance had just been announced in the Times, and for whose recovery five hundred pounds reward was offered."

"To be sure we did. I remember the advertisement perfectly. It made Brindlebun quite curious. What then?"

"Petersfeld was at that moment engaged in trying to find her. He had taken up the pursuit simply upon seeing what we all saw in the paper. He had been in Paris, upon that very business, during the morning of the day when he was last in this house."

"What on earth had he to do with her? What do you mean, Worsley? Are you going to make him out non compos? no brains—not accountable for his actions?"

"My dear sir! He has found her."

"The deuce he has!" exclaimed Mr. Buttermere, as if using up his last ounce of breath. "Went to work and found her, did he? Most extraordinary thing I ever heard of."

"I say the same. And now, to save Miss Buttermere the trouble, I will try to explain how, in the middle of his hot pursuit, he managed to commit the most unlucky mistake which has caused so much annoyance both here and to himself."

Step by step the confession was accomplished. Buttermere took his seat upon the table, between the lamps, and listened with knitted brows.

"So that Mrs. Springletop, confound her, was at the bottom of it all! I almost guessed as much. And the bank note was never intended for Linda?"

"It was intended to pay for trousers. He was writing to his tailor at the moment, and put the bank note intended for him into the envelope addressed to your daughter. That's the whole story."

"Upon my word, Worsley, I thank you very heartily for all this. What's done, can't be undone; but we shall weather it somehow, I suppose. And so Petersfeld has gone to the Pyramids?"

"Gone, in despair of ever being able to show his face again in London. I have just asked your daughter to send him her forgiveness; but, I tell you candidly, I don't think even that will bring him back."

"Well, it's all a pity. The whole thing is such a joke, if you look at it only in one aspect, that it's hard not to be able to laugh at it. Write to him, Worsley, and tell him to come back. And so Linda really took him in—this clever fellow who found the lady at last! Upon my honor, the whole thing is most extraordinary. But there is no sting about it now. We must manage to rub through. It will only be a nine days' wonder, after all. These things happen every week—eh, Worsley? If one could only box Mrs. Springletop's ears! But as for you, darling, don't fret. It wasn't your mistake. And, Worsley, I shake hands with you, and thank you with all my heart. We shall rub through somehow. It was a mistake altogether, from first to last. Mrs. Buttermere and I must talk it over. And as you said just now, Worsley, it will only be a nine days' wonder, and we shall rub through perfectly. Yes, darling, it was all a mistake—a silly stupid mistake of people who ought to have guided you better. We are all right now. We won't be too hard upon poor Mr. Petersfeld. Don't let him catch cold on the Pyramids, Worsley. You have done us all a service to-day; and, so far as he is concerned, the past is dismissed, and we hope that you will tell him so."

That self-same evening a letter, which you will never read, followed Petersfeld to Alexandria by the Marseilles mail, and an emerald-headed snake slept in an iron box on the topmost story of No. 9 Stone Buildings, Lincoln's Inn.

Let us return to Helen.

Every one, I suppose, must remember certain passages in their lives which have left behind them the impression rather of a sort of nebulous mist, than of a series of separate events, connected, yet distinct. Some rush of circumstances, unexpected and overwhelming, has blended things in one perplexing maze, and we shrink from the task of dissection, as from something laborious, long, and hopeless.

Something of this sort was the case with Helen after her return to Riverwood. A few facts only stood out solid and certain, against a general background of confusion.

Mr. Bloss himself reached Riverwood the day after her arrival, charged with the mission of bringing her up to town. Upon this occasion it appeared that her presence before the Lord Chancellor was indispensable. Mr. Salterton accompanied them. As her guardian next in succession, it was rightly considered that he would do well to be upon the spot, to accept the office which would probably at once devolve upon his hands.

Of Helen's meeting with the rector you must forgive me if I do not speak. Something of its purport you may, perhaps, presently learn. He was kind—for he never was otherwise. He was loving—for Helen was to him as his own daughter. But let the interview itself remain within the veil. It tore Helen's heart to think of, afterward. The mere recollection was like a rending of the very roots of pain. She was, at last, conscious how grave had been her fault—how blind and inexcusable her folly. But she is now in the train, and upon her way to London.

It was the first time that Bloss and she had met since the day when he received her—a little Indian baby—in Southampton harbor, and escorted her to the very station from which they were just departing. Events since then had indeed run their mysterious round; and one may imagine the interest with which the jolly old gentleman surveyed his fellow-passenger. The latter, upon her part, listened with the deepest interest to much that Mr. Bloss had to tell. He could speak to her of her own papa, when a bright and curly boy. He could talk about the making of the will—penned by his own hand—which had brought him wealth in his dying hours; wealth, alas, too long delayed. He could say something about her Indian birthplace, as it had been described to him by his correspondent of the firm of Joy, Jingle & Jump, and amused her with a description of her own tiny self, as she first opened her eyes in his face upon the deck of the mail-steamer.

"Oh, by the bye, Mr. Bloss," she said, after these topics had been at last exhausted, "I wonder if you know Mr. Petersfeld, the barrister of Lincoln's Inn. I am afraid he got into sad trouble about the bank notes which he was so kind as to take charge of for me, and I was really grieved. But that, I hope, is over now. You can not think how kind and considerate he was. I really almost wished that I had wanted his assistance—he seemed so burning to give it."

"Ho, ho, ho!" chuckled Mr. Bloss. "My dear Miss Fleetlands, it's a capital story, and I ought to have told it you before. Yes, I do know Mr. Petersfeld; and, what's more, I am indebted to yourself for the honor of his acquaintance. You may well look surprised. Never was such a droll affair known since the world began. When your guardian, the admiral, thought it right to advertise for you, he chose, as you know, to put my name in the paper, as the person to receive you in town. He pitched upon me, you understand, as being the person who first brought you to his house; independently of which there were reasons for wishing that his own London agents should not appear in the matter. Had they done so, the chances were that inquisitive people—clerks especially—would have put two and two together, and your name been discovered and blazoned right and left in no time; and this, to do him justice, he spared no trouble to prevent. My own name you see afforded nobody any clue whatever. Well, the very morning that the advertisement appeared, who should march into my office but Mr. Petersfeld himself, just as I was in the middle of my luncheon. 'Give me full particulars of the young lady, Mr. Bloss, for I'm going straight away to find her, as sure as you sit there!' That's what he said, or something like it. To tell you the truth—it was our first meeting you must remember—I doubted whether his head would ring quite sound if one tried it; but he came with the card of a very good friend of mine, Mr. Worsley, and upon his account I really told him all I dared. As to his finding you, the idea never once entered my mind. And that you should after all have encountered each other in the strange way you did, just at the critical moment, is almost more than strange. Of course he might have claimed the reward."

"Is it paid yet?" inquired Mr. Salterton.

"Paid! Lord bless you, no! We shall

have claims from half a dozen quarters. When the detectives abandoned Riverwood, they left an agent of theirs, a dirty little understrapper of the name of Tobacco, to keep a lookout upon their account. He seems to have put the Riverwood constabulary upon the scent as to the notes, at all events. Of course he will stand out for his own. I have had other notices already. It is quite exceptional, in a case of this kind, to find the reward pass peaceably into one pocket."

"I feel quite certain that Mr. Petersfeld would have nothing to say to it," remarked Helen.

"Not he! Oh dear, no," chuckled Mr. Bloss. "Not in his line at all. But now you mention his name again, it reminds me of another most singular fact. One never knows exactly how these things get wind, but I had this from the very best authority. Just fancy. Since his visit to me—that is to say while in full pursuit of yourself—he has managed to snatch a hasty moment to get himself engaged to one of the prettiest little girls in London—a daughter of one of the magnates of our Chancery bar!"

"Nonsense!" exclaimed Helen, laughing. "That was really making use of spare minutes, which, somebody says, is such an excellent habit. What is her name—her Christian name, I mean?"

"Oh, Linda—Linda Buttermere. I have admired her often, at her papa's dinners. Charming little girl, indeed! Really Petersfeld is a most remarkable young man. Never knew any thing like his energy. One doesn't know what he may not do next. I shall send him a good heavy brief, I know, before he's a week older!"

"Linda—what a pretty name!" And for the next thirty miles, Helen, with her usual impulsive generosity, was considering what wedding-present she should choose for Paul and Linda, as some acknowledgment of the debt which she felt she owed to the former.

London was reached at last, and Helen conducted to a private hotel in Cork Street. Thenceforth, for the next two days, all seemed mist and confusion. There was an interview with the Lord Chancellor, during which she was seriously taken to task, and punished with a lecture of which she too painfully admitted the wisdom. And there was a formal reconciliation with her guardian, which took place in his lordship's presence. It was not a very gracious affair; but neither party could be expected to feel quite at ease. To her great relief, nothing whatever was said in her presence about the notes, which had, as a matter of course, been lodged at the Riverwood Branch Bank.

And now, resisting all temptation to encumber my story with technical minutiæ, I will only add that the conclusion of the business was as follows: Admiral Mortlake was ordered to pass his accounts—pay certain costs—and hand over Helen to Mr. Salterton, who was appointed guardian in his room. Riverwood Rectory was to be Helen's future home.

CHAPTER XXXIV.

"I HOPE, Mr. Salterton, it is understood that these rewards are all to be paid out of my own money; and that the admiral is never to be troubled about any thing which he has received upon my account," said Helen, a few days after she had taken up her abode at the Rectory.

"That must be an after-consideration, my dear. For the next three years, the power to bind or to loose lies neither with you nor me."

Three years! A desperately long time it seemed, all things considered. Could it be possible that they had indeed to be faced? Sad or unprofitable they need not be. And yet, years of discipline and penance Helen knew that she had deserved. Wisely and bravely she resolved to submit with patience,—to trust to the endurance of a love which was all in all to her in life, —and in the meanwhile, by genuine and unfailing cheerfulness, to make Mr. Salterton rejoice that he had found a daughter. The only hope to which she permitted herself to cling was that, some day or other, long perhaps before the three years were expired, the prohibition against letter-writing might be relaxed or withdrawn. That was the real sting of the separation; and, to her, it seemed an unjust, a needless, and a cruel measure. She could not understand why she might not at least be allowed to correspond with Ferdinand. If either she or he had been actually in prison—regular convicts at Pentonville—that indulgence would not have been forbidden. However, there was no help for it. She felt that she had much to be thankful for. Mr. Salterton was always delightful; and in his sister, a quiet, lady-like person whom she had scarcely more than known by sight in the years during which the Rectory had been forbidden ground, she began to discover the makings of another friend.

In-doors, there was work in plenty. Out-of-doors, Camilla neighed from her stall. She had of course accompanied her mistress. Gigoggin, alas, was not there to attend her, and sadly the old fellow was missed. One would naturally have supposed that, after his conduct in the matter of Helen's hunting-field flirtation, the admiral would have sent him about his business in no time. But Gigoggin had lived at Riverwood almost as long as his master, and was not to be parted with upon a single quarrel, however serious. So master and man fought it out between them, and matters went on as before. The latter, we may be quite certain, would gladly have followed Helen to her new home, but the admiral was obstinate and inflexible. Not in that way, at least, should Gigoggin, with his consent, enjoy the reward of his duplicity. And, without the admiral's formal acquiescence, Mr. Salterton was firm in his refusal to allow the matter even to be discussed. It was a great sorrow to Helen, who, independently of other and more recent considerations, entertained a sincere regard for the old friend of her childhood. But, like severer troubles, it had to be borne.

So broke the morning of what appeared to be a new era in Helen's life—an era of quiet probation, and of hope deferred. Misty and doubtful in its dawning, how immeasurably distant appeared its close! Would she ever live to behold that hour—to see matters finally at rest—the ravel of her life at last combed out smooth and even?

Never, in wildest dream of the night, came a glimpse of the plan by which the knot was to be so swiftly, so instantly disentangled.

One morning, scarcely three weeks after Helen's arrival, a large old-fashioned carriage drove up to the Rectory door. A tall, elderly gentleman, of military air, with a white mustache, and a golden-headed cane, gravely alighted, and was ushered into the rector's study.

"My dear Lord St. Margarets, is it possible that I have the pleasure of seeing you again?"

"You not only see me, Salterton, but you see me with a favor to ask."

"A new sensation, I should think, if you are in earnest. Am I to take my pupil back again?"

"Why, no. I am not clear that I should trust you with him a second time," replied Lord St. Margarets. "What do you say to his late escapade? I suppose you have heard the particulars."

"I have, and with infinite concern. Of course, in one's own heart, one finds every excuse for a lad of his high spirit and perfect courage, with such a girl as Helen before him. But that he should have rushed right into the jaws of the Chancery Lion, is upon all accounts to be regretted. I was rejoiced to hear from himself, however, that he was not in any sense acting in defiance of your wishes—in fact, that he had some reason to suppose that, had he succeeded, you would not have been seriously displeased."

"Quite right. Quite true. He has acted toward myself, thank God, with the most perfect honor and good faith. I have not a word to say. Indeed, I take a great deal of the blame upon my own shoulders. I have lived too much for myself, Salterton. I have not held for him the position in the county which I might and ought to have done. But that is not the question now. Never having had the pleasure of Miss Fleetlands's acquaintance—never, in fact, having beheld her in my life—the match was not one of which I could be supposed to be personally desirous. My relations with the admiral, her guardian, were far from cordial, and I could not help feeling that Ferdinand might, after all, be acting upon impulse, without the consideration which an affair of such extreme importance demanded. Still, I was so anxious not to appear to thwart him at starting, which is worse than useless in matters of this kind, that I fear I left him in a position which was only too likely to end as it did."

"Perhaps we have not seen the end yet," suggested the rector, easily. "It is highly important, upon Helen's account, that I should be precisely aware of your views and wishes. That her heart is entirely fixed upon Ferdinand I am certain; and that she will, if necessary, wait with patience and courage three years and longer, I know quite well. But, since she has been in my house, we have never exchanged a syllable upon the subject. I felt bound, in the first instance, to learn the aspect in which you regarded the match; and I only deferred writing to you upon the subject until you should have had time to hear from Ferdinand upon his arrival out, and matters had cooled down a little after the late hurly-burly."

"My own views, Salterton," replied Lord St. Margarets gravely, "may depend much upon your answer to a question which, among other things, I came hither to put. I am come, as I told you, to ask a favor; but the question comes first. If my son has done a foolish thing, I am afraid your ward has shown herself more than his match. You will appreciate the circumstances under which I now ask you to tell me the whole story of her disappearance and return. I give no credence whatever to rumor; and, except from rumor, I have heard nothing. Let me understand, first, what we may suppose to have been her object in leaving Riverwood."

"To avoid remaining under the same roof with people who had treated your son so scandalously," replied the rector. "Helen was indignant, and with some reason. I was away from home at the time. They were upon the point of starting for the Continent; and the poor child, with nobody to appeal to, was, I verily believe, afraid of their company."

"Good," observed Lord St. Margarets, with deliberate emphasis. "You will agree with me, Salterton. The way in which they kidnapped Ferdinand was simply scandalous. I am aware that it was merely done to gratify an old feeling against myself. But she did well to distrust them, after that. I admire her spirit. But the world will ask for more."

"More is at their service. Helen left home at five o'clock on the afternoon of the sixteenth of April last; and, from that moment to this, not one half hour of her time is unaccounted for. She traveled direct to Izzleworth in company with a Mrs. Feltham, a parishioner of St. Mark's, whom she had met near the station. On her arrival at Izzleworth, she very sensibly inquired for the clergyman of the place; and, by the greatest conceivable good fortune, if we are to call it by no worthier name, found herself at once in the house of Dr. Orchard, the vicar. Orchard is a well-known man. He was some years my senior at Balliol, but I remember his name and fame very distinctly. A little crotchety, and given to physiognomy, or some humbug of the kind; but true and honorable to the backbone. Fortunately the admiral has had the good feeling to enclose to me a letter of his, describing the events of Helen's stay with him, and the sensation of love and admiration which she contrived to excite in his family. I will read it to you at once, if you have no objection."

"Good again," repeated Lord St. Margarets, at the conclusion of the letter, "and there you will agree with me, Salterton. Upon my honor, I like her better than if she had stayed at home. In fact, my good friend," continued the ex-embassador, subsiding into a diplomatic attitude, "I consider that this episode in her life may be at once consigned to oblivion. Are we so far agreed?"

"In so far that we may so consign it—yes. But not she, poor child. I felt it my duty to point out to her, in all gentleness, the greatness of her error, and I assure you I was frightened when the thing broke upon her as a reality. Her distress was agonizing."

"What a pity. Come, Salterton, I am ready to say the word. Give me your honor that she is the person to make Ferdinand happy — you know them both."

"I give you my honor that, in my opinion, he will never meet with any one as likely to do so. More than that, I tell you plainly, Lord St. Margarets, that if he loses Helen he will lose one in ten thousand."

"Good! I consent. You may tell her that at the age of twenty-three—she is nineteen, or nearly so, I think—I shall with pleasure receive her as the mistress of Saintswood, and retire upon Grosvenor Square. Tell her that my mind is quite clear upon that point."

"At the age of twenty-three?" repeated the rector, musingly.

"Twenty-three, of course. You don't seem satisfied, Salterton. Isn't that the age specified in her father's will?"

"Otherwise her fortune goes over? And the Court would of course listen to no proposal which might endanger one penny of it. Yes, I believe you are right. But, my dear Lord St. Margarets—you are in earnest, I know, in your consent—is there no possibility of abridging this deplorable—this, I must say, shameful loss of time and youth to both parties? Five years! Must they really wait five years? Is it possible that these, the best years of their lives, are to be consumed in satisfying the injunction of a Court of Equity? Could any thing be more preposterous? If we are to be ridden over rough-shod after this fashion, why not call things by their right names, and have a High Court of Iniquity at once?"

Lord St. Margarets never laughed. But sometimes, when he was really amused, a curious smile would break at his lips, and then travel quietly all over his countenance before it disappeared. It came and went, upon this occasion.

"Why, yes. Five years is a long time to wait. I am not defending the system; but it

exists, and there is only one person in existence who could strike off a single day."

"You mean the Lord Chancellor?"

"Most certainly not. Neither the Lord Chancellor, nor Guy Fawkes, nor any body but yourself. I told you that I came here with a favor to ask. I am now ready to ask it. What do you say to consenting that the marriage shall take place, say a couple of months hence, just with notice enough in fact to make proper preparation?"

"Have I really any such power, my dear lord?" exclaimed the rector, jumping out of his chair.

"Certainly. I half suspected that you might have found it no part of your duty as executor to read your testator's will. Avail yourself of the chance now! Here is the copy with which I persuaded my solicitor to furnish me."

"God bless me! Why, of course you are right. Admiral Mortlake's veto has no longer any effect. How could I have been so stupid as not to perceive the fact!"

"As not to recognize yourself as reigning guardian?" replied Lord St. Margarets with a smile. "The king is dead—long live the king! Well, in that capacity I ask your consent."

"Stay one moment. Surely my consent as guardian will not have the effect of annulling the injunction which is at present hanging over your son?"

"It will not. But upon our joint application to the court, I understand that it will be dissolved as matter of course."

"But how as to Ferdinand? It is hardly a month since he sailed. Are you about to summon him back at once?"

"No need. He is at this moment in Grosvenor Square."

Mr. Salterton returned to his seat. "No more guessing upon my part, Lord St. Margarets. I can not afford to be surprised at this rate. Will you explain?"

"The explanation is most simple. Fortunately or unfortunately, Ferdinand chose to go into a fever on the voyage out. I am not certain but that he was sent too soon—before, in fact, he was fit for traveling, but I suspect that other things may have had more to do with it. Be that as it may, he was landed at the first port touched at, and the military authorities there sent him back by the next transport. They said it was his only chance. He is now getting all right, thank Heaven. I had ambitious dreams for him once; but after all that has happened, I am content to see an augury in this last occurrence, and to accept it as the appointed termination of his professional career."

"And you have said all this, Lord St. Margarets, without even seeing Helen?"

"Why, yes. I do not intend to be told that I was myself the victim of fascination. I believe in her good looks, and for the rest I trust to you, Salterton. You have known her from childhood, and I am satisfied. It seems to me that Ferdinand's mind is quite clear upon one

I

point, and that's the great thing. Now you may introduce me, if you will."

Helen had just come in from a gallop upon Camilla. You know how she looked upon these occasions; and though recent events had stamped her features with a trace of care and sadness, they had perhaps given even more than they had taken away. Without the slightest guess as to who the stranger might be, she felt fascinated by his commanding air and stately presence. Wonderingly she allowed him to take her by both hands, and look tenderly down upon her fair young face. She stood bewildered under the clear gaze of those calm grey eyes, and the curve of that silken white mustache.

"You do not know me?" he said.

"I do not indeed," replied Helen. "But your face is not strange to me. At least, I think not."

"It will never be strange, I hope. I am Ferdinand's papa. He has asked me to be yours."

Huzza!

At last we sail within earshot of wedding-bells. Let us not linger now.

*   *   *   *   *   *

"Helen," said Ferdinand, as they slowly walked their horses, side by side, beneath the waving branches of a summer wood, "I have a surprise for you to-morrow. Whom do you think you will see?"

"That I can not possibly guess! There are so many people in the world."

"Your friend Petersfeld will be at Saintswood this evening. I made a point of calling at his chambers when I was in town yesterday, to thank him for his kindness to you. He is really a thorough good fellow. Of course, we fraternized immensely when I reminded him that we had both gone to jail upon your account."

"You didn't bring that to his recollection, I do hope," cried Helen, coloring. "It is not a reflection which I am fond of, I assure you. What did he say?"

"Quoted an old Agamemnon chorus, which I perfectly recollect Salterton trying to drive into my head—called you

"'Ταν δορίγαμβρον ἀμφινειχῆ τ' 'ΕΛΕΝΑΝ!'

I hope you appreciate the compliment. Τὸν δ' ἀπαμειβόμενος, I asked him to come down to Saintswood and stay for our wedding; and, now I think of it, he shall be my best man. That will be a capital climax to his adventures, won't it?"

"Capital! It was very kind of you to invite him. I shall be delighted to see him again."

"You must know that he has been half over Egypt since you saw him last."

"Egypt! Impossible."

"It is a fact. He only returned last Monday."

"Well! as Mr. Bloss remarked in the train the other day, his energy is something extraordinary. I feel certain that he will become a very great man."

"There is no doubt about that."

Let me interrupt the conversation. Whether or not my own letter to Petersfeld had any effect in contributing to his rapid return, I do not know. Probably another, which he received by the same (Marseilles) mail from his father, and which, consequently, reached him a few hours after he landed, may have had more to do with it. The old gentleman wrote in a rage, informing his self-expatriating son that if he chose to neglect his profession and waste his time upon the banks of the Nile, he might make up his mind to live upon the backsheesh of his fellow-pilgrims; for not one English shilling would ever be remitted in that direction.

"Now," resumed Helen, "I find that I must have another brides-maid. Mr. Petersfeld is engaged to be married to a Miss Linda Buttermere; and if you take the one, I mean to lay claim to the other. Could it possibly be managed, do you think? Ferdinand, you must really contrive it!"

"That I will, darling! My father will be only too delighted with such an opportunity of firing off his diplomacy. Nothing on earth will please him more than to be told that it is your wish, but that we fear the thing is impossible! Hey? Can't you fancy the grave twinkle in his eye, and the tone with which he will repeat the last word? It will be a whole day's employment to consider the proper scheme, arrange the exact means, and write the necessary dispatches. And the best of it is, that he'll succeed. You'll see!"

"It will really be great fun!"

"It will be a piece of luck, too, for Miss Linda," laughed Ferdinand. "What do you think that same prodigal father did when I went up to town the other day? Absolutely gave me three hundred pounds to lay out upon lockets for the brides-maids! They are, of course, all alike, with our initials intertwisted in brilliants. I think you will be pleased with the monogram."

"Three hundred pounds! I never heard of such a thing."

"Oh, and I forgot to tell you that the Gigoggin business is settled at last. The admiral has given way, and allows him to follow you. I suppose my father was right in insisting upon a regular written character, just as if old Gi had been a perfect stranger. Like Salterton, he has a strong feeling about what he calls tampering with other people's retainers. However, all is right now. Your henchman is again in your service."

"What! Another piece of good fortune! Oh, Ferdinand, how very kind you all are. I don't know how I should have managed without Gi."

"I say much the same, for my own part. In fact, I'm not so certain that I should have been where I am without him," rejoined Ferdinand, gayly. "He won't find me ungrateful. He is a made man for life."

The wedding was a brilliant affair. It took

place, of course, at Riverwood. I am not ashamed to confess that few things would amuse me more than to read a circumstantial account of it written by a snob.

"And so," said Mr. Salterton, as Helen appeared at their early breakfast-table on the morning of the eventful day, "I find that Lord St. Margarets has been considerate enough to provide me with an accomplice upon this occasion. I suppose he thought the knot would be all the tighter for a pull at both ends."

"Indeed!" replied Helen, who felt just nervous enough to be glad of an indifferent matter to talk about. "One of his friends, I suppose."

"I expect him here presently. He said he should ride over from Saintswood. He is a man whom I remember well at Oxford, and hadn't seen for years until yesterday. • And here he comes, I believe."

There was a clatter of horse-hoofs along the approach, and then a rattling ring at the front-door bell.

The door opened, and the visitor was announced.

"Doctor Orchard, sir."

"Ha! my dear Miss Fleetlands! You told me that we should meet again; but you didn't tell me how very soon it was to be. That was inconsiderate. I must have a kiss for my journey; and here are a thousand good wishes in advance of to-day's business. Mrs. Orchard sends the same. So does my sister. Three thousand in all! My dear young lady, how shall I ever thank you enough for coming to my house?"

"How can I ever thank you enough for coming here to-day?" returned Helen, ready to cry with pleasure. "Do you know, Doctor Orchard, I scarcely felt as if my happiness could have been added to; but you have made it really run over."

"Oh, dear me! If we are to compliment each other at this rate, we shall certainly be late for church. The good fortune is all upon my part. Your gallant young bridegroom was kind enough to write to me the other day, and offer me his father's hospitality at Saintswood for the wedding, in case I could manage to come and lend a hand. What a princely place it is! Long and happily may you live to reign over it. And now, Helen," continued the doctor, taking her once more by the hand—"I'm always going to call you Helen, in future, you know—I congratulate you in earnest. You have chosen well. There is no mistake about it. That cross was not won by vulgar muscle, nor by blind carelessness of danger, nor by the instinct which makes all true men happy to fight. That glorious cross fell to a man whom God had fashioned as one fit to win and wear it; and if that young fellow had touched his hat to me at a stable-door, I should have taken off mine to him in return. I should indeed. To

mistake that face would be to insult its Maker. You are a heretic as to all this, Salterton?"

"Open to conviction; *sine comburendo*, if possible. Not, I confess, upon the strength of two individual instances, and those two—Helen and Ferdinand."

Doctor Orchard ought to have made his bargain for at least ten more kisses before Helen retired to her bridal toilette. He had indeed made her love him dearly.

Of the wedding itself, one or two incidents are all that I feel it at all desirable to record. In the first place the admiral made his appearance, in accordance with a formal invitation. He shook hands cordially with Lord St. Margarets, as well as with the bride and bridegroom; and went home with a lighter heart than he had carried for some years before.

Linda was not present. Diplomacy had done its best, but had failed upon this occasion. Shortly after the ceremony, Petersfeld found an opportunity of approaching Helen.

"You must let me offer you this little talisman, Mrs. Hunsdon," he said, "with my warmest congratulations and good wishes. Will you wear it sometimes for my sake? I brought it from Egypt. We can never be quite indifferent to each other, I hope."

"Indeed, we can not, Mr. Petersfeld," replied Helen, admiring the sparkling toy. "Thank you very much indeed. Did it really come from Egypt? It shall always have a place on my chain. It is a talisman for good, I hope—but I am so sorry that Linda could not be here."

"Come, Helen, we mustn't ask questions," said Captain Hunsdon, approaching. "Petersfeld and I had a conversation last evening; but never mind that now. Petersfeld, I am going to give you a commission. Will you undertake it?"

"With pleasure."

"It is to convey this bridesmaid-locket to Miss Buttermere. I trust to your honor to present it personally. You will tell her, please, how grieved we all were that she was unable to be present, to wear it in her place."

"And tell her, from me," added Helen, "that I hope she will be as much in love with her talisman as I am with mine."

"Must I really—" began Petersfeld.

"Certainly. It is in your charge."

There was no time for more. There is not much opportunity for private conversation upon these occasions.

"Then I will carry it."

Petersfeld kept his promise like a man. But I shall not tell you what passed at the interview. I have special reasons for this reservation. Whether or not, to use ladies' language, "any thing came of it," every lady in the land is at liberty to conjecture for herself. And the lady who guesses right will have read my story to greater advantage than the lady who guesses wrong.

THE END.